THE CREMATION OF SAM M^cGEE

DEL LEONARD JONES

First published by Casey Strikes Out Publishing in 2018
Copyright © Del Leonard Jones, 2018

ISBN print 978-1-7326052-0-6
ISBN ebook 978-1-7326052-1-3

To Dianna, my light-o'-love, the love of my life

Part One
Cuba

I have no doubt at all the Devil grins,

As seas of ink I spatter.

Ye gods, forgive my "literary" sins —

The other kind don't matter.

— Robert W. Service

CHAPTER ONE

NOW, SAM MCGEE NEVER WAS FROM TENNESSEE. He was born and raised in Plumtree, North Carolina.

Sam McGee from Plumtree, Tennessee, sounded lyrical in print, so I gave myself license to nudge his feeble village across the state line. That's not easy to confess, a newspaper reporter's reputation is all he has. Truth is the coin of a correspondent's realm. It engenders trust, and without trust I'd lose a million faithful readers to other New York papers.

Our paths first crossed in Cuba in late 1897 when I happened upon a firing squad. A Cuban rebel was condemned for striking a Spanish officer, and McGee was implicated when he went to the rebel's rescue, for demanding a tribunal before a man was put to death. I appeared like a ghost from a weedy thick as McGee and the rebel were stood against the gray wall of a church to be riddled by six soldiers as lean as their Mauser rifles.

A Spanish major, arrogant of eye and as haughty as his rank, drew rein and issued orders from his high horse. The Cuban's mother wailed and begged for his life. The Spaniards made him squat, pants to knees, over a bayonet jammed upright from the ground. They called it *siéntese en infinity*—sitting on infinity. The rebel perched until his legs jellied as the Spaniards watched with cigarettes aglow. Spaniards can be ruthlessly patient until they run out of rum.

The rebel collapsed sideways and limped off with a gash in his buttocks and whatnot. The six whooped and shot rifles into the air and sang lyrics I couldn't decipher because they were in drunken *español*.

McGee refused to squat; he was an American from the ground up and preferred to be shot against the blank wall. His hands were tied with fishing line, a last cigarette inserted between lips cracked by unforgiving suns. A priest lifted a crucifix to his mouth. McGee let the cigarette fall, kissed the cross, exhaled smoke into the priest's face, muttered a Hail Mary at the sky, and stared my way as if I were aiming the fatal shot from the scribbles in my notebook.

All of Cuba went silent, save the church bells, which echoed to Hispaniola. Vultures arrived, at the ready to peck away McGee's lips when the time came. There was a stale breeze on my brow. I screwed the metal cap from my canteen and dowsed my compassion with a long drink.

McGee had one working eye; the other was crystal. There wasn't an ounce of fear in him. Or bravado. Chin high, shoulders squared. He had an impish smirk. Like the Yellow Kid in the color comics.

The barefoot Yellow Kid of *Hogan's Alley* smirks from the page at whoever happens to be reading. The smirk follows me around like the eyes of the Mona Lisa. I used that; I wrote:

> The Tennessean smirked at all creation, like the Yellow Kid.

I filled two columns with precise prose, and barbershop readers throughout Greater New York stood with me among royal palms.

> He was willing to be killed, but not to be frightened. I shuddered as if I were the one doomed. I jumped when rifles resounded.

It was a sweet piece of writing, well-sifted words that said more than volumes of Mark Twain bowel movements.

> A thousand dickey birds lifted, but McGee stood solid. We maintained eye contact as blood oozed through his nose and mouth and crystal eye and dripped onto unwashed feet.
>
> At first it seemed McGee was unharmed, his good eye fierce like that of a baited bull. He kept to his feet long enough for me to catch him, an act of charity to save a man from collapsing face first into wet grass.

In the news profession, we call it a "holy shit!" item.

> I eased him down to the bolt-action echo of reloads and, without concern for personal safety, cut the fishing line from his wrists.

I couldn't believe my fortune at stumbling upon this moment at the exact time. Had I happened along an hour later, McGee never would've existed. Neither would the blood-soaked letter in his breast pocket regarding his sister Luisa. Neither would Luisa, God forbid.

Blood dripped from that pocket and sank into black soil. He looked up with his one eye and said, "Ralph Waldo Emerson was right, sometimes gunpowder smells kinda good."

It was the perfect quotation. I jotted it in my notes. When I later wrote **THE DEATH OF A TENNESSEEAN**, I left Emerson out. A dying man deserved credit for his last words.

"Talk to me," this correspondent said. "I'm Jay Kelley, with the *New York Journal.*"

America's fastest-growing, most influential newspaper. The *Sun* is dull, the *Herald* duller. The *Times* gets all atwitter about the zoning board. The despicable *World* prints news for people who move their lips when they read.

"I have the authority to make your life—and your demise—mean something."

People tell me things, they sense I'll give them a fair shake. Dogs bark incessantly and snotty-nosed sprouts shelter themselves in their mother's skirts, but any creature with two legs and older than twelve tells me this that and the other.

He was so close to the end that he could barely speak, but his trust in me allowed for a brave effort.

"Jesus," he said straight at me. He was hillbilly to the core, but pronounced our Savior's name HAY-soos like the sad natives. "Jesus, I was hopin' for better."

I gave him a drink of rum from my flask. He spat it out and coughed blood.

"Do you have family?" I asked.

"About a million cousins. Back in Plumtree."

"Plumtree?"

"Watauga County."

"Anyone here? In Cuba?"

"A sister. They'd like to shoot her, too."

"What reason would they have to shoot a girl?"

"Don't tell her I kinda jumped into a mess and died at the hands of Spaniards."

"Family deserves to know," I said.

He coughed more blood. "Cain't you mind your business?"

"Not very well, sir, and be a good newsman."

He gasped like a snapper on the floor of a boat. "Bury me back in Plumtree, Tennessee, please."

McGee said, "Bury me back in Plumtree, North Carolina, *por favor,*" but I took the liberty, not only to rhyme Plumtree, but to translate his Spanish. My readers lead complex city lives. They were putting up with the inconvenience of a trolley strike and appreciated me helping them along.

I made McGree thirty-three because death at that age carries a certain significance in the Sunday edition thirteen days before Christmas. I later learned he was thirty-one, three years younger than me, a peace baby born nine months after the end of Lincoln's War. I was born in the smeary, bloody heat of it all. In Massachusetts. I have a smooth baby face that permits me to fib about my age like a lady. I often tell people my birthday's a day after theirs to help them remember it.

"You'll be buried in Plumtree. I promise."

McGee whispered, "*Mi Dios existe.*"

He whispered, "My God exists," and was shortly buried without coffin in a grave with a famished open mouth. A grave the lousy Spaniards shoveled in, over that eye staring bang at the Caribbean sky.

McGee went as the best of them go. He passed on to his Maker with the glory of faith, the glory of love of country. All that was left was his cigarette, rolled peasant-style, smoldering in the grass.

That was the last paragraph in the story beneath my Jayson Kelley byline, my illustrated thumbnail portrait, and the headline:

THE DEATH OF A TENNESSEEAN

Despicable Spaniards Slay
Honest American in Cold Blood
Volunteer State Mourns
Samuel McGee

The Page One item was holy shit! electric and made Americans damn incensed the Spanish had shot one of ours without provocation. It brought us to the brink until President McKinley gave a soft speech. He reminded a lawn audience in his calming voice that he'd been at Antietam with the 23rd Ohio on America's bloodiest day, and war is a last resort after every agency of peace has failed. He repeated that in an interview to Sylvester Scovel of the despicable *New York World:*

> "We shouldn't send men into the mutilation mill. For, when a man dies, he leaves anguish behind, anguish to maidens who long for lovers and mothers who grieve for sons," the President said.

My publisher, William Randolph Hearst, fumed each time the *World* printed spoon-fed drivel. Willie despised Joseph Pulitzer, the half-blind geezer Jew who published the *World,* and responded with an opinion piece that may have gone too far.

> Personal tragedies have turned the resolve of our commander–in–chief to feathers. The most mollycoddled American lives in the White House.

Politicians were fair game for such words, but McKinley had lost two daughters, one to cholera and one to scarlet fever. The grieving First Lady had public seizures that were on the q.t., but next to Willie's piece was a three-column illustration of McKinley in his wife's bonnet and apron. It was drawn by Frederic Remington, our crack artist.

You'll find no greater defender of the First Amendment than myself, but Willie had stepped beyond the pale. His words published beside Remington's aproned illustration turned the office of the presidency into a baffoonery. I winced—and I don't wince easily.

In retrospect, Willie can't be blamed. He didn't have all the facts. To this day, Willie doesn't know I fabricated **THE DEATH OF A TENNESSEEAN** while Sam McGee sat across from me at the outdoor café of the Hotel Inglaterra.

THE DEATH OF A TENNESSEEAN was fiction. That's the big secret. No one else knows. Sam McGee never stood before a firing squad, I just said so in the newspaper. He never died. He's so alive he sparkles.

Willie *can* be blamed. I've changed my mind. He demanded items with bite, one after another. I had to juice from time to time to keep him off my back. He had impossible expectations, or I never would've written one word in the *New York Journal* that didn't ring true.

Truth is, McGee was my interpreter. As I wrote a masterpiece about the circumstances of his death, he drank lemonade over crushed ice, read magazines in Spanish and English, and plucked Appalachian music on a *bandurria*. I'm a modern correspondent, a two-fingered wizard on the typewriting machine; I play it like McGee played the tiny stringed instrument. I made it sing. From time to time, I halted my industrious clacking to drink from a bottle of dark rum, rub my nose, and to ask questions.

"McGee, have you ever been to Tennessee?"

He peered over *Forest and Stream*, over the top of his spectacles.

"*Si, si.* Cy Young could throw a baseball from Plumtree to the state line. Me and ev'ryone of my cousins have stood in North Carolina and made water on Tennessee."

He seemed immune to the Cuban oven. His lemonade glass

sweated, but he never did. I doubt if my interpreter would sweat if he were facing death, so that detail was true, as were most others, including his U.S. citizenship and the letter in his breast pocket regarding his sister Luisa.

I didn't meet Luisa for the longest time and I once accused him of making her up. But she proved to be so earthly real that I still can't get her off my mind.

I'd resumed typewriting when a flash of lightning gave pause. It was a ways off but unusual in winter once hurricane season had passed.

"Come to Plumtree with me," McGee said. His invitation had a cheerful lilt as if he meant it. "We'll go in the spring, I'd kinda like that. We'll sleep as brothers with your head in North Carolina and your tired feet in Tennessee."

"Plumtree's the last place I'll go, I promise."

His feelings were hurt. I didn't have time for that, and I went back to clacking. "You want me to be honest with you, don't you, McGee?"

"Sorries, *lo siento,*" he said. "I invited you because I've wanted a li'l brother all my life."

"They're not what they're cracked up to be."

He revisited his magazine; his feelings were still hurt.

"If I were to name my biggest sin, it might be honest, blunt frankness," I said.

"You're forgiven," he said, which wasn't what I was seeking, but it let me get back to work. After a while I stopped to read over what I'd typewritten. I considered his hometown. It was so close to the state line—and I to Willie's impossible deadline—I let Plumtree be in Tennessee.

Only once did McGee circle behind and try to read over my shoulder. I glared back and said, "How'd you like me to watch you take a dump?" and, to this day, he doesn't know he died in the wet grass of Page One and almost started the war two months early.

There's no one on earth who thinks himself more alive than Mc-Gee. Only the world thinks him dead. I make that confession as an act of good faith so all who read this account forward will trust its honesty no matter how hard some portions are to swallow.

I'm the son of a Massachusetts minister. My mother passed twenty-eight years ago when I was a small boy. I swear on her garden grave that words from here forth are sincere. This account will damage my reputation and give a black eye to the entire news industry—the entire country. I soldier on out of duty to the truth. The truth is all there is.

I start by setting the record straight. McGee has both eyes. He was raised a Baptist but listened to mass outside the Cathedral of *San Cristóbal* in Havana and would never blow smoke into a priest's face. He doesn't smoke. Or drink. Only lemonade and buttermilk. He's maddening, but I came to love McGee more than my real brother Joe, the captain of the Baltimore Orioles Base Ball Club.

"Of course, we can be brothers," I told McGee before I even knew him well.

"May I be blunt, too?" McGee asked.

"No brother needs permission to say anything."

"You've a joy and a sorrow in your eyes at the same time. Like Luisa."

He pronounced sorrow, sorrah. I enjoyed his accent. I awoke mornings to take a swim in it. But the last time I saw McGee, his eyes were filled with tears of disappointment. Luisa's eyes had wild anger. I thought *we* were in love, but I suppose it was only me. Maybe none of us, but I followed them both to the ends of the earth. She said it was McGee I'd forever be trailing. She said I was a better man when he was nearby.

Luisa didn't have McGee's southern accent. Hers was solid Cuban, but she sometimes spoke gibberish like McGee. Gibberish runs in families, even families long separated. I don't speak or comprehend gibberish; I'm a disciple of the honest precision of English. I've mastered it and, by the end of this tale, there will be no confusion. These are the simple facts and I guess I ought to know. McGee, forever dead, will outlive us all.

CHAPTER TWO

TRUTH IS, I WAS THE ONE AT DEATH'S DOOR WHEN OUR FATES CROSSED. McGee was johnny-on-the-spot, and it wouldn't be the last time.

I'd been combing Cuba for a holy shit! war story when I came upon two wealthy Cuban landowners, also on horseback. They were in foul moods, that much was clear. Their cane fields had been set afire by rebels and smoke was so thick our horses almost bumped heads.

The smoke made our meeting place small and inescapable. They had the nerve to search my haversack and found a tin tobacco box full of matchsticks. I explained that I'd won them playing cards because my artist Frederick Remington was too Scotch to play for money, but they knew no English no matter how loudly I spoke it. I knew enough Spanish to realize I was an arson suspect. They must've known I was a well-situated American aboard such an animal, but they seemed set on making a citizen's arrest all the same.

Tight quarters made my pony jumpy. From the cane smoke came a calming whistle that became a man on foot. He was small in stature like most men on the island, but he wasn't Cuban. He was as fair-skinned and light-haired as the Irish, impish, a pinkish presence in a land of black and brown.

"*Buenos tardes,*" he said.

"Help me," I said. I was frightened, but I'm certain I didn't sound so. "I'm to be lynched on a whim."

He blinked over the top of his spectacles, as if someone had surprised him with a flash-powder photograph. My captors knew him, and he addressed them in Spanish and me in English. His cadence was slow and soothing. His English had a Confederate accent, with a tint of Latin, a queer mixture I'd never once encountered in my travels.

"You resemble the Yellow Kid," I said.

"Who's the yellah kid?" He didn't wait for an answer. "Don't call them two yellah. The one Spaniard's my boss, *El Jefe*, he lives in that large white house, got a wife and some li'l fellers. I'm foreman of his burnt-down plantation. The one with the gun on his hip's a loony neighbor out to shoot someone, anyone, for causin' the fire."

"I'm Greater New York's most acclaimed correspondent," I said. "Tell these gentlemen they can count on faring badly in cold type. If they shoot me, the United States Navy will visit next week."

He passed that along, which did nothing to diffuse things. "Landowners like us Yanks, but they believe the Yankee press is simpatico with the *reconcentrados*," he said.

"Every word I write is fair and accurate."

"I prefer magazines, *Forest and Stream*," he said. The word stream came out of his mouth in two syllables, as if it tumbled over Appalachian rocks. He nodded toward the landowners, his thumbs stuck in his back pockets. "These ones need convincin'," he said and walked off.

"Where are you going?" Fright was in my voice for certain and the landowner with the gun smiled.

"I was about to make water when I stumbled upon your mess. If I don't go, my eyeballs will float."

He disappeared into the cane smoke while fiddling with his fly. The second he stepped from sight, the armed neighbor tried to commandeer my pony. I started to dismount, willing to sacrifice it as a business expense, but he sneered at my cowardice. He called me "*pendejo numero uno*," and cocked his pistol.

"The U.S. Navy will be here yesterday," I said from my straddle. "*Mañana*."

He waved his pistol in the direction of my heart. I crouched for safety behind my pony's head, but the animal nickered, shook off tiny mosquitoes with a hoof stomp, and tucked her muzzle toward the ground. I'd never been so exposed and I'd no choice but to sit upright with honor.

"It's William Randolph Hearst's horse," I said. "You can have it." The loon understood not a syllable, so I cried, "IT'S WILLIE'S HORSE."

"Eats weelee, eats weelee." He lowered his aim to mock me more. Maybe he was loony enough to fire at my crotch and risk wounding the animal. "Eats weelee, *pendejo. Hasta la vista* eats weelee *numero uno.*"

That intelligent exchange caused my bespectacled friend to appear from the cane while buttoning up. "Smokier than the Smokies," he said coughing.

"Who the blazes are you?" I said.

"Samuel McGee."

The landowner kept his aim square at my nuts. "Do something, McGee," I said. "He intends to unman me."

"All's well," and McGee slapped the gunman's horse on the rear, causing all three animals to spook. I bounced an inch off the saddle just as the weapon discharged and whistled a bullet off saddle leather.

Sam McGee—and my decision to make Willie pay for more animal than I needed—saved my life. My pony bolted as an arrow leaves a bow. I leaned forward until I was flat, flogged her to speed. My whipping arm kept pace with the pounding of my heart. The pony flew as if she had eight legs, ate ground with soundless hooves. I doubt if she left a footprint. She made it to Havana's outskirts before she began to play out. Her feet caught in some roots and she broke down.

Her foaming nostrils flared cherry red. I petted her inky breast and stroked her mane before I shot her out of mercy. I hiked to the Inglaterra Hotel, grateful I hadn't taken the time to name her. I was pleased I'd gotten McGee's name. He was probably at the exact time being shot for rescuing me, and I intended to write a Page One tribute to him. And to the pony to justify the expense.

That was the first time McGee saved my life. Four years before that first meeting, I was a floundering reporter drowning in anonymity. I'd moved from Boston to San Francisco to put distance between me and my family. My items were fact-filled and helped San Franciscans lead informed lives, but that got me nowhere. I was as good-looking then as I am now, but I had empty pockets and I went unnoticed by girls shaded beneath parasols.

Willie bought the *New York Journal* with his mommy's money. It cost next to nothing, little more than the $20 gold piece he wears for a tie pin, but it bled hundreds of thousands of dollars each month. San Francisco reporters work for a whistle, so Willie transferred me from his *Examiner* to Newspaper Row, where I was a hack, ten assignments a day for two bits each.

New York's the Mecca of journalism; I was thirty-two and I had to make my mark straight away. I stepped off the train at Grand Central on Thanksgiving Day 1895, two years before McGee stepped out of the cane field smoke. I was escorted by a newsboy from the platform gate to the Princeton-Yale football match, an annual affair played to the obscene rumble of eighteen thousand fanatics in Manhattan. Half the chaps get carried off unconscious; one dies now and then.

Rarely did I report sporting news, though I'd been a swimmer and oarsman at St. Stephen's. I'm a half inch shorter than my baby brother. I'm athletic and capable of batting ahead of Joe in Orioles order. Except I've bad feet.

Yale wore white, but captain Brink Thorne dyed his jersey crimson for the occasion. He smelled of cranberry juice, but I told readers it was slaughterhouse blood. The edition sold until it was exhausted.

My colleagues believed it impossible for a serious newsman to come from outside the magic of New York. Crack reporter Ralph London convinced Willie I was a one-story fluke and I was ordered to write obituaries.

Fresh death is of great interest; funerals, an odd mixture of resentments and vulnerability. Family cesspits teeming with muck and yarns.

I produced a steady stream, and I bedded a doll now and then, rich girls who were sifting through the complications of grief. I don't kiss and tell. I'm not heartless, but that's the gist.

I met a gang of yeggmen burglars at a funeral and gained their good opinion. They went on to Sing Sing; I wrote a Page One item about the artistry of safecracking. One yarn after another. I found a headless torso floating in the East River and conveyed the news aboard one of Willie's racing pigeons.

The next day, while the *World* scrambled to catch up, a pair of legs turned up in Harlem, wrapped in stained oil cloth. Remington was miles away, so he went down the street to watch a butcher at work. He drew a diagram, and I wrote a scientific item on deadline, about how a man can best be cut into pieces.

Readers liked their news drenched in emotion, so on Day Three of **THE HEADLESS TORSO** investigation, I juiced a story about a love triangle gone sour. I learned most things ahead of the cops and, on Day Four, I leapt into a moving carriage to make a citizen's arrest. The bum was guilty, but released for lack of evidence.

My career became a fortuitous blur, no enterprise too mighty to investigate. Circulation soared six-fold to one hundred and fifty thousand in my first year. I vaulted past Ralph London out of turn to become the *New York Journal's* choice correspondent. My fellow reporters changed their tune, but I was rarely in town to enjoy the envy. I was traipsing off to the far ends. I'd happen upon a foreign land, root around, and write items that satiated parlor conversation the day long. My home was a hotel room at 8 E. 32nd but, God knows, I was never home.

The trades attacked me from the get-go. They said I made five hundred a week. That flamed resentment among my colleagues. The trades said my stories were well-crafted but riddled with unanswered questions. It was New York snobbery again and I didn't let it bother me. After all, the trades once called Nellie Bly a mere stunt girl from Pittsburgh, and the doll became the most famous correspondent in the world for trotting around the globe in the eighty days Jules Verne had imagined in fiction.

I was determined to collect more miles than Nellie Bly, which led me everywhere, to Cuba, to Sam McGee—and at last to Luisa. To get there I peed a thousand feet from the Rock of Gibraltar, played stud poker with Prince Albert in Monaco, hunted fossils in the Karoo. I didn't go to the North Pole to interview Saint Nick, though I wrote a spoof to entertain the snot monsters in the Christmas Eve edition.

> Yes, Virginia, there is a Santa Claus. But don't believe it if you see it in the *Sun*.

Thomas Edison gave me an exclusive demonstration of his moving picture invention.

> It fails to do for the eye what the gramophone does for the ear.

From the auto-car show in England, I predicted another fading fad.

> We gawk but we will never love auto-cars as we do horses.

I got a pile of angry letters, but I was right again when I wrote:

> William McKinley, sadly, will defeat the boy orator William Jennings Bryan in a bitter election of few jobs and deadly strikes.

McKinley was a captive of tariffs and big business. He was wedded to his beliefs and liked to scapegoat the press. I had no stomach for his inauguration, and I took a slow boat to Queen Victoria's Jubilee. I stayed until I grew tired of all the wine that was white and all that was red, all the pomp and powdered wigs.

"You've enough loafing for a lifetime," Willie cabled. "You'll be happy to know your next assignment's in your hometown."

He insisted I steam to Boston and write a thumb sucker about his one-time Harvard classmate Earnest Thayer, who'd accomplished nothing of note after writing the *Casey at the Bat* ballad.

I wouldn't be bothered. Like many of my generation, I have a dash of anarchist in me. I don't take orders well, and I didn't want to be anywhere near my old man.

"Great pianists aren't slaves to the metronome," I cabled Willie, and I set sail for Seattle by way of the Panama Railroad. An old sweetheart had cabled that oodles of gold were showing up from the Yukon, but she hadn't seen a word of it in the local press. I arrived to find reporters swarming Schwabacher Dock, awaiting the next southbound steamship. I hired a boat, intercepted a steamer at sea, interviewed prospectors throughout the night. Each had more than fifty thousand dollars in dust and nuggets and I landed a *holy shit!* item in the *Journal* a day ahead of the pack.

I started the Klondike stampede, Willie forgave my insubordination, and a Page One is framed behind glass on his wall:

A TON OF SOLID GOLD ABOARD
Frenzied Rush Sets the Whole World Agog
Great Adventure of the Century

I changed the spelling of my byline from Jayson Kelly to Jayson Kelley. No harm was ever done inserting a vowel. It felt right, made me memorable, gave me separation from my father and my brother, and put Willie on notice that one cross remark would send me jumping to the *New York World* with my readers tagging behind like boardwalk ants to salt-water taffy.

Willie said I was full of myself. I admit, I'm a bit headstrong, but a Sunday edition with my byline was more popular than churchgoing. My success had him painted into a corner. I had him convinced I was the taller man, although he's tall as my six-foot-two base-baller brother.

Like Joe, little things bothered Willie. Sheez, it bothered him that I was born a day after he was. I'd look younger except I've a bit of a limp on both sides. Due to my feet.

New York's a rumor mill, and there was plenty about Willie. He lived in a suite at the Hoffman House, but room service dishes cluttered his furniture. He crossed his legs frenchy at the knee.

I never spread gossip, but there were whispers. Willie took teen dancer twins, Millie and Anita, to Bustonoby's for dinner most evenings. Maybe he loved one of them, maybe both, but he kissed neither. Let's just say he'd be a safe choice to escort my sister to a coming-out dance. If I had a sister. Joe's my one sibling, and I rarely see him. I never see my old man; I miss only my mother, planted in her garden.

Willie's true love was Cindy Circulation, and that's where our ideals merged like two mighty rivers. Eyeballs are what matter, and Willie plotted a war in his spare time. No kidding, he itched to start one to sell papers. He needed to groom a war correspondent, and he dispatched me to the Battle at Thessalie where I learned my way around the bottom of a trench. If I were paranoid, I would have suspected that Willie was trying to get me killed because he couldn't sack me.

One dark night, a Greek soldier was hit while ramming a cleaner down his barrel. It must've been the third time he'd been shot because he said, "Darn, that's Number Three." That's all I got out of him. Soldiers in trench mud are as taciturn as those they slay; it was impossible to get a good quotation.

Another was hit as he was reading a letter from his lover. I'd struck a match to help him see in the pitch. He was hollering invectives at me to put the match out when a sniper, with one bullet, pierced the letter, put out the match, and found his jaw. An awful stroke of luck.

He was a good Christian, so I loaded him over my shoulder and climbed a mound of bodies in search of a surgeon or chaplain. A shell knocked us down. Over we went in a heap until my mouth filled with rock.

He never once moaned. He uttered something, but my Greek is rudimentary, and jawlessness is incomprehensible in any tongue.

He was no doubt urging me to put him down and save myself. But I can never be the skunk.

It wasn't a bit cheerful to see a man, the marvelous work of God, shot through the face.

"I won't leave you behind," I said. "I'll carry you in if I die."

I tore from his chest two war medals he wouldn't be needing in heaven.

He tore from his neck a locket with a woman's face. On the other side were the clustered faces of three small boys.

"Say a prayer," I said. "Pray this war doesn't end until you can get the chap that got you. If you croak, I'll get him for your nippers. I won't have them growing up with revenge on their plates."

He died from the next ordnance that threw us three yards. Another landed but it was a dud. Unfortunately for Willie, it wasn't my time. Chin in slush, I used the dead Greek's twisted bayonet to dig the dud out of the ground while it was hot, and it's the souvenir dolls most admire when I entertain them with fog-of-war tales.

Upon my return to New York I was called upon by clubs to give speeches, which were well received by gentlemen diners and ladies in the gallery. I'd tell them of the dangers I faced, forever under the gun to write what shall stand as history. Bravos from a hundred throats.

Dolls believe newspapering is glamour and fireworks. It is magical, but it can be tedious. There were stretches when one slow news day piled atop another. That made Willie antsy and morose. On good days he spread galley proofs on his office floor and danced over them while snapping his fingers like castanets. When a bad stretch persisted, he hollered at editors through speaking tubes until he got a chronic sore throat. I wondered if he might set a schoolhouse ablaze and position me and our crack artist Remington to await the fire brigade.

CHAPTER THREE

I LONGED TO FIND A SEA MONSTER AND I GAVE THE
PANAMA RAILROAD ANOTHER RIDE. In Santiago, Chile I got a
cable informing me that Papa'd died delivering a sermon. Fire and
brimstone had consumed him. I didn't make it back for the funeral;
I extended my trip to New Zealand to find what I was looking for
washed up on Lyall Bay Beach. Remington drew an illustration from
my cabled description: a giant, slimy serpent with a horse-like head,
spread prone on a sweep of wet sand.

Upon my return, I spent one night at 8 E. 32nd. Willie assumed
my time in South America had made me fluent in the *parlez-vous* of
español and sent me and Remington to Havana to report on Spain's
refusal to give Cubans their independence. The assignment steered my
life by providence into McGee's. Eventually, into Luisa's.

"The ideal skirmish, close to home," Willie said. I'd never seen
him more animated. "A cheap war to staff." His mommy insisted on
that. "We need a dustup to return callous to our hands. A chance for
north and south to unite for the first time since '61. Prove we're a bonafide power."

Three decades had passed since Lincoln's war, a decade since a man
of derring-do could go to Lincoln County, New Mexico and kill a wild
Jicarilla redskin in fair chase.

"We've become effete from the ground up—to the presidency,"
I said.

"You've work to do to fix this nation," Willie said.

His dancer twins outfitted Remington and me in tailored tropical suits with piping on the pant legs. Willie said we were spies taking on a dangerous mission. I'm certain the journalism community sniggered at the getup and the melodrama. But I was happy my byline had expanded to **Jayson Kelley, Special Commissioner**, as if I were more diplomat than reporter, as if the *Journal* were no mere newspaper, but a sovereign nation in its own right. Answerable to God and itself.

Remington and I traveled from Key West to Havana on Willie's yacht, *The Vamoose,* and checked into the Inglaterra, the last word in hotels, with an outdoor café brightly lit, fresh flowers in our rooms. I had a marble balcony with a view of the Rosario Mountains. Cuba reminded me of Venezuela, a lovely country with every sort of verdant green.

It was also as dull as Venezuela. The rebels had neither the heart nor the arms for a frontal attack on Spanish strongholds. They dynamited a train in Santa Clara Province when they believed the Spanish-installed governor to be aboard. Otherwise, they torched the sugarcane of landowners who failed to support the revolution. Few died. I'd seen real war and this wasn't it.

I took to sleeping late but still had time to bathe in the bay, eat a modest breakfast and smoke a cigar before Remington stirred. He needed a sustainable breakfast on a silver tray before doing much of anything. He was as useful as the breeze from an old woman's fan.

"Havana's this hemisphere's Paris," I said, "where diddle's a day's work. I'd rather loaf in France. The dolls there go unprotected by the parental gaze."

Remington shrugged and disappeared for hours. Probably to drowse like a butterfly on a flat stone with never a thought in his head. I'd been a modest drinker in France. In Cuba, I swallowed the resentments of celibacy with a daily bottle of rum. By some miracle, Remington resurfaced each evening with an armful of drawings, if not a single word of stimulating conversation. We'd deal cards into quiet evenings. He was well-situated, but the tightwad insisted on playing for matches.

We never had an honest discussion; he was a brooder with a high-hat attitude. I accused him of being a pacifist. "How does that sit with your family?" It ran the Remington Arms Company.

"I'm an artist," Remington said. "I conscientiously object to the reality of this world."

I got up and thumbed through his drawings. "You're a wonderful talent." I lied. "The one man who can draw a horse to look like a horse." That part was true, but I lose respect for men who can be so smart at one thing and so dumb at everything else. "I find it curious that you never draw innocent *señoritas* in threadbare frocks. That's what readers pay a penny to see."

I thumbed through his drawings again. "Horses. Not a single doll. You're no Renoir."

He riffled the cards. "Cut."

The next evening, Cuba's heat was boiling alcohol out of me faster than it could be replaced. Distant gunfire convinced me to set up camp in the lap of a valley on the northern coast. Remington didn't want to get off his ample ass, but neither did he want to get left behind. He sweated through his shirt more than once. He smelled of onions, and his teats jiggled as he coughed cane smoke.

Our excursion eroded into disappointment. We saw a Spaniard draw sword, but it was to poke at a cook fire. Ten feet of alligator surfaced in our canvas-duck tent and we were soon back at the Inglaterra playing for matchsticks.

A world of gators, tarantulas, chiggers and sand fleas proved too much for Remington, and he decided to go home.

"You're a daisy," I said. "A fluff like Willie. You two walk with the same gait."

"You're a card cheat."

"Who'd cheat for matches?"

He didn't fumble for his answer. "You."

He returned to headquarters in time for Christmas with a folder of sketches as thick as his wife. Good riddance. From his New York desk, he could illustrate whatever I wrote about, and I could write twice as much in half the time with him out of my hair.

The Inglaterra had crushed ice, and I chewed it while smoking cigars alone under the shade of a giant ceiba tree. Ice soothes hangovers. I wrote an item as a service to my readers, that's how uneventful life had become. I cabled Willie to tell him I was coming home, too.

Willie replied with a threat to replace me with Ralph London. "The island is seven hundred miles end-to-end. Something is going on."

I objected to his tone. "All quiet. No war," I cabled. "Coming home."

"REMAIN." Willie's sore throat ripped from speaking tubes and through the underwater cable. "You furnish the dispatches. I'LL FURNISH THE WAR!"

I walked off my frustration along *Calle Obispo*, the principle thoroughfare of Havana. Stray dogs singled me out for torturous baying, and I spent a small fortune on a black Jamaican polo pony to ride above it all and to get Willie to order me home for gross extravagance. A silver star on its forehead, white hind feet, a chest of close-knit muscle, a neigh of independence. A once-in-a-lifetime animal, its coat glistened like wet ink, it took no more than a cluck to get it to take long strides.

The mount replenished my pride, and I steered for a smoldering cane field in quest of some *holy shit!* to splatter against Willie's wall. That's when I encountered the two Cuban landowners in foul moods and ready to arrest me for arson. That's when the whistling McGee appeared from the smoke and that's when I flew away aboard my Pegasus, believing the hillbilly had sacrificed his life for mine.

McGee deserved Page One treatment. He deserved Willie's wall. But to land him there required a little juice. A lot of juice. It required something more than two angry landowners. It required an innocent American gunned down by a Spanish firing squad.

Days passed before I wrote **THE DEATH OF A TENNESSEAN** because McGee turned up alive. The morning after my grand escape, he was on *Calle Mercadores* handing out sticks of sugarcane to little peasant boys with gooey grins. Nine times in ten I would've ignored their shrills, but McGee wore a smile I could see a mile.

A four-year-old girl played among the sprouts. McGee lifted her into his arms and said something to her in Spanish that got the boys giggling.

He looked up at me as if I were expected. "Look at this *chica's* cheeks."

He kissed them both, bantered more Spanish, and the girl squirmed in contagious delight. "I told her other *señoritas* are way past nine before they git so smart and lovely. I don't want her to git a minit older. I'll put an adobe brick on her head to stop her from growin'."

He fashioned a crude doll of sugarcane and gave it clothes with the leaves. "The girls in Plumtree use rhododendrons," he said.

He gifted the doll to the girl, kissed her sticky chin, and set her on her feet to hopscotch into the jangle of boys. He watched her go as if he'd never seen a child.

"Their hearts are so busy with today they don't care what comes after," McGee said. "A simple faith." He remembered to shake my hand. "Bet you're happy to be out of the cane smoke. Say, you've got the grip of a man who picks up a tool now and then. Where's your pony? I've cane to feed her."

"Ran off. I gave her freedom. I owe her—and you—my life."

"We look out for each other, *amigo*. That's kinda what we do."

"You're unemployed—and it's my fault."

"Life turns out the way it's meant to be. I've been in Cuba five years. Found what I came for. Thanks to you, I'll not be rottenin' here another five. Canada's my dream. Canada or Alaska."

"Gold?"

"Love, maybe."

I laughed. "A hundred miners for each whore in the Klondike. Canada's for gold and cold; stay in Cuba for love. I've never seen so much promise."

"Too many girls here have been ruined," McGee said. "My sister Luisa's one. I'll take her with me to the Yukon if she'll go. She needs to be far from here. She's a right excitin' girl, never gits bored."

"A handful?"

"*Ay, dios mio*—oh, my god."

"Lucky she has a big brother to look after her."

"She's my big sister. Two years older than me, unwed in her thirties, does what she wants. I'll go with or without her, but the Yukon's not far enough for Luisa."

"Wait until after winter," I said. "I can use an interpreter and right hand."

McGee hugged me. "I knew you were good luck from the git-go. As cane foreman, I befriended poor workers and well-to-do owners with ease. I kinda run with the hare and with the hound, I'll git you interviews with the *reconcentrados* and Spanish occupiers. You'll git both sides of the Cuban question. Always two sides, but you kinda know that more than me."

He agreed to minuscule wages, which I'd bury in my expenses. He'd sleep on a cot in my room for as long as I could stand him. I'm never a cheapskate, but McGee would die soon in the *Journal* and I wanted him hidden from Willie.

"Before I can begin this new job, this fortuity, this blessin', I've somethin to do," McGee said. "A prior commitment. A Cuban rebel has been shot dead. Father John has asked me to inform his *familia*. You're welcome to tag along. Please do. Deliverin' sadness is best done in pairs."

I wanted nothing of it. That was my first reaction, but I needed a story. We hiked a half mile. McGee knocked knuckles on a solid door answered by a pretty Cuban doll. Yet twenty, she seemed too young to be a *señora*, much less a widow. A toddler was hiding in her skirt, a lap baby in her arms.

McGee's introduction was in Spanish; I understood his name and mine and nothing else. McGee must've asked if we could come inside because the widowed doll left the nipper on the front porch to play and led us to the kitchen. Her home was both bare and filled with charming things that made it quaint and restful. She invited us to sit at the table but we stood.

McGee got right to it. He said *"muerto"* two or three times, followed by *"lo siento."*

The widow stared in disbelief at nothing. I thought she was going to soldier through. She watched her baby fiddle with her wedding ring for the longest time. She handed the baby to me, fell to all fours, and wept bloody murder on the kitchen floor. She got up and found a dish to throw at McGee, slapped me, remembered I had the baby, took it back and gave it to McGee, beat her fists on my chest for a time. When the fight went out of her, she embraced me as if I were her man, sobbed and screamed, *"Por qué? Por qué?"* over and over.

It was a primal scream, uncontrollable, convulsive, and I was at a loss for words. "There, there, I know how you feel."

"Por qué, Dios? Por qué?"

I patted her. "Time heals all wounds. You'll get over this someday. Things will be fine."

McGee winced. Then he shrugged with palms up. "Say what you want," he said. "She doesn't understand a word, but speak softly, not kinda reporter-like. Tone matters, not words." McGee reconsidered. "Nothin' matters. You cain't make it better and you cain't make it worse."

Her sobs quieted as she buried her face into my chest until my shirt was soaked. At last, she pushed away and rattled off some words. McGee rattled words back, and she ran out of the house and into the thick, bawling and bawling.

"What did she say?" I asked.

"How am I goin' to tell my son?"

"What did you say?"

"'I don't know.' Sometimes the honest answer is 'I don't know,' but too few are kinda willin' to say it."

"McGee, what are we doing here? That's the honest question. Why did you volunteer us for this agony?"

"Father John asked. It never gets easier. Her life has changed and we cain't fix it."

"Do you enjoy others suffering?"

"Sufferin's not all bad. Cain't avoid it, anyway. Keeps newspaperin' a-goin, doesn't it? When was the last time you wrote about church picnics?" He kissed the baby. "I've lived a fortunate life. So fortunate that sometimes I feel guilty. Almost ashamed. That's why I do it. We'll stay until she comes back for her li'l fellers. I'll check back and see her in the morn. First thing."

"Anyone who volunteers for agony is as loony as that landowner who took a shot at my nuts."

He shrugged. "Someone has to deliver the news. Someone has to deliver the truth. Everyone kinda deserves to hear it."

CHAPTER FOUR

IT WOULD ALWAYS SEEM ODD TO ME, BUT IN SOME WAYS, THAT WAS A TAILOR-MADE DAY. I sat with McGee until the grieving mother returned at dusk. I got to know him in the periphery of her suffering. I'd never forget that day.

He had no status or special abilities, yet people loved him. McGee could talk and talk, but he was quiet when he needed to be, and his habits seldom got under my skin.

Hillbillies don't converse, they "visit." That was McGee's worst sin. That and he never smoked nor drank a drop nor gambled and went to bed at twilight so he could get up and comfort grieving dolls around Havana. He always left without waking me. Always returned to my side shortly after I awoke, arriving in a hurry, as if he would suffer if he ever let me down.

I accused him of paying secret morning visits to Luisa. "Why do you hide her from me? Is she ugly?"

"Not as ugly as you." The only time McGee retaliated with that tone was when I spoke poorly of his sister. He enjoyed me poking fun at him. He lacked a penchant for grudges and judgement. He was like me in many respects and he became so dear I insisted he call me Jay.

He settled on *El Capitán*.

"I'll never be a commissioned officer," I said. "Bad feet."

"You should be proud," he said. "You're fulfillin' duty to country as a correspondent."

I never saw a man hustle so hard for so little money. I soon had an interview with Valeriano Weyler y Nicolau, the governor of Cuba installed by Spain. Captain-General Weyler was dignified and courteous. I began with a question about the hot weather. That was a ploy of mine, be it popes or presidents. I inquire first about weather, or a favorite book, or how they take their coffee. I study them when they are at ease in honesty.

When I switch to prying, some men crack their knuckles, others clear throats, swallow, or yawn. Nobody's nose grew, but anxiety escapes man's caverns with the zig-zag of bats. Some burp, some fart, some turn white, as if I'm pirating their souls.

I once interviewed the last surviving veteran of the War of 1812, or so the world had believed. I exposed his life-long impersonation of a real war hero, who died on Lake Ontario at age seventeen. The headline **DESPICABLE ACT OF STOLEN VALOR** hangs behind glass on Willie's wall.

"Is it always steamy in Cuba?" That's the baseline question I asked General Weyler.

"You think this is hot? Come back on your Fourth of July." His English was fluent, though McGee fed him a word or two when he stumbled.

"Cuba deserves it's own Independence Day," I said.

"Not on my watch," Weyler said. He didn't sound insulted; the successful are expert at hiding that.

"I've seen nothing but peaceful, harmless, hard-working Cubans since I arrived."

General Weyler showed me a missing earlobe. "A cigar was shot from my teeth with the same peaceful bullet."

"America gained its independence more than a century ago," I said. "Hasn't Cuba waited long enough?"

"Cuba was a gift from God to Spain for driving Islam from Europe in the fifteenth century."

I rolled my eyes at that whopper, and Weyler insulted me in Spanish.

"He says you are a sympathizer," McGee said. "He says you cain't be impartial."

Weyler ended the interview and, to camouflage his rudeness, provided me and McGee with a railway car to tour the island. We were escorted by a valet who addressed me in English as "my lord." McGee found that amusing, and he called me "my lord" instead of *El Capitán* for the entire train ride. I had some choice words about Weyler, but McGee defended him.

"He's saddled with a kinda impossible job."

"He's the cause of your grieving widows," I said, and I wrote this for the *Journal*:

> Butcher Weyler is a four-foot-ten fiendish despot, a cold, pitiless exterminator of men. There is nothing to prevent his carnal animal brain from running riot with itself in inventing torture and infamies of debauchery.
>
> He's more bloodthirsty than any Turk and will be remembered as the monster of the century.
>
> Yesterday, I had a young, fresh widow sob endlessly on my shoulder. God pities widows and mothers in distress and fatherless children, but He does not pity Butcher Weyler.

This may be where I stepped beyond the pale:

> I wonder how many innocents Weyler corpsed last night. He ties the arms and legs of rebels and has them pulled apart by horses. I wonder how many Cuban girls will go unwed because of him. Weyler would plug a pal in the back.

I was given twenty-four hours to leave Cuba or be arrested. I'm never one to succumb to demands—that whiff of anarchist in me—and I was captured at the Inglaterra and escorted to the docks.

Spanish soldiers forced me onto a merchant ship bound for Key West. It cast off, but it had floated fewer than a hundred yards when soldiers on shore turned their backs and walked away. They believed they had done their duty, or they had run out of rum.

I seized the moment. I folded my notes into a waterproof oilskin packet and, as God is my witness, dove into the shark-infested sea.

I am an expert swimmer, quite the English channeler Mathew Webb, but I was thrown by a breaker against a coral ledge. Somehow I found the Cuban beach. Half conscious, I waded for miles through stagnant waters and muck black as night. I found solid ground and ran like a tom cat caught in a round of rain.

I bivouacked with rebel troops, recovered from injuries, and spent nights enjoying Cuban music throbbing through the topmost trees.

There is a ten-thousand-peso reward on my head, but I fear less for myself than for these kind rebels. They are poor as can be. They smoke horse manure. If they have shoes, they are slung around their necks with a string.

I advise them to turn me in for the money so that they can feed their families, but they refuse.

I paid the rebels to smuggle out my stories written in longhand, and I was still bivouacked when McGee tracked me down. He found me dozing in a hammock, which was unfortunate because I never take naps.

"Your items kinda made it across the Atlantic to the Queen of Spain," he said.

He was red as a berry from the days he'd spent looking for me. "Good news. Weyler's been replaced as governor to improve relations with America. You do have influence. The mighty pen. Spain says you're a distinguished journalist and welcome to stay."

Even so, I secured the additional weight of a Colt .45 revolver and a counterfeit press credential that identified me as a correspondent for the Spanish newspaper *El Pireneo Aragonés*. I never stoop to forgery, but I signed my credential with Weyler's own name.

I finally got around to typewriting **THE DEATH OF A TENNESEEAN** as McGee and I sat at the outdoor café. He droned on, he thought I could typewrite and listen to him at the same time.

"Your turn," he said. Lightning was three miles off. "Tell me a story. You have a million."

"I don't tell stories. They call them stories, but they're facts strung together in interesting ways. I was hoping to teach you how to do it, make you a cub reporter, but it's a challenge. It's not for everybody."

"Why did you decide to be a correspondent?"

"America's need to know," I said. "No mystery there. You're the enigma, Sam McGee. How did a Carolinian end up here?"

"Why am I in Cuba?" Repeating the question was a stall tactic.

"You heard me."

"Where I go, there I am. That's kinda all there is to tell. Why'd I leave Plumtree? God only knows. Land so steep nobody wants it. There's sorta lotsa reasons. Panic of ninety-three closed the mica mines. Plumtree's seldom been a goin' concern. Most prefer the company of huntin' dogs to people, but ev'ryone still knows ev'ryone's business in Watauga County."

He went on casting for his answer. "Train reached Cranberry in eighty-two. I cut cross ties for twenty cents each. I knew wheat, potatoes, fruit trees. Now I know how to grow cane as high as an elephant's eye."

"New Yorkers don't know their neighbors," I said.

McGee believed that was impossible. "Ev'rybody knows ev'rybody in Plumtree. I was an only child, but my aunts and uncles had at least six kids each. My cousins asked what it was like to have a bed to myself. 'Lonely,' I said. My paps was born on the slopes of Grandfather Mountain, my mams grew up five miles to the south. There were never two people more in love. And they loved me with all their heart. That's what I mean when I say I'm so fortunate I kinda feel guilty. My mam's name was Malinda, but Paps called her Sammy. I was named for her."

"Never knew a man named for his mama."

"I'm so fortunate, God gave me ev'ythin' except the wisdom to be fully grateful. I feel guilty for having ev'ry ounce of my folks' love, so much love all to myself. I was smothered in it."

I thought he was going to cry. "Your hambone can be both charming and annoying. I know you're lying McGee. You have a sister. Luisa, remember?"

"I *was* an only child, until five years ago when my folks died one right after the other."

McGee spoke three languages, including gibberish. I couldn't figure out how it was possible to gain a sibling upon the death of parents.

"Who's Luisa named for?"

He shrugged. "Named for nobody."

I pressed in. "Why are you both here in Cuba?"

"My mams shot better than most men. That's where Luisa gits it. I prefer a fishin' pole. Caught a string of them on Toe River, where Plumtree Creek enters from the east. You can go fishin' most anytime you want to just about. I shoot economically, I can hit most anythin' in the head close-up, but Luisa's a crack shot from a distance."

I was certain she was boyish and ugly, but I'd learned not to say so. He paused to let a peal of thunder roll past. "Hot weather never bothers me. Sooner live in Hell than be cold."

"And you dream of Canada and Alaska? Tell me, McGee, why'd you leave?"

"Plumtree?" A bolt of lightning struck ground in the Rosario Mountains. He stood to stretch. He hiked his trousers twice. "God only knows."

"Tell me."

He pointed at my machine. "You'll put it in the paper."

I laughed. "People think their lives are more important and exciting than they are."

He kept his gaze on the storm front. "Somethin' I had to do. That's all."

Why did McGee grow up in Plumtree and Luisa in Cuba? That was the overhanging question. But as I became a great reporter, I learned to hold back questions until they'll be answered.

"There's always something we have to do," I said. "I require an interpreter more than an honest answer, so I'll let you off the hook. Secrets make one sick. Tell a priest. That's my advice. Tell Father John."

I rolled a piece of paper into the typewriting machine as more thunder rumbled past. I finished an opening paragraph. "It irks me that Remington's family owns the company that makes these machines, too. I paid a fortune for this. Does the thackery bother you?"

He didn't answer. His thoughts must've still been in the Smokies. Or on Luisa.

"It bothers my colleagues. When I'm at headquarters, I set it on a velvet pad on my desk."

"Nothin' bothers me," McGee said.

"Nothing except the mention of—the truth about her."

"I love my sister. I don't have the brother I wanted. That bothers me. All the time I was growin' up I wanted a li'l bitty brother."

"I have one. They're not what they're cracked up to be."

"I've decided to be your apprentice," McGee said. "Become a cub reporter."

"Won't be easy," I said. "You'll have to quit seeing only the good."

"Maybe I'm not cut out."

"Maybe not. I'll work, we'll both drink."

"That storm's going to pass north, but it's sucking in some cool air." McGee drank lemonade, played folk songs on his bandurria, mentioned how he played a homemade banjo back in North Carolina. Picked up his magazine.

I halted my industrious clacking to drink from a bottle of dark rum. "Have you ever been to Tennessee?"

McGee peered over the top of *Forest and Stream,* over the top of his spectacles. *Si, si.* Never saw the ocean till comin' here, but Cy Young could throw a baseball from Plumtree to Tennessee. Worlds apart, but you can make water in one world and splash the next. Ev'ryone in Plumtree hates Tennessee."

"Why?"

"For no reason. There's never a reason, is there?"

He mentioned sleeping with his head in North Carolina and his feet in Tennessee. "My folks' initials are carved in a pine where, as li'l sweethearts, they held hands and watched eagles glide to Tennessee and back. Paps proposed beneath that pine on a Sunday in 1860. My folks told me ev'rythin' about those days. Except one thing."

"What one thing?"

He circled to read over my shoulder. "Are you sure you're keepin' me out of the paper?"

I glared back at him. "Don't open the outhouse door on a constipated man. How'd you like me to watch you take a dump?" He never again looked over my shoulder, never read stories that he himself couriered to the Spanish censor's office to be cabled.

He went back to plucking Christmas songs. *The First Noel.* I plucked away one of his eyes, but I left his Yellow Kid smile alone. I owed it to him never to touch that smile.

Willie so approved **THE DEATH OF A TENNESSEAN** he boosted my pay to seven hundred a week. He expected a thank you, but I knew enough to know my own worth.

CHAPTER FIVE

MCGEE WAS FAR FROM FLAWLESS. His teetotalism got under my skin for one, but he became dearer each day and, against my better judgment, I made him my apprentice.

"When war breaks out, Willie wants all hands on-deck," I said. "You're fortunate, in the right place at the right time. Willie looks down his nose at anyone who comes knocking for a job. A sucker every day in McKinley's economy. Willie plays pranks on those numbskulls. He tells them they're hired if they can skip down to City Hall and uncover corruption."

"A ploy? I won't be someone's sucker," McGee said, looking at the ceiling from his cot.

"With me as your tutor, and your knowledge of Cuba and the language, you'll cut the mustard."

"I'm lucky to have come across you in that cane field," McGee said.

I nodded. "How often is a man afforded the chance to save the life of a special commissioner? I'd make you a hero if you'd let me."

He sat up. "Tell me the most important thing an apprentice needs to know."

That was easy. "Detecting lies. Lying men wrap their ankles around chair legs and splay their knees in defiance." I demonstrated with the chair in our room. "Fibbing dolls place pocketbooks on their laps. Or put a hand to their throats as if truth leaks from the pores of uncovered skin."

McGee pushed out his cheek with his tongue like a schoolboy

practicing penmanship. "Girls are honest, aren't they?"

"Not since Eve. Do you know who Nellie Bly is?"

"Around the world in seventy-two days. I love Nellie Bly."

"We all do. Our nation's most beloved female personality. Inexhaustible pluck, I'll give you that. She bumped her knees together as if I was going after her candor with forceps."

McGee crossed his legs at the knee like Willie did. "You interviewed Nellie Bly?"

"Willie wanted a yarn about her May-December marriage to a millionaire of industry." I stood in front of the room's mirror fixing my hair. "He's forty-some years older than her, and yet he left her alone with this face of mine. For two hours while he made more money."

"What are you implyin'?"

"She's too whippet-thin for my taste, or we'd have done this that and the other. I could never live with a woman's adultery on my conscience. That's Lesson Two. Lesson One is knowing a liar. Lesson Two is that great correspondents take the high road. We stay above reproach."

McGee liked Lesson Two. He asked for a notebook to record my wisdom.

"Those two things win trust." I slowed my speech as he caught up with his scribbling. "We care for readers. More than they know, but we can't let big hearts get in the way. We can't let concern for one sap stop us from delivering to the thousands."

McGee frowned. "I don't think I'm cut out."

He thought my groan was impatience, but it was painful to push swollen feet into my boots. "Takes practice," I said. "Do you know who Blanche Bates is?" McGee shook his head no. "She's a buxom stage actress; she doesn't believe in right and wrong. She pushed me into the chesterfield in her backstage dressing room at Daly's Theatre. Leaned over me like this."

I took McGee by the back of the neck, and made him stare down my hairy chest. "Nowhere to look but at her whalebone corset and all that bubbles over. Miss Bates was already somewhat partly pregnant."

"By you?"

"By who knows who. DeWolf Hopper, maybe. She got jealous anytime I mentioned another doll, and she threw Hopper in my face. She said I could be a great actor like him with some training."

"I'll become a reporter while you become a great actor."

"That would be a demotion for a special commissioner. Blanche Bates says I know how to incorporate dramatic pause into my love making. What the dickens does that mean?"

McGee shrugged. "I'm the apprentice."

"I never write theater items, but I wrote an endless Blanche Bates yarn. She was never good enough for the New York stage, never had a drop-curtain scene. But I called her a better leading lady than Maude Adams, a heroine of the footlights, with a voice as sweet as bells."

"You write fibs for favors?"

"Hacks do. I'm the one chap who never kicks his golf ball out of the weeds. Dolls footle with me because they want to."

McGee scribbled on. "You don't have to write that down," I said but I let him finish before going on. "A little lying's OK with the Lord if it's for the right reason. Blanche Bates' performances sold out until her family way split her costume at the seams. Haven't seen her since."

McGee stopped taking notes, said my wisdom made his hand cramp.

"I'll teach you how to typewrite. Remember to use lots of paragraphs. Enormous blocks of gray look formidable to lady readers, of which I've many. Come on, class dismissed. We'll go read Willie's latest cable."

We hiked into central Havana. The dogs didn't bark with McGee along.

We arrived at the dispatcher. "I want you to teach me ev'rythin'," McGee said.

"Sure I can," I said while reading the cable.

'What's Mr. Hearst a-sayin'?'

"No surprise, he's antsy for a good story. He wants to get the war underway."

I thought **THE DEATH OF A TENNESSEEAN** would've done the trick, but McKinley took care of that with his soft speech. McGee watched me fold the cable and knew from my expression it was time to quit visiting and get to work.

We double-timed it back to the Inglaterra, where he arranged my typewriting machine and high-grade field glass into a haversack to safeguard my high-grade bottle of rum. That's what I appreciated. He helped with hidden hands. He saw something to be done and he did it.

He threw the leather strap of a canteen over his shoulder, and we were out of the hotel in ten minutes. He was a head shorter than me, but he carried each ounce every step, except for the pistol in my belt and the pencil behind my ear.

I offered to help. "Quit playing a martyr, McGee."

"Take care of those feet," he said.

We walked an hour when we came upon an honest-to-God skirmish.

> Spanish rifle fire started with a few pings. I was in a coastal forest a hundred yards from shore. Close enough to hear the surf, but in short order, the sea was drowned out by bullets that came through mangroves in sheets. Pieces of leaves twirled to my boots like green snow.

Cuban rebels responded to gunfire and McGee took cover beneath an upside-down fishing boat, where he somehow fell asleep. I belly-crawled over to extract my typewriting machine from the haversack McGee was using as a pillow. I wrote this item while seated upon a box of ammunition.

> A stray bullet about tore a trench through my whiskers as I wrote this very sentence.
>
> During this paragraph, hand-to-hand combat surrounded me. Nails dug into windpipes and eye sockets. Men fell over in heaps.

When fighting moved beyond my position, I was pleased to be alive and collapsed exhausted in a storm of aftershells bursting about without pattern.

I will never be able to explain how bullets can pick the best of men and leave the worst alone. Husbands and fathers get done in, while gad-abouts skip on.

I am no jingoist. I am the first to say that war is both better and worse than anything imagined, but the men of America must come to grips with an occasional fight for freedom. There is honor in dying if we die to win lasting peace.

War gives working stiffs their chance at glory, chivalry and romance. It teaches sacrifice, faith, fortitude and courage; it lets a man discover what he's worth.

War is the crowning hour.

I wrote with such focus it seemed I was finished before I'd started. I kicked McGee in the boot to wake him. "You missed it."

He yawned. "Missed what, *El Capitán?*"

For the only time, I invited him to read my typewritten pages. His surprise was genuine.

"How long've I been sleepin'? How long've I been rottenin' under this boat? I slept through a battle. Sorries, *El Capitán,* I'm a disappointment."

But it was Willie who let me down. His next cable arrived luke-warm. He said I was the best in the land at turning a pregnant phrase, but circulation was flat.

"Competing newspapers have no incentive to send a single reporter to Cuba," Willie wrote. "Rather, they poke fun at us."

"Then, bring me home."

Willie ignored the request even when, as a slap to my face,

Pulitzer sent a correspondent and artist to Peru in search of fossils that might disprove Darwin's theories of evolution. The *World* pretended to be high-brow like the *Times,* and cater to the *hoi polloi.* Tell things down the middle, tell the story, but not *be* the story. It was all an act and I knew it when the *World's* artist sent back illustrations of Inca girls working the salt evaporation ponds in hiked skirts.

The *World* never had any intention of ignoring Cuba. They just did it on the cheap. On our nickel. Sylvester Scovel, Pulitzer's ace reporter, was clever. He didn't plagiarize my work outright; he made mention of my items to point out each detail that might be construed as less than factual. His criticism came from the comfort of the Golden Dome.

Scovel was ambitious, six years younger than me and—by some coincidence—also a minister's son. We'd never met face to face, but we would know each other from our thumbnail illustrations. The boys at the *Journal* nicknamed him The Sniper, because he destroyed reputations with a single story. The trades loved him. They printed more than once that "Sylvester Scovel is the truth on two legs."

I hollered at McGee. "While I put my life at risk, The Sniper sits on Newspaper Row in the shadows of the Brooklyn Bridge stealing nuggets from my stories and planting doubts about me in the minds of New Yorkers."

"Lesson Three," McGee said. "A correspondent needs thick skin."

"That's Lesson Four."

He sighed. "I have One and Two in my notes."

"Never let readers guess your politics. And history never repeats itself. Everyone thinks so, but it doesn't. Learn to read upside down. Here's one more: when two eyewitnesses agree about every detail it's a lie. A detective taught me that."

"Life's simpler in Plumtree where my cousins are catchin' some beautiful trout and all that."

I could hear a "visit" coming on, which was the last thing a man needs when frustrated and angry about stalled circulation and sniper attacks.

"One time, me and Hiram Trowbridge and some other cousins were over in Linville and we stumbled upon this fistfight. We didn't even know the boys who were fightin', and we didn't know why they were fightin'. We jumped in just to mess around in it."

"Doesn't sound like you," I said.

"I was a bit of a hooligan for a time. I don't smoke cigarettes now, but I was already makin' them by then."

"I haven't time today. Get to the point, McGee."

He cut his story down to one last sentence. "Things kinda don't work out well when you mess around in somebody else's fight."

The holidays were approaching and they were ruined when Willie cabled that our circulation was still flat, but the *World*'s had ticked up because of risqué illustrations. Pulitzer published a scientific story on the anatomy of a human leg as an excuse to illustrate chorus girls wearing garter belts.

I dashed off a story about dead Cuban prisoners washed ashore in the Bay of Havana. A thousand had been shot in the Morro Castle prison and dropped into the water as shark food.

Willie buried it on Page Eight, but that didn't stop Sylvester Scovel from critiquing me. He wrote that the dead rebels were Cuban criminals and they'd been attempting an escape. None had been shot and only a handful had drowned, Scovel reported. He came this close to calling me a fabricator outright. Willie, to his credit, defended me in an opinion piece.

> Were natural selection a scientific fact, the *New York World* would have gone the way of the great auk.

That was Willie's public position. Privately, he was alarmed we were losing to the *World*'s sexful content. I got frantic cables from him most days. I read them to McGee, but he shrugged and said, "Some things are kinda more important than *chichis*," and he led me to a Cuban hospital deep in a forest surrounded by Spaniard soldiers.

> The hospital was filled with sufferers of *vomito negro*, vomit that looked like black dirt. They bled from the gums and rectums. They howled in pain, but still the Spaniards attacked.
>
> Once finished, the band of murderous soldiers turned jovial. They came upon a leper hospital that they set afire for good measure.
>
> Anyone fleeing was chased down like Billy-be-damned. Those caught were drenched in coal oil and burnt like cane in the fields until there was nothing left except smoldering hats and shoes.

From the comfort of his ass at headquarters, Remington drew children with toothpick limbs and swollen bellies, vomiting and running on fire from fat Spaniards in horseback pursuit. No one could draw a horse like Remington.

> Thirty thousand, mostly women and children, have died. More will succumb while the lying Sylvester Scovel eats his Christmas goose.

My reports did nothing for circulation, but they generated a letter to the *Journal* from Mrs. John W. Thurston, wife of the Nebraska Senator. Willie published it on Page One.

> Oh! Mothers of America, think of the black despair that fills each Cuban mother's heart as the life-blood of her children ebbs away.

Willie, eager for war votes in the Senate, invited Mrs. Thurston to Cuba on a junket at the *Journal's* expense. She died of heart failure aboard *The Vamoose*, moored in Matanzas Harbor. Willie wrote her obit.

Joseph Pulitzer is wholly responsible for her murder. The Jew Hungarian is a traitor in instinct and a traitor in deed for failing to show sufficient enthusiasm for our Cuban neighbors, who want the same independence we gained a century ago.

The only war was a war between newspapers, and Pulitzer's *World* was winning. I was in the dumps and McGee suggested we enjoy a day's rest at the Hotel Inglaterra where I drowned my concerns in an afternoon of heavy rum and the strum of his bandurria.

"I hate losing," I said. "We have to do something to get the upper hand."

McGee put down his instrument. I thought he had a plan of action.

"My mams used to cook lunch in the summertime, July and August. She didn't want to git the house hot at night, and I'd load my plate with cornbread smokin' hot and git my glass of spring water, or whatever we were havin'. I'd go eat it on the bank of Toe River and I'd wade back over those slick rocks if I wanted a second helpin', or honey in the comb. Mams knew how to keep Christmas, and she had watermelon a-waitin' if it was summertime. She said life's peelin' an onion. You can't avoid the tears. But tears were painless in Plumtree."

He choked up, so I offered a drink from my rum bottle. He declined it in favor of the canteen.

"Sunday lunch was kinda special. My aunts and uncles and cousins gathered at my grandmother's when church let out at Yellah Mountain Baptist, and my aunts would git chairs and talk on the porch, and git fanned by the breeze off Grandfather Mountain. The men would go out by the fish pond, but there were no trout in the pond, trout swam in Toe River and a million other creeks and rivers around Plumtree."

"Is there a point to this gibberish?" I asked.

"In Plumtree, it's slow, real laid-back. Lies are about fish. Plumtree's so smothered in mountains and forest it's like bein' smothered in a mother's arms. When we ate watermelon at Granny's, we'd leave pink on the rind 'cause Granny made watermelon rind pickles. We had to eat the pickles or we'd hurt her feelin's. They were the worst things I ever swallowed those years I lived in Plumtree."

"What's the point, McGee?"

My agitation hurt his feelings, but I'd a lot to drink and I hated his visiting when I was losing day after day to a stinking newspaper that didn't have a single reporter in Cuba, a newspaper that came this close to calling me a flat-out liar. McGee's eyes welled up behind his spectacles as if I'd published the stupid secrets he was hiding from me. I swear, he wanted to boo-hoo like a girl.

"What's wrong?" I said.

"Nothin'. I was thinkin' about my girl cousins and how they picked rhododendron leaves to make doll clothes."

"Why does something that stupid make you get misty? You're not even drinking."

"Nothin'," he said. He was embarrassed, and he deserved to be.

"You should have a drink." I extended my bottle, but he didn't take it.

"I'm ashamed, kinda."

"Ashamed of what?"

"Nothin'."

That agitated me more. I was losing the newspaper war, and McGee was making me lose my mind. "Don't bring it up if you can't discuss it."

McGee hollered. "Luisa never tasted pickled watermelon rind, to begin with."

I was taken aback. He never hollered at me, so I hollered back. "Luisa this, Luisa that, Luisa this that and the other. I've never met Luisa, never seen her. I think you're loony and making her up. Is Luisa a tall tale?"

McGee sniffled. "It's best if you never meet her. You're too much alike."

I had to change the subject or drink even more. Or… slug him. "Do you ever wonder what it's like to be killed in battle?" I asked.

He wiped his nose on his sleeve. "Alive again in heaven. What's to wonder?"

"America needs a dead hero. That's something to wonder."

McGee said I wasn't making sense and went back to his bandurria. After a couple of songs, he got a frown as if a terrible thought had crossed his mind. He dropped a chord.

"America doesn't need no dead hero, no glory hound," he said.

I took a long drink of rum. "No, but maybe it needs a dead reporter to bump circulation. Maybe it needs one to step forward to save Cuba."

"I won't be dyin' for this country or another."

"Not you," I said. "I'd never ask that of you."

McGee's smile was back at once. He was tickled by my idea. "I'll bury you in great style, my lord, I promise."

I was drunk and dramatic and he was making fun of me. I changed course a bit. "Maybe I'll find myself seriously wounded. Willie wants something to pop for the next edition."

McGee strummed the chord he'd lost. "Be careful what you pine for. If God decides to make a sad casualty of you, He will accomplish it without help."

"I'm unafraid of death," I said. "I write the way my old man preached. I live with muscular Christianity. I would die for God and country, but a wound might well put me in position to run for high office."

I was surprised to hear myself say it. I'd never given it a second's thought. The idea was fascinating. Newspapering was like having my nose pressed against a pane of glass and looking in on power. My doldrums were gone. Sure enough, I'd get myself shot to get elected. Washington needed an honest statesman. Two birds with one bullet. I don't know why it took me so long to think of it.

CHAPTER SIX

I AWOKE WITH A HEADACHE AND McGEE'S TWANG IN MY EARS.

"I've come up with an idea to win the newspaper war. You don't need to git killed or wounded or kinda elected."

I was groggy from rum, alive enough to half-listen.

"We need to git more razzmatazz in the paper," he said.

"Sheez, McGee. Go work for the *World*."

"More illustrations of pretty girls."

"This is a war, not a chorus show."

"Hear me out. Have you noticed the leering stares the Spaniards pay to Cuban sweethearts?"

That's all he had to say. It had been in front of my nose these weeks. I don't know how a red-blooded man could've missed it. There were stares from every corner at girls too young to be on Willie's arm.

Without a bite of breakfast, I manned my typewriting machine, so excited by my revelation that I wrapped my ankles around the legs of my chair to ground myself.

Spanish soldiers have turned eager and aggressive; they coerce the naïve into the cane fields. Officers order the barely budding into their quarters for a fate worse than death.

As America's only correspondent in Cuba, it's been my duty to be neutral. But that is out the window. I am a man, an American man first and

> foremost, and ready to lay down my life, my professional reputation, for a mistreated girl.
>
> I am, after all, a servant for the American way of life. A servant for the newspaper that acts. Don't be surprised if I do act. Don't be surprised if my next dispatch must be smuggled from the dungeons of Morro Castle.

"Paydirt!" Willie cabled.

Remington drew sketches of virginal, raving beauties. They were cartoonish, less realistic than his horses, but realistic enough to bring animus to New York parlors. Circulation climbed with my every dispatch about innocence lost. I imagined Willie tap dancing around his roll-top desk as I fed him daily titillation.

> The First American chaps to land on this island will be welcomed and rewarded as liberators. Cuba is crawling with dark-eyed *señoritas* desperate for protection. All are lovely in rustling skirts. They'll be all the more gorgeous in thanksgiving moods.

Willie couldn't get enough, but do-gooder McGee had a change of heart. "We cain't ignore what's important altogether. We've a higher calling, *El Capitán.*"

He led me to one more dull tragedy, a village being torched at night. I was being driven in one direction by the wind and in the opposite direction by the tide. I solved the problem with grand ingenuity.

> Girls ran from huts with clothing ignited. Among the human torches were five young daughters. Garments fell from their bodies. By the grace of God, four turned to black before they were seen shamefaced. One was unlucky. She escaped unscorched and the Spaniards celebrated with rum, rank cigars—and her honor.

Circulation soared. I was so busy clacking away that Christmas Eve came by surprise. McGee and I found ourselves prone in the long grass outside a Spanish camp and afraid to move for fear we would be shot before anyone knew we were Americans. Light from a sliver of the moon kept us pinned while miscreants emptied jugs.

Quiet as toads, we watched. Hours passed until McGee and the Spaniard camp were buried in sleep. Christmas dawn broke to the singular sound of the sentinel's naked knife sliding on a whetstone.

From out of the eastern forest came the pounding of horse hooves. Distant at first, like the unfelt drops of a coming rain. In charged a dozen Cuban teens in skirts, riding astride large steeds.

All were bareback and beautiful and gripping mane, each well-armed with rifle, bayonet, revolver, knife, and machete. They had a quantity of cartridges and didn't miss a shot.

McGee startled awake. "Luisa," he whispered.

"Your sister?"

Twenty of the hundred Spaniards were dead before he could dig my field glass from the kit; they lay strewn like rotting apples in an orchard. The Amazons were superior equestrians. They rode into the thick of camp with dash. They wore no shoes, much less hosiery, thin, feral and sinfully sexual without exception. The ugliest was as fair as the fairest on Madison Avenue. They whooped like drunken *vaqueras* come to paint the town.

One wore a red ribbon in long, light hair. She was a decade older than the teens, the most petite of the lot, the one lightest of eyes. She hollered orders, and I listened to McGee for interpretation.

"No Amazon may marry until she has killed a dozen Spaniards. She's telling them to christen their bayonets in gore."

They obeyed. They littered the landscape with corpses, shouted so as to alarm all within three miles. They soaked in the slaughter with pleasure, but the tide turned. The Spanish still had a numbers advantage, sixty to twelve, when they pulled two Amazons from their horses and shot them dead. A faint "*Viva Cuba*" the last cheer on their lips.

One of the riderless horses ran to our position and stopped short of trampling us in the long grass. The Amazon commander ordered a retreat, and nine riders disappeared into the mangroves. The horse near us spooked sideways, backwards, then ignored the chaos to graze.

The commander, last to retreat, had her horse shot to the ground. She was pinned for a second and fought to pull her bare foot from beneath the steed's weight. She'd never let go of her rifle and rested her aim across the quivering carcass, loose hair in her eyes.

"She loads and fires like a founding member of Boone and Crockett," I said.

McGee didn't speak, wrinkles of worry rippled his forehead. I held my breath to steady my field glass. She was exquisite for aim and beauty, if not for cleanliness. Her last bath may've been on All Saints Day, but beneath the grime was a woman, perhaps as old and light-skinned as myself, her skin dyed a deep red by the sun.

She was a prize, pretty as damnation, not in the mold of Maude Adams or any actress, but with the earthiness of a rare mineral.

"How many dunces have died for her on the losing end of dueling pistols?"

McGee didn't answer. The riderless horse near us tossed its head and went back to grazing.

She fought on single-handedly. She pumped more bullets into more Spaniards. When she ran short of cartridges, she mined for fresh ones down the front of her frock.

Her sexuality was an advantage and she used it like artillery on high ground. She killed gawking scoundrels until her carbine got out of order. She threw it away with contempt and killed one with a single overhead blow of her whistling sword, another with two thrusts in the back. The sword's point pulled out of a liver drunk with blood. She nearly killed a third throwing a knife, but it went past his ear and quivered in a tree.

The Spaniards were determined to take her alive, which put them at a disadvantage. She fought with the ferocity of a lead-ripped grizzly.

She decapitated one with the cane-field swing of a machete, his eyes blinked at her as the head rolled. She drew her revolver and three more Spaniards fell in a pile at her feet. One unknown soul was shot in the heart, but his life ended when her sword was thrust into his head by way of his mouth.

Soldiers who wished to stay alive backed behind royal palms until her revolver emptied. Too exhausted to chase them down, she dropped her sword and surrendered the empty sidearm to a one-toothed combatant. He stared at her threadbare frock that clung to the sweat of her breasts. He said something that McGee translated in a worried whisper.

"He will be first to have this goddess of fantasy."

"Not on my watch," I said, but I didn't move.

She spat on the combatant and said *"Feliz Navidad..."*

"Merry Christmas," McGee translated. "I hope you make as good a use of my weaponry as I just did."

The ugly Spaniard slapped her face, cut the red ribbon from her hair and stuffed it into his crotch. Her hair fell loose about her shoulders. She swung to the point of his jawbone, connected solid and square. He rose in embarrassment, the men jeered. He spat his last tooth at her and slit the straps of her frock. It fell to her waist, revealing a last unspent cartridge lodged between splendid flesh that heaved with labored breathing.

I was too much of a gentleman to stare; I'd had enough. I threw down my field glass, pulled the pistol from my belt and started to my feet. McGee pulled me down.

"Let me up," I said.

"It's suicide."

"I have to save her."

"We all want to save Luisa," McGee said, "but that's hardly the business of our nation's best press correspondent."

"Then it's true. That creature is your sister." I fought his grip. "Let me up. Damn you, McGee."

"You should never have become a national treasure, *El Capitán*."

My dear apprentice was under no such covenant and, unarmed and in one motion, he leaped like a cricket aboard the riderless horse, yanked its grazing head, kicked it hard in the flanks, and charged toward every man's dream.

McGee cried out, "*Vamos mi hermana,*" as he approached. She swung aboard, as if they'd performed the stunt a hundred times in Buffalo Bill's Wild West Show.

I was impotent, envious of McGee's courage, envious of his bold action, envious that the barefooted, bare-chested love of my life was holding fast around her brother's waist instead of mine as they disappeared into the thick.

As I watched them go, I ached to join them aboard that charging horse. But I was the odd man out.

CHAPTER SEVEN

THE SPANIARDS LEFT IN CHASE, LEAVING ME STRANDED WITH FORTY POUNDS OF KIT. I cursed McGee that Christmas Day for twelve miles, each step with my slight and chronic limp. The morning sun swelled. The sky had been swept clean of clouds by a breeze that wouldn't reach down to earth. I longed for shadows, I'd lost my straw hat, and evening was way in the distance. When I clung to the shade, hordes of ravenous mosquitoes too tiny to swat ate me alive. I had an unquenchable thirst—for Luisa.

Chin up, I made my way out of tangled underbrush to guinea grass and at last to Havana's outskirts and Hotel Inglaterra before nightfall. McGee sat plucking strings at the outdoor café. I expected Luisa to be there scrubbed and bathed with wet blonde hair, listening wide-eyed to McGee's endless visiting about my fame and escapades. The only thing at McGee's side was lemonade over crushed ice, charged to my account.

"*Buenos tardes.*" He kept playing. "How's the jungle weather?"

I said nothing to make a point.

"Shakin' a fist at the sun never does cool things down," he said. His grin grew wider into his smile. "I'm happy you're safe. My sorries for not wavin' *adios*. You look hot, hungry, and kinda tired."

My chair was available, but he got up in case I wanted his. "I've never been this tired," I said.

I pulled boots from throbbing feet and I dropped them on the table. My dust stuck to his sweating drink, but McGee took no offense.

"Where is she?" It was an order, and it sounded so.

"Where's who, my lord?"

"Damn you, McGee."

"The Cathedral de San Cristóbal. Well hidden. We'll go *mañana*."

"We'll go in an hour, at first dark," I said.

"As you wish. The Spaniards will be in the streets lookin' for her. Before dawn is the deadest hours."

Of course, he was right, and I used Christmas night to labor at my typewriting. I could neither sleep nor eat. I composed a long, crisp item about the Amazon raid, which was guaranteed to get Willie dancing his Master Juba. When I was almost done I blurted something without thinking.

"I'll make her mine."

"Sorries. She doesn't like men."

"She beds down in the forest with those teen huntresses?"

"No. No," McGee said. "She's never been fond of a man. I'm the only one she trusts."

"She'll one day have it bad for me," I said. "With your permission."

"You have *my* permission, but no man ever gets hers."

I read over my typewriting.

I leapt aboard like a cricket, kicked the horse hard in the flanks, and charged toward every man's dream.

The half-naked Amazon swung aboard behind me as if we had performed the stunt a hundred times in Buffalo Bill's Wild West Show.

As we charged off, something shiny dislodged from her breasts. An unspent cartridge. It kicked up and sparkled end over end in the rising Christmas sun. Upon its return flight to flesh, a Spaniard's bullet deflected off the cartridge.

Spain's bullet was headed for my heart. The timing of her bounce saved this special commissioner's life.

I pictured Willie reading it aloud to Remington, who would draw an illustration of our backside riding away, my heels digging into the steed with my half-naked wonder holding fast. I imagined one more headline for Willie's wall:

DEEDS OF A LOVELY AMAZON

SHE SUBSISTS ON MANGOES
FIGHTS LIKE A TIGRESS
ENDURES THE HARDEST FATIGUE

How a Noble and Nude Heroine Held the
Spanish at Bay Until Rescued by
Jayson Kelley, Special Commissioner
of the Newspaper that Acts

A CHRISTMAS MIRACLE

"Luisa McGee is about to become famous," I said.

"Her name's not McGee." My apprentice was trying to sleep in his chair with his feet on the table. "It's Luisa Evangelina Cosío y Cisneros." He spelled it for me with his eyes closed.

"Wish Willie paid me by the word. Who's her husband?"

"I told you she kinda hates men. Her ideal afternoon is to watch two kill each other for her. Now, if those two were best friends, it would be a blue-ribbon afternoon."

"You make her sound a monster."

"I love her, I do. I just hate to see you caught up in her mess. She doesn't kill Spaniards because they're Spaniards. She kills because they're men."

"Lying men, who've been dishonest with the Cuban people," I said. "She hasn't met an honest-to-gosh American one. Say, if she's single, why is her name not Luisa McGee?"

"God only knows," he said and pretended to nod off.

I pushed his feet off the table. "Here we go again with the half truths."

"She took an old woman's name, an old Cuban woman she grew to love. Long story."

"Too involved for my busy readers. I'll help them along. I'll call her the Lady known as Luisa. They'll like that."

"Perfect. Leave my name out, *por favor*."

That had already been decided. My readers would never be told Luisa was the sister of the Tennessean shot by firing squad. That would complicate things. Otherwise, there wasn't an ounce of juice in my item. It needed none. Real news can be more far-fetched than fabrication. If anything, I watered down the **DEEDS OF A LOVELY AMAZON, A CHRISTMAS MIRACLE** to make it less vulnerable to a Sniper fact attack.

"I can't leave you out." I valued McGee and I owed it to him to make him think so. "You're the knight who saved her from the unthinkable. You deserve to be famous."

"What kinda man rescues for recognition?"

"As you wish. It will save me having to explain how someone with an eight-letter name has a sister who fills a column inch."

"She took the name of Mrs. Cisneros, who passed in the saddest way. I cain't make it right. I've tried for five years, ever since I've known her. She got the short end, and I cain't make it right."

I shrugged. "I don't know why you got split up, and I know you won't tell me. My brother Joe and I grew up in the same house but on different planets. He hates newspapering. I don't sit in the grandstands and critique his swing, but he critiques my work from the peanut gallery."

"Joe cares for you. Brothers have no choice."

"Joe thinks we had the perfect Papa, but Mama was the angel— her name was Angela. She lived what the old man preached."

"The two of you are much alike. Luisa and you," McGee said and was snoring before I could ask why.

I thought of Mama in her garden grave. Homes can be trusted with mamas in them. Ours was solid and big and cozy. I was seven when Joe and Mama swapped places, when she died as he was born. The food was plentiful after the funeral. It was quiet; I would've heard people chew except for an infant's squalling. Twenty-seven years later, my blood boils a little when I remember him crying for a mama he didn't even know how to miss.

Joe was five when I forgave him and took him on an adventure. He convinced me to rescue a pigeon in the mud. We didn't swim a stroke, and the old man's orders were to stay away from the riverbank.

I came home wet. "This is for your own good," Papa said. "To keep you from joining Mama in her garden."

Joe was dry as a bone and the old man belted me as if I'd killed her. His expression was dull, as if he were cleaning fish. He made me sit feet first at the stove until the porridgy mud on my shoes hardened.

Mama never grew old; people in memories never do; they stay kilned like that muck I was never able to scrape off.

I didn't change, but the house did. It was no longer a cradle of safety. I fled to the attic where I wrote whatever came to mind. I wrote a child's novel about a boy who'd seen his seaman father three times in his life. I got my ideas looking out the tiny window from where I had an elevated perspective. Papa boarded it up when I made a pet of another pigeon.

My old man said I was incorrigible and sent me to visit my aunt in Chicago. I was milking in the barn when her cow started the fire. I didn't kick over the lantern, Aunt Cate's cow did. I took a step back to watch the flame spread. A Negro man rushed in to be devoured. He was the first to die. I sometimes imagine myself pushing him to the dirt and smothering the flame and screams with my own body. The bucket of milk in my hand would've saved his life. I imagine myself an instant hero like McGee was aboard that steed, but I was a lad. I did nothing but watch the Negro scream and the backside of the barn cough black smoke.

McGee was sleeping in his chair like a cavalryman in the saddle. Giant insects flew about the lantern. Cuba's insects were as big as condors, even in winter. Only the mosquitoes were minuscule. I stared at the white light and at its reflection off McGee; he had a trace of a smile even when he slept. A baby's snore. I relished the idea that he might one day be my brother-in-law. Once I'd married Luisa, McGee could never leave. Three birds on a wire. Instant family.

He snorted awake.

"I'll honor your request for anonymity." I said it in a Cambridge way, to let him know it was a favor. "I'll leave you out of the paper, but only if you tell me more about Luisa."

"Grew up in Havana," McGee said. "Educated at the convent. Speaks English as good as me."

"As well as I do."

"She taught me *español*, including words too peppery."

I was antsy to go and meet her at the cathedral, but that was still hours off.

"I wanted a li'l brother," McGee said. "What's yours like?"

"Joe's the highest-paid ball player the Baltimores Club carries. Gets an extra two hundred for being team captain."

"Must be kinda proud of him."

"I make more than he does."

"Must be kinda proud of each other."

"The Baltimores were way ahead in the standings, but they lost the pennant on the last day to Boston. Can you believe it? I make three times more than Joe and his teammates Wee Willie, Hughie Jennings, and John McGraw combined. I'm telling you because you don't care a crap about money. The whole world's traipsing north to the Klondike to get rich, and you're going to prospect for love. We're two romantics, alike in many ways."

"I told you, it's you and Luisa who are alike," McGee said. "I could stomach a li'l more dough. For a boost in pay, I'll do your worryin' for you." His smile broadened to let me know he didn't need a raise to worry for me. "What does Joe think about your success?"

"He says 'horseshit,' that's what he thinks. Ball players are in love with that word. He calls what I do horseshit leprous journalism."

A campaign was afoot to remove the *Journal* and the *World* from libraries. They were too yellow and licentious for the prudes and snot monsters. Joe wasn't behind the ban, give him that, but he voted for McKinley.

"McGee, you're more a brother to me than Joe. Joe's envious and judgmental and whatnot and full of shit. He says I've been trying to be someone else my whole life. I never try to be someone else. I'm not my old man, that's for sure. Dogs bristled at Papa, too, but he shot them cold."

"Sorries."

That reminded me to swallow my drink. One of the dogs Papa shot was a stray I'd befriended the day Mama died. I fed the dog funeral food and named him Jetstone because he was black. When everyone left, Papa shot him in the back. I buried Jetstone next to Mama. It's all in my child's novel. Can't believe we were raised together. Joe remembers parishioners mussing his hair as the worst thing that ever happened."

"Sorries." McGee put his arm around me.

"Stop saying that. Go make love to your *bandurria*."

"I know you love Joe," McGee said. "I see you."

"Joe visited Papa every time the Orioles traveled to Boston. He was there for the funeral, but I was chasing sea monsters."

"Sorries."

"For what? It was a holy shit! item. Joe has batting slumps, I don't. Joe and I see the exact same things differently. A lot of people do. Knowing that has pushed me along in newspapering."

"You've been pushed to the mountaintop," McGee said. "I'm proud to be your apprentice."

I put my feet up. They felt good without shoes. "How old is she, anyway?"

"Luisa? Why do all men find her attractive?"

"You'd know she was the most beautiful girl in the world if she wasn't your sister."

"Old enough for the Lord knows what. The Watauga County

records were destroyed in a blaze, but she's two years older than me. Thirty-two, but I don't know her birth date, and neither does she."

"If she was born in Plumtree, how'd she end up in Cuba?" I knew I'd get no real answer. "I suppose I'd have to suffer a visit to Plumtree to find out." I scooted my chair up to my typewriting machine to clack a sentence I would cut and paste into **DEEDS OF A LOVELY AMAZON** before I sent it off.

"Luisa will grow to like me," I said. "All girls do. You saw that Cuban widow doll hug me like I was her next lover. With your permission, I'll be the second man Luisa trusts."

McGee's laughed. "Go ahead and try. The two of you are one in the same."

I typed my thought.

```
     She'd be an exact specimen, except there is some-
thing missing inside her. She longs for something.
```

McGee teased. "I've completed a lot of worrying for you already, my lord. When do I git my pay boost?"

"That was the first thing you had to worry about."

"Worry is kinda an insult to God," he said as it started to rain. My item was finished and I folded it into the waterproof oilskin packet. I groaned to put my boots on, and we hurried toward Cathedral de San Cristóbal. I limped a little, but my feet loosened as I broke out in a glorious nighttime sweat imagining her face up close, and Willie's reaction to **DEEDS OF A LOVELY AMAZON.**

I'd return home soon with Luisa on my arm. I'd thaw her heart with an elegant New York courtship. We'd marry in the city's biggest church with McGee at my side. Nothing but joy and bliss, the worst of her past hidden from the press. She'd hate others, but she'd love me.

With the exotic beauty as my wife, I'd make my run for Congress. McGee would be my right hand. The two of them would be far better for my future than any war wound I could drum up.

McGee and I entered the cathedral. Father John stood beneath a life-sized crucifix. He crossed himself, said some Spanish.

McGee's smile vanished. "Luisa was taken by soldiers."

I wanted to take a sock at Father John for allowing her capture. He extended his arms from his robe, palms up. "He asks us to forgive him," McGee said.

McGee's knees buckled, and I attended to him. I'm at my best when I think less of myself and more for the needs of others. But I grew resentful when McGee righted himself and left my arms to comfort the cowardly priest. McGee put his hand on Father John's shoulder and said something in Spanish.

"Did they shoot her?" I said.

The priest pointed high, past the thorn crown of the crucifix, in the direction of the sea. He said something and crossed himself again.

"They took her to Morro," McGee said.

I looked into the distance at the ancient fortification. Morro Castle was built in the eighteenth century in solid rock to be impenetrable. It would stand another thousand years. I was eager to save Luisa, but I had no idea how to do it.

Father John hugged McGee and said something.

"Luisa had some last words as they escorted her away," McGee said.

"What words?"

"She said she may be dead soon. Or worse. She said something else—I'm hesitant to say."

"I'll cut your pay so you don't have to worry for me anymore. What?"

"Luisa said, 'Tell my brother Samuel McGee I dearly love him. Tell him he is all I have. He is all I love.'"

"Did she tell you anything?" I pleaded. "Before the soldiers came?"

"What she told me was in confession," Father John said in Spanish. "I can never speak a woman's confession made to God."

"No man yet has regretted trusting me," I said. "You should read my mail."

"She said..." The priest crossed himself. "She said..."

"What?"

"She said this: 'You'll hear all sorts of things about me. Most of them are true.'"

"What else, padre!"

"She said, 'I'm in love with the boyish correspondent who risked his life to rescue me on horseback.'"

Those are the last known words spoken by the Lady who's known as Luisa before they marched her with sharp bayonets to Morro Castle.

CHAPTER EIGHT

THE CANNON-LACED FORTRESS WAS PERCHED HIGH ON A MASSIVE WHITE ROCK AT THE BAY OF HAVANA. No beach surrounded it, sheer rock walls plunged to the sea. Anyone who tried a leaping escape would be pounded to death by the surf, no rescue possible.

Male prisoners, like apes, were locked in dungeons underneath the sea wall. In my travels, I'd never seen a site as petrifying. Groans, the clanking of chains, odors of scourge. Hair stood on my arms as McGee and I approached.

This was Sunday dawn, and visiting hours were from noon to four o'clock on Saturdays. McGee led us to the entrance and inquired in a patient way about the charges against *Señorita* Cisneros. He summed up a lengthy back-and-forth with one sentence. "Luisa's not accused of the Amazonian slaughter."

"The Spaniards will never admit to a carnage at the hands of girls," I said. "What charges have they cobbled together?"

"Coaxin' a Spanish officer to her bedroom."

"Horse apples," I said.

"Three Cuban rebels were hidin' under her bed. They listened as the officer had his way with her. They ambushed him when he fell asleep on her bosom. Luisa laid a trap."

"You tell the story as if you believe it," I said.

"Two more Spanish officers were kinda makin' water in the street while awaitin' their fair turn. When they heard their colonel cry out, they burst in to shoot the rebels and arrest her."

"Horse dung," I said. The guardsman sneered and said "*caca*" to my face. McGee seized my wrist before I could find my revolver.

"I don't understand how you can have courage one instant, and unlimited cowardice the next," I said.

"You won't git anywhere throwin' bullets around. Try throwin' around your influence."

McGee told the guard who I was. All I understood was "*Nuevo York*"— I'm sure he said I was New York's most powerful, most respected correspondent, but the guardsman confiscated my sidearm as if I were riffraff. He had a lengthy conversation with a senior guardsman in a blue and red uniform and sent two more guardsmen up the tower stairs to retrieve Luisa. They called her "*la puta*" once I was unarmed.

I smoked two or three cigarettes to measure the passage of time. I pictured her half naked, the way she was when I last saw her, but the Spaniards brought her down in a whore's red dress to bolster their charges. My blood boiled. McGee opened his arms to her, and she relaxed in his embrace.

McGee forgot his manners. At last, he gave me a proper introduction. I reached to tip the straw hat I'd lost in the forest and we all laughed at my adorability.

"*Señor* Kelley is an American correspondent," McGee said. "He kinda writes on war and high policy." I was hoping for an introduction with more spark. "He's a great friend, it's safe to speak to him."

"Men are *los niños*—small boys who tell fibs," she said. She had a thick Cuban accent made all the more exotic coming from a woman with light eyes. Her accent wasn't basted in Carolinian barbecue, but she was related to McGee. No denying it.

The guardsman hurried me. "*Diez minutos,*" he said, which forced me to skip the question that would've established a baseline for future lies. It didn't matter; I had to trust Luisa's mouth if I was going to trust her heart.

"I must ask straight away what my readers want to know while riding the trolley to dull jobs. Are the Spaniards—behaving?"

"They're in no imminent danger." Luisa's laugh was smoky. "I've more respect for dangerous horses."

I'm never nervous during interviews, but her beauty had me off-balance. I forgot my next question. "Describe your conditions," was my fallback.

"I'm in a private cell," she said. "The floor swarms with *cucarachas*. I woke last night with an obese rat on my chest, whiskers in my face. Morro rats are heavy as dogs. I let it live, but a man will be less lucky."

She scanned for the guardsmen, stepped closer and lowered her voice. She didn't smell of rats. She smelled of black earth and lilacs.

"My cell's at the top of the tower. I've one window. I'd time the tide and the rhythm of breakers and dive into the sea, except the window is beyond my reach and barred so that a squirrel can't slip through."

"The *New York Journal* is as powerful as any nation. That makes me as influential as any king. I'll get you out by way of the front door."

She gave me a flash of disgust. "What have your words done but leave ink on fingers?"

"Influence diplomacy."

"My very presence feeds rebel unrest. The Spaniards never should've arrested me. Now they've no choice but to banish me. They won't shoot me—that would fuel the rebellion—but they intend to hurry me to Ceuta off the African coast..." She stopped to whisper "*El Jefe,*" to warn me of the approaching uniform in blue and red.

I protested when he led her away. "That wasn't ten minutes by any stretch."

The guardsman told McGee it was against prison rules to converse in either whispers or English. He shoved a paper under McGee's nose.

"Orders have arrived from Madrid," my interpreter said. "Luisa is to be incommunicado from this moment." His voice wavered, his knees started to buckle, and I steadied him. It was obvious he was anxious for his sister, but he did nothing but hike his pants.

Luisa tried to embrace her brother, but the guardsman denied her access and slapped her when she spat in his face. Still, McGee did nothing. She didn't acknowledge me. I was miffed; I was the one with the backbone to protest as guardsmen escorted her upstairs and McGee and myself to the door.

"We'll see what America has to say," I barked as the guards shoved us out into the sunshine. The door slammed, then opened a crack and my sidearm was tossed after me.

We returned with urgency to the Inglaterra's outdoor café, where I clacked about Luisa's mistreatment faster than the green parrots overhead crackled sunflower seeds.

The Lady known as Luisa is yet old enough to be called a lady at all. She is little more than a child, not eighteen and locked away in a notorious dumping ground for prostitutes and psychotics.

McGee couriered pages to the telegraph office while I typewrote the next.

"We should organize a rescue," I told him between pilgrimages.

"No man gets to the top of the tower," he said.

I've been told by reliable informants that no gentleman has yet been to the top of Morro Castle and survived to tell. Morro rises like the Tower of London, the stairs leading to a dozen madwomen, many parading in the nude and routinely escorted into the shadows by mustachioed Spaniards.

The telegraph office was at City Hall, a ten-minute run. Every twenty minutes McGee made a breathless reappearance and off he went with my freshest pages. He was prepared to run himself to death, yet not stop to read a word.

She is petite of figure and graceful in movement. Her manners are exquisite, her self-possession wonderful.

Her light eyes smolder, her teeth must flash when the sun shines for a few minutes each day through a high window, barred so that no squirrel enters and no rat exits. The fates forbid her escape.

Each page made it to the tap-dancing Willie and into the *Journal* and, with remarkable speed, to authorities in Madrid. That prompted Spain's Queen Maria Cristina to write a letter of indignation to the *New York World*, which Pulitzer published without checking a single fact.

> Luisa Evangelina Cosío y Cisneros is not comely at all, though quite intelligent for a woman who paints her face to look young and travels about to commit crimes without a proper hat. She is indelicate and connected to the Cuban junta.

Anarchists have no regard for royalty and I responded.

> Her greatest crime was to smuggle medicine to Cuban hospitals. She is not well, the prison feeds her morphine to force her to give evidence, and maybe worse.
>
> The strain has aged her to look twenty, but I have examined records at City Hall. She is seventeen and raised pure in a convent. She is blooming into a young lady of rare culture. Sadly, she is safe only in America and time is running out.

Willie joined the fray. He wrote an editorial criticizing Pulitzer for being too frugal to send a single correspondent to Cuba to learn the facts on the ground. Tit for tat, Pulitzer called me a scandalmonger and my reports lies, pure and simple.

> Mr. Kelley is a word juggler and should be quarantined before he is allowed to mingle with reputable newsmen. His colleagues are embarrassed to publish their own fine work next to the tommyrot of an overpaid hack.

Sweet revenge. The *Journal's* circulation climbed up and up and my influence went along for the ride. My words became Spain's most fearsome enemy until McGee grew concerned for my safety. He advised me to let my whiskers grow, and we went slumming in a rancid hotel on the decrepit end of Havana. McGee liked the new place. I despised it. Meals tasted alike and there was no starch in the linen, but I sacrificed on behalf of my love.

> Our Lady known as Luisa is guilty of nothing more than refusing to submit to the lustful desires of a Spanish officer. She remains under lock and key; she could at this second or the next be assaulted on a cockroach-infested floor.

Willie tired of me calling her the Lady known as Luisa. In a childish display of bossiness, he settled on The Cuban Martyr Girl. The dummy didn't know there wasn't a drop of Cuban blood in her veins. I'd no time to quarrel; I was a hunted man. I wore a golf cap and kid gloves and walked with a cane to accentuate my limping disguise. Spain posted censors at the telegraph office and McGee had my dispatches smuggled through enemy lines to Trinidad and by boat to Key West, from where they were wired to headquarters.

Willie enlisted two hundred stringers back home to collect ten thousand signatures in support of the Cuban Martyr Girl. He beseeched the pope to intervene. To our delight, the *Journal* received a letter from Mrs. Jefferson Davis, a coup d'etat because Mrs. Davis was a cousin of Pulitzer's wife. Then came a letter in a sack of mail from President McKinley's own mother.

I remained modest. After all, I was but God's messenger. America was the true winner, our boys at last eager to face the chances of hungry guns. Their souls would have no peace unless they pulled their freight. Newspapers filled with prophesies of war, but our president urged more patience. McKinley's stock lagged as mine soared, and I was asked to steam home to give testimony to the Senate Foreign Relations Committee. That was certain to bolster my ambitions, but Willie ordered me to stay in Cuba to execute a scheme.

His plan was nutty and half-baked. "Break the Martyr Girl out of the clink and bring her to New York."

"I'm a special commissioner, not an escape artist."

"WE ARE THE NEWSPAPER THAT ACTS," came his reply. "We fill the vacuum for the feckless government. LEAD OR GET OUT OF MY WAY."

My squish publisher offered no advice on the mechanics of a jailbreak. I knew something of yeggman safecracking, but dynamiting the solid-rock castle would stretch my capabilities and endanger the girl with whom I'd spend my life.

McGee suggested a bribe might be a less worrisome solution. He hustled to Morro Castle and made the arrangements. The chief jailer wanted fifteen thousand dollars and an assurance he and his family would be taken to America. Willie's mommy vetoed the idea as too much of a proposition.

McGee was undaunted. "The Spanish are kinda tired of losin' this war of words. The pen *is* mightier than the sword, you're provin' that. Trust me, Spain wants Luisa out of jail as much as we do. They cain't release her, they'd look weak, but they want her out of the papers."

He found a guardsman to open Luisa's cell for five dollars, an amount my apprentice could pay from his pocket. For three dollars more, the guardsman escorted her to a side door, where I waited in cap and gloves.

I was dapper, but she scowled at me. "What took you so long, *cholo*?" She was lovely in her impatience. "Where's Samuel?"

I shushed her with a finger to her lips and smuggled her away with a superb show of secrecy. We walked for an hour until I came upon a familiar coastal forest a hundred yards from shore. I found the same fishing boat McGee slept beneath during a battle. This time, the forest was quiet, the surf soothing. Luisa crawled under the boat, as McGee had, and fell asleep with the same soft snore.

I gave her cheek a light kiss and went to work. My feelings for her gave me energy enough, and I rolled sheet after sheet of fresh paper into my Remington machine.

I scaled the outside walls, up the dark tower, to the top of Morro Castle, where I greeted the Cuban Martyr Girl through window bars. It was hell on earth inside. She had one musty volume for reading. Her red dress was in tatters, ripped away by who knows who, and she gave a glad little cry as if a miracle angel had appeared.

"Last night I rejected the advances of the Spanish governor." She fought tears as I examined the blood under her fingernails. "He left in a huff and promised to expedite my transfer to Ceuta. Hurry, *Señor* Kelley. The governor swore to return before I'm shipped across the sea."

"Take heart," I told her. "There's no one more faithful in the service of a young lady."

Through the bars from above, I handed her a package of sweets drugged with opium and told her to distribute them to the guards. The brutes were eager to accept candy from her hand and, in an hour, all were asleep.

I employed a hacksaw from the outside. It was impossible to cut quietly at bars that were not set firmly in the frame. They rattled and rang like a fire alarm, but no one interrupted my work. At last, before dawn, I weakened the iron and snapped it with a pair of pipe wrenches.

God made me athletic and the señorita petite enough to lift one-handed out of the snake pit. A fleeting smile was reward enough for my long hours and personal risk. I timed the swig of the breakers. I told her to set her jaw.

She was indeed an Amazon warrior, and showed none of the apprehension found in females. We jumped hand-in-hand from the castle's highest edge, up at first toward the white light of the high moon, and down, endlessly down, we descended to the amniotic sea.

I paused my typewriting. This was a good place in my prose for McGee to drag the overturned fishing boat from the mangroves to rescue us from the water, but again, he was dearly departed. His inconvenient demise was annoying.

The planet Earth was suspended in nothing but seawater. The Cuban Martyr Girl and I were left to swim, my golf cap still aboard my head, a cigar in my mouth to smoke away the sharks. We climbed, exhausted, up a beach where, as God is my witness, what was left of her red dress washed out to sea. She was without a stitch, but my eyes never wandered from the sparkle of gratitude on her face.

Luisa woke up. "I'm hungry, *cholo*. Where's Samuel?" I raised one hand to signal I was in the middle of something and resumed my clacking.

She removed the cigar from my mouth and replaced it with salty lips. She had not a nickel to bless herself with, and she offered this special commissioner the one thing she had to give for saving her life.

I cut her a palm leaf to cover herself. "What kind of man rescues for reward?" I said.

I stopped my typewriting. I was feeling my oats. She was thirty-two and I expected no resistance.

"Don't come near me, I'll chop off your *cojones.*" I went back to work.

At daybreak, the hunt for us began. I captured a stray sheepdog puppy on the beach and left the Cuban Martyr Girl to warm herself with it as she hid among the recesses of shoreline boulders.

She named the puppy Kelley. I was touched.

I strode to town, where the Spanish army was conducting a house-to-house search. I purchased the grandest cigar from a street vendor, boy's clothing, a slouch hat, a bottle of rum. When I returned, she dressed and pinned her hair in a coil before applying the hat. I lit the cigar to complete her disguise.

"Where's Samuel?"

I was weary of the question. "He disappears when things get hot."

"He likes you, Kelley."

I smiled. "Most do, those who take the time to get to know me."

"Don't get cocky, *pendejo.* Samuel likes everyone."

We had a marvelous conversation, she is such a bright girl with a quick wit. Time was running out, and I instructed her to wait an hour and then make her way down Havana alleys to the American-flagged Seneca bound for New York.

"Once the steamer departs, you'll be safe," I said. "Each second you remain on the street is fraught."

"Make your way to the Seneca by way of the alleys," I said.

"I've lived here since I was weeks old," Luisa said. "I'm safest along crowded streets. Spaniards will suspect a skulker."

We would have been conspicuous traveling together.
I set her free, a wild horse to her fate.

McGee, by some miracle, was waiting at the head of the Seneca's
gangplank. He never ceased to surprise, always where he needed to be.

We'd no time for greetings. Two Spanish detectives were stationed
at the gangplank to examine all comers. McGee had befriended them
with some happy Spanish. I jollied them with the rum bottle. McGee
and Kelley, we'd evolved into the perfect team.

Minutes before the Seneca was to pull from her dock,
a slim young fellow came running across the wharf in a
slouch hat and blue shirt, and carrying a puppy.

"Cómo te llamas?" they asked his name.
"Juan Sola."

Juan Sola's features were fair, his voice too feminine. He had no
luggage, which introduced suspicion. The drunkard detectives placed
Luisa under arrest. McGee pulled one last bribe from his pocket—all of
the wages I'd ever paid him—to get her aboard. The three of us were at
last safe and bound for New York.

One more holy shit! story, which wasn't drama enough for Willie
and my ravenous readers. Nothing ever was, and so I had to juice it.

CHAPTER NINE

THE *SENECA* ENCOUNTERED MILD WINTER WEATHER ON ITS VOYAGE TO NEW YORK. The Atlantic was flat for as far as I could see, and steaming ahead was riding a magic carpet above a world of teeming dreams. My dream was aboard, though I knew less of Luisa than the landscape of the deep that loomed with canyons and craters and creatures. She was the most beautiful mystery in the world waiting to be discovered. To be conquered. Trouble was, she clung to McGee. We never had a minute alone.

I at last found her unaccompanied on deck, bundled up and looking back at our wake. I described the sea monster I'd seen in the Pacific. "Small fish leapt about on its backside until they fell into the sea." She was skeptical, but interested. Journals had fed a worldwide fascination. "Some scientists say sea monsters are wholly fantasy but, due to my reporting, those scientists are now ridiculed by the consensus."

I tried to kiss away her skepticism but she side-stepped my advance. "Stay back or *you'll* be serpent food."

She was capable of throwing me overboard; I'd seen what she could do. I was too wise to attempt another kiss and she laughed and went below. McGee found me moping and invited me back into their circle.

"You're kinda part of the family," he said, but I remained the fifth wheel. McGee told her hour after hour about his childhood in Plumtree, endless visiting until I was sick of his wonderland of rhododendrons. He told of swimming holes in Toe River, of games of cowboys and Indians on its rocky banks, pirates in the caves of Grandfather

Mountain. Cousins behind each tree, cousins hidden in mountain fog.

His stories went on ad nauseam until I blurted the question I'd been holding back. "Can one of you please explain to me why you were born two years apart and, yet, McGee grew up in Plumtree and Luisa in Havana?"

McGee was eager to answer. But he looked to Luisa for permission, which she denied by staring past me at the glide of seagulls.

"God only knows," McGee said. "To begin with, Paps had a crick in his back." I knew that when McGee said, "to begin with," I was in for a filibuster.

"It kinda didn't help his back that he let some of his dogs sleep in his bed. He wouldn't let them *all* sleep there at once or Mams would've shot ev'ryone. She was a better shot than Paps. That's where Luisa gets it. Mams and I went to church on Sunday, which Paps didn't do. He didn't go to church at that time."

Whenever McGee mentioned their parents, Luisa got annoyed with me. "Does the newsman need to hear the details?"

McGee told of other relatives. "One of my cousins, Hiram—he was a year younger—they were the poorest people. We climbed to the treetops. From there we could see the fish swimmin' in the pond. Some big ones nobody ever caught. Granny had a rooster that hated li'l fellers. Me and Hiram, we lived in fear of that rooster. It was bigger than a spring turkey, as I think back. We'd be up a tree and here comes that rooster a-flappin'."

I wanted to tear my hair out. I wanted to get Luisa alone to consider our future, but she was absorbed in McGee's trivialities. I would've left to have a stiff drink, but I could stare and stare at her because she never looked my way. That made me want her the more. I drank her in. I'd never had it this bad. I suffered a malady no balm could cure. I was needy.

"We'd have to holler for Granny to git the rooster so we could git out of the tree. When Hiram started bawlin', Granny came to the rescue. Hiram was cryin' up in that tree for so long I saw a li'l boat in the middle of the fish pond, a boat someone had kinda whittled and carved. I got Hiram to stop cryin' when I told him we'd git that boat."

"Did I ever tell you I was a swimmer at St. Stephen's?" I said.

"So Granny went back inside after she chased the rooster off, and we stripped down nekked as jaybirds and we took after that boat, and here comes Granny with the switch. Toe River's wide and shallow, so you can wade it. But the fish pond's deep. We weren't to be in it. Granny was the law back then, but her switchin' never hurt. Granny said, 'You've not lived long enough to know nothin'.' She was right; I'll never live long enough to know nothin'. One thing I do know, she would've punished us more if she'd put away the switch and made us eat her pickled watermelon rinds."

Plumtree sounded so apple pie that I had to excuse myself from the conversation to keep from retching over the rail. McGee waved goodbye; Luisa didn't notice me leaving. She was mesmerized by the childhood she'd missed for an unexplained reason.

Truth be told, I was angry at McGee for the way he monopolized Luisa's hours when he knew my intentions. I decided I could be happy with Luisa, or with McGee, but I couldn't be around them both at once.

They were always together, and by the time we got to New York I was half crazy. I went straight to the *Journal* newsroom and clacked poison out of my system. My readers would never learn of McGee's bribes that freed Luisa from Morro. For the first time in a while I was happy to have written **THE DEATH OF A TENNESSEEAN,** I was glad to leave McGee out.

I typewrote that there was more to the story of Luisa's escape from Havana. I'd spared readers the entire truth because of it might be banned from libraries. But my voyage home had given me time to reflect. I filled them in about the boy Juan Sola when he came running to the *Seneca's* gangplank with a puppy and no luggage.

While I jollied the two detectives with the rum bottle, they sent for a third to bolster their numbers.

There is no delicate way to describe the matter from here forward. Children should stop reading, as should all ladies and squeamish gentlemen.

The three brutes escorted the Cuban Martyr Girl up the gangplank and strip-searched her on the deck. Down to her slouch hat and stockings.

Willie read over my shoulder. He ordered me to describe each dimple on Luisa's buttocks to Frederic Remington, who sketched her standing bare and bold.

"Make her ass less equine," Willie said. "Draw sinister mustaches on those Spaniards. They need something to leer behind. Pencil their skin darker to contrast with hers."

It was after midnight when the basement presses vibrated the building. Readers would soon see Luisa again from the backside. This time they'd see more. They'd see the round derrière that was clothed when she'd escaped with me aboard the horse. The three dark detectives in this latest illustration savored an unobstructed frontal view.

Willie presented me with a copy, still wet with ink.

> The outrage was carried out directly beneath the thirteen stripes and forty-five stars of the American flag.
>
> The brave pup, named Kelley for yours truly, tried to intervene. It snarled and barked until it was tossed into the sea.
>
> The brutes snatched her hat, but had not the manners to remove their own. She stood naked as the day she was born seventeen innocent years ago.

I glanced up from my glistening, Page One, holy shit! item. The towers of the Brooklyn Bridge were out the newsroom window. I was king of this city still bathed in nighttime, but not the master of Luisa.

She and McGee were having a holiday at the Waldorf on Willie's dime.

> She was guilty of nothing more than having the best of Cuba in her heart. The best of the United States of America.
>
> The three detectives laughed and unpinned her coil of hair. It was littered with sand, which proved to them that she was a floozy. They called her a habanero, which is a Cuban pepper too hot to eat.
>
> I can't write what happened next, not without violating a number of obscenity statutes and causing the *New York Journal* further banishment from libraries.

Half-truths are exhausting. I slept two hours and awoke a new man. The frustrations had been expunged from my system. Writing had been therapeutic, ever since my days looking out at Mama's garden from the attic, watching for the return of my make-believe seaman father. It was another day, a new day to win Luisa.

She came out the door of the Waldorf dressed both stylish and wholesome in a white gown like a society woman on Fifth Avenue. She didn't blend in; her beauty betrayed her.

I was confident on my home turf and I escorted her to a reception for the Cuban Martyr Girl at Madison Square Park. She refused to go without McGee tagging along. For once, he was the fifth wheel. I took her arm, which she allowed because she'd never seen such traffic. It was comforting to know she feared something in the world. We were a handsome couple. Nobody knew who McGee was, nobody ever would. He was a fish out of water.

"This is my city," I told Luisa. "Now that I've made you famous, it's your world, too. It's a bit different than Havana, don't you think? Way better than Plumtree."

Luisa came to McGee's rescue. "A fire trap. A good place when you're sick of peace and quiet."

Tiny newsboys with large voices and ink-stained hands cried from corners until they absorbed each other in noise. One guttersnipe, wearing knickers and wool cap like the rest, caught my attention when he shouted my name.

"Read it in the *Journal*. Jayson Kelley rescues fair beauty from Spain's clutch." I welled with pride for an instant, and then hurried to walk on. I pulled Luisa by the arm and past the newsie. I'd no such control over McGee, and he stopped to examine the headline held high in the lad's hands.

CUBAN MARTYR GIRL MISTREATED BY SHAMEFUL SPANISH

Does Our Flag Shield Girls on the High Seas?

Luisa read the headline. It bothered her little. McGee's reaction was the opposite.

"This is a cock-and-bull story," he said. He saw my thumbnail illustration. "You wrote it?"

Luisa performed well, a better actress than Blanche Bates will ever be. She played off McGee's disapproval and yanked the copy from the newsboy's hands, and slapped my face with it. She didn't mind being on display to New York, but it bothered her to be on display to her kid brother.

My arms spread wide at the injustice. "I don't write the headlines. I don't draw the illustrations."

"What illustrations?" Luisa and McGee said in unison.

Willie had moved her derrière to Page Two to conceal it from old prudes. Luisa found it. Flattery twinkled her eyes, but she threw the pages at me in pretend disgust. They fluttered to the ground, landing rump up.

"You told the world she was violated?" McGee said.

People on the crowded streets stopped to gawk. A few pointed in recognition of me. They didn't recognize the older version of the Cuban Martyr Girl, but they admired her beauty nevertheless.

"I've never been raped once," Luisa said. "Until now, by you."

"For the good of your country."

McGee picked up the paper to spare embarrassment. I took it from him and showed him the opinion page.

"See what Willie wrote," I said. "The Cuban Martyr Girl's escape from Morro Castle is the greatest journalistic coup of this age. You should be proud of what I've accomplished. What we've accomplished. Not ashamed."

Luisa slapped my face again, this time with her hand.

A hundred people must've seen it. I heard general laughter. Still, no one recognized her from Remington's illustration, because Luisa was in the costume of a fine lady.

A voice from the crowd said, "That can't be her. She's gorgeous and a fighter, but she's too old." With that, Luisa hit me with the closed-fist of Amazonian force. I lost my feet.

I feared that reporters from the *Sun, Herald, Times*—or Sylvester Scovel of the despicable *World*—might be nearby. The Sniper would happily let millions know that my humiliation came at the hand of a woman dressed for shopping at Ghormley. He would accuse me of juicing. He would accuse me of shaving fifteen years off the Cuban Martyr Girl's age.

"They stare at me like I'm some goldfish," Luisa said.

"They stare because I've made you a heroine found in fairytales."

"Tall tales. I'd rather be hanged in Havana."

"Go back. Go to the North Pole for all I care."

The crowd closed in so tight I couldn't dodge her closed-fisted punch to my nose. I was knocked to the curb and she stomped into the vast Madison Square crowd. McGee said nothing. He wasn't acting; he looked down upon me with disgust. Maybe with pity. The crowd closed in tight. A hundred faces were staring, but only McGee's was in focus. He'd never looked at me that way before.

I was confused. A minute ago it was Luisa I wanted more than anything, and it was McGee who was clumsily in the way. Her rejection hurt, but less than his.

McGee stared down for long seconds. Even with my nose bloodied, he acted as if I was in the wrong. I wanted up but he didn't extend a hand. I wanted to escape his eyes but they followed me like the Yellow Kid's smirk. I'd never seen McGee's eyes like that. They were unforgiving.

I covered my face with the *Journal.* "Your sister is deranged with deep scars."

"Lyin' kinda hurts people."

I pulled the newspaper from my face. "So does your so-called honesty." Two gents helped me up and dusted me off. My arms spread wide, I argued, "I did what's best for America—for Cuba."

Blood dripped from my nose. McGee grabbed the newspaper from me, crumpled it, and threw it to the ground. "Damn you." It was the one time I'd heard him swear.

"What I write is for the ultimate good."

"Falsehood is your hidin' place."

A wind kicked up to swallow his language. I shoved him into the arms of onlookers. I wanted him to take a swing at my bloody nose. His hands clenched and unclenched, and then he flipped two cents to the newsie for the one-cent copy that had jumped the crowd and was blowing down the street like a Texas tumbleweed in a dime novel.

"Time to move on," he said.

"You're leaving me? To go with her? You're my student, my apprentice. My paladin."

"You no longer need an interpreter, *El Capitán.* I don't understand you, anyway. You're foreign to me."

"I'd never leave you for my brother, and Joe's a real brother."

He winced at the insult. "Gotta go."

"At least my father raised me alongside my own sibling."

An emotional wound came to his eyes. "Words matter, *ese.*"

"You're making a mistake." I tamped-down the pleading in my voice. "There's no brighter star to follow than me. My photograph will soon be on campaign buttons."

I seldom raise my voice, but when I do I project like the actor DeWolf Hopper. "Don't abandon the gold mine the minute you find the vein."

He kept walking.

I was confused. The tight circle of onlookers took notice until I was, again, unfairly embarrassed. I'd never been so betrayed. This was some odd contest, and I wasn't sure of the rules. Luisa had won. I'd seen her decapitate a Spaniard. Now, I'd seen she was capable of cutting out my heart. She brought to the surface something dark that had been safely sunk.

"*Ay, dios mio,*" McGee said as he disappeared into the crowd.

"You're dead to me!" That's what I hollered. I was thinking something else. I was thinking I needed him to interpret for me. To interpret my mess. To guide me through it.

The more I realized I'd lost him, the more I needed him back. I didn't chase after her. I imagined myself chasing after him, pistol in hand. I imagined the headline I was capable of creating.

TRIAL OF THE CENTURY

World's Greatest Correspondent Shoots Man He Killed Off Once Before
(A JAYSON KELLEY TELL-ALL)

That's one headline Willie would never dance around. I let McGee vanish after her into Greater New York.

Church bells pealed. Fifty thousand at Madison Square Park craned to get a look. I made my way, climbed to the stage, took hold of the megaphone, admired a vast sea of my readers.

A band playing an overture went quiet. "My name is Jayson Kelley."

The audience roared as they saw a thumbnail sketch come to life. Roman candles burst, but I couldn't smell the sulfur through a bloodied nose.

"The Cuban Martyr Girl has been delayed," I said through the megaphone. A murmur of disgruntlement. "Fear not. She is shy, but she's safely in America." Hurrahs. Extended applause.

Snot monsters sat aboard their fathers' shoulders. I could see them a half mile in the distance. It was as if I were the keynote at a grand convention. Forget McGee. Forget Luisa. This was my opening salvo into politics.

"The Spaniards disgraced the teen beauty, first with a maggoty prison bed, then with worse. Far worse. It's unjust President McKinley and his diplomatic swells beg the country for still more time. Do you want to be patient?"

Shouts of "No" and "Never" filled the air.

"That ship has sailed." Men cheered, women waved handkerchiefs. "We demand an end to McKinley's rigmarole."

The sting of Luisa's fist on my face, the deeper sting of McGee's turned back, brought passion to my voice. "Our president worries we will be bogged down in a hostile tropical climate. If he didn't agonize on this, he would agonize on that and the other. Worry is the opposite of trust. Worry is fear, and fear is an insult to God." It was a stemwinder. "Have faith. In God we trust." I employed dramatic pause. "Trust not in our president. Trust in God—and in our repeating rifles."

Men shot pistols into the air.

"Chaps will soon be climbing over each other to get to the front. Let the wolf rise in the hearts of all. God bless America, and may the Stars and Stripes fly over Havana."

The orchestra's *Star-Spangled Banner* ricocheted off skyscrapers. I stayed for hours and shook hands until long lines dwindled. The next day I was offered a captaincy by Theodore Roosevelt, the new assistant secretary of the Navy. I wrote an item explaining that I declined the commission to better serve the country as a correspondent. Sylvester Scovel published rumors of my bad feet, which I denied.

> I passed up a medal and a pension to do what is best, to do what is good, to do what is right.

Pulitzer's pitiful paper, lagging sadly in circulation, at last acknowledged the Cuban Martyr Girl had been strip-searched aboard the *Seneca*, but it claimed it was carried out with delicacy by a Spanish matron and behind closed doors. No males were present, Scovel wrote.

I wrote that the *World* was too proud to make a simple apology, and Scovel accused me of a new, dangerous brand of "jailbreak journalism." Pulitzer's paper had become a joke. It was ignored. By me, by Willie, by the public at large. The buckets of water The Sniper'd thrown at me had failed to extinguish my creative flame. I'd become a wildfire of words, out of their control.

> How many times will we allow Spain to board vessels and disrobe delicate damsels? What's next? I'll tell you what. Spain will stop an American liner on the high seas, the very liner carrying Joseph Pulitzer's two young daughters. Or yours.

I spent the next afternoon searching New York for Luisa and McGee. She was too striking to go unnoticed, and a cop at Grand Central said she'd boarded a train south to Johnson City with a bespectacled escort. Willie was cross when I told him. The Cuban Martyr Girl was magic for circulation, and he ordered me to set after her. But Willie's fickle, and the next morning he took a sharp turn.

"Roosevelt telephoned. The *USS Maine* is coaling up for Cuba."

"Holy smoke."

"It's hush-hush," Willie said. "Uncle Sam insists it's a friendly visit to Havana Harbor. Friendly, my ass. There hasn't been an American man-of-war in Cuban waters in forever."

"Holy shit!"

"Room will be made to embed one reporter aboard. Roosevelt wants it to be you—only you."

"Too bad I'm on my way to Tennessee. The night train. You can't take a powder without the Cuban Martyr Girl on Page One. Sylvester Scovel will have to go."

"Forget her," Willie said. "We published an illustration of her harvest moon. What's left?"

I chortled. "If we publish what's left, we'll both land in the clink."

It wasn't yet nine o'clock, but Willie poured me something stiff. "Here's to four centuries of Spanish naval pride to be severely humbled."

I raised my glass. A silent toast to McGee and Luisa. I'd lost him to her. I'd lost her to him. But it was time to move on; never a minute to wallow.

"God, I envy you," Willie said. "You've the chops to go anywhere, to report on any holyshitdamnthing."

CHAPTER TEN

I DEPARTED BY RAIL FOR KEY WEST, WHERE I WAS TO CATCH THE *USS MAINE* AT DOCK. Baltimore was on the way, and I hadn't seen Joe in forever. I wired ahead and met him for a musty ale at Charles Street Union Station.

Two or three dolls were aboard the southbound, one comely enough to bring my mind back to Luisa. I was in no mood for that, and I distracted myself with the train's chug and thoughts of Joe. I'd give him apologies for missing Papa's funeral. I knew of no two brothers more famous and successful than the brothers Kelly/Kelley. We'd spent our adult lives making him proud, and that's what I intended to say.

He was in a squat mood, even though weeks had passed since his Orioles finished second to the Beaneaters in the closest pennant race of the nineties. I offered condolences for his club's collapse, but Joe knew the Beaneaters are my team. They used to be his, too.

"You should've long been over it," I said. "There, there. Chin up, you'll capture the flag next season, maybe."

He took Papa's clasp knife out of his pocket, the one with the deer-antler handle, and cleaned his fingernails as if ball-yard dirt still resided under them. I was about to bring up Papa when, out of the blue, Joe complained about what I do for a living. "Why don't the papers ever print something positive? That's what this nation sorely needs."

"Crime, underwear, and pseudo science," I said. "We publish what people want."

"Keyhole journalism. Freak journalism." Joe wiped his face on his sleeve and smirked as if he knew a dark secret. "Jailbreak journalism."

"Yellow journalism."

That got a grin out of him. "I love that bald mick urchin in the comics, his nightgown the color of dry *horseshit*." Joe emphasized baseball's favorite word.

"Eight pages of comics cost Willie a million dollars in new presses, but they make the rainbow look like lead pipe."

"Say, that picture of the butt-naked girl. Why'd you print it?"

"Willie did. Wasn't my call." I took a swig of ale. "Got something against naked dolls?"

"Something against indecency."

"She didn't mind, why should you?"

"Why'd you change the spelling of your name? Papa's name."

"Abraham. Abram. People in the Bible changed names all the time."

"She didn't mind her bare butt in the paper?"

"You read *National Geographic*?"

"Sure, I read it on trains. Ball players read, you know. *National Geographic* prints facts."

"It published a Zulu negress bare-breasted. Under the guise of education and culture. Memberships to the Society are through the roof. Folks get what they want. Yellow newspapers aren't just in New York, Chicago, and San Francisco. Boston's thick with dandelion dailies. Philly. Baltimore's next."

"That's when I'll tell the Orioles to sell my contract to the Louisvilles."

"You grouse a lot for a man who gets paid to play a game."

"What you think of me is none of my business," Joe said. "I grouse because I no longer get news in my newspaper."

"Tell me something, Joe. Would people go to a ball game where the players never stole, never swung for the fence, never slid cleats up— never kicked at a stinking umpire? Who'd attend such a game?"

"Scribes, like umpires, shouldn't be the focus. The least they're noticed, the better job they're doing."

I gave Joe the last word and he went back to mining his fingernails.

Staring at that clasp knife brought a childhood resentment to my head. One day the old man wheelbarrowed Joe about the yard. Papa stopped to bark at me for performing summersetts. He gave Joe a pig-a-back ride—and that knife.

Joe wouldn't remember. Joe doesn't remember the pigeon he made me save from the mud. He thinks I made up the whole story. I make up squat. I went after that dumb bird all because of Joe. I could outrace him around the bases, except that bird ruined my feet. Joe doesn't remember the time he lent me that clasp knife of Papa's. I wish I didn't. Not even that knife could scrape away the dried mud from my boots.

"Can't believe you missed Papa's funeral," he said.

"As if sea monsters weren't a good reason."

"Sea monsters are horseshit."

"Train to catch." I paid for his ale to move things along.

"Catch this," Joe said, and he tossed me the knife. "You can have it." He mussed my hair as if he were fond of me. I resented it. I was the older brother; I was supposed to muss *his* hair.

Our visit was unrewarding and so brief I decided on a whim to swing by Plumtree. That had to be where McGee and Luisa were headed when they boarded for Johnson City. I'd surprise them, tell them war was afoot, and they might never see me again. Luisa would warm to me if she knew I was heading into harm's way for her beloved Cuba. McGee would forgive me, though, for the life of me, I didn't know what I'd done to get either of them so mad at me.

I never would've made the effort had I known there were forty miles of woody wilderness between Johnson City and Plumtree. I wound up on a contraption called the East Tennessee & Western North Carolina Railroad. It pretended to be a train with its narrow-gauge rails, a low chug, and high-pitched whistle.

The ET&WNC didn't go to Plumtree. It was to travel past a flag stop at Elk Park and on to Cranberry, but the tracks had been removed from Elk Park on. I got off where the tracks ended and the train tooted on back toward civilization.

I hiked a mile or two atop the rail bed from Elk Park to Cranberry and nine or ten steep and windy miles over Blowing Rock Road. It wasn't a road at all. It was a moonshine trail through a forest of hardwood trees growing out of solid rock. I had to pick up my feet to keep from tripping over varicose veins of root. McGee grew up in a land of giant boulders pasted with hard lichens. Rivulets of spring water splashed from the sides of the mountain and made rocks and roots slippery.

The trail was steep, and my lungs stung with altitude until I found myself behind schedule for Key West. I kept going past wrens and cardinals, chickadees and grosbeaks. The forest was peppered with deer. No other large game except a black bear sow searching for insects. It was warm for early November, but winter was squarely on the sow's mind. I recalled McGee saying it barely snowed some Plumtree winters, and it never stopped snowing in others. The sow sniffed the scent of me in the breeze and moved on.

Everyone juices when describing their boyhood haunts. Except McGee. It was as he described. The lap of the Blue Ridge Mountains was embedded in vistas, fog, and peace. I pictured McGee as a boy, a small version of himself. He had no choice but to grow up with his smile. I wished I'd been the little brother he wanted.

I at last came to a stone footbridge over what had to be Toe River. It was wide as McGee had described, flowed north to south, full of round rocks like scrubbed potatoes in a pot of shallow water. The same rocks were dry and white on both banks.

I crossed the bridge and stepped with officialdom onto hollowed ground. I thought I'd paid little attention to McGee's visiting, but there was Yellow Mountain Baptist Church, smaller than expected, a one-room log cabin with a bell dangling outside from a low tree limb. I took a nap in one of the three pews. When I awoke, an old man with weathered cheeks and three ugly dogs was waiting for me outside.

"Name's Simeon Trowbridge Philyaw," he said. "I make moon likker. I'm also beekeeper and I'm also the law. I git a dollar for arrestin' drunken brawlers or adulterous wives and two bits for summonin' a witness. Last month I went to a house where a husband said somethin' smart and the wife hit him with a pan. Never seen a wife so mad. You have a name?"

"Just passing through."

He laughed. "No one passes through. The one way to git to Plumtree is to git born here." His dialect was the same as McGee's. "You talk Yankee. You talk so near like they do. Talk real fast. Most of us were Rebels, but we had folks favorin' the North among us here and there. Those who come back, we manage to git along."

I was wary of his dogs. "They don't bark at no one honest, and if they do, we'll shy rocks at them."

"Do you know Sam McGee?"

"Ev'ryone does. Even you. You just missed him."

I'd wasted all day for nothing. I'd never see either McGee or Luisa again. I needed to come to grips with that. I had a crucial mission in front of me, and the two of them were getting in the way. I needed to get to the USS Maine. My luck would turn once I did.

"McGee come waltzin' back after five year," Philyaw said. "With a girl. Prettier than autumn leaves, you know what. They come in on train and foot. He wanted to stay, but she pushed him to leave so soon."

"Why in the world would he leave Plumtree in the first place?" I said. "It's nature's miracle."

"His Mam died of cancer and his Pap of loneliness a few months later. They left Sam a li'l land on Grandfather Mountain. The house is felled down now. He would've stayed five years ago, except his folks also left him that letter."

"The one in his pocket? What did it say?"

"Lord knows. That's the town mystery in a town with few secrets. The letter made McGee crazy is all. He disappears five year and waltzes back with her. Prettiest girl I've seen and I've been way past Boone to where the cotton blooms and blows. They're not married, you know what."

"She's his sister."

Philyaw barked a laugh. "McGee has no sisters, no brothers. His Mam gave birth to four of five after him, but they were in heaven before their first week. Ev'ryone felt for the McGees. For li'l Sam. He grew up an only child. His girl has a Spanish accent."

I corrected the insult. "Cuban."

"You sure? She spouts cuss words like a Spaniard." He pointed at the church. "They spent the night on a pew, you know what. Most women her age around here have already had their kids. They're dry as broom straw. Maybe she's divorced."

"She hates men."

"That's what I'm a-sayin'."

"Where's McGee now?"

"Run off fast as a snowmelt creek before I could arrest her for sin-nin'. Or for being Spaniard. I can't arrest a girl who belongs to McGee; he never cussed once in his life. Since he was twelve, anyway."

The three dogs circled down at Philyaw's boots. "She'll have a baby in nine month. Ev'ry girl whose been kissed on a pew in that church gits a baby in nine month. McGee's li'l miracle will come out poppin' with July's fireworks."

He squatted to dig a tick from behind a dog's furry ear. "Mc-Gee's folks, Keith and Sammy Pritchard McGee, fought for you Yanks. They come back after the war. Sam was born nine month later, a few grunts and a couple of pushes and out he come yea big. Named for his fightin' mother."

"McGee's mother fought in the war?"

"I was at Keith and Sammy's weddin' back in sixty-one. Dark blue wildflowers in her hair. She was feminine, you know what. A girly girl with pluck. The 26th North Carolina conscripted Keith, found him hidin' in a Grandfather Mountain cave. She couldn't live without him and signed up in Lenoir. Disguised herself as a boy. The Confederates took anyone, they required two teeth, one above and one below to bite the cartridge when loadin'."

I'd caught the old man in a lie. "You said the McGees fought for the Union."

"Sure did, wore wool gray long enough to git to the front line to desert. 'Rich man's war, poor man's fight,' Keith McGee called it, said he hated buryin' poor Rebs who didn't know better."

"Guilt runs in the McGee family," I said. "That and gibberish."

"Sammy and Keith were in desperate love. She pretended to be Keith's li'l brother, cropped her hair, wore a forage cap, trousers and a shell jacket. They slept in the same tent…"

I preempted. "You know what." Luisa must have resembled her mother when I disguised her to be Juan Sola. "I suppose Mrs. McGee never joined the men in a swimming hole."

"Glory hallelujah, truth is marchin' on. She was twenty, but she looked sixteen, mica thin and enough pluck to pretend she was a boy. Rode hell for leather. A crack shot with an Enfield that fired a fifty-eight caliber ball. Shot better than a man, she enjoyed shootin' officers off their saddle. Never shot one of my kin that I know of, so I had nothin' against her."

The moonshiner-sheriff sat down on a pine stump, shut his eyes, and hugged his knees like he was thinking back eons. He remembered something and laughed.

"Sammy Pritchard McGee once got a wild hair and stole a locomotive and loaded thousands of federal prisoners aboard. Made a dash to Morgantown. Shocked these parts, from Raleigh up to Richmond. "

He laughed until the dogs quit licking themselves and got up to stretch. "Sammy and Keith fought for the North, but we didn't blame them. None of us owned a slave. Fuddlin' Joe was a mica miner. No one here had a slave, never a pot to piss in. Sam was born nine months after they came home, a peace baby. Never strayed thirty-two mile past Boone—until he read that letter."

"Luisa rides and shoots like her mother. Better than a man," I said.

"Who's Luisa?"

"Sammy's daughter. The girl who slept in that church."

"I told you, McGee has no sisters. No girl in Plumtree ever had Luisa for a name. No girl had her accent. Plumtree's never had a girl that pretty.Neither has Newland, nor Rose Creek. Wish she was nicer. Her cheekbones can kill, puts the prettiest in the shade, but she's the devil, language as poisonous as pokeberries. I told her so. She spat in the dirt and said she was off to the Klondike to git stinkin' rich."

Philyaw cupped a hand over his mouth. "I wasn't supposed to tell you that part."

"Why not?"

"She said if anyone come lookin' to say she and McGee went somewhere else, to the moon, anywhere but chasin' gold. She told me two or three time. We're poor liars in Plumtree, but I should've remembered. She insisted with that Spanish accent."

"Cuban."

"I fought alongside a Cuban. He fought on our side because Cubans liked their slaves for the sugarcane. She isn't Cuban. Blonde as sour milk."

"She's Carolinian. McGee's sister."

"I ought to cuff you. You know diddle. They're unrelations. McGee's nice as can be, she's a copperhead. Cusses in Spanish. They're not kin, I promise."

The dogs took note of his irritation and circled to the ground to intimidate me with ears flat.

"Got to go." I'd conversed longer with Philyaw than I had with Joe. I needed to hike miles, toot to Johnson City, and on down to Florida before the *USS Maine* left me behind. I could use a shortcut.

"If I follow the Toe River will it take me to Elk Park?" It was too shallow to drown in.

"Meanders like a vine. Winds and winds until it returns to itself. It might lead to Elk Park, but you'll sprain an ankle on those rocks. You already have a bit of a limp. Wouldn't have gotten you out of the war. Sammy Pritchard McGee got out as easy as she got in. She showed her teats to her lieutenant smack in the middle of a skirmish, you know what, got discharged. She went to stay with family in Caldwell County."

"To have a baby, to have Luisa."

"I'm losin' patience. Keith and Sammy were married. She didn't have to sneak off to relations 'cause of some baby. Li'l Sam was born with that smile, but no big sister. Knew these mountains better than anyone. Wasn't a fighter like his folks, quite the banjo player. Drums and fiddles, harps, and bagpipes. Smoked cigarettes until he was thirteen, but never touched moon likker after he was twelve."

"Train to catch."

"I recommend you go back out Blowin' Rock. The way you came in. Come back in the spring. Flowers ev'rywhere, sourwood and whiz oak. Girls fill aprons with purple rhododendron thick as hornets."

"I won't be back," I said. But I decided right then I'd find McGee once the Cuban situation was over. Luisa didn't want me near McGee, which was reason enough to do so. I had it bad for Luisa, but I wouldn't go to the Klondike for her. I'd go for him. I'd go to spite her.

"Glad you come by and said somethin'," Philyaw said.

"Not one word you believed."

"Come back and try again. The laurels bloom in June; the apples snap in October. I'll be here until I'm stiff-backed. Maybe McGee will be back one day to get warm."

"I'm on to the next war."

"There'll never be another."

"This one won't be so bad," I said.

"Hope Sam McGee stays clear of it. Hope he strikes gold; he deserves to."

"He'd give it to the Eskimos," I said.

"That part's true. Unless that fair-skinned Spanish girl steals it first. She's the devil, you know what."

"You're wrong. She's got rough edges, but she's not half as bad as you think. Deep down, she's a McGee." The mutts bawled at me with hackles raised until I was a half mile down Blowing Rock Road.

CHAPTER ELEVEN

NAVY OFFICERS DON'T APPLAUD TARDINESS. "Grateful you arrived before the next hurricane." I knew straightaway that Captain Charles Sigsbee didn't want me aboard. "We were under orders to wait."

We shook hands. With his left, he pulled my Colt .45 from my belt. "That's what we call an Annapolis handshake." He spun the cylinder and tucked my sidearm into his trousers. "You'd sink if you fell overboard with this."

"I'm an expert swimmer and marksman. I trust I'll have it back before the Spaniards board us. Expect me to do my part."

"This is a peace mission. Loose cannons are stored in my quarters."

He handed me a wire from Willie, who wasn't happy, either. "Where were you?" he wrote. "I had to make a deal with the devil to get the *USS Maine* to delay departure. I promised the *Journal* won't print anything of the *Maine*'s mission without Roosevelt's permission."

Captain Sigsbee could've made up the time, but the *Maine* took a lazy twenty hours to travel the camel's spit to Cuba. I killed the daytime pacing as we rolled through space. The battleship was as long as a football field, its beam was twenty-six strides wide. It smelled of fresh paint, the hull white when black is the color of war.

Sigsbee hosted me for supper. His wooden quarters were small with a bookshelf of a dozen volumes at the head of a bed too short to stretch out in. I was unimpressed. There were no paintings on the walls, only a clock of Roman numerals. He took time to wind it. In one corner was a round, ceramic toilet bowl with a blue, floral decoration and a strong chain. My pistol sat catty-corner behind his gramophone.

"Orders are to befriend you so as to influence your opinions," he said.

"I appreciate your honesty. You're a man like myself, who rose from the ranks. Allergic to bullshit. May I ask, sir, what ought my opinion be?"

"The commander-in-chief wants us kept out of war," Sigsbee said. "Roosevelt wants something different altogether. He wants us to kick Spain's ass out of the hemisphere. He invited you aboard to stir things up."

"Your orders contradict," I said.

"Can't please all, this is the Navy. Write whatever you want—"

"I would, if censorship wasn't stringing me up by the balls. I'm underno obligation to fall in among your sailors. I'm here as the eyes and ears of America."

"—but nothing gets printed while you're aboard. That's the grand bargain. Take your time. Take a stab at unvarnished veracity."

After supper, it was brandy and cigars on the poop deck where the ocean filled with moonlight. Sigsbee was in his early fifties, twenty years my senior, the prime age for command, without a touch of gray on a full head of dark hair. Around his men he had countenance, an erect carriage, a direct gaze, a crisp salute.

I blew smoke into the evening. "Roosevelt was wise to leave Sylvester Scovel behind," I said. "I've never met him, but he's a tree without sap."

"Take a stab at the truth," he repeated and turned in, leaving me to drink alone.

I awoke at dawn to distant Cuban cheers that drove away my brandy headache. Havana Harbor was compact, barely a harbor at all. The Spanish fleet was wisely absent, prowling corners of the Caribbean. The *Maine* pulled into her mooring, conspicuous among the stir of tiny fishing boats.

We set anchor at buoy number four, two hundred yards from

the floating dock, close enough to hear the giggles of *señoritas* tossing bright candy into the air. The water was shallow, the sea bottom less than three fathoms beneath the keel. The rising sun burned off the sea mist. Celebrations ended and we became anchored in tedium.

Three days seemed like thirty and I asked Captain Sigsbee if I might hire a ferry to go ashore and wire a story.

"Readers will grow suspicious of my whereabouts," I said as we smoked the sunset away on the poop deck. "Their minds filled with theories of conspiracy."

"They'll know you're up to no good," he said. "What's your story about?"

"Our heroic Navy. Specifically? A day in the life of a sea captain. Your glorious reception by the Cubans and whatnot."

"Sounds more like what other scribes might write," Sigsbee said. He picked up a short piece of rope. "I trust you to have a more entertaining approach."

"Tell me how we'll win the war. That's the story readers crave."

He laughed. "We're an old, second-class battleship. Designed for sail, refitted for steam."

"Ready to fire back if fired upon?"

"Sorry, Mr. Kelley, but there will be no hostilities under my command. I've read your work. War is fun and fitness to you. When your foot is blown off at the ankle, thank heaven you won't have corns on that foot anymore."

"We're fully armed? In case of eventualities?"

Sigsbee tied a fast knot in his rope, tugged on it and on his cigar. He blew slow smoke into a pink western sky. "Anyone who starts something will be at the business end of breech-loading guns."

I employed a frown of earnestness. I scribbled some notes, which encouraged him to talk on. "Seven six-pounder and eight one-pounder rapid-fire guns. Four Gatlings, four Whitehead torpedoes. Our keel would drag bottom if they put another shell aboard."

"With your permission, I'll lighten the load," I said. It had grown dark enough to pee over the side.

"Did I mention a hundred tons of coal?"

I shook and buttoned my pants. When I turned, Sigsbee was looking at the first stars.

"We're a floating volcano," he said at the sky. "Thank God we'll be here three weeks, then we'll be gone without firing a shot. The more humdrum this mission, the more successful."

He took an endless draw on his cigar and went distant the way men do when they think about women. The night darkened to pitch, and quiet enough to hear—not just see—his tobacco draft bright orange with sea air. I mirrored him; smoke swirled from my open mouth and drifted toward the equator.

My own emotions were raw, in a constant skirmish with my mind, coaxing my thoughts from the clutches of Luisa. I'd rather be back in the trenches of Thessalie than in her gutter. By now she and McGee were traveling by rail, or ship, or some dog-sled conveyance. McGee must've realized his mistake. He'd want to be in the warm Caribbean with me, but Sigsbee would never have let a Spanish-speaker aboard for fear he was a sympathizer. I sipped my brandy. Alcohol didn't make me feel as good as it once did. I swallowed more to compensate.

Maybe they'd stopped in San Francisco or Seattle, but I knew Luisa was driven by demons to push for the Klondike in dead winter. McGee would dumbly follow; he was loyal to a fault. Intense loyalty. A dependence. Addicted to his guilt. He owed her a debt that could never be repaid. His loyalty and guilt would get him caught in a blizzard.

I pictured Luisa in the Klondike with cheeks rosy, her eyes behind long, frozen lashes. I don't think I was ever more attracted to her than I was when she was behind bars, but she would be more beautiful imprisoned inside the furry hood of a Russian parka. Warm feelings rose in me like trout for mayflies. I had it bad, but I'd never freeze to death for her. I wasn't guilt-ridden like McGee.

The captain's voice came from somewhere out of the white, snowy tundra to deny my request to ferry ashore. I blew more smoke into the hot night.

"Don't get your back up," Sigsbee said. "You've had quite a run. Your circulation's up, you're winning *your* war."

"I'll not sell one copy from this tired vessel; not under your thumb. Maybe I'll swim to Havana."

"Spain will cut the cable before it lets you wire a word," Sigsbee said. "You're under their thumb more than mine. They'll snip your gonads with that same cable cutter."

"If it's not one government snipping, it's another."

"Speaking of gonads, that jailbreak with the Cuban Martyr Girl took some."

I had no choice but to nod my agreement.

"You're a celebrity," Sigsbee said. "When I get home, my wife will want to know what Jayson Kelley is like even before we make hay. I'd best get to know you better so I'll have some Kelley stories to tell."

The cost of fame, I was obliged to share intimate information. I tossed him a bone, described what it's like to pilot an auto-car. "When, exactly, *can* I file something? Our presence here is no secret to Spain; it's a secret to the American people."

"In a month you'll be in New Orleans, no longer under my command."

The North Atlantic squadron was but a few hours north off Dry Tortuga, but a month passed and a replacement battleship never arrived to relieve us. Only the torpedo boat *Cushing* with supplies. The *Cushing* chugged back to Key West, and The *USS Maine* remained anchored to the exact spot.

Seaside *señoritas* taunted the sailors with innocence. The men asked for shore leave, but Sigsbee denied all requests. That led to sour evenings spent cooped up in quarters below.

Sigsbee and I played checkers in the evening. In the daytime, chores were few, and the frustrated crew invited me to play dice. I accepted; it would keep my ear to the ground. I was expert at dice, I'd learned from yeggmen. The boys were at first intimidated by my fame and skill, but I was the one man aboard who'd set foot on Cuban soil and they relished my descriptions of Havana after dark.

"You see nothing except lazy men and old women all day long. White-haired biddies. But when hot gusts are replaced by the caressing sea breeze the *Parque Central* fills with the magic of evening. Pretty as they are poor. None wear gowns, all wear frocks so threadbare you can see into their hearts."

The ship's chaplain, James Chadwick, was in my audience, but that didn't censor me, or stop me from taking a long drink from my flask. "The brown ones are petite. The black ones larger in all aspects. They're endowed and mature for their delicate age. All shades are shy but frolicsome and they long to be kissed for the first time. They're gentle, with eyes of rugged passion."

I was drunk. I surprised Father James with a bear hug from behind. It was beneath dignity, but I wanted to get the boys on my side. Father James' face blushed red and the boys howled and cheered when I wouldn't let go.

"Be warned, one kiss gets you engaged," I said, kissing the chaplain's cheek.

A seaman hollered. "How many Cubans have you kissed, Kelley?"

"More girls than this old boat has kissed buoys."

My clever wordplay took the sailors a second, but a few of them whooped and called me a clever punster and said they were tired of doing their duty where there was no duty to be done.

I turned Father James loose from my grip. I said, "Dolls are yards away, let's rescue them from Spanish thuggery. Are you ready to clear the decks for serious business?"

They were until Sigsbee appeared from the shadows to spoil things. He ordered me to stop fraternizing, to stay out of dice games or he'd charge me with inciting mutiny.

"Quite the taskmaster," I said and the boys laughed for an instant.

Sigsbee reminded all that he was in charge and threatened to throw me overboard to prove it.

"Sheez, this ship is here because of me."

"You're three sheets to the wind," Sigsbee said and had me escorted to quarters where, left alone, I had an angry outburst. To my surprise, the outburst escalated into a rant about being abandoned. I don't know where it came from, but I couldn't stop. I slept a while, puked, fumed, slept a while more.

When I awoke, Luisa was poisoning my thoughts. I didn't know if I wanted to strangle her or make slow love to her. I got out my Remington and typewrote a short item of fiction to keep my mind occupied.

Out the porthole, a merchant ship arrived and moored fifty yards from us. It was flying the Stars and Stripes. That lifted my mood. It was comforting to have a friendly neighbor as I finished my composition.

I fell into a dream. Willie demanded "Copy! Copy!" He hollered through speaking tubes that Pulitzer's *World* had published my obituary. I could hear newsboys hocking the *World* on street corners as I tried to compose the accurate version of my life. The *Journal's* presses were waiting, but I couldn't typewrite a word. It was one of those dreams that made me wake up tense. I've had such anxiety dreams since boyhood. I'd wake up and the dream would seem more true than reality until I convinced myself otherwise.

I woke in my cabin slumped over my typewriting machine, with headache enough. My shirt was damp with sweat. The last page of my fiction was in the machine and I read it aloud using the dawn light that poured through my porthole. I'd never before thought of myself as a fictionist, but I figured if politics didn't work out I'd have a bright future as a wordsmith with the best literary magazines.

I put my piece down and peered out the porthole at the new morning. Just then, the ominous *Alfonso XII* came into view. The Spanish warship moved in fast and anchored in our back pocket two hundred yards away, the American merchant ship off to the side. Three sizable ships in a harbor teacup small. If fighting broke out, artillery would be point-blank.

The frenzy of footsteps above my cabin convinced me to swallow my pride and seek out Captain Sigsbee for the first time since my unwarranted scolding. He was on the bridge seated in a tall, wooden captain's chair, studying the *Alfonso XII* through his field glass.

"We're still at peace, Mr. Kelley," he said. But in the same breath ordered a higher pressure of steam.

A day of energy skated by until my differences with Sigsbee were forgotten. I'm a forgiving man without resentments, and that night we stayed up smoking away our nerves with fat cigars. It had been a beastly hot day and the night was no cooler as heavy clouds swallowed the constellations.

Sigsbee received reports that all was secure, and we moved port side to watch Havana twinkle. We put our feet on the rail with the *Alfonso XII* in our periphery, and I laughed at baritone tales of his childhood in Albany.

"Where'd you grow up?" Sigsbee asked.

"Massachusetts. Cambridge. Brick home. Papa was a minister."

I changed the subject before he asked about Joe. I didn't want to waste the evening on baseball, although I would have enjoyed telling Sigsbee how I beat the tar out of my brother playing old-one-cat. The day came when Joe accused me of changing the rules in my favor. It was my responsibility as older brother to stop his whining. "You get what you get and don't throw a fit," I told him and we never played one-old-cat again.

"I suppose my childhood was perfect," I told Sigsbee.

He began a letter to his wife. I left my pencil behind my ear. I wrote stories to millions, but I had no one worth a sheet of stationery. Maybe McGee, but he'd stomped off without leaving a forwarding address.

I was eager to ask Sigsbee what yarns he was telling his wife about me when something akin to a rifle shot captured our attention. At first, I thought Sigsbee's cigar had popped like alligator juniper in a stove. His head raised like an elk's at a twig snap.

An explosion followed, not loud but sullen. It came so close on the heels of the shot, I decided the Spanish had invented a secret shell as fast as sound.

The scenes that followed felt unreal. Would be to God, I wished they were.

The USS Maine lit up.

A second prolonged and deafening explosion blew our propped-up feet from the rail. Yellow fire filled the sky. Captain Sigsbee and I were sent sliding on our rears thirty yards along the deck as the aft end folded high into the air. We slid downward through flames that followed the deck upward.

The biggest threat to my safety, other than going overboard and drowning a spit from shore, was the haphazard rain of what had been steel railings. Blocks of wood, debris of all kinds. I failed to cover my head and was struck by a cement slab.

[Editor's note: Del Leonard Jones is writing a second novel set in the dawn of professional baseball and inspired by the 1888 ballad *Casey At the Bat* as told from the umpire's point of view. Information on the publication date can be requested at https://caseystrikesout.wixsite.com/website.

Jones has written a non-fiction business leadership book *Advice from the Top, 1001 Bits of Business Wisdom from the Great Leaders of the Recent Past.* In one chapter, Fred Smith, founder and CEO of FedEx, speaks on the Pony Express and the leadership lessons that can be learned from historical figures including Alexander the Great, Theodore Roosevelt, Julius Caesar, George Washington and Dwight Eisenhower. Request a free copy of Jones's Q&A with Smith at https://caseystrikesout.wixsite.com/website]

PART TWO
PURGATORY

Bid good-by to sweetheart, bid good-by to friend;

The Lone Trail, the Lone Trail follow to the end.

Tarry not, and fear not, chosen of the true;

Lover of the Lone Trail, the Lone Trail waits for you.

— Robert W. Service

CHAPTER TWELVE

MY LANDING WAS CUSHIONED BY A DEAD MARINE, WHO PERISHED BEFORE HE HAD A CHANCE TO PRAY. I escaped serious injury, knocked down and back on my feet.

The sea flashed from dark to bright. Dark to bright. A pulse in the night sky started out as a milky green and brightened to plum-red and to a primrose haze with a wondrous sheen; colors fluttered out in a fan. Light swept about in a giant scythe.

No cannons flashed from the *Alfonso XII*, and yet explosions continued. "Our own shells are bursting aboard," Sigsbee hollered.

There came a whistling moan. It sounded human but it was air escaping below as salt water rushed the sailors' quarters.

The *Alfonso XII* approached. It didn't have far to go to board us. The war I'd worked long and hard to spark was breaking out in a bathtub. I reached to my belt instinctively. The revolver wasn't there, only a reporter's notebook. I cursed Sigsbee and his gramophone.

"Abandon ship!" the captain hollered. He ran to the wheel, and I suppose I followed. It took minutes for the ship to sink to the shallow bottom, leaving the poop and the mainmast above water. We broke in half, the foremast and the bow collapsed into atoms. I imagined the terrible struggles for life in the quarter deck, awash where the men were piped below. A flooded tomb.

The whistling noise stopped, but not the flashes of light.

"God Almighty," Sigsbee said, and I followed his eyes to where naked objects bobbed in the sea, the bodies and body parts of the dead and wounded flushed out of the hull. Those alive clung to fragments of the vessel. They came in and out of view like the flickering of Edison's moving picture show.

The fireworks at some point ended, but the scene stayed illuminated in a red glare from a fire burning midship. Someone on the wharf switched on a sear-light. The beam raked the lagoon to reveal more tragedy in the singing foam.

Sigsbee was ready to jump overboard, if only to rescue arms and legs. I hailed him with my actor's voice. It sounded otherworldly, ghostlike, and brought him back. He issued orders to flood all guncotton aboard.

I made it my duty to keep Sigsbee present and focused. "What sank us? A mine?" I hollered.

"Water's too shallow."

"A torpedo then."

"The explosion came from underwater on our starboard. Any torpedo would've had to circle like a shark."

He was back in command and none too soon, ignoring me as if I no longer existed. The *Alfonso XII* moved in tight for the kill. There were shouts back and forth over megaphones, and I cursed McGee for having abandoned me when I most needed his interpretation. Rather than fire on us, the Spaniards lowered rowboats and began a rescue of our boys from the sea. Sailors were fished out and transported to the American merchant ship, soon to be a hospital without doctors.

I convinced Captain Sigsbee we were the only two left aboard the *Maine*. I volunteered to row his gig through flotsam to the hospital ship. While plowing the sea, I again insisted we were sunk by a torpedo. He shook his head and said to himself, "No torpedo known to modern warfare."

"The Spanish have invented an infernal machine that can split a ship in two," I said. "It was in the *Sun.*"

Sigsbee blamed our own War Department. "When they refitted the *Maine* to steam, they put coal bunkers next to the ship's gunpowder magazines..."

"That's asinine."

"...on the theory that the magazines offer a layer of protection from incoming shells." He pointed at the destruction. "The fall of the smokestack, the disappearance of the big turret guns, the overturning of the deck forward, indicate the explosion has occurred from within."

I was tiring at the oars and from Sigsbee's logic. He was implying the disaster was self-inflicted. Willie wouldn't buy that—no one would.

I tried again. "Don't you find it queer the *Maine* would blow up in this harbor at this moment in history? With a Spanish man-of-war a spit away?"

"An inspection by expert divers will prove my gut right." He was still talking to himself. "The plating of the hull will be bent outward. We blew ourselves to hell."

We were hoisted from the gig and met with warmth by merchant ship Captain Frank Stevens. "Welcome aboard the *City of Washington.*"

"How many dead?" Sigsbee asked.

"How many in your crew?"

"Three-fifty."

"You've lost two hundred," Captain Stevens said. "Soon to be two-fifty. Many of your boys are holding on."

I searched for my notebook. It was gone, my pencil wet behindmy ear.

"Thank the Lord the aft magazine didn't go up," Sigsbee said. "The *City of Washington* itself might've been sunk with us. Your ship is riddled from our accident."

The use of the word accident rankled me.

"Thank God the Spanish were around for a rescue," Captain Stevens said.

Those words rankled me more, and it didn't help my mood when Captain Stevens escorted us to the injured, many with third-degree burns. Most were in their bunks dreaming of Cuban dolls when they were washed out to sea. Scores had received the sacrament from Father James. There were no nurses, and I volunteered to write letters to families.

I found stationery. One sailor had been doing punishment watch on the port quarter deck at the time of the attack. His misdeeds paid off. He went up into the open air with Sigsbee and me. Another said he was sleeping in a yawl hanging from the davits. The yawl was blown to pieces, but the sleeping man was thrown into the Caribbean and fished out in fair health.

Miracles were few. The worst-off was halved by a shell and yet alive and talkative. I didn't identify myself, I didn't want him star-struck and fishing for the proper lexicon on my behalf.

"You'll get a medal," I said.

"I'd rather they chloroform me to hell. Better to be dead than to have my little girl look at me with dread. I can't go home and give pain to the ones I love."

"There, there, I know how you feel," I said. "Time heals all wounds." My experience with the grieving widow was paying dividends. "This filthy war will soon be done. But oh, oh, never until we've won."

The sailor said some curse words that I prayed weren't for the ears of the Almighty. He gave way to ether, his lips went purple and were still moving as he died.

Sigsbee pulled a blanket over the sailor's face. The Captain looked past me and said, "How do you like war now, Kelley?"

"So, you agree this is not an accident?"

Sigsbee didn't argue. Perhaps he was coming around to my point of view. Exhausted, he asked Captain Stevens if he could borrow a log to record the events of the day, and he took leave. I hadn't the luxury of sleep, I'd readers to attend to. I used a lantern to light my feet and found seclusion on deck to compose the most important story of my life. I was without my typewriting machine, so I wrote longhand on stationery by lantern's light. I slaved two hours. Dawn broke. I put the lantern out and stretched my legs. The *Maine* protruded from the shallows of buoy number four; vultures roosted in twisted steel.

I caught a ride ashore in the lighthouse boat. Once there, I collected more string for my story, more detail.

Seven charred and bloated bodies washed against the seawall. The birds patiently swooped down from their perches to pick at the flesh of our heroes.

McGee, in his absence, continued to be a blessing. Weeks before, while I rescued Luisa from Morro Castle, he'd befriended a Cuban sympathizer in the Spanish censor's office. McGee passed along a blank cable form pre-stamped with the censor's seal of approval. I'd been waiting for an opportunity to use it. In no time my *holy shit!* item was cabled from Havana's City Hall on Weyler Street to William Randolph Hearst on Park Row. The magic of the modern age.

When I alighted in Key West aboard the *City of Washington*, this headline was the first thing I saw:

DEADLIEST DAY EVER AT SEA!
USS MAINE DESTROYED BY
SPANISH SCOUNDRELISM
DIVERS DISCOVER MINE HOLE!
Unconditional Surrender Spain's Only Course
After Worst Naval Disaster in U.S. History

Remington had drawn **WAR!** No brass type was large enough. The headline and a Remington illustration filled a Page One destined to be on Willie's wall until he was stinking up his mommy's mausoleum; destined to be behind glass in war museums for a thousand years. I had a bout of conscience and turned to Page Two in search of my mention of Sigsbee's theory, that the explosion was self-inflicted. Willie had taken the liberty to trim it out and insert his own theory.

> The Spanish, perhaps, arranged mines in the Harbor prior to the Maine's arrival to be exploded by means of electric currents sent from shore by buried wires. Such mines, filled with guncotton, carry much larger charges than torpedoes from warship tubes.
>
> We may never know the exact evildoer who pressed a button ashore and sent our boys sky high.

Willie had dared to muddle with my copy. I flipped back to Page One and studied Remington's illustration, a scene of the *Maine* seconds before the disaster, anchored over a sinister, oblong object, a Spanish submarine deep in twenty fathoms of water. His illustration did not comport with the true depth of the Bay of Havana. It did not comport with my story, or Willie's theory, but comportment mattered little to Remington.

I refocused attention on my piece. It filled the columns of four pages, my destiny as the greatest correspondent secured. "That's what matters," I said to calm myself. "That's what will matter on Election Day." I went back to reading.

> Misery will weigh heavy in American homes as our brave boys are carried by pallbearers up San Rafael Street to the Havana cemetery.
>
> Throughout the United States, businesses will close, school sessions will be cancelled and

nippers told to pray on bended knee. Choirs will sing "America" to flags at half mast as companies of volunteer bluejackets are raised from among the best of chaps and chums.

My item recommended a war resolution be passed in Congress without a minute of debate and the military be given carte blanche to spend any amount of treasure necessary.

The White House, at last, will get out of the way, or war will come knocking on the eastern seaboard. Boston's buildings present a large target for enemy fire.

The Spaniards have been capable of the worst brutality going back to the fifteenth century, and the only thing certain is that they will make more trouble if opportunity affords.

Be brave. Fortunately, the beginning of the end is at hand. Remember the Maine. To hell with Spain.

I sensed something amiss. Something wasn't quite right with my words. Something out of kilter. Willie had done substantial tinkering. Maybe I'd gotten a concussion from the cement slab, but I didn't recognize my writing in places. My prose is unlike anyone's, a bare-fisted fight. My roundhouse punches remained throughout, but missing were some feints and jabs.

My eyes gravitated again to the **WAR!** headline. Beneath, Willie had removed my byline, *Jayson Kelley, Special Commissioner.* That caused me great distress. He'd redacted the credit I deserved.

My heart sank as I read again top to bottom. I exploded at the injustice, cussing and kicking and ranting until Key West passersby stopped to gawk. Willie had edited my piece so that it was no longer a first-person account. This last paragraph had been inserted in italics next to my illustrated thumbnail portrait.

> *The Journal's famous war correspondent Jayson Kelley was tragically aboard the USS Maine at the time of the gutless attack and is feared to be at the bottom of Havana Harbor. His coverage of the Cuban situation will be remembered as one of the most prodigious feats of American journalism. His soul is in God's hands, though his corpse may be in the bread-basket of a circling shark.* **W.R.H.**

Those were Willie's initials at the end of my piece. Willie had killed me off.

I shook the newspaper violently at the gawkers. "What sort of monster does this?"

"Spain," one hollered. In unison five or six chanted my own words: "Remember the *Maine*. To hell with Spain."

"To hell with William Randolph Hearst," I said.

Below his initials, along the bottom of Page Four, was the Hogan Alley comic. The Yellow Kid's smirk was following me, except it wasn't a smirk. The barefooted little snot monster had a toothy grin.

CHAPTER THIRTEEN

I HOPPED THE FIRST TRAIN IN THE GENERAL DIRECTION OF CHICAGO. Before we reached speed, I'd plotted a half-dozen revenge scenarios, but none were vengeful enough.

Two nights in a Pullman afforded me precious time to stew. I spent much of it it in the saloon car and, if I wasn't there, I was standing in the open platform between cars. Each time I returned to my seat, someone new sat across from me. One young man, dressed in black, was with his plump new wife. He'd married the first hussy to come down the street. I spoke off-color but her man did nothing to defend her honor.

The porter was called to quiet me down, but he was a Negro, so what could he do? He shined my shoes to placate me. I excused myself to pump water in the basin to wash my face. I paid another visit to the saloon, pissed from the platform, and when I resurfaced, this blonde was seated across from me. The last thing I wanted was female companionship and she was exceedingly satisfied with herself, a tattler, one of those dolls who sits at soda fountains and gossips in whispers.

She also wore black. She didn't know who I was, but she knew I was well-situated. She spoke first. "February is the most cheerless month for scenery."

I was too drunk to respond. Too furious at Willie.

"Do you know the time?" she asked. "Or even the time zone?"

"Eighteen ninety-eight."

She smiled at my sarcasm. She said I must be in a mood because of the war. "Remember the *Maine*, to heck with Spain, pardon my

French. Cheer up, handsome, it soon will be won."

Her hair was her glory and I stared waiting for her roots to grow out.

"I'm happy for your company," she said. "It breaks up the day."

I fell asleep from inebriation.

I awoke wanting to sleep more, but I was too angry. The blonde had changed seats, leaving me alone. The last thing I needed was more time to think. I went between cars for fresh air and decided my best course was to get to San Francisco. I'd march into the *Chronicle*, sell my story for an obscene sum. Willie's lie would be exposed by his West Coast competitor, the nemesis of his flagship paper, my life restored. Within days, my tale would spread to every town.

Special Commissioner Jayson Kelley
Rises from His Ocean Tomb

I stopped for a night's rest in Chicago; infuriation had turned my insides to fricassee. I was met at the station by a newsboy. How Willie knew I was aboard that very train was beyond me, but the newsie told me to "Tellyphone Mr. Hearst before you go and do nothing lunertic."

I found a private gentlemen's room at the Fred Harvey House, had myself a tall drink, put a call in through three or four operators. I'd let Willie grovel. I pictured him sitting behind his desk of deep walnut, oversized to offset his girly voice and whatnot. I was going to expose him as a fraud.

"I understand," Willie said. "You resent being killed without your permission. Anyone would. The removal of your byline. Unforgivable. Uh-huh, I get the gist."

"A lying skunk." The mouthpiece shined wet from my spittle.

"Any correspondent would be outraged," Willie said.

Willie's self-assured tone angered me the more. Why was he calm as harp music? We'd argued often enough in the past. I always had the upper hand. Now, I was the one who sat sidesaddle.

"Don't you see?" Willie said. "This is a grand scheme, grander than the prison break by the Martyr Girl. I've hired divers. They won't find you, but the search will fill Page One and…"

A few seconds of static were followed by Willie's voice, drenched in pleasure. "The grandest ploy. Something to print while we're awaiting our boys to skedaddle down to Cuba."

I beat my fist on the copper bell of the phone. "You killed me! You pirated my work!"

"So stipulated. Made you walk the plank. I plead guilty. I already apologized. We need to get past that. For the sake of our prank. You'll love it. The search for you will keep Sunday editions popping until our troops are on the ground."

"Until I waltz a dos-i-do from Davy Jones' locker and skate into the *Chronicle.*"

"Don't overreact," Willie said. "Don't mix metaphors."

I slammed the earpiece into the fork of the phone and made myself another drink. I called Willie back five minutes drunker, negotiating my way past more operators.

"Won't America be flabbergasted to see my ghost arrive at the *Chronicle* in a couple of days?" I said. "I'll expose you and then I'll come to New York to sock you in the nose and go to work for Joseph Pulitzer."

"I wouldn't do that…" static …"you're the one who'll be exposed. We'll expose you as a fabricator." His voice was drab. Serious. Not the least bit sissy. "No choice. You'd leave me no choice."

I puked a laugh. "Don't threaten me, you hypocrite. You're the fabricator. You fabricated a man's death. Who stoops that low?"

Willie's drone came through the earpiece like he was dictating a memo. "Ralph London's been examining your items going back three years. Talking to people you long ago interviewed. Combing fact from fiction. He's been working on it for a month. All the time you were doing nothing on the *Maine.* Slow work, like picking lice from a newsboy's hair."

"Ralph London knows I'm alive?"

"No, no one knows. Me and you. That's why this scheme's so brilliant. London knows you embellished, but thinks you're dead."

"I never embellished. Never once."

"Again and again."

"I'd rather be dead."

'You invented entire people outright. I found it hard to believe, but London has the evidence. All the goods. You can get away with fabricating in San Francisco, but one must watch one's step when writing for a New York daily."

"Ralph can't find his johnson with both hands down his trousers."

"A proven reporter long before you came along."

"Journalism isn't algebra," I said. "You used to know that, Willie. I work the same equation and get different results; that's why readers love me. You used to know that. London hits singles. I hit doubles and triples. I knock the cover off the ball."

"I don't want to expose you, it'll make us all look bad, but if you sell your story to the *Chronicle,* Ralph London will have no choice but to write a long yarn telling your readers you were a crank..." *static.* "... prove you staged your own death. We'll give our Page One apologies that we ever let a hack like you come to work for us."

I threw my drink against a painting on the wall. I looked around to assure myself I was still alone in the gentlemen's meeting room.

"Go ahead, take me down. Drag the *Journal's* reputation down with me. If you want two wars going on at once."

"I'll sack a couple of editors, in good faith. Editors should've intercepted your lies long ago."

"Who killed me off? You did. Yours is the big lie; that's all you."

"There's a lot to be said for mea culpas, a humble apology for our failure to keep Jayson Kelley on a short leash will help the *Journal's* reputation more than hurt. Circulation unharmed. Memories are short when there's a war on. We'll recover. You won't."

I felt shorter than Willie, an odd thing to think when we were eight hundred miles apart.

"Half of New York already suspects you're some sick Huckleberry," he said. "Wait until we tell your readers you staged your demise to sit on the floating dock and watch brave divers search for you. Your choice. Doesn't have to be this way. We can be a team, the way we've always been."

I drooped my forehead against the wet mouthpiece. My feet throbbed. I was cooked. "I'll fight you, Willie. What have I to lose when my option is dead?"

"Jay…" Static lasted so long I thought some dickey bird had perched on a line in a cornfield and choked conversation from the universe. "Jay, that's one way to go. Or, you can stay incognito, enjoy a sabbatical."

"Dead's a somewhat long sabbatical."

"A holiday is all. The Palace Hotel…" *static…* "A month or two of leisure in San Francisco. The minute the war's over, I'll resuscitate you. Make you famous."

"I'm already the most famous correspondent in history."

Willie laughed. "I cinched that when I drowned you. More famous than Nellie Bly. You're welcome. In exchange for your loyalty, the weight of the Hearst syndicate will rally behind you …" *static …* "when you make that run for high office."

"Pretend I'm dead, come back to life to make a run? I'd be a laughingstock."

"Think, Jay. When it's time, I'll smuggle you back into Cuba aboard *The Vamoose*, to Cienfuegos on the southern coast." He had been planning for a month. "We'll say you escaped Morro Castle. Like the Martyr Girl. What a scheme. The Spaniards captured you when they sunk the *Maine*, and they're holding you in a dungeon all the while. Beneath the sea wall. You'll be set free the day our boys liberate Havana. Be a hero."

Willie was on to something. "Catch the updraft of victory fever," he said. "Hero enough to be…"

"President." My whisper carried clear as bells. I'd long considered

Congress a likelihood, but by the century's turn I'd be thirty-seven, past life's great divide, and constitutionally eligible for the presidency. The milksop McKinley won in ninety-six. Next time around, he'd be blamed for dragging his feet. For getting the *Maine* sunk. For failing to achieve victory in a timely fashion. He'd lose to any square-jawed opponent who didn't cheat at golf.

"Someone gets elected because of what we did," Willie said. "Might as well be you."

My hands quit strangling the telephone. I grappled for modesty. "Any man who wants to be president should be disqualified from being so."

"With my backing, of course, the backing of the Hearst syndicate. I'm buying another newspaper—one there in Chicago. Hush-hush. I'm taking our circulation war to Pulitzer's home turf in the Midwest. I'll win you delegates in Illinois, Wisconsin and Missouri. I already own the electorate in California and New York. A landslide."

"What am I to do with myself in the meantime?"

"You're more difficult than my twin girls. Draw your salary. Float on a cloud. Dream big dreams."

Willie danced around his phone the instant I agreed, and I kicked myself for not demanding more of his mommy's money. His taps faded and his voice was back on the line.

"What a holy shit! scheme. Two months will be good for your constitution, get you rested for your campaign. Say, did you hear? Your brother quit playing ball to sign up with Roosevelt's Rough Riders."

"Joe quit the Baltimores?"

"To go kill some stinking Spaniards. God bless him, to avenge your death. All in tomorrow's edition. London's writing a long yarn."

"Joe quit for me?"

"Tomorrow. Page One. A masterpiece. Patriotism sells better than garter belts these days. Everyone wants in on this war. Girls too. Annie Oakley offered fifty lady sharpshooters. America's own Amazon force."

"Joe prefers his world neat as a ball diamond, each safe base ninety feet from the next."

"This country sorely needs heroes. We'll give her brother heroes. You'll be our biggest hero. Bigger than what's-his-name. The one-eyed Tennessean from Peachtree. What's his name? Shot by firing squad?"

"Plumtree."

"It's a holy shit! scheme. Your part is simple. You can't drop a stitch. Stay incognito or it falls apart. No one can know. Me and you. Our secret forever, we'll take it to the grave. Got to go. Damned war to cover. Look what you've gone and done. This will be the last time we talk. Alex Bell won't let me telephone you all the way to San Francisco, not yet, damned Scotsman."

"McKinley would tax it, anyway."

Willie laughed. "Be good. Wire me from time to time, but use an alias. Wear a disguise. Shouldn't take more than a month or two to kick Spain's ass. Don't drop a stitch; that's your one job. Enjoy the Palace Hotel. After the war, we'll do a series about your desperation in the dungeons."

He hung up. I put the earpiece on the hook, hid the drink-stained painting behind a chesterfield. Things work out for me; they do. I was still the best-paid correspondent in the land and, truth be told, happy to be free of deadlines. There was no better place for a holiday than San Francisco. My second home. Illustrious dolls of the West are wide open to wonder. A place to lick my wounds, forget McGee—and my lost Luisa.

The search for my body slipped to Page Two, then behind the color comics and out of newsprint altogether. Hoopla faded and I felt the same as dead. As the days passed, I struggled to be content. I wore out the wooden sidewalks of San Francisco. The place had changed since I'd left in 1895, it was as if I'd visited a childhood home that was owned by strangers. I couldn't throw my fame around to get the dolls. Willie'd forced me to be a damned nobody.

One day, I was no longer bored and I wished I were. My whole world fell apart when Sylvester Scovel wrote an item in the *New York*

World accusing me of juicing. I was dead and forgotten and, still, he called me a liar. I was a stiff and I couldn't defend myself.

How Sylvester Scovel came up with the story was obvious. My colleague Ralph London never did like me after I passed him up out of turn at the *Journal*. Once I agreed to the scheme, Willie put London's tell-all on ice. He made London write puff pieces about Joe's devotion to his dead brother.

London couldn't use his ammo, so he gave or sold it to Scovel at the *World*. Thank God, readers cringe when newspapers urinate on the deceased half of hero brothers. Had I been alive, the accusations would've stuck. Pulitzer buried Scovel's items deep behind the brevities, but that didn't stop Willie from criticizing the *World* for peeing on a man who couldn't defend himself.

> What muck will Pulitzer rake next? Will he report that First Lady Ida McKinley takes bromide salts to dull her public seizures? The *New York World* is beneath all dignity.

Popular opinion always lands on a dead man's side, and the story faded after two days. Willie wired that he'd sacked Ralph London without fanfare. London went to work for the trades where he railed against me and Willie. In a week, London was sacked again for carrying out a vendetta against a man at the bottom of a bay.

God, I missed reporting. I was a shell of a man without it. I dangled my legs at the docks, frittered away my life talking to prospectors. Men landed from the Klondike goldfields most days, but no one had seen a Carolinian mutt with a mile smile. No one had seen his unforgettable sister with loose hair that sparkled like the waves of the bay.

Unanswered questions were endless inside the confines of my boredom. McGee or Luisa? Which trail would I follow if they split up in the Klondike? Were they both drowning, which one would I save? I'm a man from the boots up. Of course, I'd save the damsel. But the decision wouldn't be easy. How often does a man find a McGee-like friend? I never had.

I wondered if McGee and Luisa had heard of my death. He'd weep. Maybe she'd weep on the inside for the man who rescued her on a charging horse and again by sawing through cobwebbed iron bars and diving with her hand in hand into the sea.

Who would I save? I whispered, "God only knows." The one honest answer. I dismissed the exercise as farcical. I'd never have to choose between McGee and Luisa. They were joined. Inseparable.

Afternoons I attended town hall meetings and student war rallies at St. Ignatius College, soaked my feet in sulfur at Skaggs Springs. American flags fluttered from the Tenderloin to Golden Gate Park, even outside the laundries of Chinatown. The same chant around each corner, "Remember the *Maine*," followed in unison by "To hell with Spain." My slogan appeared on buttons, matchbooks, penny candy, and in the cries of newsies.

My slogan lived on, but I'd been forgotten. I removed my disguise. San Franciscans stared right through me. I spent nights drinking and scheming of ways to blow on the embers of my legacy. Plotting ways to get me remembered. I walked crazy with the blues. I'd way too much time to think. To drink.

Why did she grow up in Havana instead of Plumtree? Why, after years and years, did McGee get a letter and go looking for her? Why'd she hate men? Did she hate me? The answer to that question was no. Girls had no reason to hate me. I loved them all. I loved everyone, I appreciated Negros for their Christian values. I prayed that I'd put out the fire with that bucket of milk. I hadn't an ounce of prejudice against anyone except Spaniards. I respected girls. With Cuba's independence, the world would be a better place, safe from Spain's rapists. I'd been swallowed up by chaos, but at least I was still an honest man. Honest with myself.

Once Willie's scheme played out, I'd prepare for the presidential campaign. I'd head to the Klondike and make her my bride. Make Mc-

Gee my best man, my brother-in-law. If I found one, I'd find the other. McGee and Luisa would be down the same path. With them aboard, I'd capture all of Appalachia.

Willie wired to brag the *Journal's* circulation was approaching one and a half million, more than any newspaper in history, and our boys hadn't yet landed.

"No one man's death has ever meant so much," he said.

CHAPTER FOURTEEN

MCKINLEY WAS A SLOTH; it took him forever to secure one hundred and twenty-five thousand volunteers to swell the twenty-eight thousand regular army. A million answered the call, but the weeks passed and no one had fired a shot.

I took an afternoon walk along the damp sidewalk of O'Farrell Street. I hadn't gone far when the gloved hands of a maiden covered my eyes from behind. A monstrous kiss was planted on me.

"I'm performing for a stock company at the Alcazar Theatre," Blanche Bates said, wiping her rouge from my cheek with a handkerchief that smelled of sweaty boobies. Some dolls can bathe and bathe and never smell half as good as Luisa did in Morro Castle. "I'm fed up with New York."

Only then did Blanche Bates realize I shouldn't be alive, but the delay wasn't long enough for me to come up with a plausible lie. I'd no choice but to trust her, and she was thrilled to be let in on Willie's grand secret.

I'd launched her career, I'd convinced Greater New York she was a better leading lady than Maude Adams. The biggest whopper ever to make print. She owed me far more than her silence—and it was liberating to at last confide in someone.

"Keep it our secret. If things fall into place, I'll go head-to-head against McKinley in 1900. Start the century with a new generation."

Blanche Bates was too buxom to be First Lady material, but I let her yammer about how a bachelor will never be elected president, and how wonderful it would be to raise snot monsters in the White House.

The Alcazar had a chesterfield backstage like the one at Daly's Theater in New York, and we fell into it like a wagon wheel into a rut.

"Mind your Ps and Qs," she'd say, but she proved to be the one with an insatiable appetite.

I hadn't seen her since she split the seams of her sequined costume. The newsman in me wondered what had become of her pregnancy, but there was never a good time to ask without seeming indelicate—or interrupting things.

As San Francisco grew colder and wetter, Blanche Bates grew more taxing. All she wanted was to spend my money and wear me out. We dined at the finest restaurants, where she talked nauseously about the actor DeWolf Hopper. Anytime I mentioned the Cuban Martyr Girl, she'd get jealous and counter with DeWolf this and DeWolf that. DeWolf this that and the other.

I'd never been saddled with a doll so expensive. I had a hoard of cash saved, but I was blowing my entire salary on her and unable to squirrel away any more. She never wanted to do anything that didn't set me back a dollar.

Bedding Blanche Bates twice a day became a chore. She was the one actress in the world without good timing. I'd crawl atop her and close my eyes. I'd imagine Luisa naked beneath her Russian parka, and that's when Blanche Bates would open her yap.

"Don't go back to Cuba, my love." She sounded nasally, nothing like my accented goddess.

"I won't." I hid my irritation. "The hacks down there write little except each other's rumors."

The one thing I ached for, other than Luisa, was to create grand journalism again. I had ink in my veins, but there was no point in going to Havana. The *World* and the *Journal* had a dozen correspondents down there, and one or two press credentials went to second-rate sheets throughout the land. There were no American soldiers in Cuba, but the hotels were overrun by hapless scribes.

Staying hard inside her was hoisting well water with a bucket full of holes and it didn't help matters when she teased, "Maybe you're dead after all." I couldn't keep my mind on the task at hand. Everyone was in Havana, except the army and me.

"Original reporting under such conditions is stealing a bite in a famine."

"What?" she said. I'd interrupted her pelvic rhythm. Turnabout is fair play.

She shushed me. She had her eyes closed. Thinking on DeWolf Hopper. We never finished. She didn't mind. Her true enjoyment came from having the goods on me. Her ticket to the White House. She rose to comb her hair bare-chested in front of the mirror. I'd seen enough of her for a lifetime, but she moved into my room at the Palace Hotel.

Willie wired, this time to say my salary would be cut in half on June 1st. "Cuba's filled with our correspondents feeding off my teat. The Caribbean's dotted with my yachts, but an invading armada has yet to set sail. This war is bankrupting me, and it hasn't yet started. McKinley needs to be shot. I'd rather him dead than you."

I'd make Willie pay me back wages down the road. In the meantime, I wasn't going to let Blanche Bates chew her way through my savings. I quit taking her out, trimmed back except on my drinking. She groused. She said she was tired of being treated a whore and she was going to tell the world Jayson Kelley was alive.

"I'll pay for your pheasant dinners," I said. "I'm broke, but I'll hire on at the *Chronicle*."

She embraced the idea. I hated it. I'd have to pretend I was some no-good hack. She was expert with stage makeup, and I walked into the *Chronicle* in complete disguise, in case I bumped into someone who knew me from my formative days at the *Examiner*.

The *Chronicle* was in a marvelous new building, San Francisco's first skyscraper. A clock tower seen from Oakland. It was a rare sunny day but I was in the dumps. I was back at the bottom, back to where I was before Brink Thorne soaked his jersey in slaughterhouse blood. The spendthrift Blanche Bates was forcing me to empty cesspits for a living.

I told *Chronicle* chief editor Charles Wood Dryden my name was Jack Blaire from Boston. "Blaire with an 'e,' and I'm pretty good at obits."

Wood Dryden wore his hat inside the building, so I left mine on. I'd prepared for conceivable questions, but he didn't want to talk about anything except himself. He'd been quite the reporter at the *Examiner* a decade ago.

"You've heard of me," he said, and I nodded as if I had. "I tossed myself over the side of an Oakland ferry to show local authorities they are incapable of timely rescues. My biggest feather came when I found the gutless umpire who vanished after striking out Mighty Casey."

"That was Nellie Bly. She found the ump."

Wood Dryden stopped talking for a second, but his lips kept moving like a horse eating oats. "I found the ump," Wood Dryden said. "I cracked the story."

I'd insulted him and it was time to leave. I looked for my hat that was still on my head. To my astonishment, Wood Dryden offered me a first assignment so terrific I wondered if he knew I was Jayson Kelley come back to life.

"The tenth anniversary of Casey's historic strikeout is approaching," Wood Dryden said. "Children of all ages still recite that damn ballad by what's his name?"

"Earnest Thayer."

"That's right. I forgot you're from Boston. Who's the actor who keeps reciting the ballad on stage to thunderous applause?"

"DeWolf Hopper."

"You're quite the encyclopedia, Mr. Blaire with an 'e.' Casey played but one season after Thayer's *At the Bat* ballad. Eighty-nine. Imagine, a few rhymes taking down a legend. Casey gave Nellie Bly a batting lesson you know."

"Maybe she gave *him* the lesson," I said, and we chuckled.

"Girl reporters can't be taken seriously, not when they have the unfair advantage," Wood Dryden said.

I nodded agreement. Wood Dryden and I had chemistry. "Why hasn't Casey talked to the press in ten years?" I said.

"Dammit if I know." Wood Dryden removed his hat, and the smell of oil drifted through the room. "Always two sides. See my hair. I part it down the middle, exactly down the middle, same as each item in the *Chronicle* now that I jumped across the street to be chief editor. Nothing yellow here. Casey's ready to talk. I still have a reporter's nose, and he's ready. You stick around, Jack Blaire, and I'll teach you a thing or two. For now, I expect you to hop on over to Casey's and come back with a Page One scoop."

Blanche Bates came along. It was the first time she wanted to do something that didn't cost me an arm and a leg and I figured a buxom actress might get us in Casey's door. She made me buy her one of those licentious dresses, which I considered an investment.

On our way over I thought of my brother Joe, who'd turned courageous. He became a professional baseballer right after Casey quit. Spectators dwindled, the game went into a drought. Today's players get paid horseshit. Casey's the only one who ever got rich at the game. He had a mansion on the outskirts of Golden Gate Park, which we reached on the McAllister and Haight Street lines. I had an extensive knowledge of baseball and I'd tell Casey I was a chum of Joe's, who'd put his baseball career on ice to join Roosevelt's Rough Riders. I'd tell him Joe and I were boyhood friends who used to play old-one-cat.

From Casey's door I could hear someone shooting billiards inside. I let Blanche Bates knock with her gloved hand. Casey answered with a stove-up sheepdog that barked at me until he hollered, "Shut up, Hope." The dog was nearly dead with age. It was male, with a bitch's name; he licked his sore tool as Casey smiled at Blanche Bates.

When I introduced myself as a reporter with the *Chronicle,* he stepped from the stoop, kissed Blanche Bates fat in the mouth, and let go of her ass to sock me in the jaw. I was on the ground before I knew I'd been hit. I thought that something fantastical would've happened now that I'd become a reporter again. But the old magic was gone, the sting traveled to my feet where the toothless Hope was growling and gumming away at my boot. Casey whistled the dog inside.

"I never struck out," he hollered. "Earnest Thayer made up that horseshit." He slammed the door, and that was the end of the interview.

The fiasco was a ploy by Wood Dryden. He knew I'd get socked because he'd played this same trick on greenhorns a hundred times. I kicked myself. It was the same kind of trick Willie played on those who came begging. He told them to expose corruption at City Hall. It disgusted me to be treated like an ignorant cub reporter. I wasn't a prideful man or I'd have told Wood Dryden I was Jayson Kelley, put him in his place. That would have felt good in the moment, but a disaster nevertheless. A disaster that would have cost me the presidency. At least my apprentice McGee wasn't there to see my humiliation.

Blanche Bates was mad because I gave Casey a reason to slug me before he had the time to look down the cleave of her breasts. "You've been played a fool," she said, and made me pay for skating and dizzying rides on the Golden Gate carousel before she'd take the cable car back to the Palace Hotel without whining.

She wanted a matinee performance out of me. She was still bubbling over in that costly dress but I was worn out. She pouted and I should've given her the slap she deserved, but I'm a modern man. I left our room for the Barbary Coast to take care of frustrations. She followed me to a groggery. At first, she had the pride to stay outside. She stewed across the street long enough for me to go on a spree. Things were reeling around when she left the sidewalk and found me drinking with a tootsy-wootsy.

"Why do you play the big-shot act?" Blanche Bates said. "I'm the big shot now."

"You're some act, alright."

"You've heard them cheer me at the Alcazar. No one knows Jayson Kelley anymore."

I shushed her for saying my name aloud, but the drunk boys

couldn't remember their own names. I bought a round and they gave me three cheers.

"You can't sneeze without costing me a few bucks," I told her and I gave my tootsy-wootsy a kiss on her puss. Blanche Bates slapped me so hard my feet got a sting.

"I suppose our budding romance is dead," I said. She slapped again. I don't know why the slaps were calming. She warned my new doll not to waste time on me. "He can't get hard and he can't keep a job and he's stingy to boot." Blanche Bates gave me a smeary kiss atop my blistered cheek and another on the sore jaw Casey had socked.

"You'll miss me," she whispered in my ear.

I handed Blanche Bates my empty stein. "Fill this with beer. Put my johnson in it, pull it out. That's how much you'll be missed."

My fresh doll laughed until she got a side stitch. I planted a long one on her and the boys cheered until they'd earned another round.

"Say hello to DeWolf for me," I said as Blanche Bates went out the door.

She found me in the dawn. Some boys had chucked me under the sidewalk slats along Geary Street, and Blanche Bates woke me so I could suffer both my headache and a stolen billfold. I couldn't escape either her stare or the tight space. I had to worm-wriggle to move a few inches.

She had me trapped and said her sorries down at me through the slats. Sincere sorries for making me get so drunk, but I was in no condition to forgive. I needed nothing at this awful juncture except a true drink, my true love, my true friend.

"Whatever came of your pregnancy?" I said.

The first cable car of the morning passed; maybe Blanche Bates didn't hear. I hollered up her skirt. "Shouldn't you have a lap baby by now?"

She got spitting mad. "I drowned it. Tossed it from the Brooklyn Bridge."

We both knew she was lying. "This that and the other," I said.

I army-crawled out of the mud, lit a smoke and walked on without looking at her. She followed me down to Lotta's Fountain. I tried to clean off, but all I did was smear mud on my best suit.

"It was yours." She was teary and wiped her eyes with the back of her gloved hand. Like she did each night on stage.

"The daddy's DeWolf," I said. "It's Hopper's, or some yeggman's in Sing Sing."

She sobbed. No one wants a scene in the street, and she was trained to cause one to the last row. I shushed her, and she took a swing at me closed-fisted. I ducked. Like I said, she didn't have good timing. Many hours later, she barged into my room, unashamed her one eye was swollen tight due to her temper and her big yap.

"I wired Joseph Pulitzer in New York," she said actress-like. "I told him Jayson Kelley's alive."

"What've you done?" I grew adamant. "You've got to wire him back, tell him you made a big mistake."

"I told him Jayson Kelley's alive and well and socking young ladies about the San Francisco Bay. You socked me for knowing what's what."

I threw up my arms. "Next time I'll roll dice to see if you have it coming." I hadn't changed my suit, and dried mud that had originated from beneath the sidewalk flew into the air. I worked up an apology. "I got testy. Next time, I guess you'll do as I say."

She didn't accept my apology with grace. I pondered the consequencesof her telegrams to Pulitzer. My reputation was no longer protected by my death; whatever Sylvester Scovel knew about my juicing would become fair play. If I were found alive, it would abort my ambitions—journalistic and politic.

"The Sniper's on a train and heading our way," I said. "To see if your story holds water. To put my mug all over Page One. Pulitzer must've known you were a crank."

"Mr. Pulitzer knows who I am. He's seen me on stage in New York. That's how much he believes me."

"He's blind. Can't see his hand in front of his face. Crazed. Everyone knows. He suffers from insomnia, asthma, neuralgia;

he's ugly as a root dug from dry ground."

"And, by the way, he might bring Nellie Bly out of retirement, sick Nellie Bly on you, is what that lonely, rich Hungarian wired me."

"You're an effing harpy." I called her a few other things, but I made amends. I was boxed-in. "Wire Pulitzer and tell him you were mistaken. Don't play-act a bitch."

"Wouldn't matter if I did. Mr. Pulitzer already knew you were alive before I said anything." She went on to say Pulitzer got a phone call from a switchboard operator days after the *Maine* was sunk. The operator told Pulitzer she had connected a call from the Fred Harvey House in Chicago to William Randolph Hearst.

"The operator stayed on the line, listened to each word you blabbed," Blanche Bates said.

I kicked myself. Why had I never courted operators? I could've had *holy shit!* sources all over the country.

"Guess who's on the line with Hearst? You, that's who. Jayson Kelley, who's supposed to be a ghost."

Anger overwhelmed me. Anger at Willie for killing me. Anger at McGee and Luisa for abandoning me. Intense anger that unearthed something long dormant. I wanted to strike out at them, but no one was around except Blanche Bates with her shiner. She wanted another one, she was begging, but I wouldn't give it to her. "If Pulitzer's known all along, why hasn't he published something?"

"Mr. Pulitzer's a smart Jew. He wants it nailed down tight. He's in no hurry. He said Hearst started a war, and the lie must be exposed. That means sending his all-star correspondents to find you."

"Christmas. And you told him where I'm living?"

"Mr. Pulitzer spent a fortune on telegraph tolls to tell me I'm the finest actress. He said I was doing a service to my country because liars and their lying newspapers need to be weeded from the game."

"I don't lie. I'd rather chew on quartz."

"He's sending Sylvester Scovel and Nellie Bly, if she comes out of retirement. I love Nellie Bly."

"You promised to keep me a secret. That's the curse of truth-tellers. We think others tell the truth, too." I needed air. "Look at me. I'm sweating like you do when we footle."

My mind was off in a million directions. I'd been forced to make a big, greasy move, and I made it with long strides into the fog of my future. Blanche Bates trailed me out the Palace Hotel. I walked too fast for her. From a distance, she hollered terrible things at me.

"I pray you will one day fall in love and get no affection," she said.

It was so unjust. First my death, and now betrayal from a doll I'd trusted. I'd never see the promiscuous, back-stabbing actress again, so I gave her the last word.

"Was a boy, by the way."

The last line in a drop-curtain scene.

CHAPTER FIFTEEN

I WITHDREW A PILE OF CASH FROM WELLS FARGO AND
MADE HASTE FOR THE ARCTIC. I was being both pushed and
pulled, pushed by The Sniper Sylvester Scovel and the stunt girl Nellie
Bly, pulled by Luisa and McGee.

In Seattle, I hit a snag. Every square inch on anything that floated
north to Alaska was booked through September.

"I *have* to get to Skaguay," I told the clerk at the dock. "Now."

"Don't we all," he said.

Respect never sees what a man is, only what a man does, and no
one knew I'd launched the whole stampede right there at Schwabacher
Dock with my **TON OF SOLID GOLD** item. I seethed as a stream of hu-
manity ticketed aboard the steamship *Queen* out of turn.

"Mother Mary, I'm tired of being treated like a nobody."

"Aren't we all," the clerk said.

My life was inside out. Willie killed me off and came up with a
hare-brained scheme that forced me to go incognito. Blanche Bates
shared a few flirty telegrams with Joseph Pulitzer that dashed my ambitions. I was once a man in control of my destiny, a man who could
ignite wars. Now, I couldn't secure a job in journalism. I was powerless
over a dock clerk. A fugitive—who couldn't find steerage on a damn
boat. I was pathetic.

"My storybook life is gone," I said to nobody.

"Unspectacular lives turn out best." This voice was weak, but had
a lilt. It came from a sick young man in line to board the *Queen*. Before

I could tell him to mind his business, he coughed up blood.

Those along the gangway stepped aside like he had something worse than the third-day auge. I recognized opportunity. "No fortune is worth your life."

"Righto," he said between coughs.

"I'll buy your passage," I said. "So you can afford a Seattle doctor."

An undertaker, more likely.

He claimed to be a Canadian banker for a British concern, but his accent was Scottish. I've found the Scottish to be unhelpful but polite and overly appreciative. I found him a cup of tea and his coughing eased. "There, there," I said. I fetched him a second cup and he agreed to sell me his place aboard with one condition.

He gave me a buckled satchel filled with papers. "I'll catch up to you in Dawson Town. If I don't, you must promise to get my scratchings published."

The satchel had heft. "A tremendous amount of effort went into this," I said.

"It's verse; some rhymes a fellow might say in a pub. It all popped into my head."

"You're in luck. I'm an accomplished writer with New York connections."

"You've the soft hands of a professional. Any money from publication goes to my sweetheart, Constance MacLean of Vancouver, who I court by mail. I've seen her only in this photograph."

She was pretty enough. I assumed the poetry was less endearing, unworthy of publication, but I agreed to his terms. On June 10th, 1898, the day the Marines at last landed at Guantanamo, I steamed for Skaguay with twice as many nobodies as the tug was made to carry. I found isolation at the aft and read a bit from the satchel.

GRIN

by Robert W. Service

If you're up against a bruiser and you're getting knocked about —
Grin.
If you're feeling pretty groggy, and you're licked beyond a doubt —
Grin.
Don't let him see you're funking, let him know with every clout,
Though your face is battered to a pulp, your blooming heart is stout;
Just stand upon your pins until the beggar knocks you out —
And grin.
If the future's black as thunder, don't let people see you're blue;
Just cultivate a cast-iron smile of joy the whole day through;
If they call you "Little Sunshine," wish that
THEY'D no troubles, too —
You may — grin.

Not Walt Whitman, though it lifted my spirits. I didn't scatter the papers into the sea as I thought I might. McGee would enjoy the verse. It would nourish his smile, and comfort me when I needed comfort most.

I grinned myself for the first time in God knows when. I read more Robert W. Service ballads; they put me in a good mood, caused me to warm to the boys aboard and the obnoxious hopes they harbored. They were much like the rebels of Cuba, their fervor contagious, and I grew happy to be in their company for the great adventure of the century. I took secret pride in my part. I'd set the world agog with **SOLID GOLD** in the north and **WAR!** in the south. Maybe I was a nobody now, but no man alive had accomplished as much.

I warmed to five boys in particular. Shate Allen of Le Roy, New York, had invented a menthol shoe powder and balm to cure frostbite. Happy Jack was a red-haired well digger and wool grower from Meteetse, Wyoming. He said he hadn't been blue one day in his life. I distrusted any redhead who said that.

A kid named Bubbles MacKintosh of the Scottish Highlands said he could handle any ragtime tune on any music box. A pair of baseball umpires said they could handle any amount of ragging from fanatics. They shared a house back home with a Negro ball player. One umpire was old with a handlebar mustache, in his late forties, but in athletic condition. He called himself the Judge. The other was a decade younger, kept to himself, didn't get my jokes, didn't let one food touch another on his plate and walked away from unfinished conversations. His name was Avocado Jones, but that had the ring of a lie for sure.

The umpires lived in New York City. The Judge had the appropriate accent, but Avocado Jones sounded Californian and I concluded they were concealing something more than a Negro.

The six of us spent nineteen days aboard the *Queen* playing cards and talking of gold from the grassroots down, a hundred dollars of gold in each pan of dirt. Fortune hunting is the ultimate lie the disenchanted tell themselves but I played along. When we tired of gold, we talked of wasting it on auto-cars and mansions with velvet lawns.

Happy Jack announced he would join the Mounties. "The scarlet police. Search the solitudes for the freezing-to-death." He saluted. "Duty first and duty last."

Going to the Klondike to save random lives was asinine, but everyone had an asinine reason to go. McGee, after all, went to find love.

"What's your reason?" Happy Jack asked me.

"No reason. A lark."

"You can be a Mounty, too."

"You have to be Canadian to join the Mounties," Shate Allen said.

"The Wind Rivers in Wyoming can get cold as Nome," Happy Jack said. "I came upon a dying man in a lean-to last winter, wrapped him in robes of fur, dragged him through a blizzard. So cold I'm still not warm. I pulled him through the anguish with an ache in my fingers and ice between my toes."

"Saved a life?" the kid, Bubbles MacKintosh, said. "That's something."

"Saved his and changed mine," Happy Jack said. "Gave me a purpose."

There was something off about him. Always cheery, as gay as Avocado Jones was gruff.

"Doesn't matter who you saved in Wyoming," Shate Allen said. "You have to be Canadian to be a Mounty."

"I've been put on earth to rescue folks," Happy Jack said. "I'll die happy if I save one more. The Mounties will take me." He looked at me. "They'll take you, too."

I shrugged. "I make my own luck no matter what I do." By some method of alchemy, I'd make Luisa my wife. I'd escaped San Francisco with a small fortune unspent by Blanche Bates. If prospectors in the Klondike played cards as these five, I could make a living off my poker. I had to keep that in my back pocket, and I resisted the urge to clean them out aboard the *Queen*.

I drew my third consecutive unbeatable hand, threw the cards face down in the middle. I moved my attention to a miner outside our six-man circle, a Slav the size of a whale. He'd been to the Klondike, said he could find goldfields blindfolded.

"I once wore parka so frozen a sloppy whore broke it off with ice axe to get at my johnson," he said. Everyone laughed except Avocado Jones.

The Slav was clean-shaven, an oddity for a man from the cold, where shaving's a travail. He had giant hands, which he never extended to anyone in greeting. He shoved them down his trousers when he conversed. He spat tobacco like a grasshopper; half his teeth were black. From his mouth spewed "goot" but patchy English. He was loud, his voice carried to the Wekweeti northland, which he pronounced the "Vekveeti norzland."

He owned a pocket watch with a pedometer. Any man who counted in one direction so he could retrace his snow-blown tracks back to safety was in high demand for a conversation. He said he'd made one small fortune, pissed it away on one exquisite whore, and was on his way back for more gold so he could get more of her.

"It not gold that I'm needing, so much as just finding gold," he said, while prospecting his trousers so thoroughly I regretted being a trained laureate of observation.

His left ear was missing and his face on that side paralyzed, nicked, and scarred. Shate Allen diagnosed it as severe frostbite, but the Slav insisted it was a knife fight in the Malamute Saloon.

"Called me son of slut. Mmm. Agreed on knives, threatened my nose with butt of gun."

Be it frostbite or a knife, he was left unable to smile on one side; and so he attempted no smile at all. He just gripped your eyes and held them hard like a spell.

"Whores give me half-off for half face," he said.

I laughed at the Slav's joke. I sized him up as a man accustomed to getting what he wants, a man to have on my side now that nothing went my way. I mirrored him to get him there. If he made and lit a cigarette, I made and lit one, too. If he stuffed it half-out, I'd stuff mine to an identical smolder. I did what he did except go fishing for my privates.

He initiated our first conversation. "That redhead boy from Vyoming is merry."

"God bless him," I said.

"I'm atheist," the Slav said. "I've looked for Him at clouds and dirt clods. He not around."

"I've my doubts from time to time. What's to be gained by praying from a Bible that makes no sense in places?" I showed him the two war medals I'd taken from the Greek soldier. "These will get me past Saint Peter."

"Heaven's in the arms of my whore at Dawson Town. So pretty she hurt. Plays heartstring. She'll cost the king his crown someday."

"Reason enough to stay clear."

"Of Dawson Town? If two of you six make it, I bet one will be you. You swim, don't you?"

"Float like a damned dam duck."

"The rest of the ladies should go home, teach Sunday school," the Slav said. "You got name?"

"If you do."

"No one needs it for anything. Except sons-a-bitches."

"Then I'll not ask where you're from."

"I'm hound of hell. Lots men from Australia, California, South Africa, find gold, you ladies never do. You six are city, except Happy Vyoming. Me and him never set paw in a city. Windswept Skagvay and Forty Mile, no town any bigger."

"You must visit San Francisco," I said.

"Mmm, too many ooh-and-ahh girls. Dawson Town a marsh two year ago, nothing but snowshoe hare. It big as a Kansas City now, signs and canker and borried money all over. Too big. I'm going back only for her."

"She must be something," I said.

"I got letter from my dying mother," the Slav said. "She has to see me before she gets called away. But here I am, headed the other way, headed back for her as Mother croak in loneliness."

"A whore keeps you from your dying mama?"

"I'll go home. In two year, maybe three, cross gurly sea, her on my arm. A baby or two on my knee. They'll meet Mother at cemetery. Father's already there. Mother did the cooking; father gave the whooping. They'll be there waiting, buried beneath the smell of clover, new-mown hay and damp loam. Drenched in silver rain. Where you from?"

"Massachusetts. Missed my papa's funeral because of a sea monster."

He pondered that. Said he'd never seen a sea monster but he was a believer. "I grew up pissing on rocks. Orange lichen and ants as big as bear. Shiny ant, shiny and black. You can go snow blind staring at blackness or whiteness. Step foot along the blue Yukon, you'll change. Forever."

"A place to get rich."

"If you open saloon. Men pay anything to escape skeeters and loneliness. The Pistol Shot takes in three thousand a night of dust. There's less gold at the crick-bed sand than down the neck of my whore. Lost this ear over her."

"How?"

"Fight started at Malamute Saloon. Ended on the bank of mighty Yukon. Ear fell into the river. Picked apart by a boil of starved trout. Ear's trout shit at the Bering Sea by now. I'm lucky it wasn't a gun fight. Can't shoot; frostbite in my hand."

"What's her name?"

"Nobody has name. Especially you. What is it? Massachusetts McGuire, I bet. My whore's the Lady known as Lou."

"Luisa?"

"Lou. Just Lou. She talk like a Luisa, but blonde as hay. Perfect as Sunday turd in a preacher outhouse."

CHAPTER SIXTEEN

THE SEA PASSED. Nothing was visible at night except white churned up by the *Queen*. The rest of the world was black and unknowable. That was how life had become. I scanned for the future but I saw churn.

Luisa was a whore? Just when I'd hit bottom, my life had turned worse. I was determined to forget her, but I stewed all night. Sunrise arrived before sleep. Our sea journey drew near an end as we steamed past islands to the west, mountains to the east, and great glaciers calving into the sea like President McKinley to action.

Havana's harbor was small, but Skaguay had no harbor at all. We anchored a mile off, and barges took us within spitting distance of shore from where we waded the last five yards. Half of the crew splashed to shore to seek fortunes. The *Queen* would have to steam home short-handed. I almost went with them, but I decided to keep going to find McGee. Girls found pig-a-back rides on broad shoulders; a fat one wanted to board me, but Happy Jack took my place. He said he needed practice at saving damsels. There was no damsel on earth worth saving.

Late June was barely spring, Skaguay a wind-swept goulash of ice and mud surrounded by an infinite wilderness of new leaves. Afternoon melt lasted two hours when the main road named Broadway became a gully wash the color of chewed peanuts. The place smelled of thawing earth, and I was tempted to bottle some air and ship it to Nellie Bly and Sylvester Scovel as a taunt. To let the *World* know I was out here where a man can find himself, but can't be found.

Nellie Bly had never left New York. I was sure of it. She once possessed the pluck to storm around the world, but she was ten years younger then. Something changed her heart, I saw it when I interviewed her. She'd gone soft. She'd tired of chasing holy shit! stories, or had grown content with the ones she'd caught. She'd quit chasing fame. She'd become the bride of a millionaire. Sylvester Scovel was the only sleuth on my tail.

Skaguay was more dense than London. Men lived packed together in cabin squats dug into the sides of hills. Every foot of flat ground had been claimed, sold, divvied up, and rented as campsites at fantastic prices. We chipped in for two nights on the corner of Fifth Avenue.

The old umpire, the Judge, bought salmon from a native woman gutting on the bank and I boiled potatoes in a tin coffee pot. The wind was kicking, and my cooking would've set Skaguay afire but the canvass of our tent was too wet to burn. We lost the Slav to a cathouse and our fish heads to wandering sled dogs, but the worst luck arrived in the morning when two Mounties in scarlet coats rode up. They weren't letting prospectors cross Chilkoot Pass without a ton of supplies.

"We're grouchy from a winter of prospectors with insufficient means to survive," Captain Steele said from the saddle.

I asked how we could carry that much over the pass, and he proffered useless advice. "Tear the covers from books, you betcha. Get rid of that satchel of useless papers. Better yet, go home. That's my best advice, but Yanks never take advice. Get out of the Yukon by fall. The winter ended produced famine beyond Dawson Town. The coming winter will starve the town itself."

Happy Jack stepped forward and saluted. "Came from Meteetse, Wyoming to join the Mounties."

Captain Steele spoke past him as if he wasn't there. "My best advice is stay out."

Happy Jack, desperate to be heard, took the captain's horse by the bit. "I'm here to save lives. To join up. Duty first and duty last."

"Got to be Canadian," Captain Steele said. "That's the second thing. The first thing is let go of my horse, you betcha."

I expected Happy Jack to be demoralized, but he stayed chirpy. "I can save folks, can't I? Even if I'm no Mounty?"

"Save all the idiot Yanks you want," Captain Steele said. "Start with yourself and turn back."

Once they rode off, Happy Jack grinned like a dope. Everything ran off his back, but my other shipmates were in the dumps. They didn't have the funds for the necessary supplies, and that's when a Georgia man named Soapy Smith made a timely visit. He said he earned his livelihood following doomsday Mounties around and offering hope in their place.

"Someone has to be a man of faith, and I fashion that's me," Soapy Smith said. "I own the telegraphy office in Skaguay. The one telegraph until Juneau, and I charge five dollars to wire any bank or sweetheart in the world."

The boys said they couldn't afford five bucks, they said they needed that and more for the fare back to Seattle.

"Five dollars gets you a hundred words," Soapy Smith said. "You can write a book with a hundred words, tell your girls you love them and to send money and you'll buy them gew-gaw if they'll wait for you. Five dollars is five minutes' work in the creek beds, a piss in the pot when the alternative is to drag-ass home a nobody."

"I'm well-situated, I don't need to wire for money," I said and Soapy Smith pulled me aside to tell me I'd need my friends along if I wanted to get to Dawson Town.

"Unless you're John Wesley Powell, it's impossible to escape the rapids of the Yukon without comrades. It's a rampageous river, a moving carpet to the-devil-knows-where. You'll need all hands to negotiate the lather. River's glutted more than ever this spring. You swim, don't you?"

"Like a mountain muskrat."

I needed McGee in my miserable life, so I dug deep and paid Soapy Smith twenty bucks so everyone could wire for funds. He pointed in the direction of his telegraphy office. We headed that way and bumped into the Slav, returning from his night of carousing.

The Slav laughed without a smile. "There's no telegraphy wires into Skagvay. Soapy Smith fleeced men here to Denver with that gambit. I go gallivanting for a minute, and you get swindled."

I should've been suspicious. Soapy wore a business suit in the land of mud. Without a newspaper to write for, I was off my game. I stomped off double time to get my money back.

"Forget finding it," the Slav boomed with his whaler voice. "You're Soapy's newest pigeon is all."

I hated to be duped. I hated being called a pigeon. Had I been a correspondent, a special commissioner, I'd have done something, anything, something vengeful, something phantasmagorical. But I'd been abandoned by newspapering and stripped of all magic.

"I know it come as big surprise, but some men lie for money," the Slav said, loud enough for a public shaming. "Don't feel bad, Soapy makes a pigeon of many other men. At least he does it with all manner of day gone by. Skagvay's a scrofulous town."

I wasn't to be duped again, and I struck a deal with my cohorts. I had enough of Willie's money sewn into my clothes to fund the supplies. They were to repay loans at fair interest, or give me a twenty-five percent stake in their fortunes to come, whichever proved greater. Shate Allen was first to sign on, and I was a one-fourth owner in a frostbite venture.

The others came around without a moment's thought, and I kicked myself for not insisting on more favorable terms. Even so, just one in five needed to make a strike for me to prosper and I intended to expense unpaid loans to Willie once I escaped Morro Castle. They'd have a parade at Madison Square Park, McGee leading my horse.

The Slav required no stake, but he demanded thirty-two dollars to lead the six of us to Dawson Town. "The lightest food can hoof it," he said, and I bought sheep and pigs at inflated prices. "The rest must be packed over Chilkoot Pass. Trail's too rugged for horses, and horses scarce, anyway."

Something was off about Happy Jack, and I tried to convince him to stay behind. "You'll never save a man's life, but you can save your-self—and you can save me your stake," I said.

The Slav overheard and insisted Happy Jack tag along.

"It's my money," I said.

The Slav gave me back twelve dollars and said, "Stop bellyaching. At least he's not city. He's forthright. The boy has digger's back and stranglehold on joy."

"He's too dumb to save a life," I said.

"Nothing in his head, sunflower seeds in rattle, but nothing get under skin. Let the Medder Lark throw in."

The sun set on Skaguay. The Slav pulled his hands from down his trousers and tugged on the chain of his pocket watch. "After ten," he said and nodded toward the dizzy mountains to where we were headed. "This is cussedest land I know. Some say God got tuckered when He made it. Goot thing I'm atheist. This land grip like sinning. "

He cocked his good ear to listen to nothing except red evening clouds.

"War is underway, but this end of the earth was never at peace," he said. "You're all galoots, pitiful and unfit. The outfit will drown in rapid of Whitehorse Canyon, and I'll float into Dawson Town. I'll pilfer from your caches. It OK to steal from the drowned."

The Slav stuffed out his cigarette. "God, I wish I could forget Lady Lou. Others are plain to me now."

I about crushed my cigarette, but decided to let it burn. I was done mimicking the Slav. A cold crawled up my back. The slush on the outskirts of the fire's warmth had solidified to ice in the dusk.

"Clambering uphill tomorrow, straight uphill for days," he said, farted, scratched. "A farting man never tire," he said while turning in. "A farting man is the man to hire. Add that to your satchel of poetry."

I farted because I needed to, not out of camaraderie, and stayed up to finish my smoke. Enough sunset reflected off clouds to read some of the banker's verse, but I couldn't focus on it. Her whoring was weighing on me.

I steered my thoughts elsewhere. The idea of endless, painful walking up the mountain made me obsess on my chronic feet and my childhood rescue of that pigeon in the riverbank mud. I never shed one tear as Papa had me sit feet to stove. Joe bawled and sniffled and did nothing to help, like the day he was born, the day Mama passed giving him life.

Joe was in Cuba with the Rough Riders on my account. I couldn't believe it. When I saved his pigeon, my old man sat me on the floor with the Book reading verses, the soles of my wet shoes snug against the heat. Papa's version of sitting on infinity. Joe did nothing.

"He that conquereth his soul is greater than he who taketh a city," Papa said. He wouldn't let me pull my feet away until the last whiff of steam curled out. I prayed he'd kick them away before any damage was done. No one did anything.

When I'm honest with myself, I give my father the credit he deserves for my success. When my feet were roasting, I vowed to gain control of my life and never give it up to anyone. It's why I became incorrigible; it's why I've that touch of anarchist. I question authority, so Papa's the reason I became the best at newspapering, at exposing sham, afflicting the corrupt, being a pain in the ass to the comfortable, writing holy shit! items to decorate Willie's wall. I had no friends. Except McGee. But I always get my girl, and a man who gets all the dolls never becomes infatuated with one.

Except Luisa.

The Slav's snoring put me on edge. He was the lucky one; he was resting easy because he didn't yet know we were adversaries. I got back to my reading, but it was too dark and I wasn't paying attention to the poet's words. I was in disbelief that the Slav and I had it bad for the same goddess.

The chill of unease invaded me, but it had nothing to do with Joe. Nothing to do with Sylvester Scovel breathing down my neck. It had everything to do with me and the sleeping Slav. There were two of us—and one of her. Maybe there were a hundred of us—and one of her.

I had it bad for a whore. I was in utter disbelief.

CHAPTER SEVENTEEN

I DEPENDED ON THE SLAV FOR DAY-TO-DAY SURVIVAL AND COULDN'T LET ANY GIRL COME BETWEEN US. That proved a wise decision when, on Day Three, the last blizzard of spring blew in on Chilkoot Pass. The air filled with snow thick and dry as the ash that had floated upon the sinking *Maine*. I couldn't see three yards.

Unable to find flat ground, we pitched tent in a defile so narrow the Judge cooked dinner on the trail. Parties of men, like deer without pasture, trudged past. On Day Four, we passed men dug in a drift and eating raw bacon. The band was headed out and they warned us to turn back.

"Summer lasts five minutes," one said. "Then winter, when the abyss is served for breakfast."

The Slav ordered me to buy their whipsaw. I refused, the anarchist in me reared its head, but the men gave it to me for nothing. I could've had their entire cache for nickels, but we hadn't the energy to pack another ounce up and over the saddle that led to a higher saddle between peaks.

I was already lugging my share, and I burdened Happy Jack with the saw. He accepted it with courtesy, but the Slav gave it back. "Push on with your old-man limp. Get to the top of Devil Hill. From there, it downhill and sunny."

I have a knack for bluff and stagecraft and I pretended no offense. I couldn't let the Slav know that we were at loggerheads. I redirected my ill will at the well-digger, who the Slav had let tag along. The redhead was the perfect foil; he was oblivious to boorish behavior.

The ancient trail was made of slate rock buried in hard ice. Wet by midday, it became slick, but hundreds of wayfarers slogged up the switchbacks like iron filings toward magnetic north.

Near the top, an enterprising stranger had rigged a cable. He employed Siwash Indians to hoist freight over the last mile at a cent a pound. The Slav ordered me to pay it. I blasphemed at Happy Jack, and that night when I turned in, I put him in charge of drying my boots by the fire. That made him last to get to bed. He was OK with it; I could've got up and kicked Happy Jack in the head and he'd have been OK with it. Something was off.

The Slav was warm under blankets thinking of Luisa, but I couldn't do the same. She'd made it clear she wanted nothing to do with me, and there I was climbing an insurmountable mountain. Something was off about me, too.

The trail at last aimed downhill. The sun shined radiant off each blade of bunch grass. The livestock wanted to graze, but we shooed them with impatience. Our exhaustion turned to energy as we scrambled for Lake Bennett. We skipped downhill, where I lay on my belly gulping glacier water so cold it hurt my teeth.

We were children for a time. I was half-dozing, watching a bee swing clover to clover, when the Slav, in his godawful, godlike voice, announced how we'd accomplished little. "Trail of land over," he said. "Trail of river begin. Ladies, there's no time to dance the mazurka. Get ready for five hundred mile of soaking cold."

Lake Bennett's shoreline was a tent city lined with a variety of half-built and shapeless flotation devices. Handymen with sawdust in their hair constructed scows and auctioned them off. I convinced the Slav I was flat broke and we set about to build three makeshift scows.

"It no beauty contest," the Slav said. "It race to get into the lake ahead of our loving neighbor, who hammer nail round clock."

He pointed at the whipsaw. "A spanking investment." He had to rub my nose in it. He had to rub my nose in everything.

We used a packing case for each bottom; we patched holes with hemp rope others had discarded; and we covered it with tar. Jackets of plaid wool made due for sails.

The Kid MacKintosh climbed the trail one night and counted the wicks of 832 campfires within a hundred yards of Lake Bennett. There seemed to be no room for wildlife among humans, but coyotes were thick. The Slav shot at them for fun, but he shot as if by guess. The coyotes were left standing, without fright, and sniffing the wind.

He cursed. "Frostbite damage down my arm to my trigger finger. I'm better taking wing shot at bird with a scattergun."

That was good to know. If I ever had to battle the Slav, I would insist on an old-fashioned duel with pistols. Duels were honorable, but out of fashion in these times of milquetoast McKinley.

I had no reason to fight the Slav. Not over her. I sat next to him by the campfire. Someone had to bridge our divide, someone had to be the bigger man. "I don't know why our friendship has soured."

"Because you got corncob up your ass."

That annoyed me and I ordered Happy Jack to make himself useful and find firewood. He'd be gone an hour; any dry wood within a mile of Lake Bennett had been burned or floated downstream as a piece of vessel.

I conjured up a sunny disposition for the Slav. "Tell me stories of the Malamute Saloon. Whisky interests me."

He ignored me. I stirred the fire with the whipsaw, poured us both coffee, added something with kick to our cups.

"It has a piano," the Slav said, "but nobody play a note. Mother taught me to play goot, but there's no reason to go into Malamute for music; no reason to go except drinks are honest. And to be driven mad by her."

"Who?"

"Lady Lou."

"Oh, yes," I said. "I'd forgotten about the whore."

"If you saw her, you wouldn't forget, you'd want to promenade her across Porcupine Flats." He took a long draw on his coffee and I freshened it with more spirits. I seized upon our diplomatic thaw to ask if he'd ever seen McGee.

"Can't help you. Except for Russians and pinochle-playing sauerkrauts, each man up here's McGee or McGraw. Bet you're a liar McGuire. I smell lies on you like skunk cabbage."

"You don't like me, do you?"

"There's things about you I don't like. Why do you maltreat the Medder Lark?"

I had no answer. The Slav saw the glowing eyes of a coyote off in the dark. He drew the pistol from his belt and fired three rounds, but hit nothing except mud in the bank.

"I've known men like you," he said. "No flies buzz your shit."

"I've been called uppity, but I do what's square."

"Mother taught me piano and still had time to teach me right from wrong."

"Mine died when I was seven."

That dampened the Slav's criticism. He poked at the fire and looked at his watch. "Time to turn in."

"We should wait up for Happy Jack." I knew the Slav would like me saying that. "If you like Happy Jack, you'd love McGee. Everyone does."

"Don't like Scotsmen. Never have."

"He's Scots-Irish-Welsh, with a Cuban accent that carries a whiff of Carolina."

He whistled. "Crapola, sounds made up. Is he smug as you?"

"His sister is. McGee's humble to a fault."

"You didn't mention a sister." He poked at the fire, weighing the new information. "I came upon man out there. Talked about a sister. Nice night. He had smudge fire to smoke away the skeeter but it was her eating at him. He sat tight to the fire like he was chilled. Friendly guy, Happy Jack friendly, except smart. Thin, his belt hanging slack. I asked if he was looking for treasure. '*Si, si,*' he says in Tex-Mexican, 'but never down in the dirt, always up at the heaven.'"

"Did he wear spectacles?"

"Ate Siwash pemmican, ate half, gave rest to my dogs. I thought they'd bite his hand off, but nibbled from his palm like squirrel. 'The trail to anywhere is both magic and tragic.' He kept saying stuff. Dumb stuff that didn't sound dumb at the time. I've listened to lots of voices, but never a voice so pregnant."

The Slav raised his pistol and aimed squint-eye at a coyote. "None of it makes sense now. Said he hadn't been warm since he left Peartree."

"Plumtree," I said, but he jerked an errant shot at the exact time.

"Smudge fire became a confessional," the Slav said, aiming another round that strayed. "Spent night thinking and ruminating. I'd never in my life had conversation like that. Spoke of death a-grinning, and we thought about our crimes." He jerked another. "He spoke of God some, but never proselytized or I'd've slugged him."

"You told him you're an atheist?"

"I make no secret. If there's God, this is forlorn land He forgot. If there's God, He doesn't care or He doesn't know."

"What did McGee say?"

The Slav lowered his pistol. "Said he'd rather know His presence than His absence."

I envied the Slav's conversation with McGee as much as I envied his night with Luisa. The Slav had stolen my place within her arms— and with him beneath the ceiba tree. If Happy Jack had returned at that minute, I would've slung a rock at him.

"Your friend gazed into smudge fire. Didn't ask questions like you. A big sin of yours, your pie hole. This McGee's goot man, told me I'd figure things out myself. He wrestled for my soul, but in quiet way. I made a confession. I confessed I had revenge in my heart. I need to even a score. Your McGee told me that revenge and resentment are poisonous baneberries. You eat them and hope other person dies."

The Slav tucked the pistol in his belt and stuck out his hand. I took it. "Riley," he said. "Name's Riley Dooleyvitch. Got nothing to hide now that I know you have goot man for friend."

"Robert W. Service—at your service," I said. It was OK to borrow from the poet. He wasn't using his name; the grippe surely killed him. I was making fair use of a dead man's cache.

"I drank coffee most the night with your McGee as fire rose, fell. He a nighttime coffee drinker. I need my likker, but for some reason coffee tasted goot as peach brandy that night."

The Slav Dooleyvitch raised his cup, and I sweetened it. "You're the opposite, Mr. Service. The more we talk, the more likker I need."

"You mentioned his prodigal sister."

"He never knew he had a sister until folk died and left him letter. She was born before him and shipped off as an infant to live amongst finest relatives. Rich American sugar magnate and barren wife. Letter said don't fret, she happy, but his folks were dead and he had to go find her. Found bitter whore at Havana."

I don't know why I defended her. "She's no whore."

"You pine for her?" Dooleyvitch tried to pucker and make kissing noises, but he couldn't with face paralysis on the left side. "You're right. She got caught up fighting Spaniards in the Cuban situation."

I feigned disbelief. "Dolls don't fight."

"Amazon."

"Don't believe in them. Sea monsters. There's no Amazons except in storybooks."

"Your McGee said it's true." Dooleyvitch drank coffee grounds from his cup and chewed on them for the whisky. "Your McGee said his own Ma fought as a Yank. His Ma and then his sister fought square on with men."

"What else did he say?"

"Lordy, isn't that enough?"

I made and lit a cigarette and gave it to him. "Where was McGee headed?"

"Said he'd been on his own, saw nothing but caribou for month. On sunny day, bull moose charged. Rifle jammed. He faced moose head-on with knife. This Siwash squaw pop up from the willow scrub and shot it with a bow made of whalebone. That how they met, been yoked up since. Does that McGee know any female who doesn't shoot a weapon?"

"McGee's married?"

Dooleyvitch laughed a mouthful of smoke without a smile. "Squaw aren't real girl, dummy. Go eighty mile nonstop at fifty-below. No female does that except cougar and nitchie squaw in snowshoe. I spent a December night in a Siwash hut. I'm offered a squaw and two daughter as gesture of hospitality. They don't speak English or Russian, nothing except turkey gobble. But I partook. Ever have squaw?"

"I've had everything under the sun. Siamese twins."

"You're a liar McGuire."

"Service. Bob Service."

"You got a Mrs. Service? It OK to have squaw if married. Mingling with squaw isn't adultery."

"I'm a bachelor, and I'm a modern man. I treat dolls right. I'm in support of the women's vote. I don't mistreat Eskimos and I don't chase whores into the distant corners of the earth."

"Don't get high-mighty," he said. "Men get lonely, tire of staring drowsy into smoke of small fire. Hunger for velvet breast on frosty night. Hunger for Lady Lou."

I wanted to decapitate him with the whipsaw, but the road to victory was on the smart end of a firearm.

"Something wrong?" he said.

"I need to find McGee. Is he coming back to civilization soon?"

"Some men spend a night or two with squaw, a month or two," Dooleyvitch said. "Other disappear forever. Said his squaw named Laughing Eye. Squaw are farm animal—you never give squaw a name like a pet. I told him to his face, but his fist clenched and he said he's in love enough to cry in Laughing Eye arms. I laughed at the joke, and he got mad."

"I've seen McGee get mad. Something to behold."

"Little guy, couldn't hurt me. Gets his kit and leaves me by smudge fire. Said if his sister had seen the way their parents loved each other, she'd've turned out OK. He's on rack about sister's awful life." The Slav poked at the fire. "Is she pretty?"

"She isn't butt-ugly."

Dooleyvitch tried to make kissing sounds again. "She must've been butt-ugly infant to get shipped off at Cuba. Her ma wanted to kill Rebel instead of nursing her butt face."

Dooleyvitch put his hand to his chin and felt his face. He unfolded a knife, cut the stubble down. He bled on his numb side, cursed and vowed never to shave again.

"Where'd McGee go?" My voice was impatient.

"Stop asking. You don't go finding folk above Circle. Your friend stomped off into night with that guilt. Live with squaw in hollow of spring grass with musk-ox and a birch canoe. Live in hollow flooded with sunset purple. There's a million meadow that never felt no human footprint. Plumb-full of hush to the brim."

I made and lit two more smokes.

"He's squaw man now," Dooleyvitch said. "For year, maybe two, maybe forever. Maybe an ugly half-breed on way. You can't bring half-breed in from tundra; they inherit vices of both squalid Siwash and civilized man. They inherit virtues of neither. Half-breed take no coffee in their likker, that's their single virtue."

"Wonder where his sister is?"

He attempted his awful kissing noises, but stopped when it brought fresh blood to his cheek. "Married," he said. "They all get married up here, even homely uglies like your sweetheart. They're hidden in tent and lean-to. Men get shot day after day over gold. They get shot that much more for claim-jumping girl. There's better halves hidden all over Yukon."

"She's no man's wife. That much I know."

"Look for her buried in snowbank. No girl survive the Klondike winter without pimp or husband. I'm tired of trying. She a made-up girl. I'm thinking you made her up. Imaginary girl skate up and down frozen river round here like hare. Maybe she mermaid, slap-dab under the polar ice. What's her name?"

I didn't say and he kissed air again. "My Lady Lou exotic, get a bullet casing full of nugget for half night. I had the gold and I summoned up the nerve."

I'd never hated a man more than I hated Dooleyvitch right then. He was ready to describe their love making. My next question was pre-emptive, I asked because I knew the answer would come unsolicited.

"What's she like horizontal?" I heard an edge to my voice.

He walked twenty yards, wrestled a stump from the ground. He left his pistol behind. I don't know why I didn't plug him in the back. God would've forgiven me for shooting an atheist. He brought the stump back by the fire to use as a stool. I'd rarely seen a man as strong. But upon inspection he was crying. I looked away from his tears and at his giant hands. They were shaking.

"God sakes, what's the matter?" I said.

"I've yet made relations with her."

"You haven't done the deed?" My voice had glee in it. "You're lying. You're the liar McGuire."

"I was duped. Conned. I got her upstair at the Malamute Saloon and gave her all my dust. She say she's a shy new girl, so I beguile her with conversation. She has to pee. I tell her to use thunder mug, but she say she can't pee in front of me. I stayed hard the whole time she gone. She come back with Dangerous Dan McGrew."

"Dangerous Dan McWho?"

"She wasn't shy when she come back with him. She called me 'pendjejo,' and said men stand in line to propose to her, and I've wasted her time. Dangerous Dan's big as a mountain, big as me, but I'm not afraid of him. I'm afraid I've been cheated of my one chance. I'm afraid I'll never have her."

He blubbered a minute. "I was duped and conned."

"There, there, we've all been duped. Me, too," though I couldn't think of an example. "Who's McGrew?"

He wiped his nose on his sleeve. "A card player and Malamute pimp. Dawson Town has no mayor; he might be that, too. He tell me Lady Lou is his best girl and I need to pay more for extra time or make room for the next gent."

"Sheez."

"I'd no more money, so I fought for her. The knife fight last an hour. Moved downstair, outside, and to river bank, and ended when I lost this ear to the boiling trout."

"What doll's worth an ear?"

"If you saw her lay aside her robe, you'd lay aside both ears and an eye."

"Dangerous Dan must be some animal," I said.

"A specimen, alright. I could've lost my dick. I was out there, a frankfurter curled over hot coal. Lucky he cut off my ear."

"But for the grace of God." Lilt was still in my voice. "Are you sure you haven't known her?"

"That's your stupidest question yet. What man lie about his defeat?"

I turned my face away from the fire. I didn't want him to see the delight. Luisa wasn't a whore. She was a con artist. Happy Jack appeared into the light dragging a snag. I wanted to hug him, but he saw the Slav's tears and went to his rescue.

The Slav kept blubbering. "I can't stop thinking of her. Lady Lou stayed on my mind. Stayed on my mind night after night, even as I humped the squaw two daughter. Even after I was spent. She on my mind now, thanks to you, Bob Service. Her bosom a breast of snow goose."

"I'd never risk my life for a pair of teats."

"Shut your yap. You're the one who wants to help McGee's butt-ugly sister take laundry off the line."

"Luisa's not butt-ugly." I could've kicked myself for saying her name. Fortunately, Dooleyvitch was lost in his weeping. Happy Jack draped his arm over him.

"I have a plan," the Slav said. "I plan to get rich. That's the plan. Stinking rich before I step foot at the Malamute. I may freeze trying for that much gold, but better to be eaten alive by frost than by longing. I'll swap all the gold underground for a gold wedding band. I'll bring Lady Lou home to Mother. Or die trying."

CHAPTER EIGHTEEN

THE THREE SCOWS WERE LOPSIDED AND FLIMSY. We flattened discarded tinware and nailed it along the water line to protect our armada from floating ice. Dooleyvitch shot the livestock point-blank, ordered it butchered, packed in glacier ice, and put aboard.

We sailed Lake Bennett until it narrowed into Lake Tagish, the longest, skinniest lake I'd seen. Happy Jack didn't see the peril we were headed into; he saw Canadian springtime and peaks forever wrapped in clouds. "The lake's a-flop with fish," he said and pointed out a cow moose wallowing with its calves.

At some point, Lake Tagish became Marsh Lake, where Happy Jack saw a mother duck with a brood of ten squattering behind. There were scows along the shore, abandoned by dreamers like him, but he didn't comprehend what those dead scows said about our own prospects. If he happened to save a man from Klondike hypothermia, he'd kill him with gaiety and his mop of red hair.

I'm competitive to a fault, and I envied those who'd entered the water in the days and weeks before us, and dreaded those closing in from behind. I cursed the absent current, prayed for a tailwind. Luisa was waiting to be rescued from thievery in Dawson Town and I was on my way.

The skinny lake narrowed into a canyon where the shoreline built speed. We became a part of the mighty Yukon, and we fought to keep our scows from spinning. I wished for tedium again and, soon enough, we slowed into sunlight's rest on Lake Lebarge.

"This lake named for trapper who survived War of 1812 to die slipping here on damned ice," Dooleyvitch said.

Happy Jack convinced the Slav to stop at an abandoned boat in the marge, a derelict with *Alice May* painted on the aft. We stepped aboard and I shivered with the all-overs. The *Alice May* was haunted, I was sure of it. Had I been a working correspondent, I'd have written a yarn to make teeth chatter. We stripped down to our unmentionables, lit the boiler to dry our clothes and cigarettes. The chimney had a strong draft. Dooleyvitch gathered us around to rally the troops for what was to come.

"On my last trip, I watched three salty chap drown over coming stretch," he said.

He drew a map in the floor's coal dust with his boot heel. "The river ahead enter canyon. It narrow from quarter mile to fifty foot. Tomb cliffs rise seventy-five foot on either side, sheer and smooth. Riding aboard the breast of Horse Rapid is riding a Fort Boise bronc. Horse Rapid end at waterfall where drowned Siwash have been churning the bottom a thousand year. A mummy bubble up from time to time. No sense joining them. No sense bubbling up a thousand year from now. The scow are to be burned to save the nails. We'll climb to the bottom and build three more."

He looked at me. 'Did you bring the whipsaw?" He said it with a certain tone. He drew a circle with his heel boot. "Mud Lake. Make it to here, Mr. Service, and you'll make it to Dawson Damn Town. You ride in my scow. The umpires and Shate Allen in another. I'll need the Medder Lark's strong back in with the Kid MacKintosh."

Back when I was aboard the *Maine* and the *Queen*, it was the water I watched slide by. On the river, it was the land. I was happy to see the *Alice May* shrink out of sight; the derelict gave me the willies. Its chimney smoke was behind the first river bend when we heard the rumble of thunder without thunderheads, a musical roar, which in minutes was a seething rage.

Dooleyvitch and I were working the rapids together when his frantic paddle slipped off a shallow boulder, struck me in the forehead and sent me over the back of the scow and into the water without a splash.

I would've kicked myself for being taken by surprise, except I was in a battle for air. I went under and came up coughing. From the churn, I saw Dooleyvitch make a half-hearted attempt to throw a rope; it landed a yard from my reach. I went under and came up to see him unconcerned at my inability to swim. I went under and came up to see the second scow with Happy Jack and the Kid MacKintosh aboard. Happy Jack hollered, "Duty first and duty last," and dove into the boil.

I crashed into a mossy boulder and clung to it long enough to watch the third scow sweep ahead, through a gash, and out of sight. Long enough to have my shirt stripped from me by the current. Happy Jack washed by and he grabbed onto my boot to dislodge my grip. The two of us rushed downriver, as if by flume. The din in my ears kept me from hearing my wild heart but it filled my throat, as did the water.

Reaching shore was an impossibility. I knew I'd soon drown all because the Slav must've figured out we ached for the same girl. He knew I was handsome and charming and well-situated. I couldn't be defeated in a fair competition for her affections and I couldn't be defeated in a duel. I was to drown because I was blessed with superior attributes.

My arms flailed in the swirl. I swallowed half the river and half its pollen scum. Oddly, my dying thoughts were of McGee asleep in Cuba beneath the upside-down fishing boat as bullets tore apart green leaves.

From underwater came his whisper. "El Capitán?"

I was afraid to answer.

"El Capitán, worry about things in your control."

I surfaced to holler, "What do I control?"

Back under. I came up gasping and flailing. Back under. I gasped liquid life.

"El Capitán, my lord, let go."

"I don't believe I will."

"What do you believe?"

"Two plus two equals four."

"But you worry about it."

Red hair appeared like a ball of flame in the whiteness of the rapids. I was captured in a bear hug, but in desperation, I pulled Happy Jack under. We bubbled up, and my rescuer socked me in the jaw.

"You'll drown if you don't surrender to me. I'll drown with you."

I did my best to succumb. We traveled downriver in tandem, feet first. Sometimes our heads were above water, oftentimes beneath. I gasped each time the river churned us up. We used feet to defend against boulders. We slammed into one and were sent spinning like wood chips in a mill.

He used well-digger legs to push off rocks and us toward shore. We got lucky when a river bend let us drift sideways. We came into water a yard deep, but too swift to stand in, and we swept over more submerged rocks eager to crush my skull.

Inch by inch, Happy Jack kicked us toward safety until I was able to stand in a peaceful, chin-deep pool buried in a blanket of thin mist. The mist ended six feet above my head where the sky was blue. Geese, larger than anything on wing, came in a wedge and landed about.

I was breathless, speechless. For the first time since Dooleyvitch knocked me in with his paddle, I realized the water was numbing. We gained the shore, where my lifeguard built a fire. Happy Jack stripped to his indispensables. I was without a shirt and tugged off my trousers with shivering hands. My lips were too purple to thank him, but it made no difference. Happy Jack wasn't expecting gratitude. He thanked me through chattering teeth for letting him fulfill his duty.

"Your chum, the Slav Dooleyvitch, tried to murder me."

"Naw," he said.

When my trousers were dry, we hiked the shore, past pools of lilies and by a bluff so steep we saw a balancing bighorn falter and fall sheer from the sky. Wild animals were abundant; we passed a she-wolf so near we could see yellow eyes. She'd nowhere to go that wasn't straight up or straight down, and she stood staring.

We caught elevation to see ahead. Two miles in the distance were our five mates circled around a fire. They'd stopped short of the water-fall and were burning the scows as planned.

Anger took ahold of me. "I almost went over those falls. I would have if Dooleyvitch had clubbed me with his paddle a minute later."

"An accident," Happy Jack said.

"You never see nefariousness in anyone."

In the distance I studied the Slav. I couldn't distinguish between Shate Allen, the Kid MacKintosh, and the umpires without a high-grade field glass. But Dooleyvitch was larger than the others. I'd need patience to get even. I'd need a scheme involving pistols.

"They're having a service for us," Happy Jack said. He walked on ahead and sang *Ta-ra-ra Boom-de-ay*. He said he was hungry, and I found a soggy onion in my pocket to stop his singing. We caught up in three hours. They'd clambered to the bottom of the waterfall and were building two scows with the leftover nails.

They were delighted to see us climbing down after them and gave three cheers. Dooleyvitch slapped Happy Jack on the back, knocked the wind out of him. "You're no goot, Vyoming, but you buck up and do your damnedest."

"It was Mr. Service here who did the saving," Happy Jack said. "I was going under for the last time when he pulled me out by the scruff."

I'd no idea why he lied. I was ready to set the record straight, but Dooleyvitch scoffed at Happy Jack's story. The Slav doubted my heroism. Out of friendship for Happy Jack, and despisal for the Slav, I yielded to the fabrication. I held my tongue. I now had two friends, McGee and Happy Jack.

The seven of us crowded into two scows. I took care to stay out of the Slav's. As we shoved off, I looked back at the waterfall. For the first time since Skaguay, there were no crews behind us or before us.

"Countless soul have perished in rush for riches," Dooleyvitch hollered. "Lucky we lost not a man. Cheer up. You flower are going to survive after all. Never predicted it, never wagered on it, but you'll soon be picking up nugget size of Chickasaw plum."

We floated through a night, which was a blessing. I would've stayed awake on shore, anyway, to keep from being ambushed by the crazy Slav. The mosquitoes on the banks were in clouds but troubled us little in the middle of the river. I was glad for that, too, being shirtless. The night air was cold, but I forgot when we hit another patch of water that snatched us up and carried us swiftly along. Come daylight, we shot the Five Finger Rapids and the Rink Rapids without trouble.

We at last floated upon the tents and shanties of Dawson Town. "For the love of Mike, you all made it," the Slav said. "The test of river is over. You're home, ladies, you're home."

He poled one craft to shore. I poled the other, as our mates leapt over the sides and splashed to shore. We arrived in time to eat hearty and to see the town boys play baseball beneath the sunset gild of the dome. It was the start of high summer, the Fourth of July. The temperature was approaching its best.

Happy Jack went to town and bought me a shirt. Dooleyvitch bought a jug of chokecherry fire and passed it around. The umpires danced a rigadoon. As dusk settled near eleven o'clock, we spotted campfires fringing the mouth of old Bonanza Creek three miles above town.

One or two fireworks were set off between twin peaks and distant prospectors chanted, "Remember the *Maine*, to hell with Spain."

I stayed awake a second night and took a sunrise walk up old Bonanza Creek. There were sod-roofed cabins with mossy walls and piles of tailings where men had toiled with pick and pan. I felt accomplished for completing the journey, for surviving the Slav's machinations. Accomplished for making my way to a vast hiding place, where Sylvester Scovel would never find me. The Slav wanted my scalp. Rather, I'd take his by taking Luisa. I'd soon find her in a nearby establishment known as the Malamute Saloon.

I was sleep deprived as I walked up Bonanza Creek, and yet nervous as a groom. I whistled at the red morning sky to relax when I came upon Happy Jack. He was naked, strangled, his neck tightly wound to a dead tree. It was as if he'd been tied by the neck like a horse to the snag and a grizzly had chased him round and round until he ran mad out of hempen rope. I'd never known a man to hang himself that way, but there were no tracks except his own.

The temperature dropped. I felt an evil presence. Maybe it had followed us from the *Alice May*. I can describe anything, but I couldn't describe this. If I had to—if someone put a gun to my head and demanded a description—I'd say it was the cold isolation of the neverworld.

I didn't feel sad, not as sad as I thought I should, as sad as I wanted to be. I felt exhaustion. I shuddered. My mind went to McGee. I wondered if he was safe. I rushed back and rousted Dooleyvitch from sleep. I rousted Shate Allen, the Kid, and the umpires for protection from the Slav and I escorted them all to Happy Jack's strangulation.

"Lot kill themselve up here, but I'm wishing it'd be somebody else," Dooleyvitch said. He spat a brown stream that dribbled down the left side of lengthening whiskers. He was keeping his promise never to shave.

"I knew he wouldn't make it," I said. "I warned you back in Skaguay."

"Glad you came across him," Dooleyvitch said. "There are others out here who will slide off rope into pile of maggot and never be found." He spat again into a bilberry bush. "Least he had the manner to do it in July, give him that. Ground thawed to bury him."

The Slav and I found a blacksmith in town named Tellus, who made pine boxes six by three. Dooleyvitch made me pay for one and the umpires had the digging done atop a hill when we got back for a Christian burial.

I put Indian head pennies on Happy Jack's eyes. I was angry at him for dying, for falling on his sword without explanation. Sorry for the way I'd mistreated him, sorry I was back down to one friend—one lost friend—and sorry I'd once told the Slav I was a minister's son. I was expected to say a few words when that chore would've fallen on the Judge.

I cleared my throat. "My old man wore out a number of Bibles, but nothing much sticks with me."

I remembered how Papa's face cast its own light when he spoke of heaven and went dull when he closed the church door on the last congregant and took a drink. His God was a consuming fire. His face was my clock, and I knew the time of day by how dull it was.

I'd been to a number of funerals, but this was the first one I'd officiated. Dooleyvitch offered me a pull from his chokecherry concoction. I didn't want to relinquish the jug, but I let it travel hand to hand as they awaited my eulogy. They weren't mourning; they'd already said their goodbyes to Happy Jack and me when they thought we'd been lost on the river. I wondered if anyone would care when I died—for a third time.

My travelmates urged me to hurry up and patter a prayer so they could prospect. "He dug wells and grew wool in the Wind Rivers and whatnot," I said. "To him, it was duty first and duty last."

Funny how I can be the best in the world at digging for scandal and dark secrets, but I'd yet been to a funeral since Mama's where I knew squat about the deceased.

"He had a strong back, stronger humility, and is soon to be under a mound on a ridge," I said. "I'm dead tired and that's all I'm going to say. It isn't right to make things up. I leave that to hack obit writers."

"Hear, hear, " Dooleyvitch said and gave me a second turn on the jug.

I recalled the time back at headquarters when I was bored and wrote my own obit as a lark. Every man should do it, to see where he stands. A Bible verse came to mind then, and I borrowed it now.

"When thou passest through the waters, I will be with thee; and through the rivers, they shall not overflow thee: when thou walkest through the fire, thou shalt not be burned; neither shall the flame kindle upon thee."

"Damnation, that thick," Dooleyvitch said and spewed a volcano of broadsides. He calmed down after a full minute and tugged on his bally hat. "Cursing work where prayer fail."

I looked at clouds larger and whiter and more poised than they ever were in Cuba. "Smile at us from wherever, Happy Jack," I said.

"Bury me like this when I go," Dooleyvitch said. "A little spot on a hill. Bury Lady Lou atop. Bury me face up, Lady Lou face down. Put a lid over us for privacy."

That was that, except I wanted to clock him with the jug. The Kid MacKintosh sang a hymn, while Dooleyvitch shoveled in clods of clay without help.

"Shit, maybe I'm no atheist," he said. "I don't have enough faith to be atheist." He looked at me. "We're all an hour nearer to finding out who's right."

Dooleyvitch lifted his last spade and let the dirt scatter into the four winds. "Little more of the Medder Lark should ever be said."

The umpires collected flowers from the southern slope and I made a wooden headstone. I carved:

Atop I fashioned a willow cross. We set rocks on the grave to foil the next bear. The shadow of a cloud skated by. I stretched out and fell asleep for the first time in three days as eagles glided over in search of uncovered mice.

PART THREE
THE KLONDIKE

You'd follow it in hunger, and you'd follow it in cold;

You'd follow it in solitude and pain;

And when you're stiff and battened down let someone whisper "Gold,"

You're lief to rise and follow it again.

— Robert W. Service

CHAPTER NINETEEN

OUR CLAMBAKE SPLIT IN HALF. Dooleyvitch vowed to stay clear of the Malamute Saloon until he was properly rich. He hustled off to the goldfields, and the umpires trailed. Shate Allen and the Kid MacKintosh accompanied me into Dawson Town, past the sawmill, the Pistol Shot Saloon, the length of Good Luck Row, and into the Malamute. I'd champion the con artist Luisa before the Slav panned a fleck.

The Malamute was two stories, which made it and the Pistol Shot the tallest structures. They bookended Dawson Town. It wasn't yet noon and the first floor was empty. An old codger slept it off in the corner. Not another human in sight until a Chinese bargirl came out from a closet and wiped the counter.

We sat at the back table and she came and shooed us. "Dangerous Dan's," she said. "Back of bar reserved for Dan McGrew."

We stepped to the front across the sawdust floor. Her name was Guan-yin and she poured us generous tin cups for being compliant. We'd put a few under our belts when Luisa came down the staircase. I knew it was her even before the Kid MacKintosh gasped at her beauty;

her ankles on display beneath a hiked skirt. She didn't look our way, she didn't look any man's way, but I saw enough of her face to know it wasn't flush from sex.

Still, I half believed she was a whore and I was ready to sock the first man to follow her down. There were two. One was a miner and he was hollering that he'd been cheated. The other was a Yukon giant, equal in size to the Slav. He could've been Dooleyvitch's clean-shaven brother, but this brute was without the Slav's nicks of battle, and better looking for it. More broad at the shoulders, more thin at the hips. I might've described him as handsome, except he had pig eyes.

The miner vowed to forever take his business to the Pistol Shot, but he went back upstairs when the giant told him to select another of the Malamute's six and tell his friends he'd bedded Luisa.

"Lady Lou's out of commission," the big man said. "Girl troubles."

I knew he was Dangerous Dan McGrew when he and Luisa took the chairs from which we'd been shooed. They sat side-by-side, their backs against the wall, the world before them. There wasn't a hint of warmth between them, but they were more than business partners. They were like the Yukon River I'd survived; he made treacherous by her current. They were attached by a common goal: To put the screws to others.

Guan-yin hurried drinks to them. Dangerous Dan shuffled a deck and laid down cards to play solitaire. Luisa never glanced up. She sat there, lovelier than ever, and watched his luck. Only at his luck, never at him. Never at my longing.

I wanted to surprise her out of thin air, but I froze on my barstool. Luisa and I had parted in a bad way. She'd punched me in the nose, and stomped off into the Madison Square crowd. Maybe she'd put it behind her. I knew I had the second I saw her, but I don't find as much forgiveness in others as I find in myself. If she stood and walked across the Malamute toward me, I'd remember the good, the times I'd rescued her. But if I walked her way, she'd remember her butt-naked illustration and forget it was Remington's fault.

At some point, she'd feel my presence. I shifted my eyes from time to time to make sure Dangerous Dan didn't catch me coveting what was his. Was she his? The cards were his world. She was there for the danger.

Shate Allen left for a nature call on the banks of the Yukon River. It seethed a few steps from the Malamute door. The proximity of the riverbank up and down was what kept Dawson Town from stinking to high heaven.

While Shate Allen was gone, the Kid found the piano in the corner. Luisa was taken by the sound, as if the music box had never been touched. Guan-yin moved to stop the Kid's keyboard intrusion, but Dangerous Dan gave her a nod, and the bargirl let the Kid be.

He filled the place with tunes and patrons. That encouraged him to play a jag-time ditty with force enough to be heard to Juneau. Twenty more boys, numb to the world, arrived to whoop it up.

Dangerous Dan sent Guan-yin to invite the Kid over to his table. The Kid listened to the giant, shook a hand as big as a ham, and rejoined Shate Allen and me. Luisa looked the Kid's way and I prayed that she caught me in her periphery.

"I've been offered a job, two dollars a week," the Kid said. "You get four bits, as agreed, for your grubstake."

He played until it was twilight outside, nearly midnight. Luisa rose, stretched, pulled light hair up from her long neck, and climbed the staircase. I'd never felt more anonymous in my life. I might've believed myself invisible except Dangerous Dan finished his game, gave me a frosty stare, and climbed after her.

We three newcomers napped at the bar until the sun rose at four. I used the morning to teach Shate Allen rudimentary canvassing and salesmanship.

"Tell bald men your frostbite balm sprouts hair like squash vines. That'll juice sales," I said. "Shake a man's right hand while putting a tin cup of menthol powder in his left. "A Malamute handshake."

By noon, he'd sold twelve dollars' worth and gave me three in dust. Enough to drink away Happy Jack, to drink away Joe off being a hero where bullets were buzzing bees. Not enough to drink away Luisa. The more I drank, the more I watched the staircase, but by afternoon, she hadn't swept down. Neither had her business partner. Or, was he her pig-eyed paramour?

I unbuckled the satchel and did some reading to take my mind from things. The ballads were drenched in war and nature and capers, which made me miss creating high-grade journalism. I feared my skills would atrophy. To keep them from going to seed, to feel alive, I asked around.

McGrew was described by the codger as a powerful man in more ways than one; so much power he never had to use it. He'd stayed out of brawls, except for one gunfight and one knife fight when he'd cut off another man's ear.

"Dooleyvitch," I said.

"McGrew's dangerous the way an avalanche is dangerous," the codger said. "Sits still until the second you look over your shoulder to see a mountain moving at you. Ever been in an avalanche? Snow is white, but avalanches bury you in blackness."

"Seen volcanos, earthquakes," I said. "Everything kills. Even dolls."

"Never seen a girl kill anyone," the codger said. "Giving Dangerous Dan lip is the fastest way to the greedy grave."

I continued my barroom interviews. I learned that Joe Ladue founded Dawson Town two years before. He owned the better half with the sawmill and the Pistol Shot. Dangerous Dan owned this half. The Pistol Shot had nine whores, the Malamute six. The Malamute was home to fair whisky. Home to the Lady known as Lou.

Boys could pay huge sums to be alone with her and were free to lie about their success. Or, tell the truth about their failure. Lying and truth-telling stimulated business, convinced other boys to try their luck.

People tell the same story in different ways, so a good reporter can pick and choose the truth *du jour*. Most said Lady Lou shared a bed with Dangerous Dan McGrew. A few said they shared a bed but didn't touch each other. He let her bring him to a boil. The suffering made him feel human.

Some said he'd once been shot in the chest by Ladue. Dangerous Dan was saved when the bullet found a deck of cards in the pocket of his jacket, but he was bruised too badly to climb aboard even the softest breast. He and Ladue split the town in half to settle the feud and they enjoyed a year-long truce.

"There's a million dollars of gold dust spilled into Dangerous Dan's sawdust floor," the crotchety codger said. "Another million lost between the teats of Ladue's sirens. Are you going to pay a visit to the girls upstairs? Three in one room, two in the other. She's his. He has a nickname for her. My Petalflower."

"I've had my share of flowers. Siamese twins, joined at the hip."

Guan-yin laughed, flashed gold teeth. "Nobody touch her. Nobody touch her, not even him. Maybe they kiss. What Lady Lou lack in human feeling, she make up for in pretty. Some say she's witch." The bargirl winked at me. "You handsome, boss. You touch her."

She was reading my mind.

Guan-yin laughed harder. "All boys interested in Lady Lou. She deluged with marriage proposals. She make lousy wife. Except maybe for a dirty politician. She sparkled about when she first arrived. When she went upstairs, her own brother left Dawson Town in disgust. Sam McGee. He good man, but he said, 'Only God can change her,' and he walked into the wild along the Alaska-Canada border. Never come back. I miss Sam McGee."

The saloon went quiet. Luisa breezed down the staircase, followed by him. Dangerous Dan took his seat in the back for his first solo game of the day. I was encouraged; frustration filled his face. Suffering. But no hint of romance. He laid his cards regimented in a way that he'd never laid her.

I grew drunker from an hour of quiet celebration when, in the back of the bar, up stood Dangerous Dan. He wore a dinner jacket as if the Malamute were a London restaurant; a string bowtie like Shate

Allen's around an inflated neck. Despite his refinement, he reminded me of hippos in the Congo, bored with life until it dawned on them to kill something.

I was sweaty under the collar as the pachyderm walked a straight line toward me. At his side was Luisa. She pretended to not know me from Adam. She was protecting my anonymity from his animosity, her gesture of thanks for the times I'd saved her life. She had warmth for me, which made my long journey worth every inconvenience.

She wore a Paris gown that displayed a carnival of bust. I couldn't believe that this girl, who'd decapitated a toothless Spaniard, bubbled so feminine. I had it bad. Worse than ever.

The Malamute seated thirty-some, but forty boys formed a semi-circle around Dangerous Dan, the effervescent Luisa, and me. No one had a square inch except Guan-yin behind the bar. With the proprietor making a rare visit to the Malamute's front end, the bargirl moved with energy. She had the expression of a girl expecting rain as she wiped the counter with her dry rag.

"That's the first time she's cleaned since the Ming Dynasty," Dangerous Dan said to sound smart. The boys laughed; Luisa examined her nails, which had grown out since her Amazon days.

Dangerous Dan removed his hat and bowed deep. "The Arctic brotherhood welcomes you to this great white land."

I'm one to play along. I removed my hat and bowed in return. I was familiar with the timing of comic opera on the New York stage, and I froze deep in my bow until the boys up and cheered.

Dangerous Dan shifted weight, and the crowd quieted. "Boys, hail the great cheechako."

A cheechako was apparently a tenderfoot. His minions chanted "Cheechako, cheechako," their boots pounding sawdust until Dangerous Dan held up his hand.

"We intend to make you a bonafide sourdough," he said.

A sourdough is a man who's earned his stripes. I bowed deep again. "That's ripping. I'd be honored, indeed, sir."

I enjoyed stealing the show in Luisa's presence, and this didn't sit well with McGrew. It grated on him all the more when I bought the boys a round, though it's not in my character to give people the big-shot act. They drank to my health.

"I fear you don't appreciate the gravity of this accolade," Danger-ous Dan said. "We're making you a bonafide sourdough before your bona-damn-fide time."

His cursing carried a certain edge, but I remained polite and comedic. I crossed one leg in front of the other and curtsied. The boys whistled through short, summer beards. Dangerous Dan's voice remained harsh.

"No immigrant has ever become a sour-damn-dough until he sur-vived a damn winter."

"Why, sir, would you promote me out of turn?" I said. He had no answer. "I was once caught in a storm that swept the Macedonian plain from the Balkan highland. That was the most bitter cold I survived."

Maybe it wasn't the best moment to be pompous about my travels. "La-di-da," McGrew said, and the boys whooped and said their la-di-das and curtsied about.

"I've seen a sea monster." I raised my voice to quiet the fun. "In the chasms of Cook Straight. Head raised above the surface, cleaving the waves. The backside was as big as an English mile and enveloped in seaweed and inky fecal matter."

The boys were impressed, though the monster I'd seen on a New Zealand beach was a fifteen-meter squid.

"Its breath was stench. Horns up and down its back the size of masts. One unblinking eye. It sunk beneath the surface, causing a whirlpool that sucked the scenery down with it."

Luisa was my target and her disinterest took the wind from my sails. Dangerous Dan didn't like me changing the subject.

"No one passes muster until he's watched the Yukon ice go out," he said. "Don't matter where you've been. Don't matter what you've seen. Don't matter who you are. Dutch, Dago, Swede, Finn, Portugee,

Irish, Scotch, Cornishman. The title of sourdough must be earned. I don't care if you've ridden a unicorn bareback. I don't care if you're Prince Effing Albert."

There were more la-di-das and curtsies, but I took them in stride.

"I'm known as a man who can absorb a little ribbing," I said. "I've no doubt your winter's awfully fine, but my visit will be abbreviated. I'll soon join Roosevelt's Rough Riders to teach miscreants a hard lesson. I'll be leaving for Cuba long before the break-up of your ice."

I bought another round and the boys toasted in unison. "Remember the *Maine*. To hell with Spain."

"I'm here to accommodate," Dangerous Dan said. "I'm here to expedite your sourdough commencement so you can skip off to a soft climate."

Guan-yin handed Dangerous Dan McGrew a tall glass of green liquid. Steam—or some kind of mist—rose from it.

"To become a bonafide sourdough, you must drink this ice-worm cocktail down," Dangerous Dan said.

The boys cheered, and I paused to give them their good fun. "I've never seen an ice-worm. What does it cure?"

"Sobriety," Dangerous Dan said. Laughter and boot stomping vibrated a hatrack of deer antlers on the wall. A coffee cup or two fell from the shelves. Cups and utensils in the Malamute Saloon were made of tin, except Luisa's glass and the glass steaming tall in McGrew's ham hand.

The production was choreographed, and I played my part. I accepted the green drink. I was drunk enough to down any poison in good fun, but Luisa looked up from her nails with a cocked brow of concern for my well-being. I asked a question to stall.

"Excuse my ignorance of such matters. I've downed my share of foreign cocktails, but what is an ice-worm, please?"

"It's peculiar to Blue Snow Mountain," Dangerous Dan said. "Few men have seen the mountain, which stands solitary. Rises higher than any peak, lost forever in clouds, its forests never touched by the profanity of the axe. The peak is white, its base a blazing blue."

"By all surveys, there is no mount higher than McKinley, not on this continent," I said.

"See boys, he doesn't know everything about everything," Dangerous Dan said.

"Nothing about nothing," they chanted and whistled with derision. The ingrates had already forgotten who'd paid for the round.

"Truth changes," I said. "Grandfather Mountain in the Smokies was once the tallest, until wagons dead-ended at the Rockies. Now, it's McKinley. I wish it weren't."

"Blue Snow's the tallest, least so far," Dangerous Dan said. "Two times taller than Pike's Peak and growing each time it snows. It snows each day, except when it's too cold. I visited a second time. No other man has been twice. No white man."

"Where, precisely, is it?"

"Some say it moves from place to place," Dangerous Dan said, "but it's always at the end of the last moose trail. In Rory Bory Land at the white top-knot of the world. It stands at the end of creation. Within the polar rim at the foot of the throne of a god. A god of severity."

Word must've spread cabin to cabin, tent to tent. Attendance swelled. One boy carried squirrels in with him, and the squirrel rifle he used to kill them. I projected my voice like actor DeWolf Hopper to accommodate all ears. "Did you ascend it, sir?"

"And descended. Climbed until I reached the last scrubby willow that fights to survive. Climbed three miles higher into fog. Fear dwells there. Shuddering fear and famine." Dangerous Dan took back the drink and spoke deep into steam. "Climbed blind, didn't stop until I bumped into the —Almighty."

McGrew extended the steaming glass back to me, but I didn't take it. I didn't believe a word; I don't know why I shivered with the all-overs.

"I climbed. Climbed in a whirl of Northern Lights, high o'erhead in green, yellow and red. Cut steps up the side with an ice axe. Shivered in the wind at the top. Air cold and thin, I breathed bayonets. Peered o'er its jagged brim."

Dangerous Dan peered over the brim of the glass. His nose dripped with green sweat. "Fewer men have seen an ice-worm than have seen the Burning Bush."

The boys listened in silence, as if they believed his horse dung. "On the way down, I survived an avalanche, dug out like a sickly snail and crawled into thick pine. In hunger and cold I wandered to and fro, above timberline and below. The Almighty took pity and led me to the sea, where ice-bound whalers heard my moans. They fed me, sheltered me through winter. I was a feeble scarecrow."

I looked him in the gut. His girth made me small. "Thank the Almighty, you seem to have fully recovered."

His swinish eyes bulged at the insult. His ham hand clenched the glass until I worried it would shatter. "Stop staring at my Petalflower like you ache for her."

The boy hunter cocked his squirrel gun and pointed it at me. Lots of men carried firearms into the Malamute, but it was of concern to have one presented.

"You've got a big mouth," the delinquent said. "Nothing but brags escape your puss."

I moved my gaze from anywhere near Luisa and beyond to the open door. I had no escape. Boys boiled in. There were eighty or ninety inside and forty more pushing in from the bright, late-evening. None wanted our playact to end.

"I brought back two," McGrew said.

"Two what?"

"Ice-worms. Are you daft? The other I pickled to show the scientific guys. Yours is alive and simmering up this glass." He extended it my way once more. Guan-yin tried to cool it down with a spoonful of beer, but it bubbled like pea soup on a forgotten stove.

I searched out Luisa for a woman's intuition, but saw the squirrel gun pointed in my face.

"My advice?" Dangerous Dan said. "Chew and swallow. Quick."

I saw no choice but to take the glass again. Despite the boil of the liquid, the outside of the glass was cold enough to weep frost. "I enjoy spicy hot. I've enjoyed the peppers of Tibet."

"It's hot, guaranteed," Dangerous Dan said. "If it weren't for ice-worms, Blue Snow would be smothered in glaciers. All white. Ten thousand foot higher. Unscalable."

I inhaled the mist. "Smells Icelandic, like war without breeze. I can't see the worm. What, sire, does it look like?"

"A greasy thing that coils in queasy rings. A belly of bilious blue."

"What do they eat?"

"At each other's tails; work their ways up to the head until, come springtime, the strongest are left."

"Elegantly Darwinian," I said. "How big is it?"

Bargirl Guan-yin cackled. "It a beaut. Why your face white like dread?"

"I'm unafraid of bugs. I lived on them for a week in Persia." I put the drink to my lips. Luisa softly shook her head in warning.

"I'd be a sport," I said, "but I eat nothing alive unless I can look into its eyes."

"Eyes a bulbous red," McGrew said. He stuck his fat hand into the steam and fished around in the glass I held. He snapped his paw away as if he'd been bitten. Blood ran from his thumb and dripped into the cocktail. Again, I got the all-overs. Pain and impatience filled his voice. "Drink," he boomed.

The multitude chanted, "Drink, cheechako, drink."

Guan-yin tried to wrap Dangerous Dan's bleeding thumb in her dry rag, but he shouldered away. The cocktail shook in my hand. I wasn't play-acting. It shook on its own. Green liquid splashed to the ground and sizzled on sawdust like hot grease. Fear stirred in Luisa's eyes. She wasn't play-acting, either.

"It digging," Guan-yin said. "It chewing through glass bottom. Drink and drink fast."

"It'll taste like crap afire." Dangerous Dan's voice had urgency. "Don't swallow it whole or it will live in your gut and chew you a new asshole."

"Chew through permafrost on down to Hong Kong," Guan-yin said. "Grab onto something, gadabout."

I would've already swallowed it down, if not for the general fright on Luisa's face. I peered into the green liquid one last time, saw nothing, and put the glass to my lips.

"No! *Alto!*" The order came drenched in Luisa's accent. "Stop!"

The sulfurous odor and the thought of the scalding worm gave me the pips. I went chicken, removed my lips from the glass, and the boys jeered." Cheechako, cheechako, drink your cocktail down."

I had no choice but to lose honor and leave Dawson Town, or fill my mouth with smelly hell. I took it in one mouthful. The worm was fat and oily on my tongue and halfway down when I remembered I'd forgotten to chew. I heaved it from my throat and down Luisa's décolletage.

She slapped me. "You puked into my *chichis.*"

Booze, mixed with green foam and blood from Dangerous Dan's thumb, stained her Paris gown in various colors, as if I'd eaten an eight-page section of comics. Luisa captured the worm trying to bury itself between her boobs. She took the glass from my hand, returned the worm to its liquid, tipped the cocktail to her own painted lips and drank it down, hooch, puke, sweat, blood and all. I'd never felt so small. Her lips smacked as if the worm were smoked salmon. Dangerous Dan threw his arms around her and she kissed him heavy with closed lips. Pretending to be affectionate.

The boys roared, half in appreciation of her and half in despisal of me. She grabbed me by the collar and kissed me full in the mouth, in a hateful way that tasted of cigarettes and sulphur. She'd somehow saved the worm in her mouth and she shoved it into mine. Her tongue pushed down my throat until my heart burst.

I swallowed. She curled her tongue into the shape of a straw and thrust it down my Eustachian tube for good measure. "You've been raped, too," she whispered.

I pulled from her clutch and shoved through the crowded door and into the street. I ached to turn around, to tell all I was Jayson Kelley, special commissioner, to tell everyone I was alive. But the young squirrel hunter chased after me. "See the growed man deer tail it out of here."

He plunked a couple of rounds over my head. I ran down Good Luck Row, past the liquor shops, the barber, the quack doctor, and a thousand chords of wood. Past Tellus the blacksmith, still at work, heating irons to a reddish-gold and hammering a coffin identical to Happy Jack's. I wanted to crawl into it.

The town dogs barked at my shame. I kept going, but I'd nowhere to go. I ran through a choral society of yips and snarls toward the other end of town. Nothing would stop me from charging into the unknowns, up toward the Circle. I swore I wouldn't stop until I got to McGee's hollow of spring grass. To his musk-ox and canoe. I ran from Luisa and the Malamute and down Good Luck Row like a man on fire races from his flame.

CHAPTER TWENTY

I HAD NO WORLDLY IDEA HOW TO FIND MCGEE IN THE VAST ARCTIC AND I STOPPED AT THE EDGE OF TOWN. A whisky or two at the Pistol Shot rescued me from the labyrinth of my mind. I was the man Luisa desired. She'd kissed me full with an open mouth.

The Pistol Shot was more classy than the Malamute and I decided to stay and let Luisa stew that I might never come back. She'd lost her brother to the wilderness and she was no doubt fretting she'd lost me, too.

The Pistol Shot had a dance hall and a pine floor, but the piano player was a gift-less hack, the hooch watered-down, and the rules of billiards cooked up. I considered the nine whores but I had no interest. The skinny one, the fubsy one, the delicate oriental. On Day Three I passed up the blonde. Although she bleached in a bowl, I told her her hair was lighter than Lady Lou's.

"Whose are bigger?" she asked.

I yawned. "All teats have the odor of toilet water." Except Luisa's. I slept like the dead, inhaling and exhaling dreams of lilac and salt air.

I awakened to a commotion rising from downstairs. The boys were whooping, "Remember the *Maine*. To hell with Spain." I joined them to learn the news. The Rough Riders had conquered San Juan Hill. My war was winding down with me stuck four thousand land miles away.

I was shamed here and forgotten there. Life was vastly unfair. My baseballer brother was certain to march at the front of my parade. He was in a better position to win votes. I couldn't get elected Dawson Town dog catcher, though they sorely needed one.

I'd nothing to do but resurface in the Malamute. No one had noticed me gone for three days because Luisa had vanished as well. On the very night I puked down her décolletage, Dangerous Dan had accused her of having the glow of love's wooings for me. She'd stormed out and a gap-toothed whore named Tipperary L'Envoi had taken her place at McGrew's side.

The codger and Guan-yin filled in the story. Even before I played my first game of billiards at the Pistol Shot, Luisa knocked on a stranger's door. It was the middle of the night, a random cottage in the forest. She, no doubt, had become lost chasing after me. The door was opened by the blacksmith and maker of pine boxes.

"Tellus and Lady Lou got hitched," Guan-yin said.

"The next day?" I said.

"We'd all marry her if she knocked at our door," the codger said. "Tellus got Bathsheba in shivering glory. Ain't this the land of bonanzas."

I was broken-hearted. "She's a sick puppy dog," I said, which was true. I'd seen her strip-searched without a hint of shame. I'd seen her lop off a Spaniard's head. I had an unrequited love for a crazy woman. A crazy married woman.

"Nothing adds up," I said. I was the sicker puppy.

"Don't try," the codger said. "Life isn't mathematical. It takes a trained man to figure people out. All I know is Tellus is a grateful oaf. He'll toil all day pounding steel for her. He'll keep her secluded high on a hill."

"Isn't Dangerous Dan jealous?"

"He's satisfied with Tipperary L'Envoi," the codger said. "She loves like a dead silverfish, but at least she lets him touch her."

"You go twitting over to steal the blacksmith's bride," Guan-yin said.

"Married women should be left alone," I said.

An hour drunker, I swung by the shop, where Tellus clanged at his anvil. He remembered me, and we had a warm conversation about Happy Jack. Tellus was from Scotland by way of Fond du Lac, Wisconsin. He was in a good mood for obvious reasons. He was hairy and thick, the last man on earth to satisfy Luisa unless he heated his johnson in red coals alongside his poker. He said he was joy-filled going home after a day's work.

"We've yet made love. We will soon. We've known each other but a few days."

I trailed him that evening. His cottage had windows and was well-shingled; it was meant to be lived in forever. Half-drowned in greenery, bee-kissed morning-glory clung to the door.

She burst out that picturesque place to greet him. I was hidden by the husky sun over my shoulder that set sideways and directly in their eyes. Their long shadows climbed up and over the cottage. She mocked his frown, won a smile from his fatigue, teased him until he sang a Scottish song. I could barely hear. I was but yards out, but Skookum Creek rippled between us.

She was a different woman, little like the Luisa I'd known three days before. She wore a colorful frock, as fresh as the hillside choked with flowers. She wasn't the barefoot Amazon I'd once seen whoop like a drunken *vaquera*. Not the cold, card-watching seductress of the Malamute. She moved with a degree of innocence. The weight of her arms around his thick neck was light as cottonwood snow. Sweet past all hope of recovery. If Tellus were handsome, he'd have her forever. If wishes were horses, beggars would ride.

I slept the night on the other side of the creek; the forest surrounded me like a great cathedral. Woods athrill with secrets. Tellus left for town first thing. She was humming his Scottish song when I quieted her with a knock. She answered straight away, as if she'd been praying at the door for my arrival.

"Jayson Kelley, you piece of skunk shit." All verve and glow.

Her accent was bells, and I told her so. "Your spoken name arouses you," she said. "You're a dog who's content licking itself."

I took her hand. "Marriage doesn't suit you."

She pulled away. "I'm Luisa Evangelina Cosio y Cisneros y

Tellus. So go away, *pendejo.* You violated me in print, while your millions drooled."

"It was Remington who sketched you butt-naked on the *Olivette's* deck. I warned Willie not to publish it—not across five columns." I held my arms wide to emphasize the size of the illustration and my innocence.

"I'd go for the law, if there was one."

"You rather enjoyed being on display in your glory."

She didn't try to be offended. "New York enjoyed it more than I did. You're scum, *escorio.* Samuel trusts you. That's the reason I'm letting you into my home."

We sat at the kitchen table. "If Tellus finds you here, I'll tell him to strip you butt-naked like your newspaper stripped me. If he doesn't cut off your *huevos,* I will."

She was teasing, in all likelihood. "I'm here because McGee's my best friend in the world. I hurried to the Yukon to lend you comfort. I knew he'd gone into the Circle and left you alone. A Slav goldbug told me. He bumped into McGee out there by a smudge fire. The Slav knows you, too. He's out to even some old score; I'm here to protect you."

She laughed a hard, smoky laugh. "It's Samuel who needs protection. From you. From me. From the two of us. He's far away, where we can't hurt him."

"I'll find him. I'm leaving tomorrow."

I had no intention of hiking a thousand miles through a mosquito infestation, but I craved her reaction.

"Leave my brother alone." A dash of witchery came to her eyes. "You have no idea where he is."

"I told you, I met this goldbug. The one who got his ear cut off over you. He drew me a map to a hollow with a musk-ox and a canoe."

She remembered Dooleyvitch and was convinced I had such a map. She filled the stove with flame and took me by the hand. She'd do anything to keep me from roping McGee back into our lives.

"Maybe we two are alike," she said. "Just as Samuel says." I felt for her wedding ring. It was missing. "I was cleaning the stove when you knocked."

"You must be lonely," I said. "The Yukon's more isolating than an island. More gold than good."

"Tellus is the most humble, hard-working man in Dawson Town. I'll stay with him forever. I'd be a fool to leave."

"Do you love him?"

"He loves me, the only one now that Samuel's gone. He's gone forever. I conned a few miners and off he went."

I raised an eyebrow, and she accused me of being judgmental, which I never am.

"Samuel walked out of the Malamute and kept walking," she said. "We're going to leave him be."

My eyebrows remained raised. "I suppose conning's the same as newspapering," she said. "Whoring is, too, but more honest. Too honest for us."

Willie had pimped me from time to time to sell a copy of his miserable sheet, but her comparison was hogwash and I told her so.

Luisa looked at the wall clock, which meant she wanted me gone. "Don't breathe a word to anyone. Don't ever come back."

"I promise."

I knocked the next morning. And the next. She let me in. I wanted to take her on the bearskin rug, but I was patient. I wanted to be her first *and* the first to wholly satisfy her.

She was satisfied with kitchen conversation. "Samuel took me from New York to Plumtree."

"I know. I followed after you. I arrived too late."

"Samuel said my soul needed to heal, said my cousins would teach me to swim in the Blue Ridge rivers, teach me the crags of Grandfather Mountain. Plumtree is the loveliest place on earth, but I couldn't stay among aunts and uncles I never knew. We looked related, but we didn't sound alike. We didn't seem alike. I couldn't step where my parents had stepped. It hurt too much. I had to get out of there and Samuel came with me because Samuel is loyal to a fault. He said I couldn't travel to the Klondike alone."

"The Klondike is as peppered with more hillbillies than the Appalachians. I'll take you back to New York. You'll get an annulment in the city." It would be easy. They hadn't consummated.

"I wish Samuel never showed me the life I missed. Our parents were wonderful and deeply in love. Do you know how that hurts?"

For once, I had no answer.

"Plumtree tortures Samuel, too," Luisa said. "It tortures him to know I wasn't there all those years."

I no longer knocked; I stepped into her cottage each morning after Tellus left for town. I needed to make something happen soon. She had a handsome, interesting, understanding man around all day. If I wasn't careful, she'd light it up for him at night. If her breasts heaved for Tellus, he'd have me to thank. I'd have myself to blame.

"I'll never understand why Samuel put up with you," Luisa said. "Honest to God, I suppose there's something decent in you somewhere." She opened the kitchen window and listened to the singsong of birds. "Samuel didn't know I existed until his—our—parents passed. I thought my parents were the rich sugarcane assholes. Samuel arrived in Havana to tell me he was my brother and that my real parents had died in Carolina. He showed me their letter. Until then, I believed I'd been born in Cuba, to those *gilipollas*."

I touched her hand to lend comfort. She didn't pull away. "Why were you sent to Havana?"

"Cuba was meant to be temporary until Lincoln's war ended. But my real parents decided the assholes could give me the finer things."

"There, there. It was the loving thing."

That offended her, and she pulled away her hand. "The *gilipollas* abandoned me at the convent."

"Why?"

"They thought they were barren when they adopted me. One day, they had a daughter of their own. They kept me until I was thirteen. Their *real* daughter was attractive, but I eclipsed her, so off to the convent I went. They said I was ornery, though I was far sweeter than I am now."

"Life changes us," I said. "You wouldn't have wanted to know me as a younger man. I'm quite evolved."

"I thought I was their real daughter, too. They told me nothing different. I was beaten by nuns for two years. One day, I was taken in by a poor old woman. My *abuelita*. We pretended she was my grandmother. She was the first kind person in my life. The only one until Samuel."

"How awful, going from riches to the convent to abject poverty."

"It was wonderful," Luisa said. "I loved my *abuelita*. She told me I wasn't born; she said I was made in the foam of the sea, the foam the island of Cuba floats upon. My *abuelita* and I toiled, sewing sacks into the late hours, four busy hands and her sweet, tired face beside the candlelight. My *abuelita's* gone."

Luisa teared up. My instinct was to go after more truth, but I didn't. I wanted her to feel cherished more than I wanted the facts. She looked past me at the clock and I left.

My next knock came with pleas to pack her things and run away with me before Tellus came home. "A beautiful woman can have the life she wants in New York. San Francisco. You don't love Tellus."

"I wounded my brother; I chased him into the Circle. I won't wound Tellus. I'm done hurting the men who are kind to me."

I set my coffee down, circled the table and pulled her into my arms. "Tellus'll never take you away, you know that. You'll rot here."

"He cares," she said. "He has a heart."

"I've that in spades, and derring do. Men like Tellus chase after righteousness like kittens after string. They grow old on hills all over the world. Come with me, I'll give you a life."

She resisted my kiss. "I once gave you a delicate brush on the cheek as you slept under a fishing boat in Cuba," I said. Her scent was as earthy now as then, and I regretted I'd applied enough musk to pollute a bat cave. "The world thinks me dead. Wives can't commit adultery with dead men."

I held both of her hands. No hurry. Hours left on the clock. Time enough for dramatic pause. But this was no scene in a stage play and I wanted her to know it.

"I care," I said.

"Never breathe a word of this."

I unbuttoned her frock. "Dead men don't talk."

"We're both dead. We deserve each other." She initiated the next kiss. It brushed my lips as the wings of a dragonfly. I searched under her frock for skin. It had a mistiness, as if she'd stepped flush from a hot bath.

We stood over the bearskin. She softened in my arms. A tear of hers ran down my cheek. I'd never dreamed she was capable of crying.

"Is it McGee?" I said. "I love him, too."

She shook her head no. "Forget Samuel. He's gone. Never try to find him."

"Then… your grandmother," I said. "How did she pass?"

"You must promise me one thing."

"Tellus will never know. I promise. Neither will McGee."

"No, not that. Promise me you'll leave Samuel be. We both must. Our lives got meshed with his, but he's happiest without us. Don't go looking for him." She grabbed me by the scruff. "Promise."

It was a whisper, but it was a demand. I made that promise. I expected to keep it; I had no map, anyway. She helped me off with my shirt and trousers. For a long while she had no interest in removing her own clothes. When at last she stripped, she twirled for inspection.

"Better than a newspaper illustration?" She didn't wait for an answer. "Get down on the bearskin." Again, it was a whispered demand. "Now."

The stove popped, and I jumped. Luisa did not. Her heart pounded for me. Passion ripened her.

"I hate you," she said.

The feel of her was more silky and electric than other women. She was eager to take me, but she was on top and kept her knees together. She made us both wait. My toes curled inward. The glory of expectations.

I caressed her. It had become the perfect moment, a moment like none other. A moment of freedom from my hidden flaws. My throb was in my ears, so I didn't hear his approach until his deep singing forded the creek. She clamped tighter at the sound of him.

Oh, beloved, sweet will be your surprise; today will we sport like children, laugh in each other's eyes..."

My inner self trembled in place. Luisa threw herself off me. "Shit, he's never come home this early."

His singing closed in nearer.

"*Crown each other with flowers... rifle the ferny bowers. Today with feasting and gladness wine will flow; today is the day we were wedded only a week ago.*"

"Sheez, he thinks it's your blooming anniversary."

"He closed the forge at noon."

The vines that honeysuckled the windowsill were too thin to hide us as Tellus peered in. I'd hiked my breeches as he had the hill, but I was bare-chested and Luisa without a stitch. I expected his hand to hold a bouquet of anniversary lilies. Rather, it gripped a branding iron.

He knew. Even before he peered into his cottage, he knew.

CHAPTER TWENTY-ONE

TELLUS ENTERED IN A BURST, INTENDING TO USE THE IRON. "It's not what you think," I said. "Luisa's my best friend's sister, she's a sister to me."

The cottage had been cozy before he arrived. Now it was cramped, no room to breathe. Tellus was too close to the door for me to gamble on a run and my pistol was rusting away in Havana Bay.

Tellus took his sweet time stoking the hearth fire.

"We never, Luisa and me," I said, but Tellus was unwilling to reason with a half-naked man who reeked of musk. "She's McGee's sister. She's the same as a sister to me."

"You've sent me headlong into the nethermost," Tellus said to her. At me, he glanced once, his eyes too shamed to give me an up and down.

He was determined to heat the iron in the embers and sear his bride, who he flung naked into the chimney corner. She was more than capable of fighting back, but she seemed to have lost her pluck when she needed it most. I was unsure of his intentions for me once he finished with her, but bloodlust leapt from his eyes. He wouldn't dare look at me in his despair, but he was plotting me a terrible ill.

"One thing led to another but I never touched her, as God is my witness." I said nothing more. The less one defends oneself, the more he is believed.

"I'll hang you with that four-pronged buck that swings on this cottage's north side," Tellus said. "I had to track it by the river, trail it in the cover, and kill it on the mountain miles away. You, I'll gut on the stoop."

"I'm no stag, sir."

He pulled the iron from the embers and wielded it like a lance. His breath was on my face, his voice in my ear. His eyes at last found mine. "I shaped this iron with savage blows of sparks. I forged it with the might of this arm."

He positioned the brand an inch from my nose. ꓘꓘƎH

And it wasn't to hell with Spain.

He hadn't cooked it in the coals long enough to get orange, but enough smoke rose from the black iron to make it worrisome. While I was distracted by the mirrored design, he knocked me out with a left cross.

I came to with such a headache I thought I'd been bucked off and kicked in the head. Tellus had shuttered the windows, which made the cottage a sparrow's nest at dusk. No air to breathe. Nowhere to fly. The dark accentuated the glows; a glow from beneath a log in the fire, another from the end of his iron. He'd taken advantage of my state to heat ꓘꓘƎH to fruition, bind my hands behind me. Thongs cut into my wrists, but it was my feet that hurt.

During my loss of consciousness, he'd dragged her from the chimney corner into the center of the room and gagged her with a silken mesh meant to smother her scream. If only she had the wherewithal to muster one.

In the glow, he saw me twitch and knew I was awake. With the sizzling iron in his right hand, he pulled me left-handed to my throbbing feet, and beat me into a bookshelf along the wall. A number of dusty volumes fell upon me. I didn't mind a reasonable amount of trouble, but I was bound and he was unfairly strong. I was compelled to beg for my life as he dragged me beside her. The bloodlust in his eyes left him. He seemed more sad than angry but determined nevertheless.

Luisa remained naked and shivering at my side. Tellus threw the bear skin over her. He stepped on her loose hair to trap her to the floor, although she'd made no effort to get up. Tellus twisted her fingers from their grip on the bear skin. She turned her head to me. She searched my eyes. But when I wouldn't let her find them, she let him open her hand, and he forced the glowing haft into a palm full of stiff, black hair. He pressed it downward and downward until the tiny cottage filled with the odor of grizzly hair seared into flesh.

I expected her to scream. Maybe she did, but I heard only the screams of Tellus filling the cottage. I screamed, too. Two male screams that originated in pain and fear. She absorbed the haft quietly as the duet of male screams echoed through the Klondike.

He branded her other palm in eerie quiet, barely a moan from either man. He stabbed the iron back in the coals and brought his attention to me. "He who seeketh his neighbor's wife shall suffer the doom of the brand."

I begged to live, and he said I would if I put up no struggle. "I don't believe in taking life," he said. "I will brand you once on the forehead. You won't be fair anymore. You'll be hare crap in fresh snow."

I begged again.

"First in the balls. It's the right thing."

"I'm Jayson Kelley, you've heard of me, the foremost press correspondent in the land. Have mercy, and I'll make you famous."

Tellus was unswayed, and I may have sobbed on the floor. "I'm with the *New York Journal*. 'Remember the *Maine*? To hell with Spain.' That's me, I'm him."

"The baseballer's brother? Shut your yap. That Kelley died on the *Maine*."

"Ask her," I said. "I've got a million and a half readers. Jay Kelley makes anyone a hero. I'll get you elected governor of this province."

"We'll be leaving. Tonight in the dark. There's no governor where she and I are headed."

I lay flat on the ground. My breeches had been left unbuttoned in my initial panic to dress. He yanked them down two-fisted. My voice begged, "Please, kill me, but don't rob me of my creative juices. Greater New York will never forgive you."

My trousers were around my ankles. I was hobbled or I would've fought him to the end. He pulled the iron from the fire, put his foot on my neck, and squared the orange glow an inch from my crotch.

"Grin," he said.

I felt the heat. I felt the hair singe and curl. I cursed my own courage. I was too brave to pass out. I tried to scream, but his boot was on my Adam's apple.

My lips moved. "Do it," I choked, and I meant it. I surrendered to what was to come. "Blame God. I'm to be maimed because He made me a man and He made her irresistible."

She began to sob. That made Tellus sob, too, and inside the delay, the door was opened by a third man bursting into the cottage with pistol cocked.

"*Buenos tardes*," came the playful drawl of a Cuban barker at the Tennessee State Fair.

The open door doubled the size of the room. The iron was shot from Tellus' hand with marksman's accuracy. It dropped and burned me in the abdomen, a boot width above emasculation.

"Sahm-WHALE!" Luisa sobbed.

"Sorries, *mi hermana*. For being kinda tardy."

Luisa's face regained its color as Tellus ran bawling into the wilderness. The sunlight pouring through the open door set off her corn-flower blue eyes.

McGee didn't acknowledge me. Nevertheless, my one friend was back. I'll never again be more happy to see anyone. That goes without saying and whatnot.

CHAPTER TWENTY-TWO

I'M A FORGIVING MAN, it's been a defect of mine longer than I can remember.

I forgave McGee for being tardy to the rescue. Had he burst through the cottage door a second sooner, I wouldn't have been left with a scar on my belly. McGee wasn't as magnanimous. He blamed me for ending Luisa's week-long marriage. He blamed me for this that and the other, for her naked illustration in the newspaper, for the HELL on her palms.

"You're supposed to be dead," McGee said, and he blamed me for the grief I'd caused him when I'd gone down with the *Maine*.

"I thought you'd be somewhat pleased to find me breathing," I said.

"I trusted you and I'll kinda forever be suspicious of any words out of your mouth…"

"It's Willie's fault," I said. "He has impossible expectations."

"…and out of your pen."

McGee moved to Guan-yin's end of the bar to ignore me altogether. I forgave Luisa, too, for ruining our one chance with the clamping of her knees. There would be a lifetime of opportunities for us. I wanted to tell her so, but she was back beside Dangerous Dan in the Malamute's rear. Ignoring me to ride shotgun over a game of solitaire.

Luisa, McGee, and I were estranged. We were in the same barroom, but not speaking. It was sad, three fifth wheels, and only one of us big enough to grant absolution.

She was shaken, green around the gills from the trauma of the branding, but she'd slathered herself in powder and paint to hide it. Stylish in white gloves, she bubbled from her corset. Dangerous Dan was playing red on black when he caught me staring at her. He made the effort to rise, walk the sawdust floor and make a threat.

"No one reconnoiters with Lady Lou," he said. "She watches my luck. She's my light-o'-love. I won't lose her again."

McGee made no effort to defend me. Or her.

A lesser man would've taken Tipperary L'Envoi upstairs to sweat some fury and frustration out of his system. I drank a consolation whisky. Guan-yin was joyed to have McGee back. She served him coffee; he wrapped both hands around his tin cup to tame his chill.

A man fresh from Cuba might have reason to be cold, but it seemed peculiar for a man who'd been living in the Circle. McGee was no longer brown as a berry from the sun. He'd lost weight. He deserved my concern, but he would not accept it. His attitude dragged on for two days and would've lasted ad nauseam, except a month-old copy of the *New York World* migrated into the Malamute under the arm of a greenhorn.

The boys were keen to learn the news and, on Page One, was a *holy shit!* item, that had been reported by the stunt girl Nellie Bly.

THE DEATH OF A BELOVED BASEBALLER

Despicable Spaniards Slay
A Baltimore Oriole
Hero Joe Kelly
Riddled with Bullets
Entire Nation Mourns

July 1, 1898 HAVANA—Lieutenant Joe Kelly, one of the baseball greats in both skill and decency, died a hero charging San Juan Hill.

Lt. Kelly, his soul athirst, fell to the gluttonous guns. He was shot through the brain, breast, buttocks, bowels and gall. Even so, he went on blindly crawling, leaving pieces of himself behind.

"I've done my little bit alright," he said.

His face started twitching. His blood bright. When there was nothing more of him for the awful Spaniards to shoot, they dropped rocks on his head to crush it flat like a can of beans.

Thank God, there was a female correspondent at hand. Like the kindest nurse, I swaddled his head in a blanket to keep his brains and brain matter from mixing with the San Juan soil. He went happily to his Maker in my arms.

The lieutenant is the highest-ranking officer to die in the wearisome war. Pray God, that it will end soon or young American girls will be left with nothing but bald men who creak at the joints.

Joe had died days before Happy Jack. I braced for despair, but it didn't come. Rather, I found myself angry—furious—taken aback by Nellie Bly's callousness. Her obvious exaggeration. She wrote of Joe's death like it was gory pornography. I couldn't believe anyone could be so detached from the consequences of her words.

Girls know less of baseball than they do of war, but she went on anyway because she had once reported on Casey.

Joe Kelly made his big-league debut in 1891 at age nineteen with a hit single in his first time at-bat. He was a well-rounded outfielder who could run, hit, hit for distance, and get on base.

"Joe had no prominent weaknesses," said teammate John McGraw. "He was as graceful as any man one would care to see. He threw from

> the deepest field to home plate and scooted like a jackrabbit around the bases. He never blamed an umpire's poor eyesight for a lost game, that's how much a saint Joe Kelly was."

I looked up from the newspaper. "Joe's a casualty of war," I said aloud.

> "Remember the Maine," were the last words on Lt. Kelly's lips. "Remember my big brother, Jay Kelly."
>
> Jayson Kelly was a news correspondent. He was blown to smithereens five months ago as a stow-away aboard the USS Maine.

Nellie Bly wrote as if her readers were stupid. Of course, they knew of my demise. She was taking a dig at my fame. Joe and I would be remembered as the most famous siblings since the Brothers Grimm, maybe since Cain and Abel.

> Jayson Kelly was a somewhat inconsequential figure. Popular belief is that his body remains under the *Maine's* hull. No atom of him was ever found, and my ambitious colleague, Sylvester Scovel, is at this moment in the Klondike chasing down solid rumors that Mr. Kelly fabricated his own death and watched his own funeral like Tom Sawyer and Huck Finn.
>
> Perhaps the death of his own brother will flush Jayson Kelly out.

McGee misread my outrage for despondency. He at last let go of his unmerited resentments, draped his arm about me, and said, "Sorries. Joe was a grand athlete and a grander person."

I hid the tremor of my hand in a pocket and fiddled with Papa's clasp knife. "Nellie Bly misspelled my name."

McGee shrugged his shoulders, as if a dropped "e" that made me a Kelly again was unimportant in the grand scheme. I heard him whisper to Shate Allen that he'd often seen odd demonstrations of grief from Cuban widows.

I choked the clasp knife in my pocket to keep from going berserk. Out of expedience, I let McGee comfort me, and he got me talking. I wanted to tell him Joe was the wee assassin who took Mama, but instead I described the baseball pitch I invented as a child when Joe and I had that catch by the riverbank.

"It was a thing of science. The ball swerved like a pinecone. It curved so much the great Joe Kelly failed to catch it."

Never mind Joe was a tot at the time and had a better chance at catching his shadow. He went to fetch the ball, and that's when he saw the pigeon stuck in the mud and begged me to save it. I didn't tell McGee that part, or what my old man said as he baked precocity from my wet feet.

"There's something absent from you, boy. The midwife pulled you out of my dear wife. Otherwise, I wouldn't know you're my son."

McGee smiled with warmth at my curveball story. He embraced me; he said losing a sibling is the worst pain a man can endure.

We jawed a while on matters small. I was at last forgiven. For what crime, I'll never know. I long ago forgave everyone for everything, even Joe for spoiling Mama's funeral with his baby bawling, may he rest in peace. May she.

Luisa was unhappy with the rekindling of my friendship with her brother. She caught up to me when I escaped into the sunshine for a pee in the river. "Leave Samuel be." Another demand, but this one wasn't whispered.

"He's good for me," I said, leaking a tributary.

"You are a better man when he's nearby," she said. "But you're no good for him. We both must leave him be. Let him go home to his Laughing Eyes."

"My brother's dead. I can't let my dearest friend disappear forever."

That dash of anarchist; no one tells me what to do.

"Let him go and I'll come back to you."

"I'm better for him than some tundra squaw."

"Your one dear friend, Jayson Kelley, is the knob you're holding in your hand."

Spain soon surrendered, we learned of it in September. The whores distributed kisses to celebrate the end of the "splendid little war," and McGee toasted me with his cup of steaming coffee. "Your war cain't be over yet. But it is."

I shushed him. "Nobody knows I started it. Nobody in the Klondike except you and Luisa." And Sylvester Scovel, wherever he was lurking.

Luisa was the greater threat to my anonymity; I had to establish peace with her if I didn't want another Blanche Bates on my hands. No longer green around the gills, Luisa was in the pink, more stunning than ever.

My chance came one evening. She kept her eyes cast down on Dangerous Dan's luck so I could safely get my fill of her. A large rat vanished up her skirt.

I'd heard her scream once, and that was a war whoop when her band of Amazons invaded the Spanish camp last Christmas. A second scream should've come when Tellus branded her palms; the memory of the odor was fresh in my nostrils. She didn't scream this time, either, as the rat scrambled to the bend in her knees and beyond.

I was presented with an opportunity to win her favor and I was sober enough to seize it. My slight limp slowed me. I was half-way to her when she stopped the rat at the exact place I'd been stopped by her husband's anniversary singing. She grabbed a wad of skirt, enough to expose her ankles and calves, twisted it, and crushed the whiskered invader without another man seeing. She stared into my eyes as the demon of tooth and claw wriggled in the textiles between her thighs.

Rats worldwide die with a high-pitched, pig-like squeal, but the Kid MacKintosh played the music box with glory throughout the invasion. Dangerous Dan must've heard something. He glanced up from his cards at me as she snapped the beast's neck with her scarred hands, her dead eyes locked to the longings of mine.

"Leave Samuel be," she mouthed from across the room.

The demand was inaudible, but I'm a trained expert at lip-reading. I also know what's in a woman's heart, and hers softened a bit for me that day. I'd made the instinctive effort to protect her. It's what girls want from a man. Even Amazons. Someday she'd give me another chance, but that day she kept twisting the dead rat's neck for emphasis.

McGee and I had long walks and long conversations. He harbored guilt about Luisa's childhood and for the way she turned out. So much guilt that, when October came, he organized a dance for her birthday, although he felt guilty for not knowing what month of the year she was born.

He hung paper snowflakes from antlers until the Malamute looked like a grammar school. He ordered the Kid MacKintosh to play for all he was worth. "You'll kinda shame us if you stop," he said. "Remember you're of Scottish birth, keep playing till you drop."

Dangerous Dan caught the party fever. It'd been months since I'd seen a man in a high hat. He imported fresh Jezebels from nearby towns and gave them gowns from Paris that he'd bought in San Francisco. A *les seins fiesta* floated by, a Mardi Gras of red paint.

I sat at the bar throughout the *soirée*. McGee kept himself busy making the party a delight. That left his barstool wide open and an overdressed doll of sorry fame plopped down. She said she was Medie Lark of Finnmark and she'd never seen a man look so bored. She had arrived from Moosehide, and I asked if she knew Sylvester Scovel.

"One might fit the bill." She bit her lip and said not another word. She was a slim girl with a tilted nose, pretty as she was poor. I looked past her paint. Practically a child.

I slid her a couple of Liberty nickels, told her it was for nothing except information.

"Is this Scovel an athletic chum, like you?" she said. "A decade younger than you, much older than me? That's neither here nor there. Does he make friends easy? Sunny personality?"

"Was he from New York?"

"Said so. Didn't have your Yankee accent, got raised up in Wooster. Don't know where that is."

"Ohio."

"Say, Ohio's where McKinley's from. Don't you love the American president, winning the war so fast and all? Wooster was a newsman. Said he was looking for a man who wasn't. A man who pretended to be. Showed me a wrinkled newspaper clipping from his billfold, spread it flat on the bar and pushed it under my nose."

"What did it say?"

"It had a portrait of the man he was after, but the picture was the size of this nickel and yellowed. The man he's looking for could be any white man here to Nome. Could be you."

"What did the item say?"

"I don't read. I do other things. Anything except read."

"How old are you?"

"Fifteen next week, if you want me to be."

"Get yourself married."

"Better to make a lot of men happy than one man miserable."

"You're small. Barely budding. Barely ripe."

"Not growed yet. If you want me to be. I can be from a villa in Paris. I'm dressed the part. I can be a young widow in mourning, I can be a cocotte. You can be second to have me, the first was my cruel husband, but only part way on our wedding night."

"Be Medie from Moosehide. I hate it when people pretend to be someone they're not."

"In that case, my last man was your chum Wooster. Paws soft as yours. A tickler mustache. Kept calling me Frances. She's his honeypot." Medie Lark touched my arm. "Do you want to be my first? Do you want me to be your honeypot." She nodded toward Luisa. "Want me to be her?"

"You're thin," I said. "You live on your own air."

"Lady Lou's too pretty to be real," she said. "The kind of girl you can put in a book, but never in a bed."

I laughed. "What does an illiterate know of books?"

"What does your blonde girl know of men?" She let go of my hand, bounced my coins into her hard-boiled whatnots. Her hem swept the sawdust as she gamboled away.

I wanted Luisa, though my infatuation had subsided with McGee's return. Joe's annihilation had given my one friend back to me, and I was determined never to let loose of him again.

I went above and beyond to make him my equal. My new brother. He appreciated me going the extra mile but insisted it was unnecessary. He said service made him happy, and we went back to the way things were. We grew as close as we ever were in Cuba.

Luisa stayed distant. McGee would've turned himself inside out for her, we both would have, but she isolated herself at Dangerous Dan's side.

"It's hard to believe you're related," I told McGee. "She clings like lichen to him and to insignificant grudges."

Those words bothered McGee. It was OK for him to weigh in on Luisa's disposition and shortcomings, but I had not earned the right.

"She has reasons to kinda be at loggerheads with the world," he said.

I let the conversation drop. In the uncomfortable silence an awful thought returned to my head. If need be, who would I save? Who would I sacrifice if I had to choose? In a crisis, would it be brother or sister? It nagged me for no reason. I saddled up to McGee, and she to Dangerous Dan. I'd save the damsel, of course, a man always saves the damsel, even a damsel con artist who pretends to be a whore. A pretend whore who consummates with no one. Not even her husband.

McGee detested the Malamute Saloon for the harm it had brought to her. He was forever needing fresh air, and we went on walks past chords of wood growing higher in anticipation of winter. One day, on a walk that took us well beyond the sawmill, he made a confession.

"I suppose I'll kinda never make a good brother. That's the one thing I've wanted since I was an only child. I've wanted it more since I learned of her existence. I've tried, but I cain't be good for her. I've gone and failed."

"There, there," I said. "I know what a bad brother is, and you're not it."

"Joe kinda died for you," McGee said.

This time it was he who weighed in where he had no right, but I stopped short of scolding him. Keeping company with McGee day after day was changing something inside me. "Joe's death taught me something. It taught me that you're my *real* brother."

"I failed you, too," he said. "I'll kinda never be a good reporter."

He was right, though I couldn't put my finger on the reason. He'd so many of the right qualities. He could spin a story, for one, albeit boring. People trusted him; they liked his authenticity and told him things. But McGee's other qualities got in the way. He was more an artist. Artists know the details left out are as important as what's painted in. Journalists know that, too. But when an artist paints a landscape, he leaves out the factory smokestacks. I had the wherewithal to leave out the rainbows. To an accomplished correspondent, smokestacks are what bring a yarn to life.

"It matters little," I said. "Dawson Town doesn't even have a newspaper."

All it had were whisky, needy whores and Luisa. I traded it all for long walks with McGee. It was a joy to be with someone who knew me, understood me, who knew of me, who knew I wasn't the hapless balladeer Robert W. Service.

McGee knew that I'd changed the world. The rest of Dawson Town had treated me like a scoundrel worse than Soapy Smith. With McGee back, I could look anyone in the face and tell him to go to the devil. It was pleasant to be that man again. Pleasant to have my one good friend, my new brother, drinking coffee at my side. He was always drinking hot coffee; he was always cold. And always worried for Luisa. He knew better, but he couldn't help himself.

CHAPTER TWENTY-THREE

I'M A MAN WHO LEARNS FROM MISTAKES, but I couldn't identify the precise missteps I was making with Luisa. I never knew if she had fallen in love with me in the cottage by Skookum Creek, or if she manipulated me for reasons known only to her.

We remained estranged as her brother and I grew closer. One afternoon on a long walk, I told him I wished I could take his sister back to New York, to my element where she'd find me irresistible. He picked a long piece of grass, chewed one end and said, "I kinda prefer it out here in the wilderness."

"You must enjoy being sucked dry by mosquitoes." Not tiny mosquitoes in myriads like those in Cuba, but giant insects of prey that were dissuaded only by stiff wind. "Humans venture outside because that's where the gold is."

I made a course back to the Malamute. I knew McGee would follow. I was the boss, *El Jefe*.

"We all need fresh air," McGee said at my back. "Just as we're all in need of human companionship, but you shouldn't be expectin' it from Luisa. Your longin's for her is rottenin' your soul."

I turned to face him, but he kept talking. "You'd be better off gittin' a sharp stick jabbed in your eye."

With that worthless piece of advice, we returned to the saloon. We hadn't yet sat down on our barstools when Luisa hurried our way, kicking up sawdust. Her fast approach was unnerving. She never left Dangerous Dan's side and, if she did, she walked so the boys could take her in. She was in a panic now.

"Got a visitor today," she said. "Man from Moosehide. He recognized me as the Cuban Martyr Girl."

"Sylvester Scovel," I said. "The Sniper."

"That's certain. A mustache. Thin and long. Said he would splash my sins across Page One if I didn't point him in the direction of the fabricator Jayson Kelley."

I flinched at the sound of my own name spoken in public. But I was cheered that Luisa had warned me. She cared for my well-being. McGee was wrong.

"I confessed I was the Cuban Martyr Girl, but I told the reporter I hated Jayson Kelley and I hadn't seen him since I socked him to the ground at Madison Square."

"Where is he?" I said.

"I told him, 'You're looking for a dead man. Kelley's dead as his baseballer brother, and if he wasn't I'd've killed him myself. You've come a long way chasing a grand conspiracy.' That's what I said."

"The Sniper won't buy that."

"He did," Luisa said. "He admitted he'd been trailing a ghost. He had a dry cough. He put his head in his hands and barked like a dog and said, 'I'm giving up, heading back before I get trapped by winter. Who wants to die here? A steamer to Seattle. A train to Florida. A yacht to Cuba. I missed the war looking for Jayson Kelley where no man can be found. No man dead or alive.'"

"Shush with my name," I said, but no one in the saloon cared. Which bothered me some after the effort I'd put into playing the moody poet.

"Sylvester Scovel's a whiner," Luisa said. "Do all reporters whine on and on? He missed the triumph of the war. He barked a cough into his hands and said, 'Pulitzer sent me on this goose chase.' He barked again and said Pulitzer heard of some ploy from an eavesdropping switchboard operator. 'Jayson Kelley's dead, I'm sure of it.'"

I was in disbelief. "The Sniper's given up?"

"He's ill, he's homesick," Luisa said. "He coughed and whined, 'I'm tired. I miss my Frances.'"

Luisa had pulled my chestnuts from the fire. She harbored the warmest feelings for me, there was no other plausible explanation. I gave her a smile to let her know I was on to her.

"I suppose it's difficult to track a man whose shit don't stink." She said, "sheet don't steenk," to torment me with her accent. She walked off in the direction of Dangerous Dan. Slow enough to torment me all the more.

That night, after McGee had gone to bed, Dangerous Dan climbed the staircase toward his bedsheets. She peeled off from him and walked my way. I waited for her to stop and confess her feelings, but she kept going out the Malamute's door. I thought she was off to tame her attraction to me, but she didn't come back. She had it that bad. I'd driven her deep into the woods.

McGee and I searched for her day after day. One day, our search took us to Happy Jack's grave. Long gone were the flowers and the willow cross I'd fashioned. I told McGee how the Wyoming well-digger saved me from the drink and he'd let everyone believe I was the hero.

"What kind of man does that?" I said.

McGee shrugged. It was the last Indian Summer day. A dusting of snow had fallen, but it melted dry from a flat rock. McGee stretched out. I joined him, and I described our impossible journey by land and white water under the thumb of the Slav Dooleyvitch.

"What we do in the peaceful water matters li'l," McGee said with fingers laced behind his head. "What we do in the *rápidos*, that's what matters, *ese*."

"What do you fear most?" I asked.

"Winter away from Laughin' Eyes."

I was toasty in the sunshine and tuckered and lost in reverie, and I fell asleep for a minute. I would've slept forever, but I awoke to his voice.

"Tellus the blacksmith was good for Luisa," McGee said.

"My God, he branded her."

"Wish I'd stopped him before the brandin', but I'm kinda sorry I ran him off. She's plum out of good men."

I was offended. "Don't you see me?"

"I see you, Jayson," he said. "I see you." It was the first time he ever used my name. "She needs to be cared for."

"I care. And, anyway, she's out here somewhere, proving once more that she takes care of herself."

We went quiet watching clouds. Maybe McGee was right. I wanted to care, but great newsmen haven't the luxury. I cared as a child. I felt pain back then—more than others. Not physical pain. Caring pain. The blues went away when I stopped caring and, without the pain of the blues, I became a great success. Caring was in my nature, but it wasn't in my best interest.

I thought a thunderhead had appeared but it was the shadow of McGee's head blocking the sun from my face. He was over me, looking down. All I could see was an eclipse caused by his head.

"I'll be leavin' soon."

I closed my eyes and ignored him so as to make it untrue.

"Laughin' Eyes must wonder where I am."

"It's October. You'll freeze to death."

He agreed. "Even in August, the morn stings up there like birdshot. I'd sooner live in hell than cold, but I'll live anywhere with Laughin' Eyes and my rosy son."

"You have a son?"

"A hip-baby a-waitin'. He was born before I left; she named him *Kungak IssoKangitumut*—Smiles Forever. He likes to watch the movin' marvel of his own hand."

The mention of his other life relaxed his face but set my jaw tight. "I have a nipper somewhere," I said. This would have been great news to him another time, but he was escaping my life as he already had Luisa's.

"How long will you be gone?" I asked.

"*IssoKangitumut.*"

My eyes opened. "Forever?"

His head remained silhouetted. "To you and me, this land is new. To my family it's kinda ancient. I plan to stay until it grows ancient to me, too. Until my ev'ry bone is rottenin' under ice."

"I have a scheme that'll make us rich. You and your Siwash family will live in a mansion."

"When I'm with Laughin' Eyes—*Ijik Ijuk*—I'm well-to-do," he said. I couldn't see him tear up, but one splashed on my face. "My one regret is that my son will never taste the snap of apples from the Smokies."

"I thought you loved Luisa."

"I do, *compañero*. I love you, too, kinda more than you know."

"Luisa needs saving, and I can't do it alone."

He sighed and rolled over on his back. My face was no longer shielded and I was blinded by the flame of the sun.

McGee had made his decision, but he didn't leave straight away. He waited hoping to say a proper good-bye to Luisa. We walked each day to Tellus' cottage, but she wasn't there. She wasn't anywhere. McGee grew more absent as well.

"We can fix her when she comes back," I said, walking down Good Luck Row in light snowfall.

"I fail at fixin' people," McGee said. "I can change myself, *compañero*, and li'l at that. I cain't wait for her any longer. I'll kinda be gone in the morn."

We spent our last night camped outside the Malamute in the cold. The light of our fire was tiny next to the vast Yukon where he was headed.

"Why don't you ever let your feet warm against the coals?" McGee said.

The question jolted a memory. I could hear hoofbeats outside our Cambridge home. Hoofbeats trampling Mama's garden grave. Maybe a parishioner had come to visit and I would be rescued from the torture, but the beats passed on toward Boston. The mud on my shoes dried. My father's breathing slowed. I hoped he would fall asleep so I could scoot back from the stove an inch. Joe pouted, whimpered enough to keep Papa awake. Steam stopped rising from my shoes. I recited Bible verses in my head until the porridgy mud kilned hard.

McGee didn't press for an answer. He would've starved as a correspondent. He let me limp away alone. I had nowhere to go but to the Malamute Saloon. I always believed it to be safe, sealed off from the Klondike's misery. But it had grown drafty as cold weather coasted in.

When I had enough whisky in me to soothe the canker in my head, I returned to pee. McGee had left our campsite to stretch his legs. His outline was in the dark, a few steps from the bank, watching the Yukon flow by.

"Soon this river will fill with ice large enough to rope," he said, shivering and unbuttoning himself to join in. "Let me contribute my last share of yellah warmth."

Up the bank a sled dog joined in under a cocked leg, as if peeing was contagious. It finished and ate grass. The dog and I were feeling sick.

"Was Luisa inside?" he asked.

I shook my head no. "She's gone. She gets that from you. I don't know why you always leave."

We buttoned up in unison and said in unison, "God only knows."

The dog vomited sour. I bent and splashed river water on my face but the tears and nausea moved to my voice. "I'm tired of you saying that. You left Plumtree for her. Now you're leaving the both of us."

"I'm leaving for my wife and son. My real family. My future, not my unfixable past."

"You're my family," I said. "You're my future. You *and* Luisa."

McGee took me in a bear hug. The size of us together spooked the dog, and it loped into the thick.

"Let me tell you a story about Luisa," he said. "When I first found her in Havana, she was a girl of the street and oh so fair."

"She's no whore."

"Only once."

"Whores don't whore just once."

"She never wanted to be. She was conned. That first day, we took a walk in the plaza. A street artist saw her beauty and painted her a-sittin'. He kinda hid all trace of her wounded heart and painted a babe at her breast."

"He painted her as she might've been?" I said. "If the worst had been the best."

"He painted her eyes heaven-lit with dream, the bloom of love red on her cheek. Weeks later, I saw that paintin' again. She hangs in Cathedral de San Cristóbal for all to see. The artist put a halo round her hair."

"It's a painting of the Madonna?" I laughed.

"The farther she is from the cathedral the closer she is to God," McGee said. "Laughin' Eyes is as far away and as close as one can git."

He handed me a parting gift, a pair of mukluks made of caribou leather. "Chewed soft by *Ljik Ljuk*," he said. "To keep your sore feet dry and warm."

I pleaded. "Stay."

"I've kinda found the place where I belong. I wish the same for you."

I gave him Papa's old clasp knife, the one with the deer-antler handle. "For you, my brother," I said. "Give it one day to your son."

McGee accepted the knife and he left without a word. One final time he left. I sat an hour on the bank before I remembered his gift. I removed my boots. The sled dog came from out of the thick and snarled. I was barefoot or I'd have kicked it sideways into the river.

My sobs quieted the dog. It returned to its own puke. I pulled on the mukluks and made my way back toward the Kid's jag-time. I returned to my own puke, too.

I've come to know that storing health

Is better far than storing wealth;

That smug success has little worth

Beside the simple joys of earth;

That fame is but a bubble brief,

And glory vain beyond belief;

That it is good to eat and drink;

That it is bad to over-think

— Robert W. Service

CHAPTER TWENTY-FOUR

I'D NO REASON TO STAY IN THAT GODFORSAKEN PLACE, but I feared being caught in an early blizzard, disappearing before the world knew I was alive. I dug in for winter. I'd wait for Luisa. I'd show McGee that a man who cares is a man who stays. That's the sort of thing a man does for a damsel—and a brother.

I'd use the quiet winter to pen detailed tell-alls of my capture in the waters of Havana Bay and my incarceration in the dungeon beneath the sea wall of Morro Castle.

I'm a realistic man. I let go of political ambitions. President McKinley would win reelection in two years and the thick-fingered nincompoop would have me to thank. The war had been won without cost, and so would his second term. Joe was already forgotten, one of but four hundred forgotten souls.

I kicked myself for making McKinley popular; he never believed in the war one whit; he thought it jingoistic tosh. Deep down he was weak-kneed enough to think the Spaniards loved their homes and children as much as Americans did. His dead daughters and his wife's seizures placed him above fair criticism. He was a straddler and a waffler, who should've been the most ridiculed president since Andrew Johnson. Thanks to me, McKinley would serve a decade.

I couldn't even attempt a slapdash run for New York governor. Teddy Roosevelt did that because he never had to put his heroism on hiatus. Willie ruined my political ambitions by killing me off and there was nothing his Hearst Syndicate could do about it now.

I had to do something to keep from going mad. I decided I'd make an impossible escape from Morro Castle, readers would expect nothing less.

I swam through weedy shoal water. The currents, like a river, pushed me outward toward the Tropic of Cancer.

An Olympian would have passed out in exhaustion against the riptide, but I fought my way ashore and collapsed. I awoke after dark beneath a circle of fishermen holding a lantern to my face. My body throbbed with fatigue, but I found my wits and set out to get a closer look at Spanish gun placements.

I broke trail for six steep miles to gain a cloud-high vantage of the harbor and discovered weaknesses in the defenses.

I had little time. The entire Spanish army was hunting me down. The wild tattoo of a thousand rifles should have cut me to ribbons but only one bullet found my right shoulder and lodged in my back.

I was carried to a hospital of grass where rebels in bandages were strewn like dung in a pasture. Many were dead. The wounded groaned. The only other sounds were distant fire and nearby horseflies buzzing coagulated blood.

My shoulder was red hot, but I told the surgeon I'd danced with death a dozen times. I told him that I was busted up a bit, but

I'm hard as cats to kill and to attend to the most needy. I turned down anesthetic so others might have it.

Lord, I missed creating high-grade journalism. This was fiction, I never fool myself, but it was far from hogwash and good for the soul.

"Go on and leave me down to die," I said.

A surgeon inserted a wood peg between my teeth so I wouldn't bite my tongue. He extracted a blood-soaked handkerchief from my wound and felt around for bone fragments with an iron probe.

They must have believed I had died. An American flag was draped over me. Pride welled In my heart, proof I was bloody alive. I passed out. I awoke, not In a grave, but back in Morro from where I'd escaped.

I wrote a number of additional items aimed to dispel rumors concerning my dishonesty, to shame Sylvester Scovel, Nellie Bly and other skeptics. I'd torpedo circulation records with a series of Page One items, or maybe I'd snub Willie altogether. I'd enough ammo to write a *holy shit!* book. I'd get the sis-boom-bah I had long sacrificed.

The Kid's hours at the music box were long, and I was there for most of them. The Malamute never knew when to close; it merely emptied. I tinkered with chapters of my book until I sunk into despondency that she might stay away forever.

Out of boredom and despair, I took it upon myself to get rich. I'd a head for business, and a boomtown was the best place to employ it. Hundreds of scows and boats were arriving before the freeze. Attendance at the Malamute Saloon rose until I couldn't vacate my barstool without a stranger climbing into it. Dawson Town had more wistfulness than gold, and I convinced the Kid to switch from mirthful songs to songs about lost love. That earned him sizable gratuities and a three-fold boost in my stake.

I directed Shate Allen to secure inflated prices for his frostbite powder by informing miners he would run out within days. With winter casting about, the umpires surfaced. The Judge and Avocado Jones were loafers and had little dust for me, so I had them work for wages at Claim Twenty-Three. Each got fifteen dollars a day, but I convinced them to quit and hire on at the sawmill on Dawson Town's outskirts. It operated seven days a week to produce fresh wood for houses that were built without paint or windows in a race to beat winter. The race was being lost. For each house, twenty more tents were pitched until lanterns through frosty canvasses shined like moons through wisps of clouds.

The umpires moiled for twenty dollars a day. They put their shoulders into it and put seventy bucks in my pocket each week. I had no stake in Riley Dooleyvitch, which proved fortunate. Rumor had it the Slav was dead or half-starved and trapping for skunk hides. The umpires hadn't seen him since the day he spaded dirt on Happy Jack's pine box. Maybe the Slav's life had, like Happy Jack's, been snuffed by his own hand or a grizzly's paw. That was the speculation and I'd no reason to doubt it.

The housing shortage would tempt someone to move into Tellus' empty cottage, so I swung by afternoons. Luisa's smoke was never curling from the chimney and I'd return to the Malamute for another long night of whisky and wondering if she were married again, or dead, or conning some schmuck in Juneau.

A boomtown is an incubator for ideas. Money snowballs. Business is brains, that's all. I imagined Luisa panting for my wealth and that inspired me to cook up a scheme to jockey my sum into a small fortune. Dangerous Dan and Ladue had already cornered liquor, whores and gambling, so I extended mercy loans to placer miners. I'd finance them to rush off on concocted stampedes; I fed their dreams and convinced them to drive tunnels horizontally into the sides of hills and to sink shafts to bedrock.

It was stagecraft, the same script every time. "Where should I go?" asked one cheechako after another and I told them, "Last Chance

Gulch. In the Bunker District. Your sluicing-box will be choked with speckled earth."

I knew from my reporting days that an abundance of authority overcomes a lack of knowledge. "Your neighbors hydraulic their ground beside a bedrock ditch. They hurl heavy rock like heaps of fleecy wool. With my money, you'll do the same."

"We've heard of men who stake a hundred claims and each one a blank," they'd say.

"Your fields will never play out. You'll be stinking rich." I'd reach into my pocket. "I extracted this nugget from the Bunker District. Weighs thirteen ounces by its lonesome."

"I'll mine all winter," they'd say.

"That's the way to go. Burn a fire at night to melt the ice. In the morning, shave the thawed gravel out and build another fire the next night. Sink a shaft. You can succeed if you have the endurance, grit and perseverance."

I'd put my hand on their shoulders. "It may not be for you. Others are in line to borrow my money. Even the Siwash are after my wampum."

They'd admire the nugget. I'd reach into another pocket and pull out a fruit jar secured with paper and twine. It was filled with gold dust. I'd hand it to them like it was shoe sand.

"The cold is not to be considered," I'd say. "When the mercury is long past frozen and the ground solid to China, that's when you come back to the Malamute and pay me fair interest."

I knew they'd default and sign over their claims at pennies on the dollar. My fortune required a new batch of cheechakos come spring, when I'd make a thousand percent on the resale.

I ordered an assayer's scale from Anchorage. I'd some ideas about new methods of weighing gold—all aboveboard. Meanwhile, I sold fire insurance to half the town.

I wished McGee had stayed; I'd have made him rich as I'd promised, for playing a tiny role. The boys liked his disposition and they'd have crowded around us at the bar, laughed at his warm wit, and grown to trust me by osmosis. When they needed a loan or insurance, there I'd be to extend them at fair rates, considering the risk I was assuming.

McGee had made his choice to be a do-good squaw man. The only face in my head now was Luisa's and her absence was driving me to greatness. I was regaining my self-regard. I needed a newspaper. Come spring, I'd have the money to launch the Klondike's first, *The Dawson Daily Digger*. At last, I would be whole again, the fantastical life I'd once led would be returned to me.

I longed for that life. Willie despised New York dinner parties and I remembered when he had me step in as his surrogate. I'd sit left of the hostess, two Greek war medals pinned to the lapel of my velvet suit. Hostesses wore diamonds the size of brown sugar cubes. They wintered in Thomasville and laughed when I said, "I've been from the Horn to Honolulu and never yet met a man more important than my barber."

I remembered one middle-aged lovely at one dinner party. I'd just returned from Thessalie, before I'd set foot in flyblown Cuba. When I smiled at her with interest she scarcely believed it. "What's war truly like?" she asked.

"Anyone who hasn't been, can't be told. I had to go to see what it meant."

"America will never fight another war, will we?" She was from Virginia tobacco.

"If we don't stand up for ourselves, we're anyone's mutton. But war can't be taken lightly. I saw so many bodies, I swear they must've been plugging each other in the backs."

"I read your items first, Mr. Kelley. Before turnin' to the women's page. You have a wonderful talent for takin' me places I've never been."

I shrugged. To deny it would be false humility. "Waiters are never rude to me."

"Mr. Kelley, you should author a book."

"I have one in me. Each line so dense with honesty I doubt it will ever be published."

"About the magic isles of far away?"

"Wanderlust lures me to the seven lonely seas," I said. "There will never be rest or peace for me, Mrs.—uhh..." Shame on me, I'd forgotten her name, so I tossed out a compliment. "I enjoy your accent. I find it—sexful."

She blushed. "I like yours, too, I like men from *Bawsten*."

That annoyed me; I'd shed my father's idiom with my travels. I looked up from champagne bubbles into crinkled eyes. She was older than me with few precious years left to be pretty. Men like cheeks of chalk, but she'd painted hers too thick.

"I'll be first to own your book," she said. "I'll never lend it out, for fear it won't be returned."

We finished dinner to take the obligatory stroll. American women are, by nature, warm and open to life's wonders. She said her husband was at home. Richmond. Husbands were always back home.

"Weeks in a trench can make a bed heaven on earth," I said. A devilish thing to say. She didn't drop her eyes, said she liked men with full hair. She resisted my kiss to seem proper, but I filled her arms with wild blossom until she had no arms left to push me away. The instant she turned willing, I made her wait.

I talked about myself, and she sopped my words like a bathhouse sponge, interested in hearing more until, at last, I fed her some inside stuff that never makes it into print.

"It's a shame I'm married," she said while smothering me in her bosom.

I wanted to go home to my empty hotel room at 8 E. 32nd, to crap in the john down the hall. I resented Willie for making me do his chores. She was rich from tobacco but had to bum one of my cigarettes. I struck a match and lit two. Her face had changed color after the deed. It looked younger, flushed with a natural seashell pink. I no longer minded a conversation.

"Mr. Kelley, what might you be doin' if you weren't a famous press correspondent?"

I'm forever asked. "I suppose I'm doing the Maker's will. I couldn't sit and study for the law, and banking's worse than Blackwell's Asylum. My one sad talent is being in the right place at the right time."

She touched my hair. "Your sweet baby face has been bronzed by the open air of travel."

I laughed. "Better than being jaundiced from office light. I long ago said my good-byes to life in a cage. I intend to play my part in every epic. There's a race of men who don't fit in, and I'm team captain. Be happy I'm no taller or I would've caught a bullet in Thessalie."

She gasped and put both hands to my face.

"God saw me through," I said. "I'm grateful for my blessings. I'm well-situated at a time when decent men struggle to find work in McKinley's economy." The news war had driven the price of the *Journal*, the awful *World*, and the sneering *Times*, down to a penny. "The industry struggles to survive but there's a gold rush for reporting talent."

"You're the biggest nugget," she said, straightening the lapel of my suit. "Five hundred a week."

"You've been reading the trades," I said. "Pencil-pushers still make nothing. Newspapering's a bare-fisted prize fight. Winner takes all. Many scribes walk home in thin shoes to wives serving meatloaf pie."

We boxed another round. In the morning, she journeyed home to her hubby. If a gun was put to my head, I still can't recall her name.

I didn't realize at the time how extraordinary those days were. They vanished the day Willie killed me off aboard the *Maine*. The *Dawson Daily Digger* would at last give me a platform from which to counter unmerited attacks on my honor while promoting the Accumulator, a wooden box I invented in the blacksmith's to extract gold flecks from sea water. Shate Allen said he had an idea for a canteen that would keep coffee hot for hours, but that was far-fetched. Too far-fetched for any newspaper to make true except the *Times*. Everyone in New York believed the *Times*, but nobody read it. Everyone in the booming Klondike would read *The Dawson Daily Digger* and believe every word.

I'd never get appointed governor of the District of Alaska with you know who in the White House. But I'd get ever-richer while awaiting Luisa's return. I was soon to be a captain of industry, but I couldn't enjoy it without someone dear to share it with. God willing, I'd wrestle financial control of the Malamute, Good Luck Row end to end. I might one day own this that and the other up from Seattle. Dangerous Dan was stupid for neglecting so many opportunities. I was taking him to school. This put a big target on my back, and I had to tread carefully. At least until my newspaper was up and running. Without a printing press, I was without armor. Without a printing press, I wasn't alive.

Shate Allen, the Kid and the umpires resented me for my percentage. My one Malamute friend, the old codger, staggered over through green cigarette air to inform me the Northern Lights are a phosphorescent glare of radium off the ice.

"I've been twenty years in the Great Uncertain, back when we didn't know what lay underground," he said. "I pitched camp under that lone birch tree on Bonanza. That's right, where George Carmack made the big find. It could've been mine, I was there first."

"The Lord giveth and He taketh," I said.

"He's giveth me a second chance with the radium. My last chance."

We'd always been pleasant to each other, but I was becoming an embarrassment of riches, and the old fogey a greedy tramp in tatters, slouching along in smelly rags, a no-good with a slow step.

"I tell you now, and if I lie, may my lips be stricken dumb." The codger had a practiced speech. "Radium goes for a million dollars a pound and there's tons and tons and tons. It's mine, all mine. But if you have a hundred plunks to spare I'll sell you thirty-two percent."

I chose to turn that down.

The codger's one arm was withered and he groped for his pipe with a shaking hand. "Look at my eyes, been snow-blind twice. Look where my foot's half-gone. We'll make it ten. C'mon my friend, I'll give you a quarter share for ten plunks."

I rolled a cigarette for dramatic pause, to let the codger know I was declining his proposal.

"Say, don't be hard," he said. "Have you a dollar to lend?"

McGee would've turned over his last two bits. McGee was always broke, never a dollar to bless himself with; never a cent to his name. I bought his coffee, so any two bits he might've given the crazed codger was by all rights mine and would've come from the goodness of *my* heart.

"You're greedy as the grave," the codger said. "You're putting on weight." He wouldn't stop pestering me until a stranger came to my rescue. He was a representative of the Alaska Commercial Company. He sat on McGee's abandoned stool and bought me a drink. In a low voice he warned of the famine to come. "Once ice seizes the river."

He said he had crates of reindeer steaks aboard a sled, tinned tomatoes, and pemmican, gunny sacks of corn meal and evaporated potatoes, for delivery to Dawson Town's five stores.

I slipped him some dust for the information and he sold me the crates for the thirteen-ounce nugget and a stake in the profits. We were in cahoots.

"No one starved last winter," he said as he helped me hide crates inside the empty blacksmith's shop. "But moose hams and grouse breasts soared to two bucks a pound. Even the price of cribbage boards doubled."

"Any market can be cornered," I said. "Even bacon furred with mold. Buy cheap and sell steep."

I'd once been the reporter who exposed corruption and ill-gotten gains in others. Perhaps I'd lost my moorings.

It was nearing Thanksgiving, the snow deep and getting deeper, when I made my customary detour to Tellus' abandoned cottage. Smoke curled from the chimney. I wanted to believe it was Luisa come home to me. A sled was parked alongside the half-frozen creek and six dogs rested in fresh snow. The cottage hadn't been taken over by squatters. The lead dog was a fine animal that only a well-situated man could afford.

There had to be a pair of men inside, it was a two-man sled. I stepped up and knocked firmly, but no one answered. I heard a doll's cry, and I peered through the window Tellus had once peered through with his branding iron from ⅃⅃ƎH. I burst in, as Tellus had, except I was unarmed. As then, Luisa was cheek naked. She wasn't atop this time with her legs clamped tight to stop me, she was on the bottom. She was no longer crying. Neither was she struggling. Only submitting.

"Sheez," I said, but my presence went unnoticed in the man's commotion. I wanted him to be her husband. His crazed love-making would be easier to accept if it were Tellus. Whoever he was, he was conquering her and oblivious to all else. I couldn't identify him with his face buried in her breasts. He was coughing into them, coughing up a lung, as he whooped like a *vaquero* come to paint the town.

Had I been a bigger man I would have intervened. A lesser man would've looked away. I was a trained correspondent to the core, no matter how difficult the circumstances. Upon inspection, I couldn't believe my eyes. Luisa wasn't being loved by her husband. She wasn't at last being taken by Dangerous Dan. She hadn't even been boarded by some lucky greenhorn with a buck to spare. This man had a long, thin mustache, like the whiskers of a rat. Aboard was Sylvester Scovel of the despicable *New York World.*

I wanted Luisa to snap his neck, but she had the distant expression of watching solitaire being played out on the ceiling. I swore and she heard me as The Sniper reached his utmost throes.

I was in Sylvester Scovel's line of site, but I didn't spoil anything for him. With his face smothered in Luisa's teats, he capstoned for long seconds like a Gatling gun. At last, his entire body went limp atop her, as if he hadn't survived the event. The nightmare ended with one more dry cough from Joseph Pulitzer's overrated hack.

The Sniper climbed exhausted to stand. I wanted to murder him, enjoy his high-pitched, pig-like squeal. He extended a hand, but I don't shake the hands of naked men. I couldn't even sock him with his trousers off.

Luisa blurted an embarrassed apology for the scandalous act I had to witness. She mumbled something to me about it being her second time. "Once to save my *abuelita,* and now to save you, *pendejo.*"

"No story's bigger than a dead man who pops up alive," The Sniper said. "Mr. Kelley, your resurrection would have been one for the ages, but I traded a *holy shit!* story for an hour with her."

I may have lashed out at Luisa. "Who'd whore for an old woman?" I said.

She lashed back. "I hate you," she said. "I always have. I saved you as a kindness to Samuel. I whored for him. Never for you. I hate you."

The more a girl repeats herself, the less she believes it. Whatever Luisa did she did for me, but I prayed never to think of her again. I might never again be able to make hay with anyone. She'd ruined me. I'd never forgive her.

I gathered her clothes. I wanted her dressed. I was numb, but I pretended otherwise.

"The Sniper's a yellow journalist, he won't live up to his end," I said, throwing her dress in her face. "A man would say anything to have you."

She'd given him what I wanted. She'd given it for nothing. McGee had told me that she'd been conned the one time she'd whored before. Now, she'd whored again. She'd been conned again. I felt duped as well. I felt like the mark, like the pigeon.

I gathered her stockings and my wits. Hard winter was on its way. Sylvester Scovel and his version of the truth would be trapped in Dawson Town until spring. I'm a fine actor, and though I suffered heartbreak and a host of unthinkable emotions, I pretended to be thick-skinned to the degradation visited upon me. We three mushed together to the Malamute Saloon. There were three cheers for Luisa's return. The boys wiped beer foam from their beards. She plopped down in the back of the bar next to Dangerous Dan while they were still tucking in their shirttails.

Sylvester Scovel coughed and I used it as an excuse to move away from him down the bar. He whined, accused me of ruining his life. "I could've been in Cuba. I've been stuck looking for you. I missed the bunting, caps tossed in the air, music drowned out by a thousand bells..."

"I missed high office," I said. "The glory of the age has passed me by." I'd missed ever having her.

This got him to dry-coughing all the more. He hacked and hacked. He sounded like Robert W. Service before I'd given him money for a Seattle doctor. The satchel of the poet's ballads was with Guan-yin behind the bar, dusty from neglect. I was long ago bored with it, too busy growing rich to read one more word.

In frustration and despair, I walked the satchel across sawdust to the sheetmetal stove. The Malamute was cold and getting colder. I lit the stove with the papers. A flame rose from Robert W. Service's scratchings. His words spread to wood.

Come spring, Sylvester Scovel's story would spread like a wildfire and my life would be swallowed in the flame.

CHAPTER TWENTY-FIVE

ON THANKSGIVING DAY, IT WAS TWENTY BELOW, thirty-two below a few nights later with the rise of the full moon. By December, the sun made its appearance in time for lunch and set at three-thirty. The temperature had nineteen hours of dark to fall to minus forty.

The boys left guns and knives outside the doorstep to prevent condensation and rusting. Inside was safe, cozy lamps lit here and there. The Malamute's altar remained in the middle. Guan-yin kept the stove stoked with short firewood. Whores circled. Jag-time spewed from the Kid's fingers as steam did from the boys' slouch hats and beards.

Upstairs was warmest with feet against thick thighs. The value of all I'd stashed at the blacksmith's went up by the day, but the price of Dangerous Dan's plumpest soared until an hour against a fatty became confiscatory. I could afford them all, but Luisa had ruined me forever.

I had a perpetual headache caused by wood smoke and the nothing I ever ate for supper. I slept in fits, swigged into the wee hours whatever rot-gut Guan-yin poured into my tin. I struggled to maintain my business accounting atop my barstool. Once, maybe twice, I fell disgracefully. Sylvester Scovel was ready with a pencil to scribble this that and the other into his notes.

Guan-yin, the smallest person in the room, helped me from the sawdust. "You know what Sammy McGee used to say about you, boss?" she said through her gold-tooth smile.

"Who cares an owl crap what McGee said."

She shut her yap and used her dry rag to mop the spilt whisky around my elbows.

"Everything in the Klondike is a bald-face lie," I said. "The water that riffles the smooth stones of Salt Creek was the freshest I ever drank."

Guan-yin got my point and cackled. "Fortymile River has no end. Bad luck on Good Luck Row."

"Our dear president has never been within a thousand miles of Mt. McKinley. McGee, the most faithful man on earth, has abandoned me." I couldn't even verbalize the atrocity Luisa, the Madonna of Cathedral de San Cristóbal, had executed.

The next day cost the earth another ten degrees. A blizzard's howl swallowed the town for hours until drifts piled against the Malamute. A hike to the Pistol Shot was a frigid safari no man dared. The wind's whistle didn't ease when the sky cleared to let the horizon swallow the red ball of setting sun. The whistle became a roar in the afternoon dark and our refuge swayed in the gale.

The umpires sat in a far corner where a draft kicked sawdust up around their legs. Sylvester Scovel joined them, interviewed them, scribbled ammo he'd use against me come June.

A bunch of the boys started whooping it up for no reason but to drown out wind that crashed the saloon walls like Aleutian waves. Back of the bar in one more solo game sat Dangerous Dan McGrew. The giant drew from his deck and drew pig-eyed on a big cigar. When each game ended, he regimented his cards for the next. Watching his luck was my lost light-o'-love, which exacerbated my headache. It was a loo-loo and I forgot the raw throb in my gelid feet. Dangerous Dan was lost in a world of alternating red and black. I was lost in the red ribbon in Luisa's hair, my manhood buried in her black furs of fox. I'd never forgive her.

I don't recall what time it was, nobody does, when a stranger gusted in from out of the night and into the din and the glare. When the door swung wide, the blizzard collided with tobacco spit and the perfume of whores. The difference between inside and out was a hundred degrees. At the doorstep—only at the doorstep—it snowed a quarter inch to dust the stranger's mukluks. The black barrel of his firearm frosted before the first flake graced the floor.

"Man traveling alone in winter carries malignant spirit," Guan-yin said.

This nomad had spirit enough to halt the Kid's playing in the midst of an unstoppable tune. The stranger pushed the door closed against the gale. "It's a scorcher out there, I promise," he said.

The strings of his parka hood were drawn tight. All was covered except his eyes. One was bloodshot from peering through the scratch of fur edging. The other was frozen shut from exhales. His trousers were fur. He wore caribou mitts with the hair inside, his mukluks stuffed with straw.

He was as huge as any Highlandman, but weak as a flea. He mustered the energy to wave his mitted hand and said, "Evening, ladies" to the huddled whores and "Evening, girls" to the rest of us.

No one responded. No one yet believed he existed. He had a godlike, godawful voice that warred against the outside storm. He removed his bandanna to reveal a face mangled on the right side with the frozen blood of a fresh wound. He had a thick beard, ripped off on that side.

He struck his right arm over and over with his left hand to restore circulation. This repetition failed, and he removed both mitts with teeth half black. He loosened the drawstrings, opened and closed his mouth to test his jaw. The left side of his face wasn't working. I found that queer; it was his right side that was ripped with the fresh wound.

"Nothing lives out there," he said. His lips were black from frostbite, which made him difficult to understand. "Barely a marten track for mile and mile. Walked three day without sleep. Can't stop. Too bitter. My dog crawled forward at the wind sweep. The bitch dead for meat. Last one. I'm musher no more."

I've interviewed men who can somehow grip your eyes and hold them hard like a spell. Sitting Bull comes to mind. Billy Sunday. Such was he, and I searched his grizzled face for a clue. I was first to recognize him as the Slav Dooleyvitch, the instant he pulled out a frosted pocket watch with a pedometer. The Kid, the umpires and Shate Allen recognized him as well, as did Luisa. Everything was out of focus for Dangerous Dan McGrew beyond the reach of his cards.

"Hundred-thirty-two mile on foot," Dooleyvitch said. "Three day in deep snow, didn't stop or I'd be a statue. Lot's wife."

No response was offered, so he talked on. "It not the cold, forever the wind. Wind keen. Wind to force one into crick bed. More snow in distant cloud. Dark cloud, endless dark. The Malamute ablaze with saving grace, or I might've walked on at San Francisco. Never been, but it a hike, I promise."

The reporter in me stirred. The gales were from the northwest, and Dooleyvitch's right side was numb from the torment. He'd been traveling south.

"Tired, like I'm still out there," he said through black lips, half-black teeth and a black, blood-caked face. "On clear night the light from the Malamute swallow the Milky Way. Malamute bright as fishing moon. I feared I'd walk right past her in the storm. When I saw her, I shouted hurrah and wept."

The boys stared at him like he was a Martian. "I'm no crazier than all you. If you were sane, you'd be somewhere else."

He kept his sealskin cap on, made no attempt at his coat buttons. They were sewn with sinew, too tight for inert fingers. He took an interest in the sisterhood circling the stove. "Sorry, lady, too tired," he said. "Hungry, cold, dog tired. Too dog dirty to behave human being."

Not one whore blinked. They stared at him like painted dolls from Shanghai. He stared back, his one eye still frozen shut.

He tried to stir them alive with a question. "Has anyone looked back from outside? Icicle hang from roof like tusk. Anyone step out?"

"To take pees," I said, and the doll heads swiveled my way.

The Slav's eye stared at me. "Piss freeze hard before it hit ground. Piss hard as harlot smile."

Sylvester Scovel barked a dry cough, and the Slav's eye moved to him, then to the drafty umpire corner, to Shate Allen, and wandered back to land on me.

"Most you boy squat to pee," he said and the dolls giggled. "Outside, vapor squirt from every crack of this building. Heaven afire. A sleeping dragon. How cold is it?"

No one answered so I said, "Fifty."

"Fifty? Seem colder. Breath made cracking noise last hour-so. My gun barrel will burn any scoundrel. Coal oil in my lamp froze. Nothing work except candle in tin can and what goot that in wind?"

"No skeeters, that's one thing," Tipperary L'Envoi said from the stove. "Alcohol's thick as a milkshake. Mercury's in a frozen ball."

Dooleyvitch chose to laugh, but without smile. "I'll gyrate you a milkshake," and the gap-toothed Tipperary L'Envoi said, "Anytime."

"Fifty's a town record," the codger said, "though the town's but two years old."

"Terrible two," Dooleyvitch said. "On verge of tantrum. Anyone got chewing tobacco?" I had a fortune of it stored in the blacksmith's, but no one had any to spare.

"Do I know you?" Tipperary L'Envoi said.

"If you was raised in hell," Dooleyvitch said.

"Come over here, devil, and get warm," she said.

He obeyed and joined the whore's circle. "No man freeze with you angel around."

Tipperary L'Envoi put her arms around him, but he nudged her away, said her heat made him itch like poison oak. "Killed a grizzly, crawled into its carcass to warm up."

Dan McGrew scoffed. "That's the lie all prospectors tell."

Dooleyvitch craned his neck to present the right side of his face to McGrew. "Where'd I get this, arsehole? Grizzly stood twenty foot on hind leg. He was still gnawing on the limb of another man, which gave me a second to react. Had flensing claw. Might've been wooly mammoth."

"No mammoths anymore," I said. "Sea monsters."

"A few mammoth around. Said so in paper. New York paper, so it true. Take it to the bank. This one sniffed at me. I held gunfire till it slobbered. Frozen slobber on me. Shot in time, I couldn't aim so cold. A flash, dead as stone it fell."

He showed us brown blood under his fingernails, but Dan Mc-Grew said it was fish guts for sure.

"No one gut fish in this cold. Scoff all you want, but I dined on liver. Stuffed steaming wooly mammoth liver into this pie hole, or I wouldn't be here to buy you snow pea a drink."

The boys applauded the offer.

"Those who believe me drink first," Dooleyvitch said. His frozen eye melted open and, that instant, he looked at Luisa for the first time, square at her as if he knew she sat there showcased in fox fur before he ever came through the door.

"Dined on heart. Mmm. Ever dine on heart, my lady?"

Luisa looked back with the pierce of her eyes. Doll heads turned like flowers tracking twenty hours of summer sun. Dangerous Dan was mesmerized in his solitaire, or at least pretended to be. Tipperary L'Envoi's eyes went jealous.

"Each day and night you do heart dining I bet. I bet you dine on the heart of this squat-to-pisser." The Slav moved his eyes to me and back to her. "Give me an hour to thaw, and I'll show you a man."

"A rake of a man," Luisa said and I laughed too loudly.

The wind broke a giant icicle from the roof outside. "Hear that?" the Slav said to me. "Wooly mammoth tusk." He squeezed his hand open and shut. "Your lucky day," he said to Luisa. "My magic finger are working."

He stripped down to a buckskin shirt glazed in campfire smoke. "I thaw faster with fewer clothes. Bet you do, too."

He beat the frost from his parka, walked to the umpires' corner, and stuffed it in a crack to plug the draft. He plodded back past the stove, turned his mitts inside out, and hung them on antlers to dry.

Caribou hair lifted and floated and mixed with stove ash in the churn of warmth. His mukluks plodded to Guan-yin. He produced a spent rifle cartridge and poured from it nuggets the size of bird shot. They rattled on the bar.

"I panned this near Havilah, from the source of a stream, like of which you never saw. Here's a taste; there's a feast in the mountain."

He pulled a poke from his pocket and sprinkled dust onto the bar like cake flour. "China girl," he called, "Everyone drink on me."

The boys cheered like they were starving for booze. Guan-yin ignored them and fed the stove; light from it splashed across the ground. The Slav's eyes followed the trail of that splash to me. "Even the doubting Thomas get a free drink." He looked at Dangerous Dan. "Even the big kahuna." Dangerous Dan, eyes down at his cards, shifted in his chair.

"I won't have to borry to pay for them drink," Dooleyvitch said. "Or for anything else at Dawson-damn-Town. What say to that, Miss ooh-and-ahh?"

"Your stench thaws first, that's what I say," Luisa said, and Dangerous Dan laughed and put his arm around her in an uncharacteristic demonstration of possession. Tipperary L'Envoi moved to the Slav's side, regaining lost ground.

Nothing chases away evil spirits like free whisky, and the place erupted in conversation loud enough to compete with the wind's roar. Guan-yin delivered drinks in brandy glasses to the back of the bar, but Luisa hardly touched hers. Dangerous Dan didn't pick his up at all. I thought Guan-yin had forgotten me. At last, she poured into a tin and told me to make a toast.

"To your health, sir," I hollered to the Slav, and the boys clonked tin with their neighbors.

My toast caught Dooleyvitch off-guard. He had both hands shoved down his fur trousers. He pulled one out, farted long to stall, picked up his tin, and toasted back. "To life, my friend. Be it short for some, horseshit for other."

Dooleyvitch again abandoned Tipperary L'Envoi and took a seat on McGee's abandoned stool next to me. I took a mouthful of whisky and let it stay hot against my throat. I held my cough inside until my eyes watered, but my headache was vanquished. Everyone drank their liquor, except Dangerous Dan and the Kid MacKintosh, who resumed their playing.

The Slav's eyes rubbered around the room until they parked again on Luisa making love to her glass. The jag-time stopped. Dooleyvitch and the Kid MackIntosh traded places. The Kid took the stool next to me. The Slav strode across the room in three steps and sat on the piano bench. Hands as big as badminton racquets flopped on keys. The room went quiet, the outside howl eased at the exact time the bench groaned beneath his weight.

"Mother taught me," he said. "I've no formal training, I know music the way coal stoker know geology. I know women the same."

He repeated note for note what the Kid had finished. He had the faster rhythm of a train running late, but it was the same tune, down to the last vibration of sounding wire. In his buckskin shirt that was glazed with dirt, he sat and swayed.

"My God, that Slav can play," the Kid said.

I answered. "An idiot savant."

He finished his tune, stood, and bowed. Dangerous Dan put his dealing deck down to applaud and lifted high his glass. He was the last to drink.

"Where you from?" he hollered. The wind had died and his voice sounded aggressive.

"You don't recognize me?" said Dooleyvitch. He pointed at me. "This son-a-bitch does, the slobbering sissy."

He told Guan-yin to fetch a second brandy for Luisa, though she had barely touched her first. She combined them into one glass and swirled.

"What's your name, mister miner?" Luisa called out.

"My dear," he said, "were you ever out at the great alone, when the moon shined awful clear?"

"You passed through here before," Luisa said. "I see you've had some luck in the fields?"

"My poke is full of dust, my heart full of sin." He raised his tin for another toast. "To Eve—who introduced sinning to the world. The one thing in the Bible that's true."

He emptied his tin and traveled to the back in three steps. He grabbed Luisa hard at one wrist. Her glass fell unbroken to sawdust, splashing two rounds of brandy across Dangerous Dan's boots. His eyes sported a fistfight, but he hesitated at the Slav's size and insanity. I considered going to her rescue. McGee would've appreciated the gesture, but McGee wasn't there and I owed her nothing for the disgrace she'd visited upon me.

"I'm a half-dead thing at a stark, dead world, clean mad for muck," Dooleyvitch said. "It hell to be alone, alone, alone and hold your own. There are time when I feel I'm the one living thing."

Luisa put her white-gloved hand to the unclawed side of his face. "Loaded for bear, are you mister miner?"

"I hunger," he said staring down her figure. "Not the belly kind banished with bacon and bean. The gnawing kind for four wall, a roof, and fireside."

"A home and all that means," she said.

"I've all this gold, and I'm starved for affection. I've hungered since the last time." He threw a fistful of gold dust into the air. "This time I can afford all I want, and all I want is the mystical magic inside your fox fur. What say to that, Lady Looeessa?'

Dangerous Dan looked up in surprise that he knew her name. "Not without my say-so," he said. He wanted to his feet, as did I, but she put her hand on his shoulder to hold us both down.

"Not without *my* say-so," she said. She folded her arms in about her breast. "My say-so is what counts."

Dooleyvitch took a step toward her and she strangled his lunacy with her cruelest expression. He was another nothing, another man-rodent who'd worried her skirt. The Slav froze still. Dangerous Dan sat satisfied. The Slav watched her until he grew hypnotized by the rise and fall of her breathing. He came alive to fling another fistful of dust like a child. It settled in her hair and brought glitter to her furs.

He seized her elbow. "Don't be queening over me."

"Let go," she said. I would have intervened for any damsel at that instant. Except her.

"You make a man go bug," the Slav said and embraced her until she disappeared in his arms. He coaxed her toward the stairs. "Crown me with a woman love."

Luisa pushed him off and slapped his blood-caked cheek. That pleased Dangerous Dan and Tipperary L'Envoi. But they didn't enjoy it when Luisa kissed the place she'd hurt. For some reason, neither did I.

"Play me another ditty, mister miner," she said.

The Slav stepped back to the music box. The wind was dead and he delivered a soft tune. His arms were relaxed from shoulders down, his hands at once afloat and glued to keys. His eyes teared from more than the sting of the slap. He kneaded with fingers light and fat. He charmed eager ears, stirred a roomful of shame. My shame mixed with their shame and floated with ash and caribou hair in the kneading of warmth. The music box was but a barrier, a wall between man and sound, a sound wedged between fact and fiction. I strained to hear.

I know a number of languages, English, a little Spanish, and up-side-down reading. I can lip read and I can read HELL without holding it to a mirror. Music's the most honest language, and the song mined emotions from deep within. As the wires vibrated the last notes, Dool-eyvitch rose and returned to Luisa with eyes still moist, lifted her at the waist, carried her across the room, sat her on the bar above me and the Kid. The breeze from her skirt smelled of willows in bud.

Dangerous Dan rose in murderous anger. Luisa raised her gloved hand to put him back in his chair. The Slav stared up at her as a baby stares while sucking a mother's teat. I had to defend her, someone did, and I was mustering the sand when I realized I was staring at her the same.

"Dare leave my side and I'll clamber outside and die," Dooleyvitch said to her and I may have nodded my agreement.

Dooleyvitch sat at the box to play a third song, something loud, like a church pianist delivers a hymn. Music and sweat and malignant spirits poured from him.

Music can't be taught. It's like writing. Words are the same as musical notes, arranged by a higher power to confront us with brutal honesty. The Slav stopped mid-song and went to her, put his arm around her waist and set her feet on the ground. He caught my eyes, he caught my longings. His cracked lips broke open as he failed at a half grin.

He looked at Dangerous Dan. "You know me, but you don't care a damn."

His burning eyes revolved into his head until all I could see were the whites. He swung his poke around and around in a windmill circle like an underarm baseball pitcher of yesteryear.

"I want to state, and state straight, and I'll bet my poke it's true..." Nuggets sprayed from his swinging poke, rattled off the ceiling and walls and sheetmetal stove. Dust showered down like Niagara mist. "...that one of you is a hound of hell..."

The Slav's pupils resurfaced from his brains, and he looked right through me to the solitaire game. He pounded his fists on the bar, and tin cups jumped. "...And that one is...DANGEROUS DAN McGREW!"

The sound of his name froze his riffling shuffle. McGrew's head raised like an elk's at the crunch of snow. Pig-eyes flared. Dooleyvitch lifted Luisa again and forced a hard kiss on her chops. She bit him in the lower lip and hung on with clenched teeth.

I didn't understand the Slav's next words. They sounded from somewhere on the outskirts of human lexicon. Who could read his lips with Luisa clamping down and drawing vicious blood?

CHAPTER TWENTY-SIX

THERE ARE FOUR SUITS IN A DECK OF CARDS, ONE FOR EACH SEASON. Thirteen cards in each suit for the thirteen phases of the lunar cycle. Black cards for night, red for day. One for each week in the year.

Dangerous Dan threw them into the air. They fluttered down like fate, each one landing in its predestined place. Thin slices of McGrew's soul scattered about the saloon.

Large as lumberjacks, they didn't fit in the tight quarters of the Malamute Saloon. One had to leave, but there was no place for either to go. The Slav yanked off his sealskin cap to reveal the clue Dangerous Dan was missing. Our once clean-shaven guide up mountains and down white water, who swore never to shave again, had no left ear. It was Dangerous Dan who'd cut off that ear in an epic fight that ended when the Slav's auricle plopped into the Yukon River.

She kissed Dooleyvitch on the bloody puss. She kissed Dangerous Dan, leaving the Slav's blood on his lips. "I want a family," she said. She stood between them holding hands and the Kid played a mock wedding march in double time.

Dooleyvitch was crazed. He had never sealed the deal with Luisa. Neither had McGrew. They longed for justice, they longed for her. On another day, the smart money was on the Slav. I'd never seen a man made so insane. That would play in his favor. He wanted Luisa more than Dangerous Dan did, but he was weak from sleepless travels. He hadn't the strength of a louse.

With the sweep of one arm, he wiped me out of his way. "I paid for her once," he said, "I'm here to get what I paid for. I prayed for this fight. I'm getting the scrap I prayed for."

"She's the creature that makes the whole earth groan," Dangerous Dan said. "No matter what you paid, no matter what you've prayed, you'll never have her."

"I'll marry you, Lady Lou, take you and our flock of children to Mother," the Slav said. "Or die here fighting, and be taken to Mother by the Goot Lord."

I'd never seen so much passion. It was at that moment that I forgave Luisa again. After all, I'd done some whoring of my own, newspaper whoring on behalf of Willie and my readers. She had long ago accused me of raping her in print. Maybe I had. I bore some responsibility for the brands on her hands. I had no choice but to give her one last chance. I craved her as much as my readers craved my words. All three of us had to have her, or curl up and die.

Dooleyvitch bolted at Dangerous Dan like the polo pony I'd spurred to death in Cuba. The sea of boys parted, making room for the two largest humans of the Klondike.

Luisa fainted. The unlikelihood of her swoon took me by surprise, and I missed catching her by a step. When I went to pillow her head, Dooleyvitch again shoved me aside. He knelt to tend to her. Dangerous Dan called him a Pollack and cracked a stool over his back to send him headlong. Luisa was on her feet, her collapse a ruse to give Dangerous Dan the edge. From second to second it was impossible to know whose side she was on. I had to believe she was on mine. She had whored with Sylvester Scovel on my behalf. She had it bad.

The boys crowded as buzzards. They closed the circle as the Slav vs. Irish bare-fisted Klondike championship took root. Luisa and I were trapped inside the circle. Nowhere to go, little air to breathe.

The two came to square. Teeth clenched to trap the heat of their breath, the odor of hot whisky. Fury blazed their eyes as they exchanged strokes. They swung once and again, connecting but a fraction of the time like the five-year-old Joe swinging at the pinecones I pitched to him.

With each occasional fist that found flesh, the boys roared and leaguered them back into the ring with foreign cuss words. Dutch, Dago, Swede, Finn, Russian, Cornishman, Yiddish, Lapp—you name it—until Dooleyvitch spat black teeth like stones. I was on my toes, dancing, or a fist would've caught me. I took a position behind Luisa. It wasn't cowardice. It was Klondike smarts. They'd never take a swing at the Lady known as Lou.

The ring was three-deep when it parted to let Luisa to safety, then closed like a clam to trap me. She hiked her skirt to take a seat atop the bar. I was left to dodge combatants, nothing but color and size and sound.

They threw thunderbolts at each other until Dangerous Dan went down, mouth to sawdust. The Slav jumped aboard and choked him by his string bowtie. Dangerous Dan's groping hand found Luisa's fallen brandy glass, broke it against a stool, and the Slav had matching ears.

That didn't go over. The Slav's left hand sent Dangerous Dan to the Promised Land. He was leaguered back. The two redwoods wrestled, clenched, came apart, took turns socking stomachs and grabbing gullets and kneeing crotches until neither had the wind left to blow out a candle. I lurched to the left, wrenched to the right, as they fought like starving dogs over a mildewed bone. But this wasn't a fight over a bone. It was a godawful fight for the ankles of Venus dangling from the bar.

Once in Paris I'd seen a man crushed between boxcars. The Slav and Dan McGrew were worse off than that. Still, the slogging advanced like the river Seine overflowing its banks. Neither had a bone in his hands that wasn't broken. Both were bloody head to toe as if they'd sheltered tandem inside that wooly mammoth.

The blizzard had passed and word found its way to the Pistol Shot. An eruption of fresh spectators came helter-skelter through the impossible cold. They arrived in time to see a McGrew uppercut cause the Slav to bite his tongue in two.

The fighters clung to each other like football tacklers for three or four hours until the boys' ribaldry wound down. It became tedium, the two stout men holding each other up. Dangerous Dan swore to keep on until one was dead. The Slav, mouth full of blood, blubbered agreement.

The whores grew bored and climbed stairs to resume commerce more animated than the fight. No longer trapped, I took a position on the stairs.

Five years before, I was at the Bowen-Burke prize fight that went a hundred and ten rounds. I wrote a yarn about the Homeric scrap that lasted seven hours and nineteen minutes. While I was asleep from liquor and gumbo, the referee declared a draw. No referee was around this time. No draw possible. This time there'd be a victor, and I swore I'd stay alert to the finish.

Awake throughout was Sylvester Scovel, scribbling notes for a *holy shit!* item. The know-nothing ignoramus was unaware that Dooleyvitch had abandoned his dying mother. He didn't know Luisa had been abandoned by two mothers. He didn't know why her hands were in white gloves, or that Luisa orchestrated it all because she had deep and complicated feelings for me. Sylvester Scovel, scribbling and coughing away, didn't know squat. As always, I was the one correspondent to see both the big picture and the intricacies.

Guan-yin retired to her closet, but the love-fest between giant combatants lasted into the drooling dark of predawn. Luisa, The Sniper, and I were the ones to see each sock, hear each gasp for air.

I studied Luisa on the bar. She knew how to fulfill a grand scheme. She'd figured out how to clear the deck for us. She was the champion of intrigue, but I feared she'd miscalculated. The Klondike's two most powerful specimens were growing too weak to kill each other and leave her to me.

Something needed to be done or we'd still be there. A half hour before midday dawn, I made a big, greasy move. I extinguished the lamps one by one. The combatants didn't notice the room dimming until the Malamute went pitch.

Two guns blazed, one from Dangerous Dan's position, one from atop the bar. A pig-like squeal came from McGrew. I fired up one lamp and two men lay stiff and stark. Their bodies covered the entire floor. Riley Dooleyvitch, the Slav prospector from the creeks, lay motionless, his mouth wide in a tongueless shout. Pitched on his head and pumped full of lead was Dangerous Dan McGrew.

This was no mystery. The Slav had no aim; I'd seen him hit mud when plunking at coyotes. I'd seen her shoot Spaniards in Cuba. She had a deadeye inherited from her ancestors of Plumtree. She had made her play and it was over in an instant. Dangerous Dan had shot the Slav. McGrew might have gone on living, but he met his death at Luisa's hand.

The Sniper scribbled like a dunce. I nudged the bodies with my foot. "Each one gone to Kingdom Come."

Luisa kissed Dooleyvitch on his frostbitten forehead, on each missing ear, on the lip she'd all but bitten off. She pinched his poke and pedometer. She fished his half-ear from beneath a barstool and laid it on his chest while planting her pistol in his hand. She lifted her skirt to the knee to step over him. She smiled at Sylvester Scovel. He'd witnessed her tampering, but she was unconcerned. She took the body of Dangerous Dan in her arms and lifted his wallet.

"Men are *los niños,*" she said at Scovel, and he wrote it down as if he was the first dope to hear it.

Guan-yin exited her closet with sleep in her eyes. She refilled the stove, refilled my tin, and wiped around my elbows. I was both elated and guilt-ridden about the two rivals at my feet. They'd get themselves pulled by the boots to a charcoal-and-salt embalmment. They'd get themselves buried come spring.

I stared long at Luisa as the green haze of stove smoke took on the yellow tint of sunrise. We didn't speak, but I knew she shared my exact thoughts. She'd completed her subterfuge. Justice served. Luisa and I were born for each other. Fate accomplished at last. The dead two, like the fifty-two, were strewn on ground in their predestined place.

She made me wait for her eyes until she'd lit a second cigarette. I was the one to speak. "A pity good men had to die."

"Good men?" Luisa blew hot smoke my way.

I had to ask. "What would McGee think? About what we've done?"

"Samuel?" She blew smoke my way. "He loves us, Jay Kelley. He loves us no matter what we do."

"You love me," I said. "That's all I ever needed to know."

Luisa whispered in my ear. "You're incorrigible." I couldn't imagine more loving words.

And though you come out of each gruelling bout,

All broken and beaten and scarred,

Just have one more try — it's dead easy to die,

It's the keeping-on-living that's hard.

— Robert W. Service

CHAPTER TWENTY-SEVEN

THE SUN ROSE LIKE A PENNY AND MOVED ALONG THE SOUTHERN HORIZON. Luisa swept downstairs wearing the gewgaws and frills Dangerous Dan had given her before she'd shot him cold.

The weather turned, and the temperature soared to twenty above. Sylvester Scovel seized the opportunity to mush south to Juneau, from where he'd wire two stories to New York. The first was the shooting of Dan McGrew, a fantastical murder at the hands of the Cuban Martyr Girl.

"It'll be the trial of the century, bigger than Moses Fleetwood Walker's," he said, and there was no reason to disagree.

"The second story's even grander." He offered me a cigarette and the chance to explain why I had fabricated my own death aboard the *Maine* and hid in the Klondike behind a tin of whisky.

"Four hundred American souls were lost fighting Jayson Kelley's war—including the soul of your own brother."

They were *holy shit!* items, the two shittyest of my lifetime. He was going to pass me and Nellie Bly out of turn as the finest American journalist. Luisa would be in the clink as a murderess, as would I for treason. I'd fade into history as the First Amendment's blackest eye.

I warned Luisa. I recommended that she stop Sylvester Scovel, to shoot him as she had Dangerous Dan.

She shrugged. "Page One has accused me of worse," she said as The Sniper mushed away.

I planned to stay drunk on free Malamute whisky when Luisa declared she was McGrew's rightful heir and took ownership of the saloon. She raised the prices and cut me off until I paid my tab.

The weather turned May-like in time to boost my spirits. A warm breeze brushed clouds away from the sun's face. The temperature rose to thirty-two above, and the boys went outside to shoot scatterguns at flung snowballs. Their time would've been better spent with a hunk of soap for a bath and laundry, but they wasted the last daylight playing baseball in shirtsleeves.

Luisa watched for an inning. I was about to bring home the winning run with my elegant swing when a black cloud appeared and raindrops as heavy as cherries fell, which was as plausible as a Havana snowstorm, but true nevertheless.

We dashed inside, leaving the game a tie. Luisa went to bed and I drank into the wee hours when a chorus of dogs barked in the distance. Minutes later, Sylvester Scovel came through the door, soaked through to his moccasins.

He'd made two mistakes. He'd attempted to pilot a two-man sled to Juneau single-handedly. And he left prepared for snow, not rain. No one bothers to pack waterproof garb in winter, and The Sniper had turned around a hundred miles into the five-hundred-mile trip. He'd been caught in a torrent, hugged rocks for shelter. Nothing was dry, especially his cough.

I helped him upstairs and into some body linen Tipperary L'Envoi was holding as collateral until a miner could pay what he owed. I shooed the whore from her bed and laid Scovel into it. He coughed a confession. "I envy you," he said. "You pulled off the biggest caper ever. I'm a little saddened I'll ruin you."

The quack doctor stopped by in the morning to mix turpentine and camphor into a bowl. Luisa volunteered to rub it into Sylvester Scovel's chest as if she were Florence Nightingale.

"You plan to write a story that accuses me of the worst crimes," Luisa told Scovel. "The shooting of Dan McGrew was nothing more than a bar fight gone bad."

He said he was sorry he'd ever conned her, but he owed a duty to the free press.

"Do I get your dogs? If you die?" It was an obscene question. An odd question, too. As heir to Dangerous Dan's fortune, she was situated enough to afford all the canines in the Klondike. "The lead dog must've cost you ninety dollars in Juneau. I'll take the sled, too."

His shivers found their way through the hard mattress. "My sled, my six dogs. The dust in my poke if you can get my Bible to Frances."

Luisa rubbed into his chest more elixir, which I assumed was slow poison. But his health improved by morning, so the whole fiasco was a waste of time. The Sniper was still in control of what did—and what did not—find its way into the *World*. He remained in control of Luisa's freedom. And mine.

Luisa was a mystery. Fires are a mystery, too. This one started near the end of The Sniper's recovery. The cause was guesswork. It may have been the turpentine in his bowl. Sylvester Scovel may have been smoking in bed, but that's unlikely because he was recovering from sudden pneumonia. More likely, a draft blew a curtain against a candle, but it may have involved a rat chewing on the phosphorus of a match until it was ignited by the friction of teeth.

I wasn't going to sit back and watch like I'd watched that Negro burn when Aunt Cates' cow kicked over the lantern. I wasn't eight anymore; I had a moral obligation. But I could do little once Tipperary L'Envoi's body linen ignited and enveloped The Sniper. He ran in a senseless panic spreading his flame.

No investigation would conclude Luisa caused the fire. After all, it was her Malamute Saloon that went up. I was an unlikely suspect as well. I'd sold a volume of fire insurance without ever lifting a finger to organize a volunteer fire brigade. I was soon to be ruined, which insulated me from rational suspicion. Neither of us would go to prison. Neither of us to the chair. Neither of us to Page One. Luisa and I would be forever bound by our secrets.

The Sniper's screams were short-lived, replaced by whisky bottles exploding into atoms. I knew enough to keep the second-floor window shut to fresh air until we'd tied bedsheets together. Luisa clambered down first. Once my sore feet were aground, we watched the Malamute go up like the *USS Maine*.

We raced to the supplies I'd stashed at the blacksmith's and loaded evaporated potatoes and reindeer steaks aboard her inherited sled.

"We'll pick up the trail from Fort Churchill to Nome," she said.

"Nome?" I hesitated. "In the dead of winter?"

"Past Nome." She promised a Christmas wedding. "We're going to Samuel. Your best man."

The idea of seeing McGee increased my energy. As did the idea of being the only white man within hundreds of miles of Luisa. The town boys set up a bucket brigade from the river. Their valiant efforts were in vain, except to give us the diversion we required. I cinched my squaw-chewed mukluks tight around the knees and we mushed away in the dark as fire consumed the doctor's next door. I prayed the blacksmith's be spared, God's gift to a town aflame and in dire need of my cache of food and a makeshift hospital.

The fire must've encountered gallons of turpentine at the doctor's. It tripled in size, though it was contained by the river on one side. On the other side, it jumped Good Luck Row and ate the soap-maker's shop before fanning out through a thousand cords of wood. The noise was as an approaching tornado and increased in volume with the collapse of roofs caving in. Ground snow went liquid and the flame licked up the melt. Windowless, new-built houses were swallowed whole as we mushed from obligation. I feared the flame would catch us from behind. Ahead, I feared the ice might swallow us. Those fears, like all fears, were a waste of time and energy.

I'll never comprehend the full measure of the catastrophe. It may have consumed more lives than the war. I stood on the after-runners at the handlebars. She sat at the gee pole, and six eager dogs pulled us from guilt. I won't lie, I was saddened by the tragic loss but cheered to be alone with Luisa in a world of endless dark and white, the hot glow of the sawmill at my back. I had her to myself. And I had her to myself in quest of McGee.

I urged the dogs forward, but I controlled nothing. The outfit responded to her touch on the gee pole as a kayak does to a back-paddle. She steered our lives northward for miles until the black smoke and screams of Dawson Town's blaze was less than a dream.

We mushed away from the rising arctic sun. It was another warm day and the huskies bit at the noontime slush. She said we had no time to camp before the weather changed. We mushed through a second twenty-one-hour night and came upon American soldiers building Fort Egbert.

I knew we should stop, but Luisa skirted the fort and steered us northward. I heard the whistles and sniggers of soldiers, who stared like starving coyotes at a girl they'd never see again.

"Are you sure this is the way to McGee's?" I hollered.

"It's the way to the crypts of hell, if we don't change our ways."

We at last rested under stars. When she spoke, they shone brighter. I asked for an early honeymoon, but she was too exhausted. I rose first in the morning, refreshed at long last. It was colder, and I found a tin tobacco box with matches among the supplies. There was no dry wood, and I soaked strips of cloth in kerosene for kindling. I got a campfire flaming, melted snow, boiled fish and rice for the dogs, who drooled round in a ring. I heated more snow for coffee.

Luisa rose, and I gave her my side of the fire to keep the smoke from her eyes. The breeze shifted that instant into her face.

"Smoke follows beauty." I was still in control of my charm.

"I had a dream last night," she said. "About my dead mother."

I showed off my knowledge. "Sammy McGee was her name, your brother's namesake. She once stole a locomotive and made a dash with Union prisoners to Morgantown. I know where you get your pluck."

"Another mother, *pendejo*. I never knew that one. My third mother, the *abuelita* who adopted me in Cuba. She made sacks for wages. She sang songs and died for lack of a teaspoon of medicine."

Tales of the poor are never appreciated by readers. I'm trained to dismiss them, but I made every effort to listen.

"My *abuelita* coughed and coughed; shadows darkened her eyes. The day came when she could not rise. The doctor wrote a prescription, said she stood a chance with proper care, but we'd no money. Shelves were bare, every cupboard. Nothing to sell, nothing to fix."

This was a story for the Sob Sisters, but I listened as a lover should, and I changed topics when she teared.

"Say, do you have names for these dogs?"

"'Please take my hand, I'm cold,' my *abuelita* would say from bed. I muttered prayer after prayer. I couldn't bear her moans. I sought the street. I begged for pennies."

I came to Luisa's rescue again. "You should name the swing dog Shadrach, the wheel dog Nebuchadnezzar, and the two in between Abednego and Meshach."

The lead dog had one eye half closed from being raked with the claws of another. "What will you name him? The dominant one who keeps an uneasy truce."

"I was sixteen. I clutched the prescription in my hand. I was a virgin for sale." She was determined to go on. "I bargained for a piece of gold and I got it. My childhood for a gold coin. Icy hands on my breasts. He slapped me across the cheek, but that wasn't what hurt."

When I caught her with Sylvester Scovel, she had confessed that it was the second time she'd been a whore. I now knew about the first, and I knew the precise thing to say. "Maybe you did wrong, but you saved a sweet old lady. When I do wrong, it's for the greater good. That's what

McGee meant when he said we're alike."

"I took the prescription and pressed it into the hand of a chemist. The chemist frowned. The coin was counterfeit."

Readers love stories about innocence lost. It's what got them interested in the Cuban situation in the first place. But no one wants to hear the ugly side of the girl he adores. I wished to be spared the granular details.

She glared at me. "Are you listening?"

"Of course."

"The chemist ordered me from his shop. 'Get out, your money's bad.' I'd been duped. I'd been conned. My *abuelita* died that night."

"Sheez."

"Since then, I ruin men. They grovel at my feet; I've pity for none. I bleed them all."

"Thank God I'm different." I put my gloved hand to her cheek. It was at that moment I saw past her beauty. I saw what McGee had seen. "Loving you makes me like myself."

"You never had a problem with that," she said.

It was a teary tease and I laughed.

"You're a pompous ass," she said.

"There's one in every crowd and it's frequently me."

She got out Sylvester Scovel's Bible and tore a page from it. She used the paper to roll a cigarette with tobacco from my tin box.

"I love that you're attracted to my humility," I said. "My readers love you, too. A million of them had an affection for the Cuban Martyr Gil. A million spent more time with the Sunday Journal than they did with that Book."

"They didn't fall in love with me. They had a romance with your half-baked tall tale."

"Readers want to believe."

"As a child, I believed my doll would come alive if I'd enough faith." She drew in the smoke and extended the cigarette to me. "Samuel still has faith. Samuel's still a child."

I refused the cigarette. "I don't inhale anything ecclesiastical." Campfire smoke shifted into both of us at once until I thought we'd smother. "You said you dreamed of the old woman you failed to save?" I coughed and fanned with my hand.

"My *abuelita* told me to find Samuel. She told me to travel to the highest north until I reach a lonely moose trail."

I coughed. "There are a thousand moose trails."

"I'm to follow the trail to a grim valley."

"All valleys sit grim this time of year," I said. "Grim as a hanged man."

"She said to trust my star. That's the last thing my *abuelita* said in my dream. 'Trust your star.'"

The breeze shifted to usher fresh air. "I'm your star," I said. "Trust me. We'll mush for Juneau. I rescued you from the Spaniards. I rescued you from Morro Castle and I'll rescue you from the coming freeze. There's little time."

"I'm naming the lead dog Kelley. In your honor."

"The last dog you named Kelley got tossed from the *Olivette*'s deck and into the sea."

She shrugged. "He'll answer to Kelley or he'll answer to the whip."

What is the moral of all this rot?

Don't try to be what you know you're not.

— Robert W. Service

CHAPTER TWENTY-EIGHT

"WE'RE ENTIRELY LOST, I'M SURE OF IT. WE MUST TURN BACK TO FORT EGBERT."

Luisa ignored me. The land became treeless. The temperature dropped at once. We donned each stitch until we appeared round. The slush crusted hard, and our after-runners glided without resistance.

I lapsed into a trance induced by the vibrations, with only the crash of a bull moose to rouse me. The dogs were driven with my weakened voice, and Luisa steered us toward her star. Toward trusted McGee, as if our lives depended on him.

We may have gone two hundred miles in three days. Sledding on river ice was effortless, almost soundless. Each hour colder. Each hour quieter. Each hour whiter. The cold and quiet and white bludgeoned me dumb. We mushed on into corpselike land. The howl of a wolf would've been welcome, but there were no sounds until a raven interrupted the quiet and the white, but not the cold. The temperature had no floor.

We at last stopped, exhausted, and unharnessed the dogs. Luisa rolled a cigarette with Bible paper. The smoke lost heat and curled to the ground. I checked the thermometer. Thirty-two below.

"We're near the Circle." The breath from her speech surrounded her head, floated down and froze to willow twigs.

Behind me, Kelley stole aboard the sled and swallowed whale fat. It was sled-dog sacrilege to rob supplies, but Luisa didn't thrash him as he deserved. She whipped with a venomous voice. More exhale for her halo. The dog yelped and crawled shamefaced next to me and shivered in cold and fear.

We'd neglected the dogs. Experienced mushers would've cleaned the ice from between their pads, but Shadrach and Meshach limped and we slowed. She ignored my pleas to stop, determined to gee-pole us northward inch by inch.

"We're sunk," I said. "Hundreds of miles from the last human," but a sled appeared from behind. It was pulled in the distance by starved malamutes, but caught us in no time. I begged the Siwash for help, but they knew no English. Only jabberwocky. They waved from behind wooden snow goggles, passed, and disappeared into the void of infinity.

I was crestfallen, hopes dashed. My longing for Luisa, my longing for McGee, would kill me. I was certain of it now.

"Be grateful, *pendejo,*" she said. "The Siwash have gifted us a trail to follow."

It was December twenty-first. The shortest day, the deadest day. Everything made final by the solstice. Luisa mushed through the day-time dusk and into another twenty-one hours of dark. The night had no beginning and no end until the sun rose with a banquet of pinks and greens and radiant reds and deep purples, but the color did nothing to raise the temperature a notch. Thirty-two. No colder, but it felt so. The scarf around my mouth and nose froze hard with my breath, and the dogs limped and whimpered from inattention.

Luisa fell ill, and I drove harder until Shadrach and Meshach toiled to their bellies. They didn't have long and so neither did we.

A miracle. The toboggan trail led to a hot springs. A grove of cottonwoods were an arrow's flight away. I'd soon caper like a boy into steam so thick I wouldn't see my hand in front of my face. Ice would melt from the feet of wading dogs. I'd hear Luisa naked in the water, but I wouldn't see her in the hot cloud. The bottom's ooze would heal my feet as they waded toward her splash.

The runners scratched ahead. A bitter breeze cleared the steam and the cottonwoods away. There were no trees. No scalding water. A tundra mirage. Endless ice. Endless flat ice. Ice that cured hangovers in Cuba was impersonal and brutal in the northernmost north. A raven's cry. Thirty-two below. Always thirty-two. Made colder by the breeze; it set fire to ears and fingers. Endless, hot white fluttered before me.

What happened next was a grim accident that came in and out of view like the flickering of a moving picture show. Our sled caught an edge and slid broadside. The dogs fell, splayed on their bellies, legs moving like the flippers of sea turtles seen from Captain Sigsbee's warm deck. The sled almost ran the dogs over, slid past and dragged them behind. It jumped a large chunk of ice, flipped, flickered in the air, and capsized, scattering us and supplies across glare ice.

Luisa lay broken beside me. She raved and puked and tried to bite me and spat forth blood on the snow. Her hood had fallen off. Ice crystals sparkled her loose hair. She'd soon be dead. I was unhurt, but I wasn't far behind. No one survives thirty-two alone. Her Bible was in reach and I tucked it to my body beneath my coat.

"Samuel," she whispered. "Save me."

"I'm Jayson, and I will at once."

We knew it was a lie. I put my arms around her and she wept and slept. She was dying in my arms when a sound broke the quiet. A traveler cheering on his team. Dogs bayed in the distance. Slowly, like a dream on morphine, came their approach from true north. I listened for the language of Siwash, but a voice alighted in English and Spanish.

"All is well, *compañero*." A lone man squinted down upon me with concern. He checked on her. "She's alive. Kinda."

He covered us deep in animal skins and built a fire a yard away. I lay clutching her. Too cold—too stunned—to get up.

I soaked in his Texican. "In-laws of mine, Laughin' Eye's cousins, passed a crazy white man and a crazier white woman mushin' toward certain doom. Who else could it be but you two? That's what I deduced. You see, I use the skills you taught me. I use them sorta all the time, but for real life, not for newspaperin'."

McGee pushed pemmican into my hand. "I packed firewood aboard my toboggan, kissed Laughin' Eyes goodbye, followed my in-laws' trail, and here I am."

I ate on my back as he unharnessed his four malamutes. "Bet you're a-wishin' we were kinda back in palmy, balmy Cuba. You may lose some toes, *compañero,* but a correspondent needs but two fingers to peck a type-writin' machine."

Never a loafer, McGee upended his toboggan sideways and aligned it with our sled. He packed snow in the gaps for a windbreak, tossed moose noses to Luisa's dogs, then to his.

"She's badly off," he said. "I'll kinda need you to git on your feet."

A cup of coffee dregs by the fire, and I was ready to be of service. He heated broth for Luisa, pushed a rifle into my hands. The last thing we needed was more wood, but that's the errand he assigned to me.

I tried to return the rifle. "There's nothing out there to shoot except cold."

"Stay within sight of the smoke so you don't git lost."

When I lost track of the campfire, I realized the value of the fire-arm. My shot into the air echoed in vastness. McGee answered my volley. I was dragging a snag toward him when I saw Luisa a thousand yards off and running willy-nilly in my direction. McGee and the lead dog were in chase.

Kelley, his brush high, caught her in eight playful bounds. McGee was closing in when she went through the ice. It was the oddest, most horrible sight I'd ever seen. One second she was a moving speck in the tundra, the next she was gasping in a hole so small it made her head ap-pear large. A sheet of white ice extended for a million miles, except for that hole, which imprisoned her more decidedly than the cobwebbed bars of Morro Castle.

Even from my distance, I could hear her first deep gasp. If her head were underwater she would've drowned right then from the involuntary fight for air. I was sprinting toward her when she managed a loud "sahm-WHALE!" through rapid panting.

I reached the scene. I stopped because McGee had stopped. He was five yards out and keeping his distance.

"What are you waiting for?" I said.

"A window of calm will soon replace her panic. Build a fire. We'll be needin' it."

She floundered and gasped for a minute more and mellowed as McGee had predicted. She worked her arms and shoulders over the hole's edge and tried to pull herself from the water. She hadn't the strength.

"I'd come git you, sister," McGee said, "but it would do no good for me to join you in the river."

"Sahm-WHALE!"

"Kick," he said with impossible peace. "Kick. Git your legs high in the water. Git flat and pull yourself out."

She grew weaker. Tears froze an inch beneath my eyes. The hole appeared to be shrinking in upon her.

"You can do it, big sister." McGee's words had no fear, no urgency, only encouragement. "Others cain't, but you can."

Luisa's fright stayed locked on McGee. Suddenly, her eyes peered past him as if she'd found me hiding where there was no place to hide. The hair on my body prickled. I would've done something, but I had grown fat while growing rich. The ice around me groaned under my senatorial weight. She hollered at me, spouted words of the gutter. Her gaze went through the thickness of me and into forever.

Her outstretched hands kept slipping. Layers of wet clothes weighted her down. She bit off her mittens and dug into the ice with scarred palms. She kicked and clawed with bleeding brands but made no progress. Her muscles spasmed. The dogs from two teams surrounded the hole and bayed.

"Out of time. We'll have to git her."

"We've no rope." The snag I'd been dragging was big enough to stretch across the ice hole, but I'd dropped it far behind with my rifle.

"I told you we need a fire," McGee said. "You crawl out there and git her while I start one."

I shivered with the all-overs. "It's suicide," I said, and McGee told me to build the fire and belly-crawled himself to the hole.

My matches were a distance aboard the sled. I was helpless, left with nothing but a duty to observe. Observe. That's what correspondents do. The great ones are simply born that way.

McGee made a valiant attempt from his belly, but clinging to Luisa was clinging to a jellyfish. He couldn't pull her from the water by her hair, but he managed to soak himself in an extended effort. He persisted, even as she ran out of time.

My burning tears didn't blind me enough to spare me from her last, gray, expression. She quit reaching for McGee. She pushed away from him. Her arms went upright and stiff like tree branches. She reached her hands into the air and was swallowed by her desire to be with her brother. Two HELL hands were last to disappear in the river.

The poverty of language prevented me from expressing what I truly felt. "Father of heaven and earth," I said.

McGee looked up with exhaustion; he seemed surprised I was there. He looked around and was more surprised a fire wasn't burning.

"You'll freeze for having tried to save her," I said.

He didn't have to raise his voice. We both knew his need was urgent. I was confused, dizzy, nauseated at once. I was a bird that had flown into a window. I was going to lose them both. The two people I loved. I muscled a vomit. A sour, violet vomit. My shame stained the snow with pemmican.

"It's OK, *amigo.*" His voice went softer. "We did our rottenin' best. One second she was asleep, the next she went mad. We kinda need a fire."

I crawled on hands and knees to the hole. "Maybe we can fish her out."

"She's on her way to the Bering Sea," McGee said.

"Come back. Come back, my light-o'-love. I choose you."

McGee shivered. His eyes followed me around like the Mona Lisa's. I couldn't escape them. "Remember when I saved you in the smokin' cane fields?" he said. "Remember when I saved you from the brandin' iron? I kinda need you to repay the favors. I'm kinda runnin' out of time."

I searched my pockets. "Can't find my matches." I was panting like a dog in the desert. "They're way back there aboard the sled."

McGee pulled his mittens off with his teeth and beat his right hand viciously against his thigh. "My matches are in my pocket, dry in a tin, but my hands are too frozen to git at them."

I fished in his pocket and found Papa's clasp knife I'd gifted him.

"Cut open the dog," McGee said. His voice remained steady and kept me from falling back into fog. "We must hurry, compañero."

Kelley was oblivious to the real world, on his belly biting away ice in his pads, thinking of himself, too absorbed in his own sore feet to comprehend, too self-involved to sprint away from McGee's approach.

McGee captured the dumb thing from behind in a bear hug. Kelley snarled; his hair bristled as he wriggled to get free. Beneath Kelley's bristle was more hair, and beneath the hair was fur, and beneath the fur was something like wool. McGee held tight to it all, exposing the dog's underbelly to me. Kelley wriggled and flailed his legs in the air. As he did a contorted backbend to bite McGee in the frostbit face, I slit my namesake up the gut.

Kelley flailed and cried in McGee's arms, and twitched as I buried the deer-antler handle into hot bowels. McGee let the dog struggle for its last seconds, set the corpse on the ice and thrust his numb hands into the steam of putrid offal.

"I'll let them soak a minit," he said. "Feelin's kinda comin' back."

His bloody, smelly hands found his tin of six matches where he told me they were. I crumpled Bible pages on the river ice and covered them with loose kindling. I lit two matches at once. McGee cupped the flame with his red hands and we nursed and prayed it to a small flicker.

I ran to our camp, put some spilled wood aboard his toboggan, and got back as the Bible ran out of pages.

I brought it to a brazen blaze. As the fire snapped with larger wood, an ache came to McGee's body. The more the flame took command, the more he moaned. I removed his wet mukluks and laid him prone. I found myself stretched out behind him and wrapped to his backside as I had to Luisa's. At some point the sun set. I watched the fire dance in the Arctic dark while protecting his outside from the breeze.

The embrace soothed us both, but my shame persisted. There I lay, a man who could stir up a war, but unable to save the damsel of my dreams. There I lay, clinging to my one freezing friend.

He shivered and I squeezed him tight. I fought back against my thoughts. Had I helped pull Luisa out, we'd all be wet, we'd all be dead, nothing but barroom gossip. To the world, I would've remained at the bottom of Havana Bay. A bunch of the boys would've remembered Luisa, but McGee would've been forgotten. McGee was the last man who deserved to be. Thank God, I'd the common sense to stay dry.

As he warmed, he shook uncontrollably. I held tight and watched the hole she'd fallen through. It became honey-combed in the fire's flicker and froze over solid. McGee medicated his grief with tears. They rolled down, even as he slept, and froze in the hollow of his cheeks.

I fell asleep thinking of her. I woke when I dreamed of the kick Papa gave my burnt feet to at last move them away from the stove. McGee was sitting up.

"It's kinda my fault," McGee said. "She ran when I returned your shot in the air." He coughed wet like Sylvester Scovel had coughed. Like Luisa had coughed.

Had she survived, McGee would've given me the credit, so I grabbed onto the smidgen of self-respect he was extending to me. "I suppose you're somewhat right. You're always right, McGee. Good thing I gifted you Papa's knife."

"Keep thinkin' straight," McGee said. "The worst a man can do is lie to himself."

Truth is, I had to choose. I chose McGee. I chose me. I didn't save the damsel.

Day broke. Clouds lifted in the south, and I saw Mt. McKinley for the first time. It heaved to the heavens and my breath was taken by the yawning vastitude. I felt small as a louse. McGee was coughing pneumonia but I could do nothing, as I could've done nothing to save Luisa. Every man's life, no matter how accomplished, is about doing nothing.

I was awed at the savage, vertical mass of McKinley. Named for a pacifist who'd never been within a thousand miles of Alaska. A war president, who'd never been within a thousand miles of Cuba.

"Nothin' so beautiful," McGee said. He stopped shivering for a minute. "A million times bigger than Grandfather Mountain."

That was no exaggeration. It was more mountain than could be imagined. The sun was already in the crotch of its peaks. Already preparing to set an hour after it rose. McGee sat for a spell and stared at the wonder. I stood and stretched and made a motion as if I were pitching a baseball over the mountaintop. The sinking sun cast cathedral rays. I watched my long shadow; I was a giant baseballer, twenty times the size of Joe. Yet minuscule and inconsequential.

"She was the reason I ever left Plumtree, with its lightnin' bugs and crickets. God only knows, she was the reason."

"I figured that out some time ago."

McGee coughed. "Promise you won't stuff me in some li'l ice hole."

"I recommend you stay alive."

"Sooner be stuffed into hell."

"We're there," I said.

"It's the cursed cold, it'll git right hold till I'm kinda chilled clean through to the bone. I don't fear dyin'. I dread the icy grave. So I want you to swear...."

I interrupted to shut him up. He was giving me the willies. "I swear, I'll leave you to the ravens before I stuff you through ice."

"...I want you to swear that, foul or fair, you'll cremate my last remains."

"Cremation? Dead's dead."

McGee coughed and laughed and launched into one of his inane stories. "One time, me and my closest cousin, Jimmy, were campin'. We were just li'l kids, hardly smokin' yet, but we talked of dyin'. Late into the night by the campfire, he asked me if I'd rather be buried or cremated." McGee laughed more. "'Surprise me.' That's what I told Jimmy. 'Surprise me.'"

"I can't cremate you, McGee. It doesn't matter where this story goes. I can't cremate you because there's little wood. You couldn't bring enough if you loaded ten toboggans."

McGee's voice took on an edge. "You never listen to my stories. I'm tellin' you I don't want to be surprised. Cremate me. You can't drag my body to Plumtree. But you can carry my ashes. Scatter me in the Smokies. Let the breeze carry the worst of me away. Let my chaff blow into Tennessee."

"You know I'd walk on glass for you, but push come to shove, the last thing I'd do is roast you on a spit and tote your ash from here to Grandfather Mountain."

"Cain't you do me one favor?"

"Anything else."

"Swear. Foul or fair."

"Why is this important?"

"Plumtree's real. My parents fought for it. Their one mistake was sending Luisa away. My one mistake was ever leaving for her. Plumtree's more warm and more real than anyplace on earth."

I half-agreed to his demands to shut him up. "I wouldn't do it for anyone else, but maybe I'd do it for you."

"Promise," he said. "Promise me, Jayson." It was the second time he'd spoken my Christian name.

I should've agreed out of reflex. Lied and been done with it. "I'll try. I won't make a promise I can't keep." I was at peace with my answer.

"Promise!" His eyes went wide. "Swear you'll start a fire in my bones."

"Sheez."

He broke out in his endless smile. "We look out for each other, *amigo*. That's what we kinda do."

"I promise. It's the dumbest promise ever made, but I promise and whatnot if you promise to fight."

"I see you, Jayson, I see you. I see past your front page and into your color comics."

"Promise me you'll scratch and fight to stay alive. Promise you'll fight harder than Luisa did."

"I promised that from the git-go."

"Fight, McGee, fight, and I'll cremate you if you fail."

CHAPTER TWENTY-NINE

I LAID HIM FACE UP ABOARD HIS TOBOGGAN AND BURIED HIM UNDER A MOUNTAIN OF SKINS until he was in such high spirits he wouldn't shut up. I hitched nine dogs from two teams and we moved southward at ease.

He spoke at the stars. "Our cabin was where Plum Creek joined Toe River from the east. Papa said he could never fall asleep durin' the war unless he was camped where he could hear water tumblin' over stones. I never saw the ocean until I went to Cuba, but I imagined gurglin' Plum Creek kinda findin' its way to the Mississippi and the Gulf."

My own life's river took me to the world's movers and shakers before plopping me onto a toboggan with McGee. The sanest man I ever knew was going loony. He rambled his endless childhood rhapsodies, one after another.

"I guess I'll never forgit when me and my closest cousin, Jimmy—he had an old hound—and we'd go into the woods at night to hunt."

McGee sounded more Appalachian than ever, as if we'd crossed the stone footbridge over Toe River and happened upon Yellow Mountain Baptist. "To begin with, I think that hound's name was Smoke, after the Smokies. You ever have a dog?"

"Jetstone. And a damned pigeon."

"I don't know how old I was, eleven 'cause I was experimentin' with chewin' tobacco and likker at the time. I said, 'Jimmy, let's go a-huntin' a bobcat.' Jimmy said, 'Now's not a good night. The air's not right, not crisp. We wouldn't git nothin' but nettles.' I said, 'Well, what else we got to do?'

Jimmy couldn't think of anythin'. He whistled to the old hound, who wasn't happy huntin' that night, either.

"I told Jimmy to git his rifle, but he said, 'I'm tellin' you we're not goin' to do any good tonight. So I'm not goin' to carry a gun all over Blue Ridge creation.' We went way out in the woods, up and down them, when we heard Smoke a-barkin'."

I relaxed into his story. I hoped it would go on forever like the tundra.

"Jimmy said, 'Well, that hound's got a bobcat treed.' It was pitch black. This was in October, but it was a warm night. Bobcats like it crisp, and it was awful dark. Like it is now, except the ground was dark too, not white."

I listened to nothing except McGee's toboggan on ice and the glide of his voice. "The hound was right under a small tree lookin' straight up through the branches, a-yellin' at the yellah sliver of a moon until I thought the moon was all he'd treed. 'There's a cat up there somewhere,' Jimmy said. I said, 'Well, I told you to bring the rifle,' and Jimmy said, 'Well, I tell you what, you stay here so that cat won't come down and I'll go git it.'"

McGee stopped talking to see if I was listening, "A good reporter gets to the point," I said.

"I told you, I won't ever make a reporter, though it's a trade worth plyin'. The woods late at night git kinda frightenin', and the hound ran off somewhere, so it was just me there under that tree. I heard sounds, and I climbed the next tree over. A cat could follow me up ev'ry tree in the deep woods, but this tree had a trunk maybe five inches around, and I could climb up a skinny tree pretty well at that age. I figured maybe cats don't like skinny trees, and I kinda sat there in the moon-yellah dark in some branches and held on a-waitin for Jimmy and his gun.

"After a while I could hear Jimmy callin', 'Sam, where are ya?' and I'd say, 'Over this way,' and he kept sayin', 'Where are ya?' and I'd say, "Right here,' and he said, 'Where?' and I said, 'Up here.'

"Jimmy saw me and started laughin'. He told me to look up. A yard over my head was a possum, and Jimmy laughed and laughed and said, 'Boy, that sure is a plump possum. Plumper than Suzy.' Suzy was the nicest girl in grammar school, who dropped her pencil on purpose, and I'd pick it up.

"Jimmy said, 'I hate to let any possum as fat as Suzy git away,' and I said, 'Shut up and shoot it,' and he said, 'I don't waste bullets on possums, and if I'd knowed it was a possum I never would've gone back for the gun. Just bring the possum down with you.'

"I said, 'You're nutty, I won't bring it down.' Cousin Jimmy said, 'Just grab him by the tail, and tug and he'll play possum. That's why they're called possums, dummy. Just grab him by the tail and tug a li'l bit and pull.'

"I grabbed him, and that possum curled that old rat tail round my hand and I pulled it out of that skinny tree. All the while, the possum played possum."

"This that and the other," I said. "Is there a point?"

"You got somewhere to be?" McGee coughed. "I walked outa the woods with that possum by the tail upside-down, and Jimmy's grandmother cooked it and it sure was good."

"What's the point?"

"No point to Plumtree stories."

"I wish Jimmy were here to shoot *me*," I said.

"We're all playin' possum. Maybe that's it."

McGee coughed a minute and said he no longer felt chipper. He went quiet for a couple of hours as the temperature plunged to forty-nine. He woke up with delirium and sang a meaningless song.

"A grave deep, deep, with the moon a-peep,
A grave in the frozen mould.
Sing hey, sing ho, for the winds that blow..."

The morbid lyrics were out of character and put me on edge. He'd been my rock since the day we met in a cane field. I needed a pull from my jug, but there were precious few pulls left after my mournings for Luisa.

A sharp, small snow blew to batter my eyes. "I'll be home to Laughin' Eyes soon," McGee said.

We were headed in the opposite direction. Mt. McKinley was buried behind clouds, but revealed enough of itself for me to maintain a consistent course southward toward Fort Egbert.

"Plumtree's heaven," McGee said. "Hell's a place with headlines and deadlines."

I got a grip on the whip and gave the dogs all I had. Colder it grew until the last atom of heat left the earth. All that was left was McGee's singing, constant in tone, like the top layer of snow skims the drifts.

"There are strange things done in the midnight sun
By the men who moil for gold.
The Arctic trails have their secret tales
That would make your blood run cold.
The Northern Lights have seen queer sights,
But the queerest they ever did see... "

"McGee, my one friend, you belong in a bughouse."

As I drove the dogs on, I came to believe in the elegance of freezing to death. McGee was freezing, but wasn't suffering. Luisa had suffered only fear. Drowning and freezing are peaceful ways to go, once the distress has run its course and surrender embraced.

A blizzard skirted past and the dark sky broke knife-edged and clear. Mt. McKinley swaggered out of the clouds, a giant mass of white rising to a sky, bent and blue

I whipped on through the changing weather until the dogs staggered and fell. I was busy getting the team in order when McGee stripped his clothes, threw them from the toboggan, and jumped off to roll euphoric in the snow.

"The cursed cold," McGee said laughing. "I'm chilled clean through to the bone."

I calmed him with an embrace, drawing his freezing form to me. The flesh that clung to his bones felt like clay. I dressed him. Found his spectacles. Once the toboggan moved again, he sang louder, as if a brass band were at his back.

"Sing hey, sing ho, for the ice and snow,

And a heart that's ever merry;
Let us trim and square with a lover's care
For why should a man be sorry?"

He tumbled again from the toboggan. I pretended I didn't see him, let him slip small into the white. I'd make it to Fort Egbert alone. He got to his feet in the distance and stripped again. It's cumbersome to circle back a toboggan, but I couldn't stomach seeing McGee die nude and clayish. He was eating snow and offered it up as sugarcane. I collected his scattered garments, dressed him once more, and tied him aboard. I couldn't forget that damned promise.

McGee stared up at the grandeur. His eyes were clear and sane, but he didn't recognize me. "I left Plumtree."

"I know, I know," I said. "I know."

"Do you know why?"

I did, but I said, "God only knows."

"Ahhh, the answer to ev'ry question." He coughed until he remembered who I was. "I'll be cashin' in soon, and if I do, I'm askin' you won't refuse my last request."

"Look around. There's no fuel for a fire. It takes a sawmill of wood to burn a corpse. I'll try to get you to Fort Egbert."

"They'll have the fuel," McGee said.

"Sure they will, though they'll never let me waste it on a cremation."

"Get me to Laughin' Eyes. She has wood. You promised. Empires topple and fall, but a promise is a promise."

"Sheez."

"You're a good man. You have a heart of gold."

"I don't. News flash, McGee. I don't. I can't keep my promise. I would if I could, but it's hare-brained."

"We're both hare-brained, or we'd be at the outdoor café Inglaterra," he said. "Strummin' my *bandurria*, drinkin' lemonade, while you let the world know what's what."

Colder it got; I was in a clench. The Siwash lead dog went blind, and I cut him from the team. The lung of the wheel dog Nebuchadnezzar bled and I shot it out of mercy. I whipped on until the seven lay down in their traces and howled their woes. I hollered at McGee to see if he was alive.

He answered. "It ain't bein' dead—it's my awful dread of the icy grave that pains."

I gave the dogs a rest. I pulled off my mitt and put my hand to his forehead. Hot putty. His face was ghastly pale. I put a ball of snow on his mouth. He sipped the melt. His eyes popped open. "I want to feel the crackle of the flame. Swear to God you'll keep your promise."

I looked in four directions. "There's no wood, McGee, and the Almighty's scarcer."

He lapsed into his death sweat. His hands were blanched bone. His face a blackened horror, purple and green and gray. His lips cracked, the skin on his gums peeled away. Foam bubbled from his nostrils. But he kept his part of the bargain. He fought on.

I unloaded the last wood from the sled, policed the tundra for more fuel to stop the urge to put mercy bullets through the blind dog—and McGee. I built two fires, lit them with two matches, saving two. I spread spruce boughs on the snow between the two flickers, where I placed McGee. I shivered; McGee was past that.

"Fear is wasted," he said. "Regret is wasted, too."

I had fear and regret and grief. Warmth eased them but I knew the fires had no longevity. I lapsed into a swift sleep holding McGee, a sleep too deep to dream. The most satisfying sleep of my life. I thought I'd died, but McGee woke me with a tight grip. "The north is kickin' like a steer," he said.

The flicker-fires had gone out. Black sky on white ice remained like ink on newsprint. I rose and peed yellow, but it was gray in the dark. Four dogs had abandoned us in search of humans with better odds. Three and the blind dog remained loyal, curled in tight, balls, their tails tucked to cover nose and feet. The night clamped down, and I made lighter the toboggan. I emptied it except for the grub and the ice axe. The jug had a swish left of brandy and I kept it, too.

I hitched myself beside the three dogs and we pulled McGee at a funereal pace southward. The blind dog followed behind. As small as McGee had become, he about broke my back. I followed a lynx track.

The untrodden snow was powder. It would be a sweet bed to lie in, to die in. McGee strained to live and so I strained on too. I was up to my thighs in snow, the dogs to their jaws. I counted steps, and I rested every hundred. Maybe McGee was dead. I didn't care to check.

It remained night, but enormous clouds filled the chasms of McKinley. The lynx track was steering us in the right direction. I lighted a match to search for life in McGee's face. Pus filled frostbit eyes, blisters covered any skin exposed. I may have wept aloud. No man deserved to suffer that; no man as good as McGee. He woke to put my match out with a rough-edged cough.

"I'm goin' to live the night," he said. "On hands and knees I will buck it. With ev'ry breath will I fight."

He made it to the sunrise of Christmas Eve. A little ball rose in the sky, red, round and remote. It lit the tundra in dimness, made moss shine from rocks, made rocks shine like headstones. The little sun dipped behind a glacier.

"Look, McGee, the vast white makes uphill appear down."

"The other direction is the road leadin' home," he said. "I love Laughin' Eyes. I love Luisa. I love you, my li'l brother."

I melted another snowball on his forehead. "You've kinda got to amputate my foot," he said.

"After Christmas."

"Laughin' Eyes says she'll learn to love Christmas cause it comes at the end of moose huntin'." He coughed. "Cut off my foot or I'll never touch her again. Never kiss my son."

I prepared for surgery to shut him up. I sprinkled the last of the brandy on his ankle, a little more on the ice axe. I cursed the nothing left and tossed the empty jug to the dark.

"Save the foot after you chop it. I want it cremated with the rest of me."

"Sheez."

"Kiss Laughin' Eyes for me." He passed out as I applied a tourniquet. I wasn't about to hack off a man's foot who would die soon. He slept five minutes and woke believing his foot was gone.

"I'll tell you the tale of a Northern trail," he said, "and so help me God, it's kinda true."

"There's no truth," I said, but he'd passed out again. "Truth is," I said to my unconscious friend, "I should've saved Luisa without delay. If I'd let you build the fire, we'd all be alive."

The confession did me good but the cold stabbed like a driven nail. I rejoined the dogs and we pulled alongside Mt. McKinley, the world's largest lie. Each hour or so, McGee woke with a whimper.

"The worst form of slavery is being free of ev'rybody," he said. "I miss Laughin' Eyes. I miss my hip-baby. Luisa. God, I'm sorry, Luisa."

"I'm sorry, too," I said. "There's nothing left except her accent in my head."

"Grief tears a man to shreds," McGee said. "It's shakin' me top on down. I'm comin' apart at the seams. I'm broken up, invaded. I'd not be human to deny it. I miss her. I miss a lot of people I never got to know. I miss you."

He slept. He woke and raved of the gooseberries of Plumtree. "Stars like a million needles stab my eyes," he said, staring up at thick clouds. "They dance heel and toe."

He spoke of peach orchards and the scent of the Smokies. The rhododendron blooms. "The lusts that lure us, the hates that hound us."

"God is cruel," I said.

"I suppose He is. He gives us ev'rything except the ability to be thankful for it." He stopped to listen to a voice heard by him. He sang a last song into a snow that fell like feathers. He sat up with urgency and hollered. "We're not alive waitin' to die, we're dyin' a-waitin' to live."

He paused to consider his last words. "A wise man once said…"

"Said what?"

"A wise man once said…"

"What! What, McGee, what?"

He paused a dramatic pause to get a last whiff of life.

"A wise man kinda once said—nothin'."

"Nothing?"

"Nothin', my lord. Wise men often say nothin'."

His eyes trained on me, twitched and went still. His palms opened. His eyes closed and opened wide. Bang up at the sky. They froze that way, reflecting patches of bright blue.

McGee died, and I saw him go, peering up past my veneer. No matter. I would die soon, too. Luisa and McGee had but a head start to the finish.

I had an urge to mush the dogs to death. Instead, we pulled his remains at leisure. I stopped every ten steps. I was both sweating and shivering. Weeping broke from me; loud sobs calved from my chest. The dogs sang. We held nothing back, no one to hide from. I would freeze to death long before I got a chance to cremate McGee. I'd lived with lies; I'd die with this one. I cursed and groveled to my knees and kissed his cold cheek. I apologized for failing him, for failing his sister.

His arms and legs had frozen outspread. I laughed the hardest laugh of my life. As he died, he'd splayed himself into a starfish to prevent me from disposing of him through any hole chiseled in the river. His mouth had a smirk and it followed me around.

More laughter. More tears. I sobbed for Mama. I sobbed into the aching womb of night. I blubbered sobs, wailed vast despair. I laughed more at McGee. I sobbed for Joe. It dawned on me he'd never known Mama at all. She was nothing more to Joe than remains in her flower garden. Joe, McGee, Luisa, Mother and Father, the Slav Dooleyvitch, Dangerous Dan McGrew. I was the only one in the world left alive. I was the last bird on a wire.

I wiped my icy face with my fur sleeve, coughed a wad, and spit a ball of ice into the snow. I sobbed again, a sob for my promise unkept. I sobbed longest for that.

"At least I'm no longer wet-nurse to a loony." I sat there next to my one friend, wishing he'd wake up to tell me one last story. A syrupy,

Plumtree yarn that wasn't the least bit holy shit!

Another dog begged and cried to run off. I unhitched it and pulled on with my team of two into the last hours of Christmas Eve. The blind dog limped behind. Like McGee before me, I floated in and out of madness. I sang as he had. I don't know from where the lyrics came. They were never in the satchel of poems. They were original from my head.

I had the urge to sprint to shelter, but no shelter was in sight. I trudged on. I was out of rope. Like Happy Jack. I hated him for giving up; I hated myself for dragging on. I considered the cold of Luisa beneath the ice, the warmth beneath her cold. Few things are precise, but precisely a year ago she rode into the Spaniard camp, a red ribbon in her hair.

The sun at last rose into the bitter dawn of Christmas Day. Christmas again, full circle.

Every land has its own thrall of beauty, but no sky's as infinite as the winter sky of the arctic. I trudged into that infinity until I came upon a soundless lake that was a continuation of that sky. It was nestled in an amphitheater of snowy hills.

Sixty below. My exhales crackled. I was three hundred miles from the ashes of Dawson Town, two-fifty to Juneau, a mile for each sailor who died aboard the *Maine*. I envied them for going under in the amniotic warmth.

A snow fell so fine and powdery it was imperceptible, yet filled the sky. I trudged to something jammed in the ice of the lake. An abandoned boat. I had to squint to see *Alice May* painted on the aft.

It was the identical derelict I'd taken comfort in six months ago with the Slav Dooleyvitch, Shate Allen, Happy Jack, the Kid MacKintosh, and two umpires. I'd bumped upon the exact spot, Lake Lebarge, named for a hero who survived war to slip and die on this damn ice.

I studied the derelict and I thought a bit, and I looked at my frozen chum. "Hallelujah," said I with a sudden cry. "Here is my crematorium!"

CHAPTER THIRTY

INSIDE THE *ALICE MAY* WAS THE STRAY BUTT OF A CANDLE. I was ecstatic that my hands were warm enough to strike my last match and startled when the candle took flame.

A thin layer of ice covered the derelict's interior. McGee approached from behind, but it was a candle's trick. I lit an old tin lamp, and turned up the wick to kill the shadow. The *Alice May* glittered white like a salt mine. My fist banged on the boiler. It was sturdy enough. I tore planks from the cabin floor and I threw them and the lamp into the boiler.

Stray hunks of coal lay about and I added them to the flame. I went outside and drug the main attraction by the heels, from the toboggan and onto the deck. I was sorry to see the sun set but there was no heat in the sun, anyway. One flyspeck of warmth remained and it was in a promise kept.

The derelict had been an icy vault for so long it was slow to accept heat. At last, the ceiling dripped condensation. The fire became a huge success, and I had a seed of faith it might somehow grow hot enough to consume McGee. I filled with energy and I went outside and dragged high-water timber from the lake bank. As the two faithful dogs stared and the blind dog sniffed, I used the ice axe on a hill to dig down into hard earth—sick permafrost earth. I reached a vein of coal.

Anything of carbon I heaped on the conflagration until the furnace roared with the kind of blaze I'd ran from days ago in Dawson Town. The *Alice May* had a drafty chimney to make the fire pop; it made the craft cheery. A capable man could wait out the winter aboard. I smiled at the irony. I'd almost met my Maker in the coldest cold when the world thought I was steeped in slime at the bottom of the warmest sea.

My smile became a laugh. I don't know why, but I laughed until snot rheum ran over my lip and curled into my mouth. Salty as sea water. The fire burned with strength to reflect a seasonal red off the overhead.

"Merry Christmas, McGee. I've built you a fiery gift."

It grew so hot a man couldn't get within five yards of the boiler. I melted out some water, sat, and drank my lukewarm fill. I toasted her for us both.

"Season's greetings, Luisa."

Once gorged on food from the toboggan, I removed the mukluks McGee's squaw had chewed soft. My toes were lifeless and green and I laughed mad-like because they were a seasonal color, too.

It grew too hot to sit. I stretched out on the cabin floor and itched and slept. I awoke in a sweat. I had to wait another hour, then two. When I could at last crawl close to the boiler, I burrowed a hole in the coals with the ice axe. I pulled on my mukluks and limped to my starfish on the deck. Ice in his fingers, ice in his glassy stare. I picked him up in the same strong bear hug he'd used when I gutted my namesake with Papa's clasp knife.

McGee weighed little more than a sliver. He was a craven skeleton where hours ago beat an authentic heart. He weighed less than nothing, but moving him was clumsy with his arms and legs splayed gaunt.

"The way you croaked makes me doubt if you really wanted me to cremate your sorry remains. I'm no quitter, but a chum ought to consider a chum in the way he goes and dies."

The boiler was large, but its hatch small. I set him nearby and let him thaw for an hour, but it did no good. He was an obstinate stiff.

I hadn't the stomach to hack him into pieces. I threw in more fuel.

The fire swelled voracious, the derelict shook with incineration. I lifted him and staggered toward the flame, protecting my face from the heat with my starfish shield, steering McGee like Captain Sigsbee on the *Maine*'s wheel.

My energy was gone, but despair gave me the strength. With sweat pouring from me, I took aim at the burrowed hole in the glowing coal—and I stuffed in Sam McGee. He fit through the hatch like the last piece of jigsaw puzzle. I had no eyebrows, no lashes, but it was the singeing stink of *his* hair that made the air putrid. "I promise never again to make an effing promise." That's a promise I'd keep.

I carried a bucket of water outside for my three faithfuls, but they weren't around. The evening star was blinking alone. McGee's greasy smoke billowed out the chimney and sank to the ground. I had to both pray and pee, but I could do neither with McGee's ashes cooling and falling on my shoulders.

I shivered within seconds after hours of sweating in the sauna. Cold penetrated like shrapnel. It had to be seventy. Pee came at last and shattered on crusted snow. Prayers did the same.

Even from outside I could hear him sizzle so. It gave me the fidgets and I gained distance along a moose trail that hugged the lake's shore. I limped on for a half-mile to get him out of my nose. Out of my ears. Out of my pores. Out of my heart. My steps crunched, the earth groaned, my pulse was like the report of a rifle pounding from shoulder to throbbing feet. I wanted to remember McGee fully alive, but the best I could do was picture him asleep under the Cuban fishing boat.

Eighty.

I don't know how long I was out there. Long enough to wrestle with McGee's pointed and pointless words. The sky went sideways with a cruel, dry snow. The wind's sword stabbed my eyes and froze my tears where I once had lashes that had been singed away.

I set my jaw tight to stop thinking of him and to stop my teeth from chattering. Nothing stopped save the wind. The vastness of white in the dark made it hard to imagine anything existed, and yet I searched the horizon. No one was about, but I listened for someone coming.

"It's ninety in Havana and ninety here, too," I said aloud, but nothing answered except wagging tails from beneath white powder.

The three dogs had buried themselves together until only black noses were visible above a shroud of snow. A bit of jag-time whistled from my lips. No response. No more tail-wagging. Exhales from their noses sank to the lake's surface.

A hundred. Cold enough to feel every shame. Shames for wanting McGee to hurry up and freeze, hurry and die, hurry up and burn. Shames for Luisa, my damsel. Shames for this that and the other, the things I'd no right to do, the things I should've done. Shames of many colors gnawed until my body went numb and the arctic became oddly welcome.

God knows what else I bore. But a promise made is a debt unpaid. I'd paid my debt. There was warmth in that, more warmth than in the holy shit! witches' brew splattered on Willie's wall.

Stars danced out and meteors fell in distant darkness. The moon rose, extinguished the meteors, and lit a far valley. The wild grew bigger in the bigness. The cold embraced me in bitter bitterness. So cold there were no stars. The Christmas moon was two days from full, its light so bright it played cymbals in the white, starless silence.

The pulse of the Northern Lights started out as milky green, flared to plum-red, and to primrose haze with a wondrous sheen. Colors fluttered out a fan. They poured into the bowl of the sky with the gentle flow of cream. They danced a cotillion; they danced for the eyes of God. I wanted McGee and Luisa to see it with me but no man had ever been more alone. Over me and above me light swept the sky like a giant scythe. I crouched and watched the battlefield of the sky, the all-combing search-lights of the navies of the world.

The elastic corkscrew of light swallowed the heavens above, from horizon to zenith, as though gigantic fingers were afloat on the keys of a mountain-top music box. The universe was orchestrated to crescendo. The frozen earth groaned on. The blind dog stirred, rose, found me with its nose, and rested its muzzle on my knees. I teared at the touch. In my crouch I saw the world from McGee's perspective. From inside the Circle on down, all was fundamentally right.

"Don't believe what you think," I said, and the blind dog wagged its tail, whimpered, and licked air in the vicinity of my face.

The Northern Lights carried a slight chemical odor and made a swishing sound as the ever-hardening Lake Lebarge sealed everything deep. Luisa deeper. I removed a mitt, stroked the dog, buried fingertips down to its winter wool. I peered through my parka hood. I couldn't see anything except vague shapes. A face. Her face. It was his. No, it was theirs in a cluster.

I petted the dog's ears, startled it when I hollered and shook my naked fist at the sky. The Northern Lights grew too bright to hide beneath. I was the last man on earth, and yet exposed. The last man left, and looking for a place to hide. I rose and followed my limping moon shadow back to the *Alice May*.

One-ten, the utter end. "I'll just take a peep inside. I guess you're cooked, and it's time I looked."

The door I opened wide. An inch of snow fell heavy as gold to trap my frozen feet at the stoop. My eyes found the open hatch of the red-hot furnace.

CHAPTER THIRTY-TWO

THE NORTHERN LIGHTS HAVE SEEN QUEER SIGHTS. But the queerest they ever did see, was that night on the marge of Lake Lebarge where I cremated Sam McGee. Scientific journals have documented sea monsters the size of floating islands. But they'll never publish my truth because my truth is too queer to fathom.

I stepped through the *Alice May* door—not to find McGee sizzling—but to find my warm feet pacing the deck of the *USS Maine*. I was back in Havana Bay. Some kind of mental conveyance had returned me to the scene.

Captain Sigsbee was occupied, writing to his wife. Willie's old cable was in my pocket and I read it to myself. "You furnish the dispatches. I'LL FURNISH THE WAR!"

The ominous *Alfonso XII* was in our periphery. I heard something akin to a rifle shot. At first, I thought Sigsbee's cigar had popped like high-water timber in the *Alice May's* boiler. An explosion followed, not loud but sullen. It came so close on the heels of the shot, I decided the Spanish had invented a secret shell as fast as sound.

I was sent sliding on my rear thirty yards along the *Maine's* deck as the aft end folded high into the air. Fire followed the deck upward as Captain Sigsbee and I slid downward through the flame. There came a whistling moan. It sounded human; it was air escaping below as water rushed the sailors' quarters.

I escaped serious injury when my landing was cushioned by a marine. Blocks of wood rained down, debris of all kinds. I was struck by a cement slab and knocked over the *Maine's* rail. Captain Sigsbee reached for me— too late—and I alighted without splash in the sea.

The noise deadened in the underwater. I broke the loud surface once, maybe twice. I grasped at the bodies and body parts in the sea's churn and wondered how I ever came to be so alone amidst so much noise. I had no choice but to fight the waves that filled my mouth with tropical water.

My lungs filled with a warm, salty gargle. The sky above flashed from dark to bright. Dark to bright. A corkscrew of yellow fire. Like the flicker of a moving picture show, except the picture shows are black and white and gray. This was colorful. A drop-curtain scene of milky-green and plum-red poured yellow into the sea with the gentle flow of cream.

In awe, I watched the battlefield of the sky so bright my underwater body cast a shadow on the bay's floor. The elastic corkscrew of light swallowed the heavens far above the water's surface.

My feet settled into the slime of the sea floor. My view of the fire became blocked out. I was but three fathoms deep, and in utter disbelief as the *Maine's* hull, painted white in peace, sank to crush me.

These are the simple facts, and I guess I ought to know. There, somewhere in the crescendo, sat Willie at his roll-top desk, composing my one-paragraph, *holy shit!* obit. He was not fabricating. He wasn't dancing the dust off his shoes. Willie was somber, neither lying nor juicing in the slightest way.

> *The Journal's famous war correspondent Jayson Kelley was tragically aboard the USS Maine at the time of the gutless attack and is feared to be at the bottom of Havana Harbor. His coverage of the Cuban situation will be remembered as one of the most prodigious feats of American journalism. His soul is in God's hands, though his corpse may be in the bread-basket of a circling shark.* **W.R.H.**

I wasn't freezing in the Klondike. I was crushed beneath the hull ten months ago. Those who mistrust Willie can find a reliable account recorded in Captain Sigsbee's log.

I long for McGee to be with me. The *Alice May's* door I sometimes open wide. There he sits, staring bang right at me, cool and calm in the heart of the furnace roar. He wears that smile you can see a mile.

"Please close that door," McGee says. "It's fine in here, but I greatly fear you'll let in the cold and storm. Since I left Plumtree, down in Tennessee, it's the first time I've been warm."

ABOUT THE AUTHOR

Del Leonard Jones wrote more than 300 cover stories at USA Today and received a Pulitzer Prize nomination for beat reporting. His 93-year-old father Dale Jones recites *The Cremation of Sam McGee* and *The Shooting of Dan McGrew* ballads from childhood memory. See him recite *The Cremation* from the Colorado River at the bottom of the Grand Canyon: https://caseystrikesout.wixsite.com/website.

Jones is married to Dianna. They have two children, Ciera and Douglas. He officiates high school and collegiate sports in the Washington D.C. area and is writing a second historical novel set in the dawn of professional baseball, inspired by the 1888 ballad *Casey At the Bat* as told from the umpire's point of view.

Jones has edited the non-fiction business leadership book *Advice from the Top, 1001 Bits of Business Wisdom from the Great Leaders of the Recent Past*. In one chapter, Fred Smith, founder and CEO of FedEx, speaks on the Pony Express and the leadership lessons that can be learned from historical figures including Alexander the Great, Theodore Roosevelt, Julius Caesar, George Washington and Dwight Eisenhower. Request a free copy Jones's Q&A with Fred Smith at https://caseystrikesout.wixsite.com/website.

Jones is available to speak on topics ranging from 1880s baseball, the Spanish-American War, the Klondike Gold Rush, his many interviews with Donald Trump and the yellow journalism of the 1890s.

Made in the USA
Middletown, DE
04 August 2019